THE
DOLL
MAKER

THE
DOLL
MAKER

RICHARD MONTANARI

MULHOLLAND BOOKS
LITTLE, BROWN AND COMPANY
NEW YORK   BOSTON   LONDON

Mulholland Books/Little, Brown and Company
Hachette Book Group
1290 Avenue of the Americas
New York, NY 10104
mulhollandbooks.com

First North American Edition, April 2015
Originally published in the United Kingdom by Sphere, August 2014

Mulholland Books is an imprint of Little, Brown and Company, a division of Hachette Book Group, Inc. The Mulholland Books name and logo are trademarks of Hachette Book Group, Inc.

The publisher is not responsible for websites (or their content) that are not owned by the publisher.

The Hachette Speakers Bureau provides a wide range of authors for speaking events. To find out more, go to hachettespeakersbureau.com or call (866) 376-6591.

Lyrics to 'Wall of Dolls' by Golden Earring reproduced with kind permission of Barry Hay.
Lyrics to 'These Foolish Things' reproduced with kind permission of Boosey & Hawkes Music Publishers Ltd. © 1936 Lafleur Music Ltd.

ISBN 978-0-316-24473-2
LCCN 2014954840

10 9 8 7 6 5 4 3 2 1

RRD-C

Printed in the United States of America

For Mike Driscoll
Go raibh mile maith agat.

This is the wall of dolls
Secret world of smalls
Look at them all my friend
You'll be one of them in the end.

Golden Earring: 'Wall of Dolls'

THE
DOLL
MAKER

He knew the moment she walked in.

It wasn't the way she was dressed – he had been fooled by this more often than he had been right, and he had been right many times – it was, instead, the way her heels fell on the old hardwood floor, the weight of her stride, the way he knew she'd put a thousand sad stories to bed.

He remembered her from Raleigh, from Vancouver, from Santa Fe. She was no one he recognized. She was every woman he'd ever met.

The bar was long and U-shaped. He was seated on one of the short sides, next to the wall, his right shoulder against the paneling. This helped to hide from the world the large scar on his right cheek. As little as he cared about anything, he was still self-conscious about his scar, a birthday present from his father and a Mason jar of moonshine. Besides, with one shoulder to the wall, he was always protected from that flank.

The bar was almost empty. It smelled of overcooked fish and Mr Clean.

The woman sat two stools to his left, leaving an empty seat between them. As she dropped her purse to the floor, wrapping the strap around an ankle, the juke spun a new song, a tune by Lynyrd Skynyrd. Or maybe it was the Allman Brothers. He wasn't big into seventies southern rock. Oddly enough, considering his job, he didn't care much for music at all. He enjoyed the silence. There was precious little of it these days.

It was clear that the woman expected him to summon the barkeep, offer her a drink. When he didn't, she did. The barman took his time. Had the woman been ten years younger, or five years prettier, the barman would have flown.

When he finally made his way down the bar the woman looked over, giving it one more chance. When she looked back she said, simply:

'Seven and Seven.'

The barman dawdled, returned, slid a napkin onto the bar in front of the woman, put down the watery cocktail, waited. The woman picked up her bag, then fished out a rumpled twenty, dropped it onto a wet spot – a spot the barman, if he'd given a shit, would have wiped down.

The man made an elaborate process out of straightening out the wet bill. Eventually he came back with the change. All singles. He dropped them into the puddle on the bar.

Asshole.

He wished he had time to deal with the bartender.

Two songs later the woman slid one stool to her right, uninvited, bringing her almost empty drink with her, rattling the cubes.

'What's your name?' she asked.

He glanced over, got his first good look. Her eye shadow was electric blue, her lipstick far too red for a woman her age, which he pegged at forty-five, maybe more. She looked like a woman who slept in her makeup, only bothering to wash her face when she took that infrequent shower. Her foundation spackled a landscape of acne scars.

'Jagger,' he said.

She looked surprised. They always did.

'*Jagger?*' she asked. 'Really? Like *Mick* Jagger?'

'Something like that.'

She smiled. She shouldn't have. It ruined what little about her face there was to like. In it he saw every regret, every Sunday morning, every gray towel and yellowed bed sheet.

But this was still Saturday night, and the lights were low.

'You got as much *money* as Mick Jagger?' she asked.

'I got enough.'

She leaned closer. Her perfume was too sweet and too heavy, but he liked it that way.

'How much is enough?' she asked.

'Enough for the night.'

Something lit her eyes. It helped. Maybe she wasn't so banged up after all, despite the fact that she was turning tricks in a hole like this. He nodded at the bartender, dropped a fifty on the bar. This time the barkeep was prompt. Odd, that. In a flash he was back with refills. He even wiped down the bar.

'But can you *go* all night, that's the question,' she said.

'I don't need to go all night. I just need to go until the meter runs out.'

She laughed. Her breath smelled of cigarettes and Altoids and gum disease.

'You are funny,' she said. 'I like that.'

It doesn't matter what you like, he thought. *It hasn't mattered for more than twenty years.*

She drained her Seven and Seven, tapped her plastic nails on the bar. She turned to face him again, as if the idea had just come to her. 'What do you say we buy a bottle and go have some fun?'

He glanced over. '*We?* You pitching in?'

She gave him a gentle slap on the shoulder. 'Oh, stop.'

'I've got a bottle in my truck,' he said.

'Is that an invitation?'

'Only if you want it to be.'

'Sounds like a plan,' she said. She slipped off the stool, toddled a bit, grabbed the rail to steady herself. These were clearly not her first two drinks of the evening. 'I'm just going to visit the little girls' room. Don't you *dare* go anywhere.'

She flounced to the far side of the bar, drawing meager attention from the two old codgers at the other end.

He finished his beer, picked up the bills, leaving the barkeep a thirty-nine cent tip. It didn't go unnoticed.

A few minutes later the woman returned, heavier on the eye shadow, lipstick, perfume, breath mints.

They stepped into the cold night air.

'Where's your truck?' she asked.

He pointed to the footpath, the trail that snaked through the woods. 'Through there.'

'You're parked in the rest area?'

'Yeah.'

She looked at her shoes, a pair of cut-rate white heels, at least one size too small. 'I hope the path ain't muddy.'

'It isn't.'

She slipped an arm through his, the one opposite his duffel. They crossed the tavern's small parking lot, then walked into the woods.

'What's in the bag?' she asked.

'All my money.'

She laughed again.

When they got to the halfway point, far from the lights, he stopped, opened his duffel, took out a pint of Southern Comfort.

'For the road,' he said.

'Nice.'

He uncapped the bottle, took a drink.

'Open your mouth and close your eyes,' he said.

She did as she was told.

'Wider,' he said.

He looked at her standing there, in the diffused moonlight,

her mouth pink and gaping. It was how he planned to remember her. It was how he remembered them all.

At precisely the same instant he dropped the razor blade into her mouth, he poured in a third of the bottle of Comfort.

The steel hit first. The woman gagged, choked, bucked. When she did this the blade shot forward in her mouth, sliced through her lower lip.

He stood to the side as the woman coughed out a gulp of blood and whiskey. She then spit the blade into her hand, dropped it to the ground.

When she looked up at him he saw that the razor had sliced her lower lip in half.

'*What did you do?*' she screamed.

Because of her destroyed mouth it came out *whan nin you noo?* But he understood. He always understood.

He pushed her into a tree. She slumped to the ground, gasping for air, hacking blood like some just hooked fish.

He circled her, the adrenaline now screaming in his veins.

'What did you think we were going to do?' he asked. He put a boot on her stomach, along with half his weight. This brought another thick gout of red from her mouth and nose. 'Hmm? Did you think we were going to *fuck*? Did you think I was going to put my cock into your filthy, diseased *mouth*?'

He dropped to the ground, straddled her.

'If I did that, I'd be fucking everyone you've ever been with.'

He leaned back to admire his work, grabbed the bottle, downed some Comfort to ward off the chill. He took his eyes off her for a second, but it was long enough.

Somehow the razor blade was in her hand. She swiped it across his face, cutting him from just below his right eye to the top of his chin.

He felt the pain first, then the heat of his own blood, then the cold. Steam rose from his open wound, clouding his eyes.

'You fucking *bitch*.'

He slapped her across the face. Once, twice, then once more. Her face was now marbled with blood and phlegm. Her ruined mouth was open, her lower lip in two pieces.

He thought about taking a rock to her skull, but not yet. She'd cut him, and she would pay. He killed the bottle, wiped it clean, tossed it into the woods, then ripped off her tank top, used it to sponge his face. He reached into his duffel.

'That is one nasty cut,' he said. 'I'm going to close that wound for you. There's all kinds of bacteria out here. You don't want to get an infection, do you? It wouldn't be good for business.'

He pulled the blowtorch from his bag, a big BernzOmatic. When she saw it she tried to wiggle out from under him, but her strength was all but sapped. He hit her in the face again – just hard enough to keep her in place – then took a lighter from his pocket, lit the torch, adjusted the flame. When it was a perfect yellow-blue point, he said:

'Tell me you love me.'

Nothing. She was going into shock. He brought the flame closer to her face.

'*Tell* me.'

'I . . . na . . . yoo.'

'Of course you do.'

He went to work on her lip. Her dying screams were swallowed by the sound of the blowtorch. The smell of charred flesh rose into the night air.

By the time he reached her eyes she was silent.

The clouds had again pulled away from the moon by the time he emerged from the woods, the quarter-mile pass-through that led to the rest area where he had parked.

When he had parked his truck, earlier in the day, he had

positioned it as close to the path as he could. There had been three other rigs closer, but he figured he was near enough.

The other trucks were now gone.

Before stepping into the sodium streetlights of the massive parking lot – which held a fueling station and an all-night diner – he looked at his clothes. His jacket was covered in blood, large patches that appeared black in the moonlight. He took off his down jacket, turned it inside out, put it back on. He picked up a handful of leaves and wiped the blood from his face.

A few moments later, when he came around the back of the diner, he saw a woman standing there. She saw him, too.

It was one of the diner waitresses, standing by the back door, her powder blue rayon uniform and white sweater looking bright and clean and sterile under the sodium lamps. She was on break, using an emery board, sanding her nails.

'Oh, my goodness,' she said.

He could only imagine what he must look like to her.

'Hey,' he said.

'Are you okay?'

'Yeah,' he said. 'You know. I'm good. Ran into a low branch back there. Cut me pretty fine, I reckon.'

He was lightheaded, and not just from the watered down Scotch and flat beer and warm Comfort. He had lost blood.

The waitress glanced over his shoulder, back. She'd seen him come out of the woods. Bad for him, worse for her. The night was getting deeper. As exhausted as he was, he knew what he had to do. She would get the short ride, but she'd ride.

He turned, scanned the parking lot, looked at the steamed windows of the diner. No one was watching. At least, no one he could see.

'You don't happen to have a Band-Aid or anything do you?' he asked.

'Maybe.' She unzipped and ransacked her purse. 'No, sweetie.

Best I can do is a Kleenex, but I don't think that'll help. You're bleeding pretty good. You should go to the hospital.' She pointed at a blue Nissan Sentra in the lot. 'I can take you if you want.'

He chucked a thumb toward his rig. 'I've got a first aid kit in my truck,' he said. 'You any good with that stuff?'

She smiled. 'I've got a whole passel of younger brothers and sisters. Always getting in scrapes. I think I can manage.'

They walked to the far end of the lot. More than once he had to slow down, dizzy. When they got to the truck he unlocked the passenger side first. The waitress got in.

'The kit's in the glove box,' he said.

He closed the door. On the way to the driver's side he unsnapped the closure on his knife sheath. It was a six-inch Buck, razor sharp.

He opened his door, pulled himself into the cab, angled the mirror toward his face.

The whore had sliced him good.

While the waitress lined up the gauze and the foil-wrapped alcohol swabs on the dashboard, he pushed back the mirror, glanced around the lot. No other drivers, no one coming out of the diner.

He would do it now.

Before he could slip the knife from its sheath he noticed something in the parking lot, right near the entrance to the path. It was a small red wallet. It matched the red vinyl of the waitress's purse. For any number of reasons, he couldn't leave it there.

'Is that yours?' he asked.

She glanced to where he was pointing, put down the first aid kit, looked in her purse. 'Oh, shoot,' she said. 'I must have dropped it.'

'I'll get it.'

'You're a doll.'

He stepped out of the truck, walked across the lot, his head throbbing. He had a few Vicodin left. He reached into his pocket, pulled out the vial, chewed them dry, trying to recall if he had an inch or so of Wild Turkey left in the truck.

He picked up the wallet, thought for a moment about opening it, about learning the waitress's name. It didn't matter. It never had.

Still, his curiosity got the better of him.

As he opened the wallet he felt the hot breath brush the back of his neck, saw the long shadow pool at his feet.

An instant later his head exploded into a supernova of bright orange fire.

Cold.

Lying on his back, he opened his eyes, the pain in his head now a savage thing. The world smelled of wet compost and loam and pine needles. Snow whispered down, catching on his eyelashes.

He tried to stand up, but couldn't move his arms, his hands, his feet. He slowly turned his head, saw the whore's dead body next to him, the scorched holes where her eyes used to be. Something – some animal – had already been at her face.

'Stand up.' The voice was a whisper near his left ear.

By the time he managed to turn his head, no one was there.

'I . . . I can't.'

His words sounded distant, as if they belonged to someone else.

'No, you cannot,' came the soft voice. 'I have all but severed your spinal cord. You will never walk again.'

Why? he wanted to ask, but knew instantly that he could no longer make a sound. Perhaps it was because he *knew* why.

*

Time left, returned. It was morning somehow.

He looked into the gently falling snow, saw the axe, the bright steel wing glimmering in the splintered dawn like some silent, circling hawk.

Moments later, when the heavy blade fell, he heard them all – as he knew he would on this day – every dead thing beckoning him toward the darkness, a place where nothing human stirred, a place where his father still lay in wait, a place where the screams of children echo forever.

BOOK ONE

Anabelle

1

At just after six a.m., as every other day, Mr Marseille and I opened our eyes, dark lashes counterweighted to the light.

It was mid-November, and although the frost had not yet touched the windows – this usually comes to our eaves in late December – there was a mist on the glass that gave the early morning light a delicate quality, as if we were looking at the world through a Lalique figurine.

Before we dressed for the day we drew our names in the condensation on the windowpane, the double *l* in Mr Marseille's name and the double *l* in mine slanting toward one another like tiny Doric columns, as has been our monogram for as long as we both could remember.

Mr Marseille looked at the paint swatches, a frown tilling his brow. In the overhead lights of the big store his eyes appeared an ocean blue, but I knew them to be green, the way the trees appear after the first draft of spring, the way the grass of a well-tended cemetery looks on the Fourth of July.

On this day, beneath our drab winter overcoats, we were dressed for tea. My dress was scarlet; his suit, a dove gray. These were the colors of our amusements, you see, the feathers by which we cleave our places at the table.

'I don't know,' Mr Marseille said. 'I just don't know.'

I glanced at the selections, and saw his impasse. There had to be a half-dozen choices, all of which, from just a few feet away, could be described as yellow. Pale yellow, at that. Not the yellow of sunflowers or school buses or taxicabs, or even the yellow of summer corn. These were pastel shades, almost whitish, and they had the most scandalous of names:

Butter Frosting. Lemon Whip. Sweet Marzipan.

Mr Marseille hummed a song, *our* song, almost certainly turning over the words in his mind, perhaps hoping for a flicker of inspiration.

I soon became distracted by a woman with a small child, passing by at the end of our aisle. The woman wore a short puffy jacket and shockingly tight denim jeans. Her makeup seemed to have been applied in haste – perhaps reflected in a less than well-silvered mirror – and gave her an almost clownish look in the unforgiving light of the store. The child, a toddler at oldest, bounced along behind the woman, deliriously consumed by an oversized cookie with brightly colored candies baked in. A few moments after they passed from view I heard the woman exhort the child to hurry up. I don't imagine the little boy did.

At the thought of the mother and child I felt a familiar yearning blossom within me. I scolded it away, and turned once more to Mr Marseille and his assessments. Before I could choke the words, I pointed at one of the paint swatches in his hands, and asked:

'What's wrong with this one? Candlelight is a delightful name. Quite apropos, *n'est-ce pas?*'

Mr Marseille looked up – first at the long, empty aisle, then at the myriad cans of paint, then at me. He replied softly, but force-fully:

'It is *my* decision, and I *will* not be hurried.'

I simply hated it when Mr Marseille was cross with me. It did not happen often – we were kindred and compatible spirits in almost all ways, especially in the habits of color and texture and fabric and song – but when I saw the flare in his eyes I knew that this would be a day of numbering, our first since that terrible moment last week, a day during which a young girl's blood would surely be the rouge that colored my cheeks.

We rode in our car, a white sedan that, according to Mr Mar-seille, had once been advertised during a football game. I don't know much about cars – or football, for that matter – and this was not *our* car, not by any watermark of legal ownership. Mr Marseille simply drove to the curb about an hour earlier, and I got in. In this manner it *became* our car, if only for the briefest of times. Mr Marseille, like all of our kind, was an expert bor-rower.

The first thing I noticed was that the front seat smelled of licorice. The sweet kind. I don't care for the other kind. It is bitter to my tongue. There are some who crave it, but if I've learned anything in this life it is that one can never reason, or truly under-stand, the tastes of another.

We drove on Benjamin Franklin Parkway, the magnificent divided thoroughfare that I've heard is patterned, after a fashion, on the Champs-Élysées in Paris. I've never been to Paris but I've seen many photographs, and this seems to be true.

I speak a cluttered French, as does Mr Marseille – sometimes, for sport, we go for days speaking nothing else – and we often talk of one day travelling from the City of Brotherly Love to the City of Light.

The trees along the parkway were deep in their autumn

slumber, but I've been on this street in summer, when the green seems to go on forever, bookended by the stately Museum of Art at one end, and the splendid Swann Fountain on the other. On this November morning the street was beautiful, but if you come here in July it will be breathtaking.

We followed the group of girls at a discreet distance. They had attended a showing of a film at the Franklin Institute, and were now boarding a bus to take them back to their school.

Mr Marseille had thought of making our invitation on Winter Street, but decided against it. Too many busybodies to ruin our surprise.

At just after noon the bus pulled over near the corner of Sixteenth and Locust. The teenage girls – about a dozen in number, all dressed alike in their school uniforms – disembarked. They lingered on the corner, chatting about everything and nothing, as girls of an age will do.

After a short time, a few cars showed up; a number of the girls drove off in backseats, carpooled by one mother or another.

The girl who would be our guest walked a few blocks south with another of her classmates, a tall, lanky girl wearing a magenta cardigan, in the style of a fisherman's knit.

We drove a few blocks ahead of them, parked in an alley, then marched briskly around the block, coming up behind the girls. Girls at this age often dawdle, and this was good for us. We caught them in short order.

When the tall girl finally said goodbye, on the corner of Sixteenth and Spruce, Mr Marseille and I walked up behind our soon-to-be guest, waiting for the signal to cross the street.

Eventually the girl looked over.

'Hello,' Mr Marseille said.

The girl glanced at me, then at Mr Marseille. Sensing no threat, perhaps because she saw us as a couple – a couple of an age not significantly greater than her own – she returned the greeting.

'Hi,' she said.

While we waited for the light to change, Mr Marseille unbuttoned his coat, struck a pose, offering the well-turned peak lapel of his suit jacket. The hem was a pick stitch, and finely finished. I know this because I am the seamstress who fitted him.

'Wow,' the girl added. 'I like your suit. A *lot*.'

Mr Marseille's eyes lighted. In addition to being sartorially fastidious, he was terribly vain, and always available for a compliment.

'What a lovely thing to say,' he said. 'How very kind of you.'

The girl, perhaps not knowing the correct response, said nothing. She stole a glance at the Walk signal. It still showed a hand.

'My name is Marseille,' he said. 'This is my dearest heart, Anabelle.'

Mr Marseille extended his hand. The girl blushed, offered her own.

'I'm Nicole.'

Mr Marseille leaned forward, as was his manner, and gently kissed the back of the girl's fingers. Many think the custom is to kiss the back of a lady's *hand* – on the side just opposite the palm – but this is not proper.

A gentleman knows.

Nicole reddened even more deeply.

When she glanced at me I made the slightest curtsy. Ladies do not shake hands with ladies.

At this moment the light changed. Mr Marseille let go of the girl's hand and, in a courtly fashion, offered her safe passage across the lane.

I followed.

We continued down the street in silence until we came to the mouth of the alley; the alley in which we parked our car.

Mr Marseille held up a hand. He and I stopped walking.

'I have a confession to make,' he said.

The girl, appearing to be fully at ease with these two polite and interesting characters, stopped as well. She looked intrigued by Mr Marseille's statement.

'A confession?'

'Yes,' he said. 'Our meeting was not by accident today. We're here to invite you to tea.'

The girl looked at me for a moment, then back at Mr Marseille.

'You want to invite me to tea?'

'Yes.'

'I don't know what you mean,' she said.

Mr Marseille smiled. He had a pretty smile, brilliantly white, almost feminine in its deceits. It was the kind of smile that turned strangers into cohorts in all manner of petty crime, the kind of smile that puts at ease both the very young and the very old. I've yet to meet a young woman who could resist its charm.

'Every day, about four o'clock, we have tea,' Mr Marseille said. 'It is quite the haphazard affair on most days, but every so often we have a special tea – a *thé dansant*, if you'll allow – one to which we invite all our friends, and always someone new. Someone we hope will *become* a new friend. Won't you say you'll join us?'

The young woman looked confused. But still she was gracious. This is the sign of a good upbringing. Both Mr Marseille and I believe courtesy and good manners are paramount to getting along in the world these days. It is what lingers with people after you take your leave, like the quality of your soap, or the polish of your shoes.

'Look,' the young lady began. 'I think you've mistaken me for someone else. But thanks anyway.' She glanced at her watch, then back at Mr Marseille. 'I'm afraid I have a ton of homework.'

With a lightning fast move Mr Marseille took the girl by both wrists, and spun her into the alleyway. Mr Marseille is quite the athlete, you see. I once saw him catch a common housefly in midair, then throw it into a hot skillet, where we witnessed its life vanish into an ampersand of silver smoke.

As he seized the girl I watched her eyes. They flew open to their widest: counterweights on a precious Bru. I noticed then, for the first time, that her irises had scattered about them tiny flecks of gold.

This would be a challenge for me, for it was my duty – and my passion – to re-create such things.

We sat around the small table in our workshop. At the moment it was just Nicole, Mr Marseille, and me. Our friends had yet to arrive. There was much to do.

'Would you like some more tea?' I asked.

The girl opened her mouth to speak, but no words came forth. Our special tea often had this effect. Mr Marseille and I never drank it, of course, but we had seen its magical results on others many times. Nicole had already had two cups, and I could only imagine the colors she saw; Alice at the mouth of the rabbit hole.

I poured more tea into her cup.

'There,' I said. 'I think you should let it cool for a time. It is very hot.'

While I made the final measurements, Mr Marseille excused himself to make ready what we needed for the gala. We were never happier than at this moment, a moment when, needle in hand, I made the closing stiches, and Mr Marseille prepared the final table.

We parked by the river, exited the car. Before showing our guest to her seat, Mr Marseille blindfolded me. I could barely conceal my anticipation and delight. I do *so* love a tea.

Mr Marseille does, as well.

With baby steps I breached the path. When Mr Marseille removed my scarf, I opened my eyes.

It was beautiful. Better than beautiful.

It was *magic*.

Mr Marseille had selected the right color. He often labored over the decision for days, but each time, after the disposing of the rollers and trays and brushes, after the peeling away of the masking tape, it was as if the object of his labors had always been so.

Moments later we helped the girl – Nicole Solomon was her full name – from the car. Her very presence at our table made her absent from another. Such is the way of all life.

As Mr Marseille removed the stockings from the bag, I made my goodbye, tears gathering at the corners of my eyes, thinking that Mr Shakespeare was surely wrong.

There is no sweetness in parting.

Only sorrow.

I returned to where Mr Marseille stood, and pressed something into his gloved hand.

'I want her to have this,' I said.

Mr Marseille looked at what I had given him. He seemed surprised. 'Are you sure?'

I was not. But I'd had it so long, and loved it so deeply, I felt it was time for the bird to fly on its own.

'Yes,' I said. 'I'm sure.'

Mr Marseille touched my cheek and said, 'My dearest heart.'

Under the bright moon, as Philadelphia slept, we watched the shadow of the girl's legs cast parallel lines on the station house wall, just like the double *l* in Anabelle and Mr Marseille.

2

They always come back.

If there was one truth known to Detective Kevin Francis Byrne – as well as any veteran law enforcement officer, anywhere in the world – it was that criminals always come back for their weapons.

Especially the expensive ones.

There were, of course, mitigating circumstances that might prevent this. The criminal being dead, to mention one happy outcome. Or being incarcerated. Not as joyous, but serviceable.

Even though there was always the distinct possibility that the police knew where you had stashed the weapon, and might be watching that spot in case you came back, in Kevin Byrne's experience, that had never stopped them.

Not once.

There were some who believed that the police, as a rule, were stumbling oafs who only managed to catch the dumb criminals. While the argument for this was persuasive, to some, it was not true. For Kevin Byrne, as well as most of the lifers he knew, the saying was a little different.

You catch the dumb ones *first*.

It was the second full day of surveillance and Byrne, who had enough years under his badge to have passed it off to a younger detective, volunteered to take last out, the shift that went from midnight to eight a.m. There were two reasons for this. One, he had long ago given in to his insomnia, working on the theory that he was one of those people who only needed four or five hours of sleep per night to function. Two, there was a much better chance that the man for whom they were looking – one Allan David Trumbo – would come for the weapon in the middle of the night.

If there was a third reason, it was that Byrne had a dog in this fight.

Six days earlier, Allan Wayne Trumbo – a two-time loser with two armed robbery convictions and a manslaughter conviction under his belt – walked into a convenience store near the corner of Frankford and Girard, put a gun to the head of the night clerk, and demanded all the money in the register. The man behind the counter complied. Then, as surveillance footage showed, Trumbo took a step back, leveled the weapon and fired.

The man behind the counter, Ahmed Al Rashid, the owner of Ahmed's Grocery, died on his feet. Trumbo, being the criminal mastermind that he is, then took off his ski mask in full view of the surveillance camera, reached into a rack, and took a package of TastyKake mini donuts. Coconut Crunch, to be exact.

By the time Trumbo stepped out onto the street, sector cars from the 26th District were already en route, just a few blocks away. The police pole camera on the corner of Marlborough and Girard showed the man dumping his weapon into a city trashcan just inside an alley, half a block east of Marlborough Street.

Although it was not Byrne's case, he knew Ahmed, having visited the bodega many times when he was a young patrol officer. Byrne didn't know a single cop who had ever had to pay for a cup of coffee at Ahmed's. His brimming tip jar was testament to his generosity.

Trumbo took that money, too.

Rule number one for any homicide detective was to never take any case personally. In the case of the cold-blooded murder of Ahmed Al Rashid, Byrne decided to disregard this rule, as he had many times before.

Byrne knew that Trumbo would come back for the weapon. He just didn't think it would take this long.

At the request of the PPD, the Sanitation Division of the Philadelphia Streets Department had not touched that particular trashcan since the incident. It had been under surveillance, in one manner or another, from the moment Trumbo walked away.

Investigators also had the AV Unit make a big show of taking down the two cameras that covered this end of the block – three police vans at noon, taking three times as long taking down the cameras than it took to put them up. If you were watching, and if you paid attention to such things, you would think that, for the time being, Big Brother was not watching this small corner of Philadelphia.

If you were stupid, that is.

Detectives from the Firearms Unit had taken the .38 Colt from the trashcan within an hour or so of Trumbo having dumped it and, with their mobile unit parked a block away, removed the firing pin, rendering the gun inoperable. They did this on the outside chance that, if this operation went south, they would not be putting a functioning handgun back on the street, in the hands of someone who had already committed murder with it.

While they'd had the weapon, the ID Unit took the chance to dust the gun for latents, and were happy to report that Allan Wayne Trumbo's prints were all over it.

Byrne glanced at his watch. Three-ten a.m. Even this part of the city was asleep. He was parked in a nondescript black Toyota, borrowed from the Narcotics Unit. Nobody had uglier, more invisible cars than the narcos.

Ahmed's Grocery had reopened, still braving the twenty-four-hour schedule. Even in light of the terrible tragedy, bills had to be paid. The rear door was now locked, but Byrne had a key, just in case he needed to use the restroom, which was just inside the back door.

At three-fifteen he needed to use the restroom.

Byrne got out of the car, locked it, walked to the rear entrance to the bodega.

A few minutes later he walked out the back door of the sandwich shop. Before stepping into the light he glanced at his car. His iPhone was still propped on the dash where he'd left it. If Trumbo had come to rescue his now-disabled weapon from the trashcan, Byrne would at least know about it.

Seeing the alley just as he'd left it, Byrne headed to his car. He didn't take three steps before he heard the unmistakable sound of the hammer being drawn back on a revolver.

Byrne turned slowly, hands out to his sides, and came face to face with Allan Wayne Trumbo. In Trumbo's hand was a Smith and Wesson .22.

'You 5-0?' Trumbo asked.

Byrne just nodded.

'Homicide?'

Byrne said nothing.

Trumbo stepped behind Byrne, reached around, removed Byrne's sidearm from his holster. He placed it on the ground, kicked it toward the wall. He stepped back around to face Byrne, standing more than a few feet away. Trumbo had, of course, done this a few times. You don't stand within arm's length. That only happened in the movies, and only when the hero slapped the gun from the bad guy's hand.

Byrne was no hero.

'I didn't shoot that old man,' Trumbo said.

'What old man?'

'Don't *fuck* with me, motherfucker. I know why you're here.'

Byrne squared off, never taking his eyes from Trumbo's eyes. 'You need to think about this.'

Trumbo looked down the alley, at no one at all, then back at Byrne. It was street theater, starring, as always, the man with the gun. 'Ex*cuse* me?'

Byrne watched the barrel of the weapon, looking for the slightest shake that would signal trouble. For the moment the man's hands were steady.

'What I mean to say is, you need to reconsider the next few minutes of your life.'

'Is that right?'

'It is,' Byrne said. 'We have you in that store, Trumbo. Two cameras. Front and side. Not sure why you took off the mask, but that's your business.' Byrne lowered his hands slightly. 'It was bad enough you killed Ahmed, and you *will* go down for that. But if you kill a police officer, I guarantee you that you don't sleep fifteen minutes straight for the rest of your life. You need to think about this. Your life starts now.'

Trumbo looked at the weapon in his hand, back at Byrne. 'You're telling *me* what *I* need to do? Maybe *you* catch a hot one tonight.'

'Maybe.'

Trumbo smiled. Byrne felt an icy drop of sweat trickle down his spine. He'd pushed this too far.

'Let's just call it friendly advice,' Byrne said with a lot more confidence than he felt.

'Oh, you my *friend* now?'

Byrne said nothing.

Trumbo nodded at the Chevy parked at the turnoff in the alley. 'That yours?'

Byrne nodded.

'Nice car,' he said with a smirk. 'Keys in it?'

Byrne looked down and to his left. 'In my left front pocket.'

'Okay, then. Slow – and I mean slow like I fuck your wife – and with two fingers, I want you to get me them keys.'

Before Byrne could move, the night air was sliced by the sound of a young woman's laugh. The sound was so odd, in this scenario, at this late hour, that both men froze.

An instant later they turned to see two rather inebriated people – a young man and a young woman – walking toward them up the alley, arm in arm.

Byrne closed his eyes, waited for the three gunshots, one of which would certainly end his life. When he didn't hear them, he opened his eyes.

The man entering the alley was in his thirties, fair haired, with a droopy Fu Manchu mustache. He wore faded Levi's and a short denim jacket. He had his arm around a dark-eyed beauty – tight black jeans, hoop earrings. She was a few years younger. When the young woman saw the man with the gun she stopped, her eyes wide with fear.

She stepped behind Fu Manchu, doing her best not to look at the man with the .22.

'*Whoa,*' Fu Manchu said, slowly putting his hands up and out front.

'D'fuck you *doing*?' Trumbo asked. 'Get the fuck out of here.'

Byrne saw that the woman had already managed to slip out of her heels.

Nobody did anything.

'Wait,' the woman began. 'You're saying I can go?'

'You deaf? I *said* get the fuck *out* of here.'

The young woman backed up a few paces, now keeping her eyes on the man with the gun, then turned and ran down the alley, to the corner, and disappeared.

While Trumbo was momentarily distracted, Byrne inched toward his weapon on the ground.

'You too,' Trumbo said to Fu Manchu. 'This ain't your business.'

The young man kept his hands out to his sides. 'I hear you, boss,' he said. 'No problem.'

'Just back up and follow your bitch.'

A look came over Fu Manchu's face, one Byrne recognized as acknowledgment. 'I know you,' the young man said.

'You *know* me?' Trumbo asked.

The young man smiled. 'Yeah. We met in '09. Summer.'

'I don't know you, man,' Trumbo said. The gun hand began to tremble. Never a good sign, in Byrne's experience, and he had enough experience in situations like this for three lifetimes.

'Yeah. You're Mickey's cousin. Mickey Costello.'

'I know who my fucking cousin is,' Trumbo said. 'How you know Mickey?'

'Same way I know you, bro. We did that body shop up on Cambria. Me and Mickey took the door; you and Bobby Sanzo drove the van.'

Trumbo wiped the sweat from his forehead, began to nod. 'Yeah. Yeah. All right. You're ...'

'Spider.' He pulled up a sleeve to reveal a highly detailed tat of a spider and a web. At his wrist was a fly, trapped in the web.

'Spider. I remember.' Trumbo was sweating profusely now. 'Bobby's dead, you know.'

'Heard.'

'Got cut pulling that dime in Graterford.'

Fu Manchu shook his head. 'He was in Dannemora. In New York.'

'Right,' Trumbo said. 'Dannemora.'

It was clearly a test, and Fu Manchu apparently passed. He nodded at Byrne.

'What you got going on here, my brother?'

Trumbo gave the man a brief rundown on the situation.

Fu Manchu pointed at the trashcan. 'That's the can?'

'Yeah.'

'Why don't you just go get it? I got this.'

'You *got* this?'

The man lifted up the front of his shirt. There, in his waistband, was the grip of a 9mm semi auto.

'Nice,' Trumbo said.

'It stops the rain.'

As is the way of the street, Fu Manchu got bumped up a notch.

Trumbo nodded at Byrne. 'He doesn't fucking move.'

'Not one inch, my brother.'

Trumbo stuck his .22 into the back of his jeans, walked over to the trashcan. He tipped it onto its side, began to fumble around. After a few seconds he reached in, pulled out the greasy brown bag. He lofted it, feeling the heft. He looked inside.

'Oh yeah.'

Before Trumbo could stand up, Fu Manchu took a step forward. He put the barrel of his Glock to the back of Trumbo's head.

Trumbo: 'You gotta be fuckin' *kidding* me.'

'No joke,' Fu Manchu said. He pulled the .22 from Trumbo's waistband, then took out a pair of stainless steel handcuffs. 'Put your hands behind your back.'

Byrne watched Trumbo's eyes shift back and forth, looking for a play. There was none. He was on his knees, unarmed, with a gun to his head. Byrne soon saw resignation. Trumbo complied.

With Trumbo now handcuffed, Fu Manchu reached into his back pocket, produced a leather wallet, flicked it open. He held it in front of Trumbo's eyes. Trumbo focused, read the name aloud:

'Joshua Bontrager?'

'That's *Detective* Joshua Bontrager to you, sir.'

'Jesus Christ, a cop?'

'Well, *I* am,' Bontrager said. 'Our Lord and Savior, however, was not.'

Trumbo said nothing. Bontrager reached up, gently peeled away the false mustache.

If Trumbo had seen the pole cameras come down out on the block, he had not seen the two go up on the rooftops of the two buildings that formed the alley, cameras pointing directly down at them. The whole time Byrne had been in Ahmed's Grocery – less than a minute – the alley had been under video surveillance from a nearby van, where Josh Bontrager and fellow officers were waiting to step in if needed.

And *man* were they ever needed, Byrne thought.

The young woman who had been with Bontrager – Detective Maria Caruso – came around the corner with a pair of uniformed officers from the 26th District.

She looked at Bontrager standing over the handcuffed suspect. 'Look at *you*, making friends in the big city already,' she said.

Bontrager smiled. 'We're not in Berks County any more, Auntie Em.'

Maria laughed, high-fived Bontrager.

There was a pretty good chance that Allan Wayne Trumbo did not see the humor in any of this.

Byrne thought: What did they have? They had the suspect's

fingerprints on the weapon, the weapon was in the system, and they had the suspect in custody, down on his knees in a dirty alleyway in Fishtown – where he belonged, at least for the moment – and all was right in William Penn's 'greene country towne.'

Police were currently holding James 'Spider' Dimmock in the cells beneath the Roundhouse on an outstanding warrant. Although the resemblance would not hold up if the men were standing side by side, Josh Bontrager and Spider Dimmock looked enough alike for the purposes of this night detail, right down to the temporary tattoo and the stick-on mustache.

Ten minutes later Byrne walked out of the alley. He had possibly once been this tired, but not for a long time. He approached the sector car in which Allan Wayne Trumbo was safely secured.

Byrne opened the back door of the car, looked Trumbo in the eyes. There was a lot he wanted to say. In the end he said:

'He had five children.'

Trumbo glanced up, a confused look on his face.

'Who did?' he asked.

Byrne looked heavenward, back at Trumbo. He wanted to draw down, cap the little asshole for target practice, or at the very least send him off with a broken jaw for pointing a gun at him, but that would have ruined everything. Instead, he reached into his pocket, retrieved something he'd purchased inside Ahmed's Grocery, tossed it onto Trumbo's lap.

It was a package of TastyKake donuts.

Coconut Crunch, to be exact.

As hectic as the duty room of the Homicide Unit often was – at any given time there could be upwards of fifty people here, sometimes more – Byrne never ceased to marvel at how quiet it could be in the middle of the night. The PPD Homicide Unit ran 24/7, with three shifts of detectives.

At this hour it was a handful of detectives working leads on computers, filling out the endless paperwork, making notes about the next day's interviews.

Byrne put in a call to the primary detective on the Ahmed's Grocery case, alerting him to the arrest. The man had been sound asleep, but nothing woke you up faster or more refreshed than hearing that one of your cases – especially a brutal homicide – was on the way to closure. The detective, a lifer named Logan Evans, promised to pay for Byrne's daughter's wedding.

It was a figure of speech. A few rounds of drinks at Finnigan's Wake would probably do.

Byrne needed to decelerate. Nothing was more life affirming, or exhilarating, than having a gun stuck in your face, and living to tell the tale.

He grabbed a stack of newspapers, rifled through, looking for the front section. He found it, glanced at the date.

It was from six days earlier.

Doesn't anybody in this place throw anything away?

He went through the pile again, found nothing more recent. He poured some coffee, put his feet up.

Before long a short item caught his eye. It was no more than a few column inches, written by a crime beat reporter for the *Inquirer*. Police everywhere had a love/hate relationship with crime beat reporters. Sometimes you needed them to get the word out about something. Sometimes you wanted to take them to the ground for leaking information that puts a suspect into the wind.

This article fell into neither category.

CONVICTED CHILD KILLER TO BE PUT TO DEATH

My God, Byrne thought. Valerie Beckert was finally getting the hot shot.

He thought back to the decade-old case. He had investigated the Thomas Rule homicide on his own because his partner at the time, Jimmy Purify, had been on medical leave.

Investigate was an overstatement. There had been precious little to examine.

On a hot August night, ten years earlier, police dispatch received a 911 call saying that a woman was observed in Fairmount Park trying to bury something. A sector car responded, and the two officers discovered that the 'something' the woman – nineteen-year-old Valerie Beckert – was trying to bury was a dead child, a four-year-old boy named Thomas Rule.

Valerie Beckert was detained.

When Byrne arrived on scene he found the woman sitting on a park bench, her hands cuffed behind her, her eyes dry. Byrne gave the woman her Miranda warnings, and asked if she had anything to say.

'I killed him,' is all she said.

At the Roundhouse – the Police Administration Building at Eighth and Race Streets – Valerie signed a full confession, detailing how she had kidnapped the boy from a playground near his house, and how she strangled him.

She did not detail why she had done it.

When asked about whether or not there had been other boys, other victims, Valerie Beckert said nothing.

Her car – an eight-year-old Chevy station wagon – was brought to the police garage and thoroughly processed. There were a number of different DNA profiles found, one of which belonged to Thomas Rule, one to Valerie Beckert. The rest were classified as unknowns.

Investigators from the Crime Scene Unit also processed Valerie's house – a large, six-bedroom Tudor in the Wynnefield section of the city – and found even less.

If she had kidnapped and killed other children, and Byrne was convinced she had, she had either not kept them in her house, or had gone to great lengths to destroy any and all evidence of transference.

The department, with help from the FBI, used methane probes in both the basement of Valerie's house, as well a one square mile area of Fairmount Park near the attempted burial site, and found no other buried victims.

Not much was known about Valerie Beckert. She had no Social Security number, no tax ID. There was no record of her birth, immunizations, schooling. She had never before been fingerprinted or arrested.

The Wynnefield house, the deed to which was in Valerie's name, had been recently owned by a woman named Josephine Beckert, a woman believed to be Valerie's aunt. According to court records, Josephine Beckert died in a household accident a year before Valerie's arrest.

It was Byrne's understanding that the Wynnefield house had stood vacant for the past ten years. The widely held belief that the house was, in some way, a chamber of horrors, did not go over well with potential buyers.

And now, with Valerie Beckert's execution date coming in less than three weeks, it would probably go into foreclosure, if it wasn't already. Soon after, it would surely be demolished.

It was late, but Byrne knew the deputy superintendent at the State Correctional Institution at Muncy, a 1400-bed facility for women, located in Lycoming County, Pennsylvania, near Williamsport.

Valerie Beckert was incarcerated at SCI Muncy, where she would be held until Phase III of her death sentence began, and then would be moved to SCI Rockview, which was located near State College, Pennsylvania.

Byrne picked up the phone, made the call. He was soon routed to the desk of Deputy Superintendent Barbara Louise Wagner. Wagner was a former PPD detective who had worked in the Special Victims Unit for many years until she decided to enter the Department of Corrections.

They got their pleasantries out of the way. Byrne moved on to the reason for his call.

'I need you to look into something for me, Barb.'

'On one condition,' she said.

'Okay,' Byrne said. 'Name it.'

'One of these days you and I go to Wildwood, check into a cheap motel, and snog like drunken ferrets for the whole weekend.'

Barbara Wagner was Byrne's age, perhaps a few years older, married as hell, with four or five grown kids, and at least as many grandchildren. Still, this was their game, and always had been. Byrne played along. It was fun.

He needed fun.

'Sounds like a plan,' he said.

'I still have that black negligee from the first time you promised me.'

'And I'll bet it looks better than ever on you.'

'Sweet talker.'

Byrne laughed. 'It's a gift.'

'What can I do for you, detective?'

Byrne gathered his thoughts. 'I need to know about an inmate.'

'Name?'

'Valerie Beckert.'

'Ah, our girl of the hour,' Barbara said. 'Tick, tick, tick.'

'Yeah. Won't be long now.'

'She was your case?'

'Not much of a case,' Byrne said. 'At least not for Thomas Rule.'

'Sorry to say I'm out of the loop on this one,' Barbara said. 'Fill me in.'

Byrne explained the circumstances of Valerie Beckert's arrest, conviction, and sentencing. He glossed over the details of Thomas Rule's murder.

'Christ,' Barbara said.

'I'm Catholic, but I think He must have been busy that day.'

'What do you want to know?'

Byrne had thought about this, but everything he intended to say suddenly vacated his head. He went on instinct.

'There were more kids, Barb. I had her in the box for six hours. She didn't ask for a lawyer, and I didn't offer. In the end it didn't matter. I couldn't break her.'

Barbara Wagner just listened.

'I need to know if she's confided in someone at Muncy.'

'Okay,' Barbara said. 'But you know she has limited contact, right?'

'I know,' Byrne said. 'But in three weeks she's going to have *no* contact. With anyone. And her secrets are going to hell with her. I need to know. The *families* need to know.'

Byrne knew he was hitting this hard, but he couldn't seem to stop himself.

'Understood,' Barbara said.

'Do you think they'll let me see her?'

'Hard to say. If it was up to me, no problem.'

'I know,' Byrne said. 'Thanks.'

As a convicted murderer on death row drew closer to his or her execution date, contact with outside visitors became more and more limited. In the final days it was down to clergy, legal counsel, and immediate family.

Detective Kevin Byrne was none of the above.

'I can put in the request,' Barbara said. 'It'll have to clear her counsel.'

'Who's her lawyer now?'

'Hang on.'

Byrne heard Barbara tapping the keys on a keyboard.

'Her latest is Brandon Altschuld, Esquire.'

'Philly?'

'No,' she said. 'He's a PD out of Allentown.'

When Valerie Beckert went on trial for first degree murder she was represented by a rather pricey firm in Philadelphia. Now, when she was no longer news, she had a public defender.

'I'll see what I can find out,' Barbara added.

'Thanks, Barb.'

'You know how to thank me.'

Byrne laughed. 'I have my cargo shorts and flip-flops already packed.'

He had never owned either cargo shorts or flip-flops. Barbara probably knew this.

'Flip-flops you might need,' she said. 'Leave the cargo shorts at home.'

They sparred for a little while longer. Barbara Louise Wagner promised to call in a day or two.

Byrne turned back to the newspaper item. The photograph was the same one the *Inquirer* ran next to the original news item that chronicled Valerie Beckert's sentencing. It was a head shot of the woman, her eyes looking slightly left of the camera, appearing nothing like she must've looked when she had taken the life from Thomas Rule. In the newspapers she would be forever nineteen.

In the past ten years Byrne had thought of the woman often. At the time of her arrest he had compiled a list of a dozen missing children, twelve boys and girls who lived within five miles of Valerie's home in northwest Philadelphia. Every so often, during the last ten years, Byrne took out the list and made inquiries to see if the children had been returned to their families or, worst case scenario, their remains had been found.

The good news was that, over the past decade, six of the children had been reunited with their parents.

The bad news was that six of them had not.

Byrne took out his wallet, opened the much-folded index card with the six remaining names, as he had so many times before.

He knew that, when it came to finding missing children, investigators spoke in terms of months, sometimes weeks, more often in days. The more time that passed, the less likely it would be that the children would be located alive and well.

No one spoke in terms of years.

Byrne thought about asking his captain to once again put in a request with the FBI to reopen these missing persons cases. The cases were not technically closed, but over the past ten years, sadly, thousands more children had gone missing.

While the profile of men who kidnapped children was defined by a very narrow age and type for the child, the instance of women doing this – while much rarer by far – did not have such a distinct profile.

Perhaps this was the reason that Valerie Beckert had been able to get away with it for as long as she did. The Special Victims Unit had been looking for a man.

The children still missing were Nancy Brisbane, Jason Telich, Cassandra and Martin White, Thaddeus Woodman, and Aaron Petroff. Byrne had mapped the homes of the missing children – four of the twelve had been living in foster care – and Valerie's house was dead-center in the circle.

Byrne put away the list, made a mental note to run the names through the system again.

As he prepared to leave the Roundhouse, he thought about how, in his time in the homicide unit, he had interrogated thousands of suspects, hundreds of people who had committed murder. In that time he had become quite adept at rooting out those who were trying to work the system, trying to cop an insanity plea. He had never been wrong. Not once.

But when he interviewed Valerie Beckert on the night of her arrest he saw an icy tranquility in her eyes, even as she described stalking the little boy, luring him into her car, and strangling him.

Was she insane? Byrne had no doubt.

Was it fair or just that the Commonwealth of Pennsylvania was about to put an insane person to death?

This was not for him to decide.

The attempt made by Valerie Beckert's lawyer to reduce her sentence – or, her lawyer had hoped, to take the death penalty off the table – backfired. Valerie was declared competent, stood trial, and was convicted of first degree murder.

Byrne gathered his belongings, tried to push all thoughts of Valerie Beckert from his head.

Easier said.

In all, it had been a good day. The good guys took a bad guy – and two guns – off the streets.

Before leaving the duty room Byrne checked the roster, more commonly known as The Wheel. He was near the top. Tomorrow was a new day, and he had no idea where it would lead him.

When he stepped into the parking lot behind the Roundhouse he glanced in the general direction of Wynnefield, the small northwestern Philadelphia neighborhood where Valerie Beckert's house stood vacant.

For a brief, shivering moment he felt something pull him in that direction, something dark and foreboding, something he'd felt slither beneath his skin on that steamy August night ten years earlier.

THE DOLL MAKER

Six children found.
Six children still lost.
What did you do with them, Valerie?

3

Jessica Balzano looked at the two documents on her dining room table. They were similar in appearance – eight-and-a-half by eleven inch sheets of white paper, black ink, no staples, no folds.

As she sipped her first cup of coffee of the day, she looked out the kitchen window at the early morning commuters. It was usually her favorite time of day, so full of promise, the early morning light an armor against all the bad things the world could throw at you. She didn't feel that way today.

She glanced back at the documents, thought for a moment about how many life-changing events were chronicled by such benign things: birth certificates, death certificates, marriage certificates, laboratory test results, both good and bad. She had taken these two documents out of the file cabinet they kept in the tiny office off the living room of their South Philly row house. The cabinet held just about every touchstone of their lives, but at this moment, these were the only two that mattered to Jessica Balzano, her husband Vincent, and their children, Sophie and Carlos.

The document on the right was from Edward Jones, the brokerage firm at which they held their modest investments. A few municipal bonds, a money market account paying next to nothing, and some mutual funds that paid dividends.

The document on the left was a three page, double sided application form, an application she had read many times, but had yet to find the courage to fill out. At the top of the first page it read:

Pennsylvania Board of Law Examiners Application

She'd gone to law school at Temple University, taking every available class at every available opportunity – mornings, evenings, weekends – judiciously spending all her accumulated vacation days in classrooms with people who, for the most part, were many years younger than she. She'd gotten her degree in what she understood to be record time for Temple University, her alma mater where she'd gotten her undergraduate degree in criminal justice.

Getting through law school was supposed to be the hard part. From the beginning Jessica had her sights set on working in the Philadelphia District Attorney's office. Indeed, this had been her goal since she was a young girl who would sometimes watch her father, Peter Giovanni, testify in Municipal Court.

Each year the DA's office hired new assistant district attorneys from the same class of graduates from around the country. Weight was obviously given to freshly minted lawyers from the greater Philadelphia area, based on a number of factors, not the least of which was familiarity with the Pennsylvania Penal Code, as well as the knowledge of the people, the streets, and the struggles of the citizens of the City of Brotherly Love.

Jessica, having graduated top of her class, had inside knowledge that the job was all but hers for the asking.

She also knew that the salary of a new assistant district attorney was about half the pay of a veteran detective in the homicide unit, who were among the highest paid of all the gold badge detectives in the department. The debt load, in the end, she'd decided, had been simply too great. In addition to her huge student loan, there was their mortgage payment, private school tuition for both Sophie and Carlos, car payments on two vehicles, as well as orthodontics bills and every other bill that came with raising a family in an expensive city like Philadelphia.

Had she been single, or married without children, she might've gone for a period of time on Ramen noodles and tap water, but that wasn't the case.

The hard truth was – one at which she had arrived after many a sleepless night – that she couldn't afford to leave the department, not just yet. The final deadline for submitting the application, for the February taking of the bar exam, was two months away.

She sensed her husband behind her. Vincent crossed the small kitchen, wrapped his arms around her waist, peered over her shoulder.

'What have I told you about reading this stuff before breakfast?'

'I know,' Jessica said.

'You should be reading something calming. Like the Bible.'

Jessica smiled. 'You mean that part about Jesus tossing the moneychangers out of Temple University?'

'Good one,' Vincent said.

They fell silent for a few moments. Vincent knew that his wife had all but made her decision about this, just as he knew how heart-rending it was.

'Are you sure?' he asked.

Jessica wasn't. 'Yeah,' she said. 'I am.'

'We can do it, you know. We'll find a way.'

'It's too much, Vince,' Jessica said. 'We can't carry this load.'

Vincent spun her around to face him. He put his hands on her hips, pulled her close.

'We can pay this off,' he said. 'I'm a narcotics detective, remember? I take down one, two dealers – *bam*. Car loads of cash. We're gold.'

'I'm sure the IRS would have nothing to say about that.'

'Oh, yeah,' he said. 'Them.'

Jessica glanced around the kitchen, at the dishes stacked neatly in the sink, the napkins folded on the countertop, ready for dinner. She looked back into her husband's deep caramel eyes. He still made her heart flutter, even after all this time.

'Thanks for getting the kids off to school,' she said.

Vincent clearly knew how hard this day was going to be on her. He'd gotten up early to get Sophie and Carlos clothed, fed, book-bagged, and onto the bus, all while Jessica took a hot shower until the water ran cold.

'All in a day's work,' Vincent said.

'You could have done the dishes, though.'

Vincent laughed. 'Don't push your luck.'

Jessica took a moment, considered their options one last time. There was only one.

'I'm good with this,' she said. 'Really I am.'

Vincent kissed her on the forehead, then on the lips. 'If you're good, I'm good.'

'Besides, there's no way we would be able to keep this from the kids,' Jessica said. 'They'd find out about the money problems eventually.'

'They know.'

Jessica felt punched. She took a step back, the moment gone. 'What the hell do you mean, *they know*? How do they *know*? Did you tell them?'

'Of course not.'

'Then how?'

'How do kids know anything, Jess? They sense it. They know when we're fighting, they know when we're happy, they know when we have money problems. They just know. They always do.'

Jessica took a few deep breaths, tried to calm herself. 'Well, we've never had money problems like this.'

Vincent had no reply to this. There was none. It was true.

Jessica glanced at the clock. She was due at the Roundhouse.

'I've got to go. I'm meeting with the captain in twenty minutes.'

'Ross is a good man,' Vincent said. 'He'll be ecstatic. They didn't want to lose you in the first place. You know that, right?'

'I know.'

'It will be seamless and painless,' Vincent said. 'You'll see.'

Jessica felt her feelings close in on her. She wiped a tear from her eye. She promised herself she would not get emotional about this.

Where was the tough South Philly girl now that she needed her?

'Yeah,' she said. 'You're right. I'll be fine.'

Jessica reached for one of the folded napkins on the counter, probably for the cry she wasn't going to have on the way in. She saw something underneath.

'What's this?' she asked.

Vincent said nothing.

Jessica lifted the edge of the napkin. Underneath was a thin leather wallet. A five-year-old boy's wallet. Her five-year-old *son's* wallet. Jessica knew the precise contents. Four dollars and sixty-six cents.

It was all the money Carlos had in the world.

He was giving her his nest egg.

Jessica's heart broke into a thousand pieces.

She stood in the front plaza of the Roundhouse, just as she knew she would on this day. She thought about the building's legacy, its history. She thought about the nearly three-hundred officers who had given their lives to the city and the people of Philadelphia since the department was formed.

She glanced up at the huge statue that looked out over Franklin Park, the police officer holding a young child. She'd seen the statue thousands of times, but mostly as she drove by it, not affording it any significance, any weight in her life.

Until now.

On this day, the sight of that anonymous officer suddenly meant everything.

4

Twenty minutes later, having finished her meeting with Captain John Ross and her day work supervisor, Dana Westbrook, Jessica emerged from Ross's office. She felt as if an enormous weight had been lifted from her shoulders, but at the same time she wanted to gather her belongings and walk out of the building. She'd never felt this way before.

Jessica looked around for an open desk. Detectives in the homicide unit of the Philadelphia Police Department did not get their own desks. Each desk, and each computer terminal, were shared by the ninety detectives who worked seven days a week, all three tours. What you did get was a drawer in a file cabinet where you were supposed to put your service weapon while on the floor in the duty room. This made a great deal of sense, seeing as how many less than savory characters passed through the room, many of whom were not yet wearing handcuffs. Very few detectives adhered to the rule.

When she turned the corner into the center of the room she knew immediately which desk was hers for the day. Attached to either side of the desk were two huge Mylar balloons. On the desk was a white paper plate bearing a Danish pastry with one small candle burning. Jessica looked at the sayings on the huge, bright red balloons:

Break a leg!
Knock 'em dead!

Behind the desk, with two large cups of coffee in his hands, stood her partner, Kevin Byrne.

They found a quiet corner of the duty room, which was never easy, not the least of which was that the room – as was the design of almost every room in the Roundhouse – was semicircular. This had never struck anyone as a bright idea in a world of rectangular desks and square file cabinets.

Jessica told Byrne about her decision to postpone taking the bar exam, happily keeping her emotions in check.

'When did you decide this?' Byrne asked.

Jessica looked at her watch. 'About a half-hour ago.'

'You talked to the captain already?'

Jessica nodded. 'Everyone's good with it.'

Byrne looked out the window, at the bright autumn day, at the leaves changing in the park across the street. He looked back. 'How come?' he asked. 'I thought it was all set.'

So did I, Jessica thought. Just about everyone on day work was expecting her to come in today to gather her few belongings and say her goodbyes.

As Jessica was about to explain all this to her partner, she saw Dana Westbrook crossing the duty room, a look of grim determination on her face, a document in hand. Both Jessica and Byrne knew what was coming.

'We'll talk,' Jessica said.

Westbrook handed Byrne the document.

There was a fresh homicide in the city of Philadelphia, and Detectives Byrne and Balzano were up on the wheel.

'This is a bad one,' Westbrook said. 'Grab a couple of warm bodies. I want a status report within the hour.'

As Jessica and Byrne put on their coats, Jessica looked longingly at her pastry, on which the tiny candle had already burned down. She hoped this wasn't an omen. She pointed at the paper plate. 'Can I get that to go?'

Byrne reached over to the roll of paper towels bolted to the side of one of the steel desks, pulled off a few sheets, removed the candle from the pastry and wrapped it up. 'We're a full-service unit here.'

Jessica smiled. 'Thanks, partner.'

On the way to the elevators, Jessica had to ask. 'By the way, where the hell did you find balloons that say "Knock 'em dead", and "Break a leg"?'

Byrne touched the elevator button. 'I'm a detective,' he said. 'I've got connections.'

While they waited, Jessica gave Byrne a soft nudge to the side. 'Did you happen to buy them at that cute little gift shop on Second, by any chance?'

Byrne had briefly dated a woman who ran a rather touristy gift shop at Second and Race. The relationship began, ostensibly, with Byrne going in there to buy Philadelphia maps. He said this with a straight face at the time, as if the PPD didn't have enough maps of the city.

They stepped into the elevator.

'I'm done with relationships,' Byrne said.

'Here we go.'

'I am. I'm a bay leaf.'

The door closed. Jessica just stared. She knew Byrne well enough to know that something else was coming, but she had never quite figured out his timetable. When he didn't continue, she asked.

'Okay. I'm in,' she said. 'What do you mean?'

Byrne looked at the scarred walls of the elevator, read the maximum occupancy sticker, stalled.

'You know how, when you're cooking, and the recipe calls for a bay leaf, and you—'

Jessica held up a hand, stopping him. 'Wait a minute,' she said. 'You *cook*?'

Byrne nodded.

'Since when?'

'I make a few things.'

'Such as?'

'I make a nice colcannon.'

'That's Irish food.'

'What are you saying?'

Busted. 'I'm a *huge* fan of Irish food,' Jessica said, trying to dig her way out. 'Don't I always get the shepherd's pie at the Wake?'

'I think that might technically be English, but yeah. You do.'

'Right. See? So, go on.'

Byrne let her spin for a few seconds, continued. 'Anyway, in the recipe, at the end, they always say "discard the bay leaf".'

'Okay,' Jessica said. 'I've seen that.'

'So that's me. King of the ninety-day love affair. When women are done with me, they discard me. I'm the human bay leaf.'

Jessica tried not to laugh, on the slightest chance it would hurt her partner's feelings.

She failed.

5

The Shawmont train station was a former stop on SEPTA's Manayunk/Norristown rail line, running north and south along the Schuylkill River, the de facto border between Northwest Philadelphia and West Philadelphia. Considered to be the oldest passenger train station house in the United States, the Shawmont station closed officially in 1996. Although SEPTA trains passed frequently, they no longer stopped at Shawmont.

The two-story station house perched on the top of a rise that quickly descended to the bank of the Schuylkill River. Until recently, rumor had it that the small building housed a residential tenant – descendants of the original station master – but when Jessica and Byrne arrived, at just after nine a.m., the place looked sealed tight.

Because it was a popular spot for joggers and cyclists, there was a *Look Before Crossing* sign attached to the building, even though the rail traffic on the Manayunk/Norristown line was not all that frequent.

Byrne parked the car; he and Jessica got out, walked up the short path to the station. They crossed the tracks.

As Jessica got closer, she could see that Dana Westbrook was right. This was a bad one.

In fact, from a distance of fifty or so feet, it didn't even look real. It looked like some sort of diorama or display in a store window.

Jessica could see that the victim was a white female, perhaps fifteen or sixteen years old. She wore a dark skirt and a white blouse. There was a ligature of some sort around her neck. Her hands were tied around the wrists, resting in her lap.

What made this scenario surreal was that the girl was simply sitting on a bench, as if waiting for a train that would never come. The bench was painted a pale yellow.

Two young patrol officers, fresh-faced kids no more than a year or two out of the academy, stood guard. Their name tags identified them as P/O Sloane and P/O Kasky.

They both nodded a greeting to Jessica and Byrne.

'You took the call?' Byrne asked.

The two young men looked at each other, not knowing who should respond. Something in Sloane's eyes told Kasky it should be him.

'Yes, sir,' Kasky said.

'What time was that?'

'Right around seven-twenty.'

'Where were you when you got the call?'

Kasky pointed to the northeast. 'We had a call in Roxborough. Over in Green Tree run.'

Byrne wrote it down. 'Who made the 911?'

'Mrs Ann Stovicek. She was riding her bike.'

Jessica looked over to see a woman in her late twenties, standing next to a rather expensive-looking bicycle carrier, the kind with a child seat in the front. In the pod was an adorable girl of about two.

'What did you observe when you got here?' Byrne asked.

'We pulled up on Shawmont Avenue, parked at Nixon, then walked up the path. When we arrived here we saw the victim, then immediately called dispatch.'

'Who else was here?'

'Just Mrs Stovicek.'

'No other joggers or cyclists?'

'No, sir.'

'Did you preserve the scene?' Byrne asked.

Kasky cleared his throat. Jessica noticed that he was not looking at the victim.

'Yes, sir,' he said. 'I thought about pushing on the bench a little, just to see if she was still alive. But I didn't want to touch the wood. The paint seemed a little ... '

The young officer trailed off. Byrne finished his sentence.

'Fresh,' Byrne said. 'I agree. Good work, officer.'

Those three words were what the young patrolman needed. A bit of color returned to his face. Jessica remembered such moments from her early days.

'Has a train come by since you've been here?' Byrne asked.

'Yes, sir,' P/O Kasky said. 'Just one.'

Jessica made the note to check on the SEPTA schedule for this line. If the ME was able to pin down a small enough window for the time of death, they could check with passengers who might have been on the train as it passed by the station.

The good news was that there was a possibility of an eyewitness. The bad news was that a passing train all but compromised the integrity of any scientific data – blood, fingerprints, hair, fiber – that might be gleaned from the site.

Jessica stepped away, walked a little closer to the building, which was literally just a few yards from the railroad tracks. The first story of the structure was a muted blue. On the side facing the tracks there were three windows, all boarded, as well as a single door. The door was padlocked.

The second floor exterior had been scraped and sanded at some point in the last few years, but the project had been abandoned. There were four windows on the second story, all with shades drawn.

Then there was the dead girl, sitting on a wooden bench, as if she belonged here.

Carefully skirting the path the killer may have taken, staying as close as possible to the wall, Jessica knelt down and looked beneath the bench. There she saw that the bench had not been painted underneath.

She also saw something else. Something that made her heart skip a beat.

Taped to the underneath side of the bench was an envelope of some sort.

As desperately as she wanted to take the envelope and rip it open, she had to wait. They needed the investigator for the Medical Examiner's office to clear the victim, allowing the Crime Scene officers to begin their own investigations, which would include photographing and videotaping the victim and the scene. Then, and only then, could Homicide begin their inquiry.

A few minutes later the ME's investigator arrived. Jessica stepped away, walked eastward on the path leading away from the station. When she reached the crest of the slight incline she turned to look at the scene.

Why here? she wondered. Did this place mean something to the killer? Did it mean something to the victim?

Did the killer stand in this spot, seeing the same thing Jessica saw? Had he envisioned this young girl on a bench, and how it would look to someone approaching the station?

The soft glow of the victim's pale skin against the rough surface of the stationhouse wall made it look like a painting, or an illustration in a children's book.

*

Annie Stovicek was toned and pretty, probably closer to thirty. She wore a cranberry colored jogging outfit, black nylon gloves.

Jessica approached, then knelt next to the carrier at the rear of the bike, and the little girl seated there. 'Who's this?' she asked.

The woman tried to muster a smile. 'That's Miranda.'

'She's adorable.'

'Thanks.'

Byrne filled Jessica in.

'Mrs Stovicek was riding her bike down Shawmont Avenue at around seven-fifteen this morning, and was heading to the path when she discovered the victim.'

The path ran along the Schuylkill River. Since the nearby Shawmont pumping station had been razed, the trail along the river had become a popular spot for runners and cyclists.

'Do I have the time frame right?' Byrne asked.

'Yes.'

'How often do you come here?'

'Maybe twice a day, weather permitting. Once in the morning, once at night with my dog. I was going to make today the last time of the year, actually. It's getting a bit cold for Miranda.' She gestured to the little girl in the carrier. 'After this, I'm pretty sure today is the last time ever.'

'I understand,' Byrne said. 'The bench at the front of the station. Do you know if it's always there? Have you seen it before?'

Jessica knew they could probably get this information from SEPTA, or any number of rail preservation societies in the city, but it was always better to get a witness's perspective.

The woman thought for a few moments. 'To be quite honest, I just don't know.'

'Did you get a good look at the victim?'

'Yes. I came around the bend, my mind thinking about a thousand things. When I saw her I stopped. It looked so ... unreal.'

'How long after that did you call 911?'

A pause. 'Maybe a minute later?'

It was a question, not a statement.

'May I ask why you waited a full minute?' Byrne asked.

The woman looked at the ground, the emotion of all this finally hitting her. She looked back up. 'I guess at first I thought she wasn't real, you know? I know Halloween was a couple of weeks ago, so I thought it was one those things you see in the store, what do you call them ...'

'A mannequin.'

'Yes, of course. A *mannequin*. I can't seem to think straight.'

Byrne just nodded.

The woman continued. 'Then I looked a little closer and I saw it was a *person*. I guess I was waiting for her to wake up or move. I may have even said something to her.'

At this the woman began to tear up. She dabbed her eyes with the back of her glove.

'Sorry,' she said.

'It's quite all right,' Byrne said. He put a hand on her shoulder. 'You take your time.'

A few moments later the woman composed herself. Byrne moved on.

'Have you ever seen this young woman before?'

The woman shook her head. 'I don't think so.'

Jessica glanced over at the little girl. Although it was around fifty degrees, she was bundled in enough down to withstand a day in the Yukon. All that was visible was a little pink face.

Jessica heard people approaching. She turned and saw that the medical examiner and his photographer were wrapping up their processing of the scene. Although the medical examiner himself would make the final ruling on whether or not this was a homicide, a suicide, or an accidental death, they were bound by procedure and protocol to wait at least until the investigator pronounced the victim dead.

Depending on the circumstances, the next investigators to approach the victim, and the immediate crime scene, would be the homicide investigators or the crime scene technicians.

There were no tire treads, no footwear impressions, no shell casings, or blood near the body. A CSU officer took her own photographs, moved away.

Jessica put on a pair of latex gloves and stepped in.

Standing this close to the victim, Jessica could see that the girl was younger than she originally thought. She was perhaps thirteen or fourteen. Her eyes were open, and even with the naked eye Jessica could see the hemorrhaging. She was certain that the ME would rule that the cause of death was strangulation.

The girl's white blouse, dark skirt, and dark knee socks were an indication that she attended a private school. But there was no sweater or blazer bearing a school logo. Her dark hair was parted on the left side and blunt cut at her shoulders. On the right side was a rose-colored barrette in the shape of a swan.

She wore what appeared to be good quality black loafers. Even in this most undignified state her skirt was pulled modestly to the tops of her knees.

Being careful where she stepped, Jessica put one foot into the doorway behind the victim and shone her Maglite on the back of the girl's neck. She could now see that the ligature was a nylon stocking of some sort. It was the same, or similar, to the stockings that tied the girl's hands. Between her fingers was a filtered cigarette, stubbed out to a length of no more than a half-inch.

With a gloved hand Jessica gently lifted up part of the girl's skirt. She saw that the yellow paint had come off on the woolen material. The paint was indeed fresh.

Jessica motioned to one of the crime scene technicians, a female officer in her twenties. She requested more photographs of the immediate area beneath the bench, as well as photographs underneath the bench, of the envelope taped there.

'When you're done with the photographs, let's get that envelope off. Let's do our best to preserve that tape and that cigarette butt as well.'

At this, Jessica walked back to the path. Somehow the sun had come out from behind the clouds. At this dark moment, in this terrible place, the sun still shone. Long shadows draped the path.

'Any other witnesses?' Jessica asked.

Byrne shook his head. 'Not yet,' he said. 'Josh and Maria are working the nearby houses.'

They took a few moments, each to their own thoughts. They were both the parents of girls and, no matter how many times they did this, a teenaged female victim always slammed home hard.

'Are you thinking what I'm thinking?' Jessica eventually asked.

Byrne turned to look at her, a slight smile on his face. 'That's probably a trick question, but I have a pretty good idea,' he said. 'You're thinking about Tessa Wells.'

It was true. Her partner knew her better than anyone. Tessa Ann Wells was the victim of a murderer who became known in Philadelphia as The Rosary Killer. The Wells case was Jessica's first homicide investigation. And while the signature of that killer was different, the situation was the same. A young teenage girl was murdered, and posed in a public place.

For many reasons, not the least of which that the Wells case was the first time Jessica had been tasked as a lead investigator to step into the mind of the psychopath, she had never, nor would she ever, forget Tessa Wells.

A few moments later the crime scene technician approached them. In her hand were two evidence bags: one that contained the envelope taped to the bottom of the bench, one that held the short filtered cigarette butt.

'Were you able to preserve the tape?' Jessica asked.

'Yes, ma'am,' the officer said. 'If there's a latent on it, we'll have it.'

Because Jessica had touched a number of other surfaces, she took off her latex gloves, slipped on another pair. Byrne followed suit.

Jessica opened the evidence bag and, holding it by its corner, pulled out the envelope.

The envelope was of a medium size, perhaps five inches wide, four and a half inches deep. It was buff in color, and appeared to have a linen or vellum finish. It was the size and type used for thank you notes and invitations.

Jessica noted that the flap – a deeply pointed flap – was tucked into the envelope, not sealed. This was good news and bad news as far as the evidentiary possibilities were concerned.

The good news was that Jessica and Byrne could immediately examine the contents of the envelope. Had it been sealed it would have been put into the chain of evidence, brought to the criminalistics lab, and while there opened by some magic process known only to the denizens of the unit.

The bad news was that, had the envelope been sealed, the possibility of a transference of DNA to be found in the saliva might have eventually given them a direction, and a suspect.

Jessica had learned long ago that in this life she'd chosen, you take what you can get when you can get it.

There was no writing on the face of the envelope, nor on the back. There was nothing embossed, etched, or engraved. Still holding the envelope by its edge Jessica gently worked the flap out from the inside. She held the envelope up to the sun. She could see what appeared to be a single card inside. She reached in, pulled out a card. Byrne moved to the side so that they might see it together.

One side was blank. Jessica flipped it over.

On the other side, calligraphed in black ink, was an invitation. It read:

You are invited!
November 23
See you at our thé dansant!

'November twenty-third,' Byrne said. 'That's a week from today.' He pointed at the last line. 'Any idea what this means?'

'Not a clue.'

Byrne looked down the path, at the handful of crime scene investigators. 'Anyone here speak French?'

The officers all looked up, at Byrne. The expressions on their faces looked as if Byrne asked if any of them could fly. There were many intelligent, crafty, highly skilled people in the PPD. When Jessica's father became a police officer, very few of his fellow officers had four-year degrees, or even two-year associates degrees. At that time many, if not most, applicants to the academy applied after serving in the military, the continuation of the paramilitary command structure a comfortable fit. Nowadays, it was not that unusual to run across cops with Masters Degrees.

But even in this age of enlightenment, not to mention Rosetta Stone, speaking French was apparently not a common or highly prized skill set in the PPD. Spanish and Arabic, yes.

Byrne handed back the card. Jessica gave it another quick scan. She brought it to her nose, sniffed it. 'It has a scent,' she said. 'Kind of familiar. Gardenia maybe?'

Byrne shrugged. 'Can I see the envelope?'

Jessica handed it to him.

Byrne held it up to the light, gently worked the flap.

'This has not been opened more than once or twice,' he said. 'And it hasn't ever been opened fully.'

He was right. There were no creases other than the factory crease at the top.

Byrne angled it again to the sun, looking at the surface. Because it was a linen finish, the potential for latent prints was good.

Jessica glanced down the path that led to the river. Josh Bontrager and Maria Caruso were walking up, toward the station. They had canvassed the few residences on Nixon Street, as well as the houses and small commercial buildings on Shawmont Avenue. They approached the area where Jessica and Byrne were standing. Jessica made eye contact with Josh. He shook his head. They had not learned anything.

Staggering the interviews by four hours, over the next twenty-four, would give investigators a blanket coverage of the area – who came and went, when they did so, and what, if anything, they had seen.

Since the massive Shawmont Pumping Station had been razed, the number of visitors taking the path down to the river had dropped significantly. The pumping station had been a destination for rendezvous, both covert and romantic, as well as drug dealing.

As the two detectives joined Jessica and Byrne, one of the uniformed officers, P/O Kasky, approached.

'CSU asked me to bring this over.'

It was a small leatherette case, a delicate billfold of sorts. 'Where was it?' Byrne asked.

'It was in the victim's skirt pocket.'

'Right or left?'

'I don't know, sir.'

'Any other contents?'

'No, sir.'

Kasky handed it to Byrne, who flipped it open. Inside was a school ID, along with an emergency contact number. The ID had a photo on the left.

'Is that her?' the officer asked, glancing toward the river.

A few minutes ago he couldn't look at the victim, Jessica thought. Now he was having a hard time looking at his fellow officers. This was clearly tough for him.

Byrne looked at the picture on the school ID.

It was her.

The dead girl's name was Nicole Solomon.

As Byrne signed off on the crime scene log, and took down contact information from Annie Stovicek, Jessica walked back to the car. She turned and looked once again at the tableau. From her vantage she could see both the victim, Nicole Solomon, and the little girl in the bicycle carrier, Miranda Stovicek.

Two girls.

One beginning her life, one whose life was over.

6

The house was a two-story red brick row home on a gentrified block in the Bella Vista section of South Philadelphia, just a few blocks from where Jessica had grown up on Catharine Street, where her father still lived.

On the way to make the notification, Jessica called Dana Westbrook and gave her a status report. She was told that, within the hour, Nicole Solomon's body would be transported to the morgue, which was located at the Medical Examiner's office on University Avenue.

When Jessica and Byrne arrived at just before eleven the sun shone brightly. The trees that lined the street were bright with gold and umber leaves.

Before driving to South Philly, they had checked to see if there had been a missing person's report for a girl matching Nicole's description. They learned that David Solomon, the girl's father, had called 911 at just after midnight.

*

Byrne stood on the small porch, rang the bell. Jessica stood behind him. Jessica noted a mezuzah on the right side of the doorframe. After a few moments the door opened. A man in his late forties stood before them. He had close-cropped black hair, threaded with silver, and wore a navy sleeveless V-neck sweater, white oxford cloth shirt, and tan Dockers.

'Are you David Solomon?' Byrne asked.

'Yes,' the man said. 'I am.'

Byrne took out his ID. 'Sir, my name is—'

'It's her, isn't it?'

Byrne stopped. 'I'm sorry?'

Solomon turned and pointed at the television behind him in the living room. The picture showed a live shot of the Shawmont train station, taken from just outside the police cordon. The crawl on the lower third of the screen read: 'Body of missing girl found.'

David Solomon turned back to the two detectives. 'It's her, isn't it?'

Byrne asked: 'Mr Solomon, do you have a daughter named Nicole?'

The man did not answer. He just raised a hand to his mouth.

Byrne held up the girl's school photo ID. 'Is this your daughter, sir?'

A few seconds later the man nodded slowly.

'I'm sorry to say that, yes, the news report is about your daughter.'

Solomon closed his eyes. A single tear slid down his right cheek.

'May we come in, sir?' Byrne asked.

Without a word, Solomon stepped to the side. Jessica and Byrne entered the front room. The room was well lived in, comfortable. The furniture was older, but solid and good quality. The area over the sofa was cluttered with family photographs. Jessica immediately recognized a half-dozen photographs of Nicole – as a toddler on the beach, a gap-toothed grin at about seven or eight, as a twelve-year-old at what looked to be a piano recital.

'First off, Mr Solomon, on behalf of the PPD and the city of Philadelphia, I'd like to say how sorry we are for your loss,' Byrne said.

David Solomon leaned forward. His hands dangled at his side, as if he did not know what to do with them.

Jessica had seen it too many times. Productive people, active people, blue-collar and white-collar, people who made things, fixed things, put things into their proper places suddenly, when faced with a shattering loss, had no idea what to do with their hands. Some clasped their hands in front of them in supplication or prayer, some shoved their hands into their pockets, perhaps to keep from lashing out at total strangers, or the world at large.

Some, like David Solomon, simply let their hands float in space.

'I know that this is a terrible time for you,' Byrne said. 'We just have a few questions for you, and then we will leave you to your family and your arrangements.'

For a few moments, Solomon stared at Byrne. He seemed to be processing the information. Then he nodded.

'Is there anyone else here today?' Byrne asked.

'Yes,' he said. 'My mother, Adinah.'

'Where is she?'

Solomon pointed into a small room off the living room. There sat an older woman in a wheelchair. She was staring out the window. Jessica had not even noticed her when they entered the house.

'She has Alzheimer's,' Solomon added. 'It's not good.'

'I'm sorry,' Byrne said. He took a few moments. 'Now, some of the questions I'm going to ask you will seem terribly personal. Even invasive. I'm afraid they are necessary. What we're trying to do is get as much information as we can, as quickly as we can.'

Solomon nodded again.

'Are you currently married?' Byrne asked.

'No,' he said. 'I am widowed.'

'Do you have any other children?'

'No,' he said. 'Nicole was my only child.'

The second wave of grief seemed to land when he said this. He tried to hold back the tears. He could not.

While Byrne gave the man time to compose himself, he made a few notes. As he did this Jessica had the opportunity to look a little more closely at the room. She saw that the stairs had a motorized lift, for, she figured, Adinah Solomon. She also noticed that all the doorways had been widened for the woman's wheelchair.

'We have just a few more questions for now,' Byrne said. 'May I ask what you do for a living?'

'I'm a social worker,' he said. 'LCSW. I minored in Talmudic studies.'

'Are you in private practice, or do you work for a provider?'

'A provider,' he said.

'We'll need their contact information before we leave.'

Another nod.

'Did Nicole have any troubles in her life recently?' Byrne asked. 'Perhaps at school, or here at home?'

Jessica watched the man closely. It was a mandatory question in a forensic interview such as this – that being a non-leading dialogue – one that always came loaded with a lot more innuendo and suspicion than was intended. Whenever parents or siblings of deceased minors heard the question, they also heard an accusation.

'What do you mean by trouble at home?' Solomon asked.

'I'm asking whether or not Nicole had been depressed or unresponsive lately,' Byrne said. 'Maybe she spent more time in her room alone, less time with family.' Byrne leaned back, increasing the space between himself and Solomon, giving the man the impression that this was not an accusation of any sort. 'I have a daughter just a few years older than Nicole, and I know what a difficult age this can be.'

Byrne let the statement buffer what would be a second run at getting the information.

'So,' he continued. 'Have you noticed any change in Nicole's behavior over the last few days or weeks?'

In Jessica's experience parents usually thought about this question for a few moments. Not so with David Solomon.

'She was just fine,' the man said, perhaps a little more loudly than he wanted. 'Just *fine*.'

'Did she have any problems with drugs or alcohol?'

At this question David Solomon seemed to sag, to become physically smaller. Perhaps these were issues he had chosen to ignore.

'I don't know,' he said.

Jessica glanced at Adinah Solomon. Although Jessica was somewhat ashamed of herself for thinking so, she wondered if the woman was better off not knowing what was taking place in the next room.

'When was the last time you saw Nicole?' Byrne asked.

'Yesterday morning. We had breakfast.'

'Here at home?'

The man shook his head. 'No, not here. We had breakfast at the McDonald's. On Christian Street.'

Jessica made a note to contact the store's manager. If there was one thing McDonald's did well, at least in the big American cities, it was make surveillance recordings. There had been a rash of robberies, nationwide, in the past five years.

Solomon looked out the window, continued. 'She always ordered the Egg McMuffins. Never any hash browns, nothing else. Nicole didn't drink coffee, you see. She would open both

McMuffins, take off two of the muffins, and make one big sand-wich.' Solomon looked at Jessica. 'She always gave me the extra muffins, even though she knew that I never ate breakfast. I would eat one of them just to be kind.'

Jessica thought at that moment about having breakfast with Sophie and Carlos. She made a mental note to pay closer atten-tion to their habits and affectations. This man would never again have breakfast with his daughter.

'Did you often go to this McDonald's?' Jessica asked.

'Once in a while. Perhaps once a month.'

'Were you and Nicole considered regulars there?' she asked. 'By that I mean, were you known to the cashiers and employees by name?'

'No, nothing like that,' he said. 'It's a busy place, especially at that time of the morning. I don't know the name of anyone who works there, and I seriously doubt they know my name, or Nicole's.'

Jessica made a few notes. 'Do you remember anything out of the ordinary happening at McDonald's yesterday morning?'

'I don't know what you mean.'

'I mean, did anything happen between you and another cus-tomer, or Nicole and another customer?' Jessica asked. 'Anything confrontational?'

'Confrontational?'

'Did anything happen, such as someone bumping into you, something that another person might have taken as a sign of dis-respect?'

'I don't think so,' Solomon said. 'Nothing I can remember. Certainly nothing that I saw.'

'Can you recall if anyone was paying particularly close atten-tion to Nicole?' Jessica asked. 'Perhaps a young man, someone Nicole's age? Or maybe an older man?'

Solomon thought for a few moments, dabbed at his eyes.

'Young men are always looking at Nicole. She is very beautiful.'

'Yes, she was,' Jessica said, conscious suddenly of the fact that she was using past tense. She moved quickly on. 'What I'm getting at is whether or not someone yesterday morning may have paid attention to Nicole in a way that seemed out of place, or a little excessive, or inappropriate.'

'No,' he said. 'Or maybe it's just that I didn't notice. I didn't think I would be asked about it. I didn't think that it would be our last moment together.'

'I understand, sir,' Jessica said. 'Where and when did you part company with your daughter yesterday?'

'In front of the McDonald's. She had a school outing at the Franklin Institute.'

'How did she get there?'

'I put her in a cab.'

'To the Institute?'

He shook his head. 'To her school. They took a bus from there.'

'Do you recall which cab company it was?'

Solomon thought for a moment. 'No. Sorry. I don't take them myself. They all kind of look alike to me.'

'That's okay,' Byrne said. 'We can get this information.' Byrne flipped a few pages back. 'Mr Solomon, how much did Nicole smoke?'

The man looked slapped. '*Smoke?* Nicole didn't smoke.'

'Are you certain of that, sir?'

'Absolutely. She would never do a thing like that.'

Jessica had never been a smoker, but she'd snuck a few puffs from someone else's cigarette when she was Nicole's age. Whether or not Nicole was a casual or heavy smoker – or a non-smoker like her father believed – would be easily determined when the autopsy was performed.

'I need to show you something now, sir,' Byrne said. 'If I may.'

Solomon looked apprehensive. It was understandable, under the circumstances. He nodded his assent.

Byrne reached into his bag, took out the invitation they had found taped beneath the bench. It was now in a clear evidence bag.

'Mr Solomon, have you ever seen this before?'

Solomon reached into his pants pocket, took out a pair of reading glasses, slipped them on. He looked at the card, back at Byrne. 'I don't understand. What is this?'

'This was in Nicole's possession,' Byrne said. It was not technically accurate. The possibility existed, albeit extremely slight, that the bench already had this taped to it.

Solomon held it up. 'This was?'

'Yes.'

Jessica watched the man's eyes scan the text.

'An invitation?' he asked.

'Yes, sir,' Byrne said. 'Have you ever seen it before?'

'I don't ... no I haven't.'

Jessica noticed that the man's hands had begun to tremble. There was something about the card that spooked him.

'Mr Solomon, do you have a recent photograph of Nicole?' Byrne asked.

'Of course,' Solomon said. 'Yes. I'm sure I have one.'

Solomon looked to the two detectives to see if it was okay, suddenly thrust into a world of facts and procedures and protocol.

'It's just upstairs,' he said. 'I can get it for you now.' Before he mounted the stairs he added: 'I also have to make a phone call.'

'Yes,' Byrne said. 'Of course. Take your time.'

As Solomon went up the stairs, Jessica glanced at Adinah Solomon. The woman had not moved nor acknowledged the presence of two strangers in her house. Jessica then made eye contact with Byrne. A number of questions flowed silently between them.

Question One: Was David Solomon telling the truth about all

this? It seemed as if he had been. At least until he saw the invitation.

Question Two: Was Nicole's home life as stable and happy and normal as Solomon portrayed it? This was not quite as clear.

Jessica heard Solomon open a door at the end of the hallway upstairs, then close it. Perhaps two minutes later she heard the door open again.

Over the next few days, when Jessica thought of this case – the 306th homicide of the year in Philadelphia – she would think of the moment just after she heard the door open for the second time on the second floor.

That was the moment when everything changed.

In her experience, it sometimes happened. You thought the investigation was one thing, and it became something else.

Rarely did it happen so soon.

In that moment – the moment between a thought and a word, the distance that marks the chasm between life and death – a litany of remembrance and procedure rushed through Jessica's mind.

She recalled going to the firearms qualifying range on State Road with her father when she was ten years old. She recalled staying well back, wearing headphones, thinking about how there was a slight delay between the muzzle flash and the sound of the weapon being discharged.

In this moment, sitting in the front room of a small row house in the Bella Vista neighborhood of South Philadelphia, a space now red with rage and grief and loss, it all came back to her.

Jessica first saw the blaze of light, a yellow flash that streaked down the hallway at the top of the stairs, followed by the crack of a large caliber handgun being discharged.

The gunshot shook the house.

Before she knew it she was on her feet. Her first thought was of her partner.

She made eye contact with Byrne, who was also on his feet, weapon now drawn, moving to the foot of the stairs. Without saying a word they each selected their duties.

Jessica got on her two-way, and called for backup – a shots fired/officer involved call that would bring every available cop for miles.

Their immediate concern was for the safety of the older woman. As far as Jessica and Byrne knew – and this was far from known – there were no other family members in the house. The glass block along the sidewalk in front of the Solomon row house told them that there was a basement, and from that place could come any number of potential threats.

Anyone could be down there.

And then there was the second floor.

7

If Mr Marseille had ever decided to become a movie star, he certainly could have been one.

He was that beautiful.

There was a way the light touched the planes of his face that would have made a generation of young women – maybe two or three generations – swoon in their velvet seats.

I have to admit that I don't know much about new films, other than what I see in the newspaper and on television, and we do not watch much television. Most films nowadays seem to be based on comic books, which I've never read. While I do appreciate the colors of their world, I don't know that I would want to see them in the flesh.

Besides, there was so much to do that Mr Marseille and I never seemed to find the time to attend the cinema.

There is one film we both enjoy immensely, though. We've seen it scores of times. The name of the film is *Bonnie and Clyde*.

It is wonderfully acted, and the colors are beautiful, as are the costumes. The story ended terribly for Miss Parker and Mr

Barrow and, although they had done bad things, my heart went out to them.

As I looked at Mr Marseille in profile, I thought about what it might be like to lose him. I don't think I could bear it, even though we are both well acquainted with loss.

There are so many broken dolls.

I can't tell you how many we have tried to mend, only to discover that the challenge was too great. Some people are so rough with their dolls that they cannot be sewn or patched.

It's not as easy as you might think to mend a broken doll. There is the hair, for one. Mohair, modacrylic, mignonette, Toni style, human hair. Which to choose? Then there are the eyes which, of course, are most important. Are they counterweight? Paperweight? Button type?

There are some dolls that require so many parts that – and please don't think me cruel or insensitive for saying this – it is just better for them to be put back on a shelf.

Mr Marseille and I have done this many times.

Every time we've had to do this we've been sad for days. It is never easy or pleasant. We know the pain of loss, and it is only right and proper that others know this same feeling. That is the way of life.

So many broken dolls.

We learned how to care for them from our own *maîtresse des marionnettes*.

I returned from my reverie, a *déprimé* surely brought on by the knowledge that our story had turned the page, perhaps beginning our last chapter. I put on a brave face, turned to look at Mr Marseille. He held the gun in his right hand, looking every bit like Mr Clyde Barrow.

I covered my ears, just in case Mr Marseille was about to once again pull the trigger.

8

When Byrne reached the top of the stairs, he tilted his head to the sudden silence.

'Mr Solomon?'

Nothing.

'Sir?'

There was just stillness, the ringing peace that comes after a deafening report in a small space.

Byrne eased his head around the corner, quickly back. One hallway, three doors. Only one of the doors was open, the last door on the left.

He stepped into the hallway, his weapon pointed low. He tried calling the man's name again.

'Mr Solomon?'

Still no response. He raised his weapon and spun into the first doorway, took in the room in one snapshot.

Bed, dresser, nightstands, lamps. There was a cordless phone cradle on the nightstand, no phone. He peered around the door. No one standing there.

'Mr Solomon?' he tried again. No answer.

There were no curtains to hide behind. All the furniture was pushed to the walls. Byrne got down on one knee, looked quickly under the bed.

Clear.

He stood, stepped over to the closet. He could hear the crackle of Jessica's two-way radio float up the stairs. Besides the beating of his heart, it was the only sound in the house.

The closet door was slightly ajar. Inside there was only darkness. Byrne tried to slow his heart, listen for any sound coming from the closet – the creak of a floorboard, the unmistakable clang of two wire hangers touching, the quick breathing of someone else.

He heard nothing.

When he reached the closet he took a moment, then kicked the door wide. Except for a handful of suit coats, shirts and jackets, the closet was empty.

The bedroom was clear.

He rolled the door jamb, into the hallway his weapon pointed upward. He toed open the door to the second bedroom. This was clearly Adinah Solomon's room. It smelled of infirmity. There was a lift over the bed. A card table on the far side of the bed held a number of pill vials, water pitchers and bottles. Byrne checked the closet. Empty.

He heard a number of sirens rise in the near distance. This was South Philly. Sector cars were never more than a few blocks from each other, or from any crime scene. A call of shots fired, with officers on scene, would bring them all.

The third bedroom was Nicole's. Boy band posters on the walls, a laptop on a small nearly-wood desk, a coat tree in the corner laden with scarves and hats and jackets. There was no door on the closet.

Byrne noted that the bed was made, and resting on the pillow were three stuffed turtles.

The only room left was the bathroom.

The door was ajar.

Byrne knew he should wait, but he couldn't. He took a deep breath, rammed a shoulder into the door, spun into the opening, his weapon leveled.

The bathroom was a bloodbath.

David Solomon was in the tub, naked, the left side of his skull blown away, blood and brain tissue on the white tile behind him. A stainless steel .357 handgun lay on the floor next to the tub. Solomon's clothing was piled neatly on the toilet seat.

Byrne had seen it too many times before. Sometimes firearm suicide victims stepped into the tub to make the cleanup easier. David Solomon, it seemed, wanted to preserve his clothing, as well.

Byrne had been right about the caliber. There is nothing quite as loud as a .357 or .44, especially in a confined space. He stepped forward, toed the handgun toward him, even though there was no longer a threat from the man in the bathtub.

The room smelled of iron and blood and scorched flesh. The redolence of death filled the air.

Byrne holstered his weapon, keyed his two-way.

'Jess,' he said.

No response.

'Jess,' he repeated.

A few agonizing seconds later: 'I'm here.'

'Second floor is clear.'

'Solomon?' Jessica asked.

'Yeah.'

'DOA?'

'Yeah.'

'You good?'

Byrne hesitated. He knew what she meant. Still, he hesitated. It wasn't fair. He answered. 'Yeah, I'm good.'

'Backup is here,' she said. 'They've cleared the basement.'

'The mother?' Byrne asked.

Static.

Jessica said: 'Secured.'

9

Detectives Byrne and Balzano stood outside the front door of the Solomon row house. They were joined by their supervisor, Sgt. Dana Westbrook. Around them flowed the machinery of establishing a crime scene.

'What happened, Jess?' Westbrook asked.

Jessica gave Sgt. Westbrook a minute by minute recalling of what had happened from the moment David Solomon opened his door until Byrne went upstairs and found the man's body.

'Where was the gun?'

'I don't know, Dana,' Jessica said. 'He certainly didn't have it on him when he was downstairs. It's a big weapon. We would have noticed.'

Jessica instantly recognized her defensive tone. She wasn't on a witness stand – a place she had been many times, a place in front of which, as a lawyer, she might one day stand – so she softened her manner.

'He probably had it in his bedroom.'

'And what did he say right before he went upstairs?' Westbrook asked.

'We asked him if he had any recent photographs of Nicole. He said he did, and that he had to make a phone call.'

Dana Westbrook walked down the street, flagged the approaching crime scene unit van, the second one deployed to this location. Even though David Solomon's death would probably not be investigated as anything other than a suicide, it still fell under the category of a suspicious death. David Solomon's body would soon be transported to the morgue, and an autopsy would be performed at nine-thirty the following morning.

Both Jessica and Byrne were keenly interested in a toxicology report to see what, if anything, was in Mr Solomon's bloodstream. Toxicology reports could sometimes take five or six days, often longer when it involved the victim of an apparent suicide. Homicides always took precedence.

The moment the medical examiner cleared the body for investigators to step in, they would look in the man's medicine cabinet. Jessica had enough experience to anticipate certain medications. She would bet that somewhere in the medicine cabinet, or David Solomon's dresser, they would find a prescription bottle of antidepressants. Probably more than one.

When Byrne and Jessica were alone, Jessica asked the question. 'You saw him spook when he saw that invitation card, didn't you?'

Byrne just nodded.

'What do you think?'

'I think it triggered something in him. A memory of some sort.'

'Do you think there was any abuse involving his daughter?'

Byrne thought for a few moments. 'I don't know.'

The investigator from the ME's office walked out of the row house, nodded to the detectives.

Jessica would take the dead girl's room.

Byrne would take the father's.

10

The room was clean and uncluttered, a young girl's private sanctuary.

Jessica had hoped to be given permission to search the room when she and Byrne first arrived to give notification – a permission just as often denied as granted, and a victim's family had no legal obligation to allow investigators to do so – but now there was no one to object.

Jessica was all but certain that the last time the girl left this room – just over twenty-four hours earlier – she'd had no idea what would be her fate.

Jessica had made the note about asking the one question Byrne had not yet gotten to, a question about whether or not Nicole had been plagued by any bullying at school or online. She glanced at the girl's laptop. She wondered what secrets it would reveal.

Jessica put on a pair of latex gloves. She began with the girl's dresser, feeling once more like an intruder. In the top drawer were the frivolous debris of youth – ticket stubs to a concert, The

Warped Tour, as well as a Playbill from a recent performance of *Once* at the Academy of Music. There was also a small jewelry box. Jessica took it out and opened it. It was a music box. At first Jessica could not pin down the tune, but she soon recognized it as 'A Whole New World' from the movie *Aladdin*.

Inside the box was an assortment of rings, bracelets, and earrings. Nothing looked expensive or precious.

Jessica put the box on top of the dresser, letting the tune continue to play if for no other reason than to fill the room with something other than this deadly silence that echoed the sudden violent death of two people.

The rest of the drawers in the dresser contain the expected: underwear, socks, T-shirts, a few light sweaters. The drawers were neither particularly orderly nor messy. None of them contained anything covert, no stash of torrid love letters or anything of the like.

Jessica moved on to the girl's closet. Hanging there she found three or four complete outfits for the girl's school uniform. She briefly flashed on her own closet when she was fourteen. Only the school colors were different. She recalled hating the conformity of it all when she was Nicole's age. She wondered if Nicole had felt the same way. Perhaps not. There was nothing particularly rebellious in the accouterment in this girl's room. Perhaps the only thing that could be considered rebellious was the poster of a rapper named Machine Gun Kelly.

Jessica felt around the two shelves in the closet, beneath the folded sweaters, looking for something out of the ordinary, something that might indicate why Nicole Solomon's path crossed with someone who would do the horrible things he did to her. She found nothing.

Neither of the nightstands in the girl's room had drawers. Jessica gave a quick look beneath the bed, found nothing more sinister than a pair of new-looking slippers.

She sat down at the laptop, brought it to life, scanned the handful of desktop icons. She opened the browser, did a quick scan of the browsing history – a few news sources, Wikipedia, the main page for her school, Amazon, Zappos.

Jessica saw that Nicole had established a smart mailbox for email from her father. Jessica clicked on the box and saw that the mail subject lines were indexed by day of the week. Her father had sent her an email the previous morning, wishing his daughter a beautiful day.

As Jessica clicked through the mailbox, she discovered that David Solomon had sent Nicole email every morning, going back years. From just a few feet away, in the house they shared, he'd sent email to his daughter. Jessica's heart began to ache. This was not an abusive relationship.

She quickly perused the rest of the applications on the hard drive. There was no calendar application, no chronicle of Nicole's days.

Jessica would have the computer forensic team take a closer look at the hard drive and its contents, both visible and hidden.

She stood in the doorway, took off her latex gloves. For a brief second she saw Sophie's room a few years from now. The thought brought with it a surge of sadness and fear. She feared every day for her daughter's safety. Today more than most. Today especially.

Before leaving Nicole Solomon's bedroom, Jessica walked back to the music box and rewound it.

As she headed down the stairs the sound of that hopeful song filled the dead girl's room.

Then, like Nicole Solomon's brief life, it soon faded to silence.

11

Byrne stepped into David Solomon's bedroom doorway. Although there was nothing immediately visible in the bedroom – visible in the sense of evidence as it related to the deaths of David or Nicole Solomon – Byrne walked as close to the wall as he could.

A visual scan of the bedroom, now that he saw it with fresh eyes, as well as the knowledge that the man who once slept here had just taken his life, showed a scene not dissimilar to his own bedroom. The bed was a queen size, or a large double. Only one side was unmade. On that side of the bed, on the nightstand, was a lamp, a pair of paperback books, a small digital clock – set about ten minutes fast – a half-empty bottle of AquaFina water, along with a cordless phone. The handset was not sitting in its charging cradle, but rather was lying down on its side.

The other side of the bed, the side with the down comforter tucked tightly beneath the mattress, held a matching lamp, and nothing else. There were no clothes strewn about the room, no shoes lined up at the baseboard.

Byrne glanced back at the cordless phone. He had noticed, almost by rote, that just about everything else in David Solomon's house was in its place. Downstairs there were two remotes placed neatly next to the 42-inch LCD television, magazines squared on the end tables. Even the fruit in the bowl on the dining room table seemed to be purposefully arranged.

Byrne took out his notebook, clicked his pen, looked at his watch, noting the exact time. He put down his notebook, picked up the phone between the thumb and forefinger of his left hand, found the redial button, and pressed it. Keeping the phone an inch or so away from his ear, he listened. There were seven tones. The last number called was a local call. Mr Solomon, or whoever had last used his phone, had not made a long-distance call.

The line rang once, twice, three times. Then there was a solitary click as it transferred over to voicemail.

'*Hi, you've reached the Gillens. I'm sorry I missed your call. When you hear the beep, leave a message and I'll get right back to you. Or you can try me on my cell.*'

As she related her cell number, Byrne wrote it down.

In the second or two before the beep Byrne realized that he had expected someone to pick up the phone. He was not prepared with a message. He hung up.

He dialed the cell number, and once again got voicemail. When he heard the beep he plowed ahead. He left a message saying merely that he was with the Philadelphia Police Department, and that he would appreciate a call back as soon as possible. He left his pager number, as well as his cell number. He added that there was nothing wrong. That wasn't necessarily true, of course, but he had no idea what relationship David Solomon, or whoever had last used his phone, had with the Gillens, whoever they might be.

Before Byrne clicked off he read the number he had just dialed on the cordless. He hung up the phone, wrote down the number, and called the Comm Unit.

The commander of the communications unit would get back to him in short order with the name and address of the person to whom that number was registered.

12

The house was a split level in Miquon, a bedroom community on the Schuylkill River that sat just over the Philadelphia County line in Montgomery County.

While Byrne logged the evidence from the Shawmont scene, Jessica followed up on the phone call made by David Solomon. She parked in the driveway, walked up the walk, rang the doorbell.

After a few moments a woman opened the door. She looked to be in her late thirties, athletic and conservatively dressed in cinnamon tweed slacks and a beige pullover.

'Are you the police?' the woman asked.

Jessica held up her ID. 'Yes, ma'am,' she said. 'My name is Jessica Balzano.'

'Mary Gillen.'

If Jessica were pressed on the point, she would say that the look on Mary Gillen's face was not one of fear or consternation, but one of bemusement.

The woman opened the door, stepped to the side.

'Please,' she said. 'Come in.'

'Thanks.' Jessica stepped into the house. It was very well furnished, all leather and natural cherry. The living room alone was about the same square footage of the first floor of Jessica's row house.

'It was a man who called and left a message on my cell,' Mary Gillen said. 'A Detective . . .'

'Byrne. He's my partner.'

'Ah, okay,' she said. 'He didn't really say anything about what this is about.'

'All routine. Nothing to worry about.'

'Okay,' the woman repeated. She didn't sound convinced. Jessica understood. Unless you had every single of your loved ones in front of you, living and breathing and happy, there would be some doubt.

Jessica flipped a page on her notebook. 'Do you know a man named David Solomon?' she asked.

'I'm sorry?' she asked. 'Could you repeat that name, please?'

'David Solomon.'

Jessica watched the woman's face. While Mary Gillen was thinking, she looked up and to the right. Although it was far from foolproof, it sometimes indicated whether or not someone was genuinely trying to remember something, as opposed to a stall during which time they could cook an answer. Generally speaking, when people look down and to the left, they are telling somewhat less than the pure truth. Not always, but it was a pretty good barometer.

The woman looked back at Jessica.

'I'm afraid I don't know who that is.'

'Okay,' Jessica said. 'Do you work outside the home?'

'I do.'

'May I ask where you work?'

'I work for The Vanguard Group.'

'It's a big company. Is it possible that Mr Solomon might be a casual work acquaintance at Vanguard?'

'It's possible,' Mary said. 'I just don't recognize the name. May I ask what this is all about?'

'Of course,' Jessica said. 'I'll get to that in a moment, if I may.' She glanced at her watch. 'Were you home at about eleven o'clock this morning?'

Another glance up and to the right. 'No, I was shopping. At about eleven o'clock I was at Whole Foods. The one on Pennsylvania Avenue.'

At this, the woman pointed toward her kitchen, a reflexive action Jessica had seen about a million times on the job. It was usually at the point in the interview when people began to get defensive about whether or not the police believed what they were saying. Mary Gillen was pointing at the bags on the countertop, bags with the Whole Foods logo on the side.

Jessica turned to the page in her notebook where she had printed the phone number they had gotten from David Solomon's phone. She showed it to Mary Gillen. 'Is this your phone number?'

Now the woman looked a bit confused. 'Yes. It is.'

'And this is a landline?'

'It is.'

'And is your voicemail a feature of your telephone provider?'

'I'm not sure I know what you mean.'

'What I mean is, do you get your voicemail by calling a number, or do you have an answering machine here in the house?'

'I see,' she said. 'We have an answering machine.' Once again she pointed toward the kitchen. 'It's on the small desk in the kitchen.'

'Have you played back any messages today?'

'I don't think so,' she said. Then, perhaps anticipating Jessica pressing her on this point, she continued. 'To tell the truth, I don't often look to see if there are messages on that machine.' She reached into her bag sitting on the arm of the sofa. She extracted an iPhone. 'I get about ninety percent of my calls on my cell. I mention this number on the outgoing message on the machine.'

'Of course,' Jessica said. 'We're going to need to listen to your messages on that machine, if there are any. But just the ones from today.'

The woman was just about to say something, and Jessica was certain she knew what it was. She cut her off.

'To answer your question from earlier, this is merely a routine part of a matter currently under investigation. As I said, there's no reason to be alarmed.'

'And this has something to do with this . . . Solomon person?'

'Yes,' Jessica said. 'It does.'

'Did he do something wrong?'

Jessica shook her head. 'No,' she said. 'We're just following up on some phone calls that Mr Solomon made earlier today.'

'And you're saying he called here?'

'It appears that he did.'

'Interesting,' she said, perhaps meaning something else. She seemed to be lost in thought for a moment. The moment drew out.

'Ma'am?' Jessica asked. 'Do you think we could check your answering machine now?'

The woman snapped back to the moment. 'Of course,' she said. 'I'm sorry.'

The two women crossed the living room and stepped through the archway into the kitchen. If the living room was tastefully appointed, the kitchen was right out of *Architectural Digest*. Viking oven, Subzero refrigerator and freezer, a half-dozen high-tech smaller appliances on the granite countertops. The small desk to which the woman had referred earlier was really a knee-hole desk in a small alcove off the breakfast eating area.

As Jessica had hoped, the small digital answering machine showed a flashing red light, and the number 2 flashing next to it. There were two messages. Or, at least, there were two *calls*.

'I'm so embarrassed,' the woman said. 'I do check it now and then. I've just been so busy today.'

'I understand. May I ask who else lives here?'

'Just me and the boys.'

'The boys?'

'I have two sons. Twins. They're twelve.'

Jessica made this note on her notepad. The woman watched her write it, her skepticism – more accurately, at this point, her suspicion – growing.

'And your husband?' Jessica asked.

What had only a second ago been skepticism morphed instantly into the stirrings of annoyance. The woman crossed her arms, a sure sign of shutting down.

'We're divorced,' she said. Clipped, terse, final.

'May I ask where the boys are now?'

'Michael – that's my ex-husband, Michael – has them for the week. They're probably at soccer practice now.'

'Might the call from Mr Solomon have been for one of the boys? Might he be one of their teachers, or perhaps one of their coaches?'

The woman laughed. In the context of the conversation it was an odd sound. 'I don't mean to laugh, but I don't think the boys have ever gotten a call on this phone. I'm sorry to say that they've had cell phones of their own since they were seven or eight.'

'I have a five-year-old boy,' Jessica said. 'He's already asked me for a cell.' Small talk depleted, she closed her notebook. 'Shall we listen to the messages now?'

Mary crossed the kitchen, sat down at the small desk.

'Are you familiar with how to work this answering machine?' Jessica asked.

'I think so. As I said, I don't use it that much, but it's pretty straightforward.'

'Do you know how to save a message?'

Mary opened a drawer, took out a pair of reading glasses. She slipped them on and looked closely at the answering machine. 'Yes,' she said. 'After the message plays, you hit Delete if you want to erase the message. If you want to save it, you don't do anything.'

'Okay,' Jessica said. 'What I'd like to do, with your permission, is to let both of these messages play. In other words, I'd like to save them both.'

'Okay. I don't have a problem with that.'

Jessica took out her own iPhone. 'I have a memo application on my phone. When we play the messages for the first time, if you don't mind, I'd like to make a recording of them.'

The woman just shrugged. 'Sure.'

Jessica navigated through a few screens, found her memo app, touched it, beginning a recording. She saw the audio level needle jump a few times, letting her know that it was working.

She put the phone down next to the answering machine.

'Are you ready?' Jessica asked.

'I am.'

Jessica nodded. Mary Gillen pressed the button for playback.

The robotic answering machine voice began:

'*You have two new messages. First new message, received today at 10:09 a.m.*'

The machine beeped.

'*This is a courtesy call from the Free Library. Items you requested are at the main branch of the library. They will be held there until November twenty-eight. Thank you for using the Free Library.*'

Beep.

'I forgot about the library having this number,' the woman said as the machine cycled to the second call. 'I never bothered to update it with my cell phone number.'

Jessica said: 'We get the same message.'

The answering machine continued:

'*Second new message, received today at 11:02 a.m.*'

At the sound of the second beep, Jessica found she was holding her breath. 11:02 a.m. was just moments before David Solomon put a steel revolver against the soft palate in his mouth and pulled the trigger.

At first, the only sound was static. This sometimes happened with cordless phones. If you were near high tension wires, it sometime interfered with the DECT signal. Jessica was afraid the whole message was going to be static. After a few moments the static died down and, beneath it, she heard a man's voice say what sounded like:

'*. . . not now . . .*'

A few more seconds of static, then nothing.

The machine beeped again, and the flashing red readout went to 0. There were no more messages.

For a long, uncomfortable moment, neither woman said anything. It was Jessica who spoke first.

'Did you recognize that voice?' she asked.

'I really didn't hear much. But, no, it didn't sound familiar.'

'What about what he said. *Not now*. Does this have any significance to you?'

'I'm not sure that's what he said. But to answer your question, it has no significance I can think of.'

Mary Gillen was right. There was so much static, it was hard to tell what the caller said. 'That's okay,' Jessica said.

A few minutes later, Mary Gillen walked Jessica to the front door.

'When you speak to your sons, and you ask them if the name

David Solomon means anything to them, I would appreciate a call,' Jessica said. She took out her business card case, thumbed out a card, handed it to the woman.

'Homicide?'

Jessica noticed a slight tremble had come to the woman's hands. 'Ma'am?'

'This. Your card. It says Homicide Division.'

'Yes,' Jessica said. 'I'm a homicide detective.'

The color seemed to leach from the woman's face. 'This is something bad, isn't it?'

'We're not really sure yet,' Jessica said. 'But there really isn't any cause for concern. It's quite possible that Mr Solomon mis-dialed a number. It's quite possible he meant to call someone else.'

The woman nodded, but she didn't look convinced. Before she could ask the next logical question – that being, whether or not Mr Solomon was dead – Jessica moved on.

'It's all probably much ado,' Jessica said. 'Again, when you talk to your sons, ask them if they recognize the name. And if you could call me one way or another, I'd appreciate it.'

'Okay,' she said. 'I will.'

As Jessica reached her car, she took her iPhone out of her pocket, and touched the icon for her memo application. This took her to her saved memos. She opened her car door, slipped inside, closed the door, then touched the selection to play back the recording she had made in Mary Gillen's kitchen.

Static. Then: *'Not now.'*

Was this even David Solomon's voice? Jessica wondered.

It *had* to be. The timeline was a lock. She had little doubt. These were David Solomon's final words.

Not now.

13

The last time Byrne saw Theresa Woodman was eight years earlier. He had visited her at her home two years after her son Thaddeus had gone missing, two years after Byrne had plotted a map of Valerie's potential crimes.

On Theresa Woodman's refrigerator was a calendar, each terrible, passing day crossed off in red.

At that time Theresa was twenty-six years old, a slender, attractive brunette with light brown eyes. On that day, as this day, it was her posture that disclosed her sadness. Eight years earlier Theresa Woodman walked through the world with a weight on her shoulders, the burden of the unknowing. At that time – even though the numbers were not in her and her son's favor – she still anticipated that every knock, every doorbell, every stranger who approached would bring the news that her son had been found, alive and healthy, and was waiting for her at a police station.

Now the weight was different. It was just as full, perhaps even more so, but clearly one of resignation, a millstone of unimaginable grief.

Byrne had nearly forgotten that he had arranged to meet the woman. Being next up on the wheel, he'd had a pretty good idea that he would catch a case on this day, but he had not anticipated – nor could he have – the events surrounding David Solomon's suicide.

He'd thought about calling Theresa to reschedule, but in the end knew he would not. While the murder of Nicole Solomon had cut a fresh wound across his city, the disappearance of Thaddeus Woodman was no less terrible.

Byrne had told Theresa Woodman on the phone that there had been no news of her son, and had debated with himself about whether or not he would bring her the news he *did* have, and whether or not it would help.

When he found himself at a table at the Starbucks on Arch Street, a block or so away from where Theresa worked at the Comcast Center, he thought it might have been a mistake to do this. When she entered the coffee shop, and he saw her eyes, he knew it was so.

It had been ten years since Theresa Woodman had last seen her little boy.

Theresa hugged him, sat down. Despite her burden, she now seemed to float above her chair.

'Can I get you something?' Byrne asked.

'No,' she said. 'I'm ... I'm fine. Thank you.'

Byrne saw that she had in her hands a wad of damp paper towels, already shredded.

He reached into his bag, took out the document. He had clipped the article from the *Inquirer*, and made a photocopy of it.

'I didn't know whether or not you had seen this,' he said. He unfolded the photocopy, slid it across the table. He watched as she read the piece.

When she was done, she dabbed at her moist eyes, took a few moments, pointed at the document. 'The date,' she said. 'This is less than three weeks from now.'

She was referring to the date of Valerie Beckert's scheduled execution. Byrne just nodded.

Theresa put down the article, looked out the window. Byrne could all but see the conflict doing battle inside her. He understood. The death penalty, and all its attendant emotions – political, spiritual, human – was, and forever would be, a war fought on the fields of the heart.

Theresa turned back to Byrne. 'Are we absolutely sure she had something to do with Thad's . . . '

Byrne wanted to finish her sentence for her. There were only two words. One was *disappearance*. The other was *murder*.

He used neither.

'No,' he said. 'It's still only a hunch on my part.'

This wasn't true. It was more than that. It was a belief.

'But the DNA,' she said, as if for the first time. 'In her car.'

There were a number of explanations as to why Thaddeus Woodman's DNA had been found in Valerie's car, none of which Byrne, or any other cop, would buy. The boy's DNA was lifted from four strands of his hair on the upholstery in the back seat.

Byrne had first visited Theresa and her husband John the month after Valerie had been arrested. He had also visited the parents of eight of the twelve other children who had gone missing. During these visits Byrne had requested a personal item belonging to each of the missing children, something from which a DNA test could be run. He did not concern himself, at that time, with the four children who had lived at foster homes, as their clothing, hairbrushes and other personal items were almost always shared, therefore contaminating the sample.

Because the processing of these DNA control models were not

part of an active investigation, the city would not authorize – or pay for – the analyses. Byrne had paid for the testing out of his own pocket. There had only been one match.

Thaddeus Woodman.

Byrne turned his coffee cup on the table, searching for the right words. 'I would like to say I know how your son's hair got there, but I can't, Theresa. There's no proof that Thaddeus was ever in Valerie's car, or her house, or even in her company.' He thought about taking a sip of coffee, stalling even longer, but he knew the coffee was cold. 'It's possible that Thaddeus came in contact with Thomas Rule somehow, that Thomas introduced the DNA into the car. Maybe the transference took place that way.'

Byrne could hear the uncertainty in his own voice, his disbelief in this implausible theory, and it made him feel dirty.

'But how would that be possible? They didn't know each other,' Theresa said. 'They went to different schools. We went to different churches, different stores. My God, Thad was only . . .'

Six, Byrne thought. He was six years old.

Before Byrne could respond, Theresa continued. 'And when she . . . dies, we may never know what happened.'

'No,' Byrne replied. He wanted to say more, but there was nothing to say.

They sat in silence for a while, the afternoon trade at Starbucks flowing around them. Every so often Byrne would glance at Theresa Woodman. He noticed that she watched the other women in the coffee shop – women who were about her age, all of whom wore wedding rings – with what looked like a mixture of envy and a terrible sense of longing. He noticed that Theresa did not make eye contact with these women. He understood this. The connection it might make – one that spoke of a shared bond, one that whispered the silent promise that exists between a mother and her child – would be too great to bear.

In the end, Byrne thought, no matter how much you rely on others for support, the inconceivable tragedy of losing a child is something that takes up permanent residence in the darkest corner of your heart, and must be endured alone.

14

Mr Marseille enjoyed reading newspapers, and he took four of them on a daily basis – *The New York Times*, *The Wall Street Journal*, *USA Today* and, of course, *The Philadelphia Inquirer.*

Whenever there was something in which he thought I would be interested – generally speaking, something about fashion or music or theater – he would take out his scissors and carefully clip the article. Often, when he prepared my breakfast – usually something light like oatmeal, or perhaps a butter scone and tea, my favorites – there would be a small pile of articles just waiting for me to read them.

It had been a full day since our gala with Nicole, and we were already preparing for our next tea dance, to be held this coming Saturday.

'Here's an interesting item,' Mr Marseille said.

I loved our mornings together. I always have.

Mr Marseille read from the front section of the *Inquirer*.

'Police say they have no leads in the investigation of the murder of Nicole Solomon.'

'Murder?' I asked.

'That's what it says.'

'Why do they think she was murdered?'

'It doesn't say. But the article ends like this: "Police are requesting the public's help. Anyone with information should call the tip-line listed below. All calls will be kept confidential".'

'Do you think we should call?' I asked.

Mr Marseille considered this for a few moments.

'I'm not sure that what we could tell them that would be useful.'

He was right, of course. The police tend to be a suspicious lot – and rightfully so, given their jobs – and anything we'd tell them might reflect poorly on Mr Marseille and me.

As I cleared the morning dishes I thought about this strange turn of events. This sort of thing has happened before – not often, I must say, due to the fact that many of the dolls we have mended do not get their names in the newspaper – but whenever it does it fills me with the queerest sensation all day.

Murder.

I don't like that word, and I'm certain Mr Marseille does not either.

15

Jessica spent the morning pushing through the search warrants they needed to follow up on other calls that David Solomon had made in the days leading up to his daughter's murder, and his own suicide. Because the David Solomon case was not a homicide, these warrants were not given high priority.

The process involved calling, leaving messages, getting voice-mail, returning the call, faxing, waiting.

It was maddeningly slow.

While she waited for callbacks, she accessed ViCAP, the Violent Criminal Apprehension Program. Maintained by the FBI, ViCAP was the largest investigative repository of major violent crime cases in the US designed to collect and analyze information about homicides, sexual assaults, missing persons, and other violent crimes.

Jessica put in details of the Nicole Solomon crime scene. And while there had been many homicides committed by strangulation in the past five or so years – a dozen or so using a stocking as a ligature – none included the signature of a painted bench, or the presence of a handwritten note.

She made a note to try again as more forensic data came in.

At ten o'clock, as Jessica and Byrne crossed the lobby of the Roundhouse, Jessica noticed a woman speaking to the desk sergeant. The woman looked familiar, but at first Jessica wasn't sure where she knew her from. Then it registered. It was Annie Stovicek, the woman who had been their sole witness at the Shawmont crime scene. Today, instead of her jogging outfit, she wore a dark suit and overcoat.

When the woman saw Jessica and Byrne she looked up, offered a nervous smile. Jessica and Byrne stepped through the security checkpoint, into the outer lobby.

'Mrs Stovicek. What brings you here?' Byrne asked.

'I was coming to see you, actually.'

'What can we do for you?'

'Well, after you left the other day, I took Miranda to her day care, then went to work. Needless to say, I didn't get much done.'

'That's completely understandable.'

'Later in the day I went to take a photo with my phone – we're remodeling, and I take pictures of things like bathroom vanities and kitchen countertops I like and send them to my husband – and when I opened the folder that has my recent photos I saw a picture I'd forgotten I'd taken.'

Jessica and Byrne just listened.

Annie Stovicek continued. 'You see, when we were down by the river, I took a picture.'

'That morning?'

'No. It was the night before. Late. I was with Ajax.'

'Ajax?'

'I'm sorry. Ajax is my dog. He's a Sheltie.'

'And you took a photograph of him?'

'Yes,' she said. 'As I said, it was late. Maybe midnight. I couldn't sleep.'

'You have the photo with you?'

'Yes.' She took out her cell phone, tapped an icon. 'I didn't notice it at first, I guess because I wasn't looking for it.'

'Notice what?'

She turned the phone to face the two detectives. The photo was a medium close-up of a young Sheltie. Behind the dog was parked a white, late model Honda Accord.

'Can you enlarge this a little?' Jessica asked.

'Sure,' Annie said. She pinched two fingers, spread them. The photo, which was of a high resolution, enlarged. In the moonlight, the car's license plate was perfectly readable. It was an up-to-date Pennsylvania tag. Jessica wrote down the number.

'Did you notice if anyone was in the car at the time?' Byrne asked.

'No,' she said. 'Sorry.'

'That's okay. And you didn't see anyone near it?'

'No. We were only down there a few seconds.'

Jessica recalled walking the site the morning after the picture was taken. When she had gone down to the river there was no car parked there. She glanced again at the photograph on the phone. There did not appear to be anything on the ground near the driver's side.

Still, it was worth checking. 'I'll call it in,' Byrne said. He headed across the main lobby, took out his phone.

'Is there anything else you can remember about the car?' Jessica asked. 'Did you see it arrive? Did you see it leave?'

Annie shook her head. 'No. To be honest, I don't really remember it even being there. I remember seeing it for the first time when I saw that picture.'

'And you don't recall seeing it before or since?'

'No,' she said. 'Sorry.'

'That's okay,' Jessica said. Out of the corner of her eye, she saw Byrne crossing the lobby. She knew his stride. He had something. Jessica turned back to the woman. 'Mrs Stovicek, I can't tell you how much we appreciate this. Not everyone would be this civic-minded.'

'Do you think that car – or the person who was in that car – had anything to do with . . .'

'Probably not,' Jessica replied. 'But we have to rule out everyone and everything.'

Jessica took out a card, wrote her business email on the back. 'When you have a moment, could you send me that picture?'

She took the card. 'Sure. No problem.' Annie Stovicek buttoned her coat, slipped on her gloves. 'Okay, then. Good luck.'

'Thanks again.'

A little awkwardly, as if she might have been waiting to be dismissed, Annie Stovicek turned on her heels and walked through the double doors, out into the rear parking lot.

'Did she remember anything else?' Byrne asked.

'No.' Jessica turned to her partner. 'We have something, don't we?'

'Am I that obvious?'

'Seriously?'

Byrne cleared his throat, consulted his notebook. 'The tag is registered to one Jeffrey Claude Malcolm, twenty-one, currently residing on Nineteenth Street in South Philly.'

'Any wants or warrants?'

'Funny you should ask. Mr Malcolm is currently out on bail.'

'What for?'

'He attempted to lure an underage girl into his car in September.'

16

The building was a newer three-story rehab in an older block of row houses on Nineteenth Street near Reed Street. Because the city had mandated off-street parking for some new construction, a number of newer row homes had been built with single car garages.

The address for which Jessica and Byrne were looking had a narrow garage as its first floor, essentially replacing what had one time been a front porch. Jessica and Byrne parked about a block away, scanned the street for their target car. They did not see it.

On the way they had called dispatch and requested a pair of sector cars to troll the streets and commercial parking lots for two blocks in all directions. None had spotted a white Honda Accord with the corresponding license plate.

As they approached the address, Jessica peeked into the window of the attached garage. It was empty. A quick scan of the second and third floors showed white honeycomb blinds, all lowered.

Byrne stepped up to the front door, put his ear near the jamb.

Apparently hearing nothing, he rang the bell. After a few moments the door opened.

Jeffrey Malcolm looked younger than twenty-one. He had dark hair, dark eyes, and wore the vest and trousers from a well tailored suit, white shirt, burgundy tie. Before saying anything the man looked at Byrne, then around the big man at Jessica.

He knew.

'Are you Jeffrey Malcolm?' Byrne asked.

Through the screen door. 'Do I need my lawyer?'

Byrne gave it a few seconds. 'You need a lawyer to figure out whether or not you're Jeffrey Malcolm?'

Malcolm looked down for a moment, at his highly polished shoes. He looked up. 'What is this about?'

Even though it was clearly unnecessary, Byrne produced his badge, introduced himself and Jessica. 'For the second and final time,' Byrne said. 'Are you Jeffrey Malcolm?'

'Yes,' Malcolm said. 'But my preliminary hearing is next week. I'm sure whatever this is about can—'

'This is another matter,' Byrne said. 'We need to ask you a few questions.'

Malcolm's shoulders sagged. He opened the door wide. Jessica and Byrne stepped inside. The front room was empty, save for a number of movers' boxes stacked against the far wall.

'Moving in or out?' Jessica asked. She knew the answer to her question – if Malcolm was moving in there was only a slight chance that this address would have flagged when they ran the license plate.

'Moving out,' he said. 'I found a place up in Bustleton.'

Already answering questions that hadn't been asked, Jessica thought.

'Do you own a white Honda Accord, Mr Malcolm?' she asked.

Another pause. 'May I ask what this is about?'

'We'll get to that in just a second.'

'Yes,' he said. 'I do.'

'Can you tell us where the car is right now?'

'Of course.' He pointed in a generally southern direction. 'It's in my garage.'

'The attached garage?'

'Yes.'

'Were you out in the car late Friday night or early Saturday morning?'

'This past Friday and Saturday?'

'Yes.'

'No,' Malcolm said. 'I just flew in from Atlanta. I got in about five-thirty this morning.'

'And you parked your car at the airport?'

'No,' he said. 'It's too expensive. I took a cab.'

Jessica made the note. 'And you say you were in Atlanta?'

'Yes.'

'Was this business or pleasure?'

Another pause. 'Business. I work for Aetna.'

'How long were you in Georgia?'

'Five days,' he said. 'I usually fly out from Philly Sunday night, and come back either Friday night or Saturday morning. I couldn't get a flight out Saturday.'

More information unasked yet answered, Jessica thought. 'And there are people who can confirm this?'

Jessica saw that Malcolm was about to get angry with the intrusion, but checked himself. Anyone out on bail with a pending hearing – especially for a charge of Attempting to Lure – knew that a sense of outrage with law enforcement was best held in check. In the end he said, simply: 'Yes.'

To that end Malcolm reached – slowly – into his pocket, produced a US Airways boarding pass, handed it to Byrne. Byrne scanned it, nodded at Jessica, handed it back to Malcolm.

'You say this is a weekly routine for you?' Jessica asked.

He nodded. 'For the past five months, yes.'

What had begun with promise – Jeffrey Malcolm's car being spotted a few yards from a murder scene, its owner out on bail pending a sex crimes charge – was beginning to look less so. Still, it did not mean he was not involved.

'And you say your car is in your garage right now?' Jessica asked.

'Yes.'

'And it's been there all week?'

'Yes,' he said. 'As far as I know.'

Jessica glanced up. 'As far as you *know*? Why would you say that?'

'What I meant was, the car has been there the whole time I was gone.'

'Why not just say that?'

Apparently, Malcolm had no response to this. He said nothing.

'Did you loan your car to someone during this past week?' Jessica asked.

'No.'

'Do you mind if we take a look in your garage?'

Again, Malcolm appeared to want to object. He once more decided against it. 'No problem.'

Jessica gestured to the front door. They walked outside, Malcolm leading the way, down the steps, then over to the garage. Malcolm opened the garage door. It wasn't locked.

The garage was empty.

'*What?*' exclaimed Malcolm.

Both Jessica and Byrne gave this so-called revelation a few moments.

'You seem surprised,' Jessica said.

'I am,' Malcolm said. 'I don't understand.'

'When was the last time you saw your car?' Jessica asked.

Malcolm considered this. 'Last Sunday. I went to the mall in the afternoon to pick up a few things for the week.'

'And you put the car back into this garage at that time?'

'Yes.'

'About what time on Sunday?'

'Maybe seven o'clock.'

'In the evening?'

'Yes.'

'Was the garage door locked all week?'

Malcolm shook his head, pointed at the locking mechanism, a spring actuated assembly. The slide was missing. 'No,' he said. 'The lock has been broken since I moved in.'

'Was the car locked?' Jessica asked.

'Probably,' he said. 'I can't remember.'

'Who else has keys to your car?'

Malcolm thought about this a little too long. 'No one. Just me.'

'And where are those keys now?'

Malcolm made a show of digging in his pants pockets. He came up empty. 'They must be inside. Do you want me to get them?'

'That would be helpful,' Jessica said. 'We'll go with you.'

As they walked back to the house, Jessica made eye contact with Byrne. Somehow, two and two were not equaling four, at least as it related to Jeffrey Malcolm and his mysterious car.

By the time they reached the porch, they had their answer.

Before Byrne could step across the threshold, Malcolm pivoted and slammed the door in Byrne's face, then turned the deadbolt. It took only three attempts for Byrne to shoulder open the door. He drew his weapon, ran across the living room, into the kitchen. He called out to Jessica.

'The back door's wide open,' Byrne yelled. 'He's running. Call it in.'

While Byrne sprinted out the back door, Jessica took out her phone, called dispatch. She gave them their location, and a description of Jeffrey Malcolm. She ran out the front door, then north on Nineteenth Street, toward Wharton. When she came around the corner, she saw Malcolm cross the intersection running at a high rate of speed. He had something in his hands, although he was moving far too quickly for Jessica to see what it was. It was silver in color.

A few seconds later, with Jessica gaining on him, Malcolm headed down the crowded sidewalk, dodging pedestrians. He glanced over his shoulder. He saw how close Jessica was.

Byrne was nowhere in sight.

Of all the things at which Kevin Byrne was adept, running – especially in street shoes – was not his forte. She had many times been surprised at his physical strength. Never once by his speed.

At the moment Jessica caught up to Malcolm, at the corner of Wharton and Dorrance, Malcolm cut to his right, between two parked cars, running full bore. He never made it across the street. A white delivery van, moving somewhere in the neighborhood of thirty-five miles per hour, caught Malcolm on his left hip and propelled the man a dozen feet into the air. The sound of Malcolm's body hitting the pavement was all but masked by the sound of metal on metal, of glass shattering, as the van crashed into a pair of cars parked on the south side of the street.

For a moment there was no sound. It was as if the city had collectively drawn a breath.

Then came the screams from the people on the street who had seen what happened.

Even before Jessica could approach the body a crowd had begun to form. Jessica turned to see Byrne walking up Wharton Street, trying to catch his wind.

Jessica took out her badge, put it on a lanyard around her neck.

110

She noted a sector car turning onto Wharton from Nineteenth. She beckoned it over, made a whirring gesture with her finger, and the patrol officer in the sector car turned on his bar lights.

Jessica walked over to where Byrne stood. 'Did you see what happened?' she asked him.

Byrne had not quite caught his breath yet. He put his hands on his knees, shook his head. With traffic stopped, Jessica made her way to the center of the street, next to where Jeffrey Malcolm's mangled body was splayed. The impact had all but turned his lower body backwards on his frame. The bones of both legs were broken and pierced the skin. A portion of the right side of his skull was caved in, a long streak of blood and brain matter painted the asphalt.

Jessica snapped on a latex glove, reached in, feeling for a pulse, even though she knew what she knew. She found no pulse. Jeffrey Malcolm was dead. She turned, caught Byrne's eye.

'I'll start a bus,' Byrne said.

Byrne stepped away, took out his phone, requested an ambulance. When he returned, Jessica asked:

'What was he carrying?'

'I didn't see anything,' Byrne said. 'There's a fence at the end of the alley behind his house. He got over it pretty quickly. Needless to say it took me a few seconds. By the time I hit the street he was rounding the corner. I didn't see anything.'

'He had something in his left hand. Something shiny. Silver.'

Both Jessica and Byrne fanned out on the street. They looked curb to curb, and underneath the parked cars. When they reached the crashed delivery van – where the badly shaken driver was now giving a statement to one of the patrol officers – Jessica saw it. It was a small netbook computer, dented and scratched, lying against the curb right near a sewer grate. She got on her knees, reached under the cab, hoping she wasn't going to be involved in one of those movie moments where the wrecked automobile bursts into flame at just the wrong moment. Nevertheless, she grabbed the laptop and got out of there as fast as she could.

She walked back to where Byrne was standing. When the paramedics arrived, and the scene was secured, they stepped back down Nineteenth Street, found a newspaper box. Jessica put the laptop computer down on top of the box. She tore off her bloody glove, snapped on two fresh ones, opened the laptop.

The desktop had only a few icons. She double clicked the mail icon, launching the program. There were dozens of recent emails, addressed to *moneybear*. All of the email messages contained links to sites that were clearly adult oriented.

Jessica found a folder on the desktop called *virus*. She opened it to find another folder called *quarantine*. She opened that folder to find yet another folder called *travelpics*.

Inside this folder were what had to be more than a hundred subfolders, all bearing a first name.

Girls' names.

Jessica glanced at Byrne. Considering Jeffrey Malcolm's legal history, there was little doubt as to what they were about to see. Jessica clicked one of the folders, one called *Judianne*. She was right. Inside the folder were a dozen pornographic pictures of a girl about six years old.

Jessica closed the laptop. She would leave the subsequent investigation into the source of these photos to the RCFL, the Regional Computer Forensic Lab.

The truth was, as creepy as Jeffrey Malcolm was on paper, and indeed was in person, they were only about to take a stolen car report from him, and leave him alone. For the moment. They were not about to search his premises or his person. There was no need to run.

At least there was no reason immediately obvious to the two detectives.

Now they had to know.

Both Jessica and Byrne were well aware that there was a profound distinction between the interests and fetishes of adult men who were interested in underage girls – girls the age of Nicole Solomon – and girls the age of the children on Jeffrey Malcolm's computer. Sometimes the distinction could be as fine as a year or so.

With a sector car and EMS on site, and traffic being routed around the block, the scene was secure. Jessica and Byrne walked back to Malcolm's row house in silence, each to their own thoughts.

Because neither of them wanted to vault the fence in the alley, they decided to enter Malcolm's row house via the damaged front door, and do what they could to secure the premises.

While Jessica entered the house, and walked to the kitchen to lock the back door, Byrne went into the trunk of their departmental sedan and retrieved a large paper evidence bag for the laptop.

When Jessica returned, she saw Byrne standing at the foot of the short driveway, arms crossed, staring straight ahead. She knew the look, the posture.

'What's going on, partner?' she asked.

For a few long moments Byrne said nothing. Then: 'Are you ready for this?'

'If I say yes, may I take it right back?'

'You may.'

'Okay, then,' Jessica said, wondering just what could possibly be coming next. In the past forty-eight hours they had begun an investigation into the murder of a young girl, made notification to a man who put a gun in his mouth and pulled the trigger, and now had come to question a man who had run into traffic and been splattered curb to curb on a busy South Philly street. She was ready for anything. 'I guess I'm ready.'

She was not.

Byrne took a few steps forward, turned the handle on the garage door, opened it.

There, in the garage – a structure that had fifteen minutes earlier been completely empty – was Jeffrey Malcolm's white Honda Accord.

17

The crowd at Finnigan's Wake, the legendary Irish pub at Third and Spring Garden Streets, was raucous.

Kevin Byrne did not join in the fun. He sat alone at the front bar, nursing his first Tullamore Dew.

Cops always knew who, among their ranks, wanted to talk, needed to talk, and those who needed to be left alone. Byrne figured his vibe was the latter. So much so that two stools on either side of him were empty. Every so often Margaret, one of the best bartenders in the city, would glance his way, expecting him to raise his empty glass, calling for another round.

So far, the double Dew on the rocks had been enough.

Byrne thought about Jeffrey Malcolm, and what it must have been like in his last few seconds, when he knew he was going to die. People who are addicted to pornography, especially child pornography, are hoarders, and there is no one thing in their lives – not money, not possessions, not family or friends – that is more important than their collections. They never seem to be able to delete a single image. In the end, it seems, Malcolm gave his life for it.

Was the man, in any way, connected to the murder of Nicole Solomon? They might never know. Malcolm's car had been transported to the police garage, and was currently being processed for evidence.

Byrne thought about Valerie Beckert, and how it was a different obsession that drove her to kidnap and murder little Thomas Rule.

Byrne dropped a twenty on the bar.

Thirty minutes later, against all reason, he turned onto the expressway.

The drive to Muncy would take about four hours, taking Byrne northwest through Allentown, Hazelton, Berwick. Even though traffic was light, Byrne found himself following the speed limit, perhaps because he was unsure if this was something he really wanted to do. More than once he eyed an exit with the thought of turning back.

About midnight he pulled off at Rt. 54, ordered coffee at a service plaza.

He sat in a booth, took out the binder that held the case files for the homicide of Thomas Rule. He had many times gone over every page, every photograph, every scientific report. And while it was true that sometimes, even after years of staring at something, a new angle or idea might suddenly appear, Byrne did not think this would be the case with the Thomas Rule evidence.

The investigation into the boy's death was closed. Byrne was looking at the data in the hopes of finding out what happened to Thaddeus Woodman and the other children.

He opened the folder, looked at the lab reports, his eyes bleary from the lack of sleep.

He then went to the photographs of the victim. The first in

the series was taken at Fairmount Park. Valerie Beckert had wrapped the boy in an old shower curtain liner, securing it with packing tape. The first photograph, taken by CSU, showed the small figure, barely discernible through the translucent material.

The second crime scene photograph was of the victim, lying on the unfurled plastic sheet. In this picture Thomas Rule was on his back, his hands to his sides. He wore dark trousers and a light colored crewneck sweater. If it were not for the deep welt around his neck, it would appear that he was sleeping.

Byrne opened a second folder. It was not officially part of any record kept by the PPD. This folder was his own, one he kept to chronicle the disappearance of Thaddeus Woodman.

He picked up the photo of Thaddeus, an Olan Mills type. The smiling, dark-haired boy was in that painful and awkward stage between baby teeth and permanent teeth, a time when a haircut was more of an inconvenience than anything related to vanity. He had inquisitive eyes, an untamable cowlick. Byrne tried to imagine the boy as a pre-teen, a teenager, a young man.

How tall were you going to be, Thaddeus?

What were you going to do for a living?

What were going to be your sports? Baseball? Football? Basketball? Hockey?

Were you going to be a husband and a father?

Were you going to be a good man?

Byrne often wished he could be the kind of person who could hold out hope for things like this, that he would one day have the answers to these questions. He was not that kind of person. More than two decades unearthing the darkest impulses of the human heart had forever stolen this from him.

Thaddeus Woodman was dead.

And, in two weeks, his killer would be, too.

*

When Byrne went out to his car in the service plaza lot he was all but certain he would go back to Philadelphia. He knew he was on a fool's errand, and that by the time he reached the three p.m. mark later that day, he would hit the wall of exhaustion, and be all but useless in his part of the investigation that mattered at the moment: the senseless, brutal murder of Nicole Solomon.

But still he pressed on, driven by an opaque, unnamable energy, one born of the belief that Valerie Beckert was a mass murderer.

Byrne arrived at SCI Muncy at just after two a.m. He knew that Deputy Superintendent Barbara Wagner had the night off, and it was for that reason Byrne had chosen to drive the nearly two hundred miles to Muncy in the first place. Barbara was good people, former PPD, and he didn't want her to experience any blowback if his little plan backfired.

Byrne did not know all the internal politics of the corrections system, but he knew that inmate #209871 – also known as Valerie Beckert – was not mandated by law to meet with anyone, including the only three classifications of people who had access to her at this point in the process; that being her attorney, her clergy, and her family.

Byrne also realized that his credentials as a city detective would pull little weight at a State Correctional Institution – indeed, an often bitter rivalry and sense of mistrust existed between law enforcement officers and corrections officials. Still, in his experience, he found that it was harder to blow him off in person than it was on the phone, and it was for this reason he had not called ahead.

He should have. As it turned out, he'd made the trip for nothing.

Upon arriving – after nearly four hours on increasingly snowy Pennsylvania roads – he was told that Valerie Beckert had already been moved to SCI Rockview to await her ultimate fate.

In consolation, after meeting with the superintendent herself – a pleasant and understanding woman named Gretchen Allenby – Byrne was offered a small suite of rooms in which to shower and take a nap before heading back on the journey to Philadelphia.

Byrne needed both, but declined.

He stood in the all but empty visitor's parking lot, hoping the frigid night air would revive him. Before long a car pulled into the lot, parked a few spaces to Byrne's left. It was a large four-door sedan, perhaps a decade old, its finish caked with road salt. Before the driver cut the lights, Byrne saw the license plate, and the small crucifix in the corner.

The man who emerged from the car was in his late fifties or early sixties, fit and trim for his age. He wore a dark blue overcoat, charcoal fedora. He also wore a priest's collar. In his hands was a thick stack of manila folders.

Byrne walked over to the priest's car. 'Good morning, Father.'

A little startled, the man looked up. He searched Byrne's face for recognition, found none.

'Good morning,' he said. 'I didn't see you standing there.'

'Sorry.'

'Not to worry.' He pointed at the main building. 'It's a little scarier inside.'

Although Byrne was much taller than the priest, and the parking lot was dark, Byrne saw no fear or apprehension in the man's face. Even in the dim light, Byrne could see a pair of small scars on the priest's right cheek, but the man's nose was straight and true. Apparently, the chaplain had won more fights than he'd lost. Byrne wished he could say the same for himself.

Byrne extended a hand in greeting. 'Kevin Byrne.'

The man smiled, shifted the stack of folders. 'Sounds Philly Irish.'

Byrne returned the smile. 'Born and bred.'

The priest put out his hand. 'Tom Corey.'

'Nice to meet you, Father.'

'Back in the day, I spent some time at St. Anthony's,' he said. 'Do they still call it the Devil's Pocket around there?'

'Only by old-timers like me.'

The scene drew out, but it was not uncomfortable, nor a moment unknown to either man. Still, it was Byrne's duty to find entrance to the conversation.

'Do you have a second?' Byrne asked.

Father Corey closed the trunk of his car, put the folders down. 'I do.'

Byrne had no idea where to begin. He just began. 'I'm a homicide detective with the PPD. I've run up against something that I can't seem to shake.'

Father Corey just listened.

'I came up here to see one of the inmates,' Byrne said. 'I'm not even sure why, or what I would say when I saw her.'

It appeared that Father Corey expected Byrne to continue. When he did not, the priest asked: 'May I ask who it is you came to see?'

There was no reason not to tell him. 'The inmate's name is Valerie Beckert.'

The priest's face did not register surprise. Despite some widely held perceptions, the carrying out of the death penalty, especially in Pennsylvania, was not a common occurrence. For women, it was even rarer, almost unknown. The burden on a prison chaplain at such a time as this had to be heavy. It was one thing to prepare a person for the end of life in a hospital or hospice. In such a grim and forbidding environment as this one, it had to be much harder. Byrne did not envy the man his cargo.

'I was the arresting officer,' Byrne added.

Byrne knew that whatever Valerie had told Father Corey – if indeed she had said anything to him – was between her and her confessor. For many reasons, not the least of which was his own Catholic upbringing, Byrne did not ask the question.

'I'm sure you're aware that, at this late date, her contact with the outside world is quite limited.'

'I know,' Byrne said. 'It's just . . .'

Father Corey waited a few moments. 'A matter of faith?' he asked.

Byrne hadn't thought of it in these terms, but he imagined it was. 'I think it probably is.'

Father Corey nodded, looked at the prison complex, the high stone walls, back. 'In the end, what we do, it's *all* about faith, right? What I mean is, I have to have faith in the system. I have to believe that everybody along the way did their jobs, and that no mistakes were made. I have to have faith that all these women are here for a reason. Especially a woman in Valerie Beckert's position.'

Byrne understood. While it was true that many of the people he encountered in his job had broken the law, it was not part of his mandate to make life easier for them. It was just the opposite. His job was to make the lives of everyone else a little safer by putting criminals behind bars.

Yet, in many ways, the job of a prison chaplain was the reverse. Everyone Father Corey encountered was also a criminal, but it was the priest's purview to help them find a path to salvation, no matter how heinous the crime. Byrne had never considered what a difficult job it was until this very second.

'Can you tell me about your concerns?' the priest asked.

Byrne gave the man a brief rundown of the circumstances surrounding the other missing children.

'But you have no proof of this,' Father Corey said.

'No, Father.'

The priest once again looked at the prison complex, back. 'Hebrews says that faith is the substance of things hoped for, the evidence of things not seen.'

'I believe she did these crimes, Father. And if she never confesses to them, once she is gone, the families will never know peace. I feel that they deserve to know, no matter how painful it will be. I feel that the burden of not knowing is worse.'

'And what about your burden?'

'Father?'

'The burden you've placed upon your own shoulders to find these answers. How long will you carry it?'

Byrne had no response to this.

Father Corey closed his car door, locked it. He turned back to Byrne.

'May I ask you something, detective?'

'Of course.'

'Have you made peace with the fact that, when you arrested Valerie Beckert, you were doing that which you are sworn to do? That you did your job without hatred or prejudice?'

It was a good question. Byrne decided that he had done his job properly. There had been many before Valerie, and many since. He hoped he could, in the end, say the same about them all.

'I have, Father.'

'That's all any of us can do.'

The priest reached into his pocket, pulled out a card. He handed it to Byrne.

'I know there's a few miles between Philly and Muncy, but you could always call.' He pointed at the lightening sky. Byrne hadn't even noticed. 'We never close.'

Byrne took the card. 'Thank you, Father.'

'Have a safe journey.'

Byrne watched the priest walk toward the side entrance, sign in at the security checkpoint, and disappear into the building. He wondered what the man was going to encounter this day, if he would save even one soul. He wondered if such a thing was even possible.

A few minutes later, with a milky sun rising behind a bank of deep gray clouds, Byrne got in his car, and headed back to Philadelphia.

18

In the days that followed the discovery of Nicole Solomon's body at the Shawmont train station, and the suicide of her father, the neighborhood in which Nicole had last been seen was canvassed three times, at three different times of day.

The interviews had produced nothing in the way of evidence or leads.

No one had come forward with any information, despite daily items in the *Inquirer* and *Daily News* that all were tagged with the tip-line number, and the pledge that all calls would be kept confidential.

Investigators learned that, on the morning before her body was found, Nicole had visited the Franklin Institute with ten of her classmates. They'd left at just after noon. All ten of the girls had been interviewed, as had the bus driver and key personnel at the Institute.

One of Nicole's classmates – a fourteen-year-old girl named Naomi Burris – told Jessica that they had walked three blocks south on Sixteenth Street, and parted company on the corner of Sixteenth and Spruce.

Naomi, who cried the entire time Jessica had spoken with her, said that she didn't notice anything strange or wrong, or that they were being followed. She said everyone called Nicole 'Nic,' and asked if it was true that Nicole's father had killed himself like everyone said.

There was no way to sugarcoat it, so Jessica told her that it was true.

The crime scene had since been released, and all traces of the crime, except for the spots on which the legs of the bench had rested, were gone. The bench had been transported to the police garage where it was processed for fingerprints and hair evidence. None were found. The paint was determined to be an exterior latex.

Whatever scientific evidence that investigators could gather from the area surrounding the Shawmont train station – that which had not been destroyed by passing SEPTA trains – had been processed, logged, filed, and entered into the binder. Two days after the murder there had been a number of violent thunderstorms, and any evidence that had not been collected, or destroyed, had been given back to the earth.

The one piece of evidence that was unique, and therefore gave the investigation a new avenue of inquiry, was the stockings used to strangle the victim. According to the preliminary report from the lab, the stockings were not made of nylon, or any of the synthetic blends that are currently available. The stockings were silk. Criminalistics estimated that they were at least thirty years old, maybe as old as fifty.

They concluded that there was a lot of biological material available on the stockings that did not belong to Nicole Solomon. Further tests were underway.

It was not lost on either Jessica or Byrne that Adinah Solomon –

David's ailing mother – was near an age where such stockings might be packed away in a trunk or in storage. A thorough search of the house and property did not yield any stockings, but that didn't mean the Solomons had not rented a storage facility somewhere.

The sad truth was that, until concrete leads were generated, David Solomon – despite his loving daily missives to his daughter – could not be ruled out as a suspect.

Jessica and Byrne visited the McDonald's on Christian Street. The manager made a DVD of the surveillance videos from the time David Solomon and his daughter had visited the restaurant.

The video showed them entering the store at seven-ten a.m. Nicole walked to the counter, while David took a seat in a booth. While Nicole waited in line, she did not engage any of the other patrons in conversation, and did not appear to speak to anyone other than the young woman at the counter who took her order.

Jessica and Byrne watched the entire video, up until a few minutes after David and Nicole Solomon left the restaurant at 7:36. They watched all three vantage points. No one paid the Solomons any particular attention, or was found staring at the teenager for anything more than a few seconds.

They made notes regarding the people sitting around the Solomons, as well as hard copies of freeze-framed stills of the people sitting at nearby tables.

If the killer put his eye on Nicole Solomon inside that restaurant, he did not make a show of it.

Both Jessica and Byrne attended David Solomon's funeral service, out of both respect to the man, and to put their own eyes on everyone who showed up.

They walked away with exactly that with which they arrived.

There were no leads.

As to David Solomon's suicide, Byrne had followed up on both the gun David had used, as well as with David's co-workers and friends. The people with whom he worked – he was a member of the staff at a healthcare provider called AdvantAge in Langhorne, Pennsylvania – were shocked and saddened at both Nicole's murder and her father's suicide, but seemed unable or unwilling to shed any light on the reasons behind either.

By mid-week, investigators did uncover some possible motives for David Solomon's suicide. They learned that David Solomon's wife had been killed in a car accident two years earlier, and that the driver of the other car – a man ruled to be legally intoxicated – had received a jail term of only nine months. They learned from neighbors that Solomon, after burying his wife, had become morose and unsociable, all but inconsolable, and had recently been hospitalized for more than three weeks for severe depression.

A search of the Solomon home had uncovered a number of prescriptions for antidepressants and sleeping pills – all current, yet hidden in a box in the basement, perhaps to keep them from Nicole's eyes.

The weapon, a Charter Arms Bulldog .357, was legal and licensed to David Solomon.

None of the man's co-workers knew the name Mary Gillen.

The SEPTA train that passed the station in the brief window of time at which the ME had been able to presumptively put the time of death did not carry passengers who used any kind of rail card, which could have been used to identify them. Any leads generated in this area would have to go out over the media, or involve investigators taking the train themselves, and interviewing passengers.

Both avenues of investigation were being considered.

There was no link yet found between Jeffrey Malcolm and Nicole Solomon. Malcolm had told the truth about being in Atlanta the previous week. A canvass of the other residents on

Malcolm's street yielded nothing in the way of eyewitnesses to Malcolm's Honda Accord coming or going from Malcolm's garage.

Hair and fiber samples were taken from the Honda's trunk, and had been submitted to the FBI for testing.

The document examination section of the PPD was located on the first floor of the crime lab, formally known as the Forensic Science Center at Eighth and Poplar streets.

The building also housed the other science units – Firearms and Ballistics, Criminalistics, and the drug lab.

The director of the document section was Sgt. Helmut Rohmer. A giant of a man with bleached white hair, Sgt. Rohmer – who insisted on being called Hell – was a lab rat in the truest and most noble sense of the word. Among the number of artifacts and newspaper articles framed and mounted on the walls, his proudest piece was a large section of drywall cut from the lobby of an apartment building, a piece of drywall where a killer – a man currently serving a sentence of life without parole in Rockview – had misspelled a word while spray painting a taunt to the police.

It was Hell Rohmer's work that put the man away. In a job that was mostly about forged signatures, sometimes a document examiner could be the only link between a killer and justice.

When Jessica and Byrne entered the room, Hell was poring over a document from a current case, his brow furrowed, a look of intense concentration on his face. As Jessica got closer she saw it wasn't a police document at all, but rather a copy of the latest issue of *Maxim* and a photo spread of actress Lacey Chabert.

Hell looked up from his magnified swing-arm light, a bit startled. He gently slid a manila folder over the *Maxim*.

If Hell Rohmer was known for anything, it was for his collection of black T-shirts. The rumor was that he had thousands. Today's shirt read:

The last thing I want to do is hurt you.
But it's still on the list.

Hell pointed sheepishly at the copy of *Maxim*. 'Did you know Tim Burton is thinking of making a sequel to *Beetlejuice*?'

Neither detective was buying into the cover story. Hell moved on.

'It's funny that you guys are here. I was just thinking about you,' he said.

'But not enough to actually call,' Byrne said, letting him off the hook.

Hell laughed. 'I may be easy but I ain't cheap.'

He walked over to his massive bookcase, took out a file. He walked back to the examining table, extracted a photocopy from the folder. It was a facsimile of the invitation found under the bench.

'This is beautiful penmanship,' he said. 'I mean, I realize that whoever wrote this is probably a psychopath, but still, there's a pretty high skill set at work here. This reflects many hours of practice.'

'Did you run it by the ID unit?' Jessica asked.

Hell shook his head. 'Not yet. But I examined it under the heaviest magnification I've got. I don't think we're going to lift any prints from this. Or the envelope. However, if whoever touched that envelope touched the gummed part, we may get a partial.' He pulled a stool over. 'But that doesn't mean it isn't a cornucopia of information to be found within.'

'That much?' Jessica asked.

'Okay, maybe I'm overstating. I just love saying the word "cornucopia," although I only use it seasonally.'

'Maybe you just like blowing your horn,' Byrne said with a smile.

'Snap!' Hell replied. '*Good* one.'

129

Hell sat on his rollaway stool, got down to business. 'Okay, first off, I'm a hundred percent sure that the entire document was written by one person.' He put the photocopy of the invitation on the examining table, angled the swing-arm lamp over the top. 'What do you guys know about calligraphy?'

For Jessica and her partner, it was almost a rhetorical question. Jessica would say 'almost nothing.' Byrne would say 'a little.' He knew a little bit about almost everything. Jessica let him answer.

'A little,' Byrne said.

'Well, I'll just touch on the basics here,' Hell said. He opened the drawer, took out a small telescoping pointer, pulled it out to full length. 'The first thing you learn about is called the pen width.' He pointed to the top line of the invitation. 'With calligraphy pens, other than monoline pens, you are using nibs that have a narrow side and a wide side. The measurement from one edge of the wide side to the other is called the pen width.'

He pointed to the individual letters in the first line:

You are invited!

'The other important thing to know is about the pen angle. Different alphabets demand different angles, from zero all the way up to ninety degrees. Most calligraphy, however, is done at a forty-five degree or thirty degree angle.'

Hell looked up at the two detectives. 'Are you still with me?'

'Riveted,' Jessica said.

Hell opened the file, took out another document, a second photocopy of the invitation. This one had an overlay of five horizontal lines, like a musical staff.

'All calligraphy is based on five basic lines,' Hell said. 'The ascender line, the waistline, the branching line, the writing line, and the descender line.'

As he rattled off these somewhat confusing terms, he tapped

each of the five lines he had drawn horizontally across the photocopy of the invitation.

'Ascenders go above the waistline to the ascender line. Des-
cenders go below the waistline to the descender line. Keep in
mind I did this with a ruler and the finest point nib made. Look
how precise and uniform these strokes are. If we get another
example of this – and I hope we don't – I'll be able to make a
match from ten feet away. This is almost perfect.'

Hell looked up, realized he was gushing, added:

'For a crazy person, I mean.'

Jessica said nothing. What detectives in the field did every day,
and what the forensic people did in the lab every day, was as different as jobs could be. It was understandable that the scientist
sometimes yearned for the so-called excitement of the physical
chase, and that the detective yearned for less of it.

'There's a lot more to learn about this,' Hell continued. 'Some
of it involves the slant of letters in certain alphabets, but we don't
need to go into that now.'

'Can you tell if it was written by a man or woman?' Jessica
asked.

Hell thought about this for a few moments. 'That's a tough
one, but I would say it was written by a man. Men tend to press
a little harder. This is presumptive, but I'm pretty good at this.'

'What about the age of the document?' Jessica asked. 'Can you
tell how long ago it was written?'

'Oh, it's recent. I'd say it was written within a day or two
before it was recovered.'

'What about the paper?' Jessica asked.

'See, now we're getting into the factual part of our show. I love
this part.'

Hell walked over to a bookshelf, pulled out a large sample
book of papers. The name *Qena* was written on the binder. Hell
put the book down on the table, opened it to the center.

'The paper is manufactured by a company called Qena. The stock is a sixty-five pound cover, vellum finish.' On the right-hand side of the book were nine different color samples. He tapped one called *Aged*. 'The line of paper is called Lunaparche. Very elegant. This particular note was written on sixty-five pound cover Lunaparche Aged.'

For a moment, Jessica thought about asking him if he was sure about this, but besides being an insult – every scientist in the forensic sciences, especially the director of a unit, never said they were certain unless they were certain – it was clear, even to her untrained eye, in a side-by-side comparison with the original document, that he was right.

'It's a great line of paper,' he said. 'It has the look and feel of parchment. Plus it is FSC certified, and made from thirty percent recycled postconsumer fiber.'

Whenever you talk to Hell, you had to expect some fan boy jargon.

'Where is it available?' Byrne asked.

'Unfortunately, a lot of places online,' he said. 'Unfortunate for us, of course. Fortunate for the friendly folks at Qena.'

'Are the cards available in that size from the manufacturer?'

Hell smiled. 'Very good question, detective.'

'I have moments.'

'The answer is no,' he said. 'It comes from the manufacturer only in eight-and-a-half by eleven sheets. This document was cut to this size.'

'Do we know what was used to cut it?'

'It was cut with an extremely sharp blade. I would say an X-Acto blade, probably first use. It definitely was *not* cut on a paper cutter.'

'What about the envelope?'

'The envelope is what's known as a baronial. It has this deep pointed flap and a diagonal seam. It's the envelope of choice for announcements and invitations. Greeting cards too, of course.'

'I always go baronial with my greeting cards,' Jessica said.

Hell smiled. 'Once you go baronial ...'

'What can you tell us about the pen and ink?'

Hell reached into his pocket, produced a pen. 'It's a Staedtler Calligraph Duo. Black ink.'

'Just like that?' Byrne asked.

'Just like that,' Hell said. 'I do some calligraphy myself. I've yet to meet a document examiner who hasn't at least dabbled in it. I tested the ink, measured the width. It's a Staedtler.'

'Also available everywhere.'

'Sorry to say it is. Available at Blicks, for one. Amazon, of course. Under three bucks.'

Byrne studied the note. 'What about the last line?'

See you at our thé dansant!

'It means "tea dance",' Hell said. 'According to Merriam-Webster, first known use was in 1819.'

'I'm going to guess you know what a tea dance is,' Jessica said. She declined to look at her partner. She wouldn't give him the satisfaction.

'I do,' Hell said. 'But only because I looked it up. A tea dance is a late afternoon or early evening dance, often held after a garden party. Believe it or not, they were often given by officers in the Royal Navy.'

'Royal Navy as in British?' Jessica asked.

'Yeah,' Hell said. 'Weird, huh?'

Jessica looked at all the material on the table: the original document, the paper samples, the pen.

She felt as if they were just at the edge of something, but she had no idea what it was.

*

By the time they returned to the Roundhouse, the initial toxicology report on Nicole Solomon was completed. The fax from the ME's office was in Jessica's mailbox.

Jessica made a copy, put it on a desk and returned a few phone calls. When Byrne showed up she handed it to him.

Byrne scanned the report. 'Look at this,' he said.

'What?'

'There was trace amounts of psilocin in her system.'

'I'm not sure I know what that is.'

'It's an hallucinogen,' Byrne said. 'Psilocin and psilocybin are the active ingredients in magic mushrooms.'

Jessica looked up from the document. 'And you know this how?'

'I read a lot.'

'Uh-huh.'

Byrne sat down at a computer terminal. 'Plus, I'm older than slate. And I've run into it a few times.'

He got online, made a search, and navigated to a website devoted to hallucinatory drugs. He printed off the main page devoted to mushrooms and handed a copy to Jessica.

'It's a Schedule One drug,' Jessica said.

'Yes it is,' Byrne said.

According to the DEA, Schedule 1 drugs – heroin, ecstasy, methaqualone, LSD, and others – were drugs with no currently accepted medical use, and had a high potential for abuse.

How much this changed they didn't know. Yet. But Jessica had to admit that it was unexpected. After looking through Nicole's room, and cruising the girl's email and browsing history on her laptop, there was little indication that Nicole Solomon did any illicit drugs.

'So, Nicole Solomon – good girl Nicole, good *student* Nicole, never been in *trouble* Nicole – suddenly decides to start doing mushrooms?' Jessica asked.

'It doesn't compute, does it?'

'It does not,' Jessica said. 'So there's a good chance it was fed to her.'

'This is what I'm thinking,' Byrne replied. He opened up the binder, retrieved the documents related to Nicole Solomon's autopsy. He flipped a page.

'Stomach contents are consistent with the Egg McMuffins her father said she had that morning. There was some undigested chocolate.'

'So, Nicole goes to breakfast with her father, takes a taxi cab to her school, then attends a movie at the Franklin Institute. At some point in this timeline – in the taxi, at the school, on the bus, at the Institute – she decides that she is a drug user, perhaps for the first time in her life, and takes magic mushrooms.'

'What's wrong with this picture?' Byrne asked.

'Just about everything,' Jessica said. 'How much do you really know about magic mushrooms?'

Byrne put his left hand flat on the desk, raised his right hand. 'I have never once ingested a Schedule One drug.'

'Willing to submit to a polygraph on that?'

Byrne looked at his watch. 'Is it six o'clock already?'

Jessica laughed. 'We should get Vince in on this,' she said.

'I agree.'

Vincent Balzano was a detective with the Narcotics Field Unit North. If it was an illegal drug, and it was being sold or consumed anywhere in Philadelphia County, Vincent, or his partner Lou Cefferati, would know about it.

Jessica picked up the phone, dialed Vince's number at the station house. After a few seconds, there was an answer.

'Cefferati.'

'Lou, this is Jessica Balzano.'

'Hey, bright eyes. How are you?'

'Old and sassy.'

135

'I believe the sassy part.'

'How's Jeanie?'

Lou Cefferati's daughter Jeanie had been diagnosed with ALS – Amyotrophic Lateral Sclerosis, often referred to as Lou Gehrig's Disease – at the age of seventeen. There was a yearly fundraiser for the condition, one in which Lou Cefferati was deeply involved. Jessica, along with just about every detective she knew, made it a point to attend every year.

'She's good,' Lou said. 'Day at a time.'

Jeanie Cefferati had been given only a few years to live at the time of her diagnosis. That was eight years ago. Jessica had never met a stronger or more positive person than Jeanie Cefferati.

'Is Vince around?' Jessica asked.

'He's on the street,' Lou said. 'Got a message for him?'

'No message,' Jessica said. Whenever Vincent was on duty, Jessica never called his cell phone. He always had his mobile phone on silent, or turned off, when he was on the street – a poorly timed ring tone could mean death to a detective in narcotics – but it was not worth the chance that he had forgotten to do so.

'Just have him give me a call,' Jessica said.

'Does he have your number?'

'Smart ass.'

'Been accused of worse,' Lou said. 'Just ask my ex.'

'Be safe, detective.'

Jessica hung up the phone. She turned back to the toxicology report. She'd read so many of them in her time that they all tended to look the same. She looked again at the ME's report on Nicole's last meal, thinking:

Who among us, in their last hours, ever speculated that some rushed-through meal, some gourmet extravaganza, some instantly forgotten fast food would one day be a document on a homicide detective's desk?

For a crazy moment Jessica closed her eyes, and tried to recall her three previous meals. There was the sandwich she'd had for lunch, a Sinatra hoagie from Sarcone's: prosciutto, roasted garlic, fresh mozzarella, drizzled with red wine vinegar and oil. You don't forget a Sinatra hoagie. Maybe it was the garlic.

For breakfast, a pair of small croissants.

Last night's dinner? She couldn't remember.

Jessica was all but certain that Nicole Solomon had no idea that an Egg McMuffin would be her last meal.

19

'Brandon Altschuld, please.'

While Byrne waited for the public defender to come onto the line, he looked at the box on the car seat next to him. In the failing light of day he thought, not for the first time, that it looked the same as just about every other box from the evidence storage room. Unless you could see the name and case number on the outside, along with the date, you would have no way of knowing what was inside.

This box held the few scant items found in Valerie Beckert's car on the night she was arrested.

From the phone: 'This is Brandon Altschuld.'

'Mr Altschuld, my name is Kevin Byrne. I'm a homicide detective with the PPD.'

Silence. A long, protracted moment. Byrne continued.

'I was the arresting officer in the Valerie—'

'I know who you are, detective,' Altschuld said. 'What can I do for you?'

The man was throwing down serious attitude, but Byrne had

expected it. There was never, nor would there ever be, any love between defense attorneys and the police, and for good reason. Byrne knew that, at least with high priced representation, the arrogance was gilded by expense accounts, media glory and, if the case was high profile enough, a possible book contract. With public defenders – a job with low pay, long hours, and very little chance for fame – the police were the sworn mortal enemy, a protected class that broke every statute they were sworn to uphold if it meant clearing the streets of people they considered vermin.

'I'm calling to make a request regarding Valerie Beckert,' Byrne said.

More silence. Altschuld was going to make him work for everything. Also expected.

Finally: 'I'm listening.'

'I'd like to speak to your client,' Byrne said.

Byrne heard the man make a sound about as close to a laugh as possible, without actually laughing.

'Is that right?' Altschuld asked. 'What could you possibly have to talk about with my client?'

Byrne knew they would get to this, but he didn't think it would be this soon. He tried to leaven his tone with one of respect for the man's profession. 'I think that she might have some important information about other cases.'

'Really? Other homicides?'

'Well, no,' Byrne said. 'They are not open—'

'Then why are we having this conversation? I know I wasn't her counsel when she was tried, but as I recall you had her in an interview room for about six hours after she was arrested. Why would you think she's going to tell you anything now? It's been ten years.'

There was no answer to this. At least, not one that would move the ball forward. 'Look, Mr Altschuld, I know that—'

'You had your chance. The Commonwealth of Pennsylvania is going to take my client's life in less than two weeks' time,

Detective Byrne. My client has made peace with that sad fact. I suggest you do the same.'

'If you could just—'

'Have a nice day.'

Before Byrne could respond, the man ended the call. Byrne had to stop himself from throwing his phone out the window. He'd broken so many phones this way in the past few years that he'd considered buying them in bulk. Instead, he clicked off, took a deep breath, then gently put the phone in his pocket.

He glanced out the passenger-side window, tried to calm himself. The call had gone worse than he expected, and he'd expected it to go pretty badly.

This section of Fairmount Park was all but deserted at this time of the early evening. He saw a pair of joggers on the winding path; a teenaged boy and his golden retriever playing a game of Frisbee catch.

Byrne got out of his car, raised his collar to the wind and chilling mist. He crossed the field. When he reached the spot at which Valerie Beckert intended to bury Thomas Rule he stopped. He shoved his hands into his coat pocket, closed his eyes.

He saw Valerie sitting on the bench, her hands cuffed behind her. The patrol officer who had detained her stood a few yards away. Thomas's body lay on the ground at the side of the path, small and forever stilled. The tableau of these three figures were as vivid now as they had been that night.

When Valerie had looked up, and met his eyes for the first time, Byrne had seen something in them he had only seen a few times before. There was no fear, no sense of shame or guilt, no remorse. Instead, for a fleeting instant, her eyes seemed to say that she had been waiting for this moment her whole life, along with something else that had stopped him cold.

It seemed she had been waiting for *him*.

*

The finial rose into the night sky, a bird of prey on the branch of a massive oak.

The front yard was overgrown, the walk covered in dead leaves, small branches, wind-blown trash. The sign for the realty company was long rusted, its phone number and the name of the Realtor obscured by ten years of rain and snow and grime.

When Byrne turned the key in the lock he thought for a moment he had the wrong one. He'd found the key on a small plastic fob in the evidence box he'd taken from the storage room at City Hall.

He tried again. Right. Nothing. Left. Nothing. The lock seemed to be rusted shut. He tried once more, slowly rocking the key side to side. Eventually he felt the key turn, the tumblers fall.

When he entered the foyer, the feeling descended upon him in a damp and disquieting wave.

The foyer was empty, devoid of furniture, covered with a thick layer of dust. In one corner he saw shredded paper, the remnants of a roll of paper towels, the bottom chewed away and carried to some other part of the house, only small black mouse droppings left behind.

Straight ahead, through an arched opening, was the living room. It was large, even for a Wynnefield center-hall colonial. At the far wall was a fireplace, bricked over in painted blocks. To the left were empty bookshelves, half the shelves missing.

Byrne tried to rationalize why he came back here, but he knew the reasons resided in his heart, not his mind. He knew that the emotions that drew him here – the anger that accompanied the decade-old unwavering belief that the one-time occupant of this house had murdered more than one child – would cloud his judgment, but at the moment this did not matter to him.

He believed that in the dark heart of this structure lived Valerie Beckert's secrets.

Byrne shut the door.

He felt the house close in around him.

With the evidence box under one arm, Byrne ascended the steps. He ran his hand along the rail. Somehow he knew that the fifth tread from the bottom would groan, that the handrail would have an inch or so of play halfway to the top. He did not *know* these things from any sense of remembrance or recall. This knowledge did not live in a part of him connected to the first time he had entered this house.

At that time he'd moved through the space with a sense of urgency and dispatch, his training, his powers of observation, focused on finding clues and evidence that would lead him to the other children he was certain Valerie Beckert had murdered.

They'd found nothing that night. There was no clothing, no murder weapons, no hair or fiber evidence, nothing that would indicate that any child – including Thomas Rule – had ever even paid a visit to the house.

Did Valerie have another place of residence, somewhere she used as a killing room? he'd wondered at the time. They'd found no evidence of that, either.

Byrne reached the top of the stairs, sat on the landing, opened the evidence box. There were only three items inside.

There was a brightly colored box, a Happy Meal from McDonald's, itself containing an object about which Byrne had thought many times over the past decade. He opened the Happy Meal box, picked up the toy, a rather faithful orange plastic casting of Nemo, from the Pixar film *Finding Nemo*. The toy, like the other objects in the main box, still held the residue of the black powder used to lift fingerprints.

Byrne knew, based on Thomas Rule's autopsy, that the boy had not eaten anything from McDonald's on the day of his murder. He wondered which of the other children had eaten the Happy

Meal, which of them had sat – frightened and tearful and alone – in the backseat of the car, this small plastic toy in hand. Byrne moved the tail, the two fins, wondering: Had Thaddeus Woodman done the same thing?

He put the toy back into its box, picked up another item, a small bottle of baby aspirin. As he had on that night a decade earlier, he shook the bottle. There was only one pill left. Again, he wondered why Valerie Beckert had this in her car. Was she nursing the children through their summer colds, only to bring them to such a terrifying end?

Byrne closed his eyes, summoned the feelings. He could all but hear Thomas Rule's sobs in this space, hear his footsteps as he tried to escape from the monster that was Valerie Beckert.

He opened his eyes, glanced around at the rolling gloom of the drafty house, took the third item from the box. It was a key ring. On it were three keys. One was for Valerie's car, one was for the front door to this house, and a third key, an old skeleton type.

What did it open? Byrne wondered. *What secrets, what horror, would it reveal?*

Byrne put the keys back in the box, closed it, stood to leave.

As he did, the floorboard creaked beneath his weight.

20

The floorboard creaked beneath her weight.

She stopped, held her breath, listened.

Silence.

On her first night in this house, a many-roomed mansion in north-west Philadelphia, Valerie knew she was finally free.

When her aunt Josephine was a young woman, they say she was a great beauty, a nightclub singer of modest fame, working the small clubs in and around Philadelphia and Camden, catching the eye of men young and old alike.

By the time Valerie was trusted to the woman's care, at the age of seventeen, following Valerie's father's death, Josephine had gained a good deal of weight, and the only singing in which she engaged was in the shower, or while she puttered in the small herb garden behind the house.

Aunt Josephine, although often possessed of a mean temperament – a woman prone to violent, alcoholic fits – was a wonderful cook. Her waistline spoke the truth about this.

THE DOLL MAKER

It was her weight that would one day bring her life to a sudden, dreadful end.

When Josephine's husband Randall Beckert had died two years before Valerie came to Philadelphia, Josephine cashed in all his bonds, liquidated his accounts, and spirited the cash away like some mad monk.

It took Valerie less than three weeks to find it all. She was skilled at navigating small passageways, and practiced at finding that which was meant to be hidden from searching eyes.

For the first time in her life, Valerie had the run of a house.

She had never felt so liberated.

On most days, at just before dawn, Valerie would rise, make herself coffee, and take up position in the front room. Once there, she would part the curtains a few inches, and wait for the children to pass by. By seven or so they would emerge from their houses, trundling along behind their harried mothers, walking alone, standing in wait for the school bus that stopped just a few yards from the walk.

Valerie watched with something close to enchantment.

She watched the boy on crutches who took the longest time to pass in front of the house. One day the boy stopped at the end of the walk, tried to arrange his weight sent askew by his book bag, knapsack and lunch bag. Valerie was certain the boy had seen her watching him.

There was once a girl who wore a black patch over her right eye for the longest time. At first Valerie had thought it the result of some short-lived therapy, but after a few months the girl still wore it.

There was another boy who walked with a limp. He had a sweet face, even when he struggled to keep up with the others.

When she'd taken the trains to Philadelphia she'd had to leave behind her coterie of friends, but here she knew she would make many more.

But there was something she had to do first.

As she stole away to bed that night, just two days before the first day

145

of spring, she glanced down the stairs. Her shadow was as long as the staircase itself.

Valerie put her hand on the cap of the newel post at the top.

It was loose.

A few more turns and it would be even looser, she thought.

Something like that could be dangerous.

21

The newel cap was loose.

Byrne turned it, thinking about the last days and hours and moments of the children who had entered this house, never to leave alive again.

He'd known the moment he crossed the threshold ten years earlier. Maybe before. Perhaps he even knew as he drove down the street, a short lane on the northwest side of the city; a pair of weed-choked vacant lots on either side. He had the feeling he was being drawn to the end of the street, iron shavings toward a magnetic field.

He knew the sensation the way he knew any emotion that gathered inside him – anger, jealousy, or the envy he sometimes felt when he saw new, freshly minted police officers, straight from the academy, their badges bright and polished, their eyes clear.

This feeling was darker. It was one he got sometimes, a damp chill across his shoulder blades, rising to the back of his neck. It sometimes brought the understanding, the mindset of the people who committed murder, a murky second sight he acquired more than two decades earlier, a brief and hellish moment when he had been declared dead only to come back a minute later.

The knack had come and gone over the years, and was mostly gone now. He'd been wrong about things far more times than he had been right. But he had been right often enough to know that it was something he could not discount.

He never discussed this ability – if indeed an ability was what it was – with anyone. Not his family, his co-workers, even a cadre of psychiatrists and social workers he'd been mandated to see over the years. He had not even discussed it in depth with Jessica, the person to whom he felt closest in his life.

In the time since his death incident he had tried many things to come to an understanding. For a brief period he had suffered migraines, and in the aura that accompanied the malady he thought he had visions. He had been to a number of therapists, had even visited a regression therapy group, hoping to return to that moment.

But here, in this place, a house where malevolence once lived, he felt something new. Not a hunch or intuition, but rather a kinship.

It was as unnerving a feeling as he had ever felt.

What happened here, Valerie?

For Thomas Rule, for Thaddeus Woodman – and all the others – he had to know the truth.

Before he could stop himself he took out his phone, and made the call.

22

It was Saturday. It was time for our *thé dansant*.

I was beside myself with anticipation.

Mr Marseille was dressed smartly. He wore a dark suit, subtly striped, starched white shirt, and a claret tie. His shoes, as always, were highly polished.

There were so many things to consider. Not the least of which was what *I* would wear.

Mr Marseille, as always, was in charge of making the tea. Heaven only knows where he gets the ingredients – he sometimes disappeared for hours on end, causing me no end to worry. I had once thought about asking after this, but I decided against it.

Sometimes magic should remain in the realm of the magician.

Where do the birds come from?

Where does the rabbit go?

Magic was such fun. Perhaps we would do a magic themed tea one day.

Wouldn't that be the best?

There had been a time, the longest time, when we stopped giving parties. I was saddened by this, but all things happen for a reason. At least, I've been led to think so. If there was no master plan, what would be the point of living?

I sat at my sewing machine, the sunlight streaming through the dormer window. Whenever I made clothes I did all the stitching, making sure to back stitch. Some use glue guns to make their clothes, but I think that is cheating.

I put the last stich in the skirt, turned it right side out. I gave it a quick press with the steam iron. I arranged the outfit on the bed, and looked at the photograph of the original.

I thought it was perfect, but perhaps that was immodest of me. I do so hate to be boastful.

'Mr Marseille?'

Mr Marseille entered from the parlor, crossed the room. He had just finished shaving and smelled wonderfully of lavender. He bought all his products through the mail; all imported from France. He was quite strict about this. There was a time, last year, when he let his whiskers grow for five or six days when there was a delay in his order.

Needless to say, he did not appear in public that way.

'What do you think?' I asked.

He studied my work for a few moments. For me it was agony.

'I think you are an artiste, dear heart,' he said. '*Nonpareil.*'

He often said things like this, but I believed him to be sincere.

'*À votre bon cœur!*' I replied.

Mr Marseille laughed. I laughed, too.

'Do we have everything we need for the dance?' I asked.

'We do. I acquired suitable transportation this morning. I don't think the van will be missed until Monday morning, and by that time it will be back where I found it.'

'With gasoline to replace what we've used, of course.'

'Of course.'

With a spring in my step I crossed the room. I held open the door. 'It is time to dress,' I said.

Mr Marseille took out his pocket watch, flipped it open. 'We have forty-one minutes if we are to keep to our schedule.'

'Then I won't tarry.'

Mr Marseille left the room, closed the door behind him. There was no need for me to turn the key in the lock. If there are two things I know about Mr Marseille – and there is no one in the world who knows him better than I – it is that he is fiercely loyal and, beyond all else, a gentleman.

Fifteen minutes later I stepped from my room. My outfit today was a blue dress I had made about a year earlier, but never worn. I'm happy to say I am exactly the same size, and the gown required no alteration.

'How do I look?'

Mr Marseille took my hand in his. 'You look beautiful.'

I stood on the corner, in the shadows, as Mr Marseille crossed the street. My heart was fluttering as it always did at moments like this, just before an invitation.

Handguns scare me terribly, but Mr Marseille is very clever and skilled with them. Years ago, we took some of the naughtier children to the forest. Mr Marseille set them on a log. One by one they fell, like kewpies at the carnival.

He knew what to bring to the invitation.

Nobody accessorized like Mr Marseille.

At the precise moment, I stepped from the shadows.

The boys looked at me with something close to awe. I felt enormously flattered. I've never been very confident in my appearance – far from it, really, I've always felt myself the boudoir doll never taken down from the shelf – but at this moment I felt the prettiest girl at the dance.

The two boys stopped, looked at each other, then back at me.

'Hello,' I said.

'What's your name?' the taller of the two asked.

'Anabelle.'

'Awesome,' the shorter of the two boys said. 'I'm Robert, and this is Edward. Our friends call us Bobby and Teddy, though.'

I gave them my best smile. 'Might you consider me a new friend?'

'Of course!'

'Then may I say it is a pleasure to meet you, Bobby and Teddy.'

Bobby looked me up and down, perhaps searching for a clue as to how he should proceed. 'Where do you go to school?'

'Oh my,' I said. 'I'm done with school.'

The boys were of an age when an older girl might be seen as an insurmountable challenge. Bobby, clearly the more confident of the two, moved forward.

He looked over his shoulder, back at me, leaned forward, as if proffering a conspiracy of the heart. 'We have some beer.'

'Beer?'

'Yeah,' he said. 'A twelve-pack. It's Sam Adams.'

'I've never had beer,' I said.

This wasn't entirely true. I once had a sip from Mr Marseille's glass, and I thought I might choke. I don't know how or why people drink it. It seems the nastiest of habits.

'Sam Adams is great,' Teddy added. 'You'll like it.'

'I see.'

'My dad's out of town,' Bobby said. 'We have the whole house.'

'You are quite young to have your own house.'

Teddy smiled. 'We're older than we look.'

'Where are you from?' Bobby asked.

'Paris, France.'

It was a white lie.

'*Wow*,' Bobby said. 'We've never met anyone from Paris, France before.'

'We are all quite French there,' I replied with a giggle, quite the coquette.

Bobby and Teddy laughed with me.

'So, what do you think, Anabelle? Do you want to party with us?' Teddy asked.

I've never fully understood the use of the word *party* as a verb. I suppose it is now part of the lexicon, the *lingua franca* that bridges the gap between the young and the not-quite-so young.

'Where is the party?' I asked.

'Not far,' Bobby said. 'My dad's house is only a couple of blocks away.'

I glanced up the alleyway, pointed in that direction. 'I just need to get my things. Will you escort me?' I asked. 'A girl can't be too careful these days.'

'Sure!' Teddy said.

'No problem!' added Bobby.

We strolled down the alley; Robert to one side, Edward on the other. I felt quite the debutante. We soon came upon the white van.

'My book bags are inside that van,' I said. 'In the back.'

'I'll get them,' both boys said in unison.

The boys sprinted to the van, opened the back, climbed in, just as Mr Marseille stepped from the shadows, gun in hand.

It was time for tea.

23

The Aquatic and Fitness Center on Grant Avenue was a huge complex that boasted the largest indoor pool in the city.

Today's event was the first city-wide competition of the fall/winter season, for swimmers ten to fourteen years old.

A few years earlier, while watching television with Sophie – Jessica recalled the moment exactly, it was during a butterfly stroke competition on ESPN – Sophie hit the mute on the remote, turned to her mother and, in the solemn way she had, said:

'I want to be a swimmer.'

Jessica glanced at the TV, at the young men in Speedos. 'Well, that Ryan Lochte *is* pretty cute,' she said, nudging her daughter.

'*Mom*.'

Sophie was at that age where any mention of boys produced either a nervous giggle or a full body blush. Sometimes both.

Thus began an odyssey that took the distaff half of the Balzano household to pools, both indoor and outdoor, both sanitary and less so, both Center City and suburban, in the quest to get proper and affordable instruction in the aquatic arts, as well as a rhythm that coincided with Jessica's workload, Sophie's school schedule, as well as all the motivating factors that go into keeping a twelve-year-old girl focused, motivated, and reminded of the sacrifice being made by her long-suffering mother.

Not so surprisingly, Sophie had taken to swimming – competitive swimming – with a great deal of skill and enthusiasm. It was not unexpected to Jessica, because a few years before the swimming craze Sophie had wanted to take up the study of the flute. She had since won a number of competitions, and was actually making music of her own.

Since Sophie had taken up swimming she had gotten stronger and better at the sport, and now had her sights set on medals.

Now, at just after ten on a Saturday morning, Jessica and Sophie were at the Aquatic and Fitness Center preparing for Sophie's two competitive events.

While Jessica was waiting for Sophie's first meet, her phone rang. It was Vincent.

'Hey, babe.'

'How's she doing?' Vincent asked.

'Her first race is coming up. She's got her game face on.'

It was true. Sophie was sitting by herself, at the far end of the pool, her thousand-yard stare in place. She was practicing her square breathing, another recent interest.

'I found your magic mushroom dealer,' Vince said. 'Word is, if you want the kind of high-end psychedelics found in your victim, he's the man to see. We've got a meet set up.'

Yes, Jessica thought. 'You know, you just might have a future in this narco thing.'

'Tell my captain to give me a raise.'

'I'm having a late lunch with my father,' Jessica said. 'I'll bring home something for dinner. We won't be late.'

She clicked off, looked at her watch. There was still another half-hour to go before Sophie's race.

After the first few six-hour meets, Jessica discovered that one of the best ways to stay awake was to become a timer.

At most meets there were three people, usually mothers of the competitors, who volunteered to time the competitions. Each were given stopwatches, and positioned at the center, as well as each side of the starting/finish line.

The reason for having three different timers was that the judges would take an average of each score, thereby softening the possibility of bias or cheating. As if the parent of a child athlete would ever do such a thing.

In her second event, the fifty meter breaststroke, Sophie came in second. It was her best finish ever.

The three women tasked with timing gathered at the official's table. The numbers were added, an average was taken.

Before the final tallies were posted on the digital board, Jessica sensed a woman standing close to her. A little *too* close to her. It seemed that the woman was scrutinizing Jessica's recorded times.

'Um, excuse me?' the woman asked.

Jessica turned. The woman standing next to her was about her own age, a little shorter and heavier, and apparently shopped at Carmela Soprano's garage sales. The woman was a study in three different shades of aqua. She probably figured it went with the water.

'Yes?' Jessica asked.

'You have my daughter winning by 2.5 seconds,' the woman said.

'That's right.'

'I don't think so, hon.'

Hon? *Hon?* The only people Jessica let call her *hon* were her husband and any diner waitress over fifty. Miss Paramus Outlet 1992 was neither.

'What are you saying?' Jessica asked, knowing she was baiting the woman, trying to find a way to care. 'Are you saying it was closer than that? I can make it closer.'

The woman snorted. 'It was more like 4.5 seconds. You need to change it.'

Jessica took a half-step back. 'You're taking a tone with me,' she said. 'You have no cause to take a tone with me.'

The woman squared her shoulders, balled her fists. 'What are you, a friggin' *cop*?'

Jessica bit her tongue. Literally. She thought she tasted a little blood.

'Please tell your daughter congratulations for us,' Jessica said. The woman, whose name was Vicki Alberico, turned around, looking for her precious little fish.

Jessica pointed to the other side of the room.

'She's right over there,' Jessica said, putting a towel around Sophie's shoulders. 'She's the one puking pool water in the corner.'

They sat on the bench outside the girls' locker room. Sophie was crushed. Jessica combed the tangles from her daughter's hair.

'What's the matter?' Jessica asked.

'Nothing.'

Jessica knew, but she wasn't sure how to handle this one. She knew that Sophie liked to win, probably even more than her mother, which was saying a lot.

'You did great, baby girl. I'm really proud of you.'

Sophie Balzano would not be consoled.

'I came in second,' she said.

'What? Are you *kidding*? Second is awesome. That's better than everybody in the world, except for one person. Eight billion people is a lot of people to beat.'

'Yeah,' Sophie said. 'Except for Angie Alberico.'

'Okay. Except for Angie Alberico. But there's always next time, right? And think of how sweet it's going to be when you blow past her to win. Think about that scrunched-up little lemon face she's going to have.'

It took a few moments, but Sophie beamed. 'It *will* be sweet, won't it?'

'Oh yes,' Jessica said.

'Chlorine is my perfume.'

Jessica smiled. 'Go get dressed. We'll stop at Capogiro.'

Capogiro was an artisanal gelato shop on Thirteenth Street.

'Before lunch?' Sophie asked.

'What are you, a cop?'

Sophie laughed, and headed to the locker room.

Jessica sat at the light at Fifth and Washington. She had dropped Sophie at home. It was her afternoon off, but there was paperwork piling up on her. She intended to stop by the office for an hour.

The city had other ideas.

Jessica's phone rang. She thought about letting it go to voicemail, but she saw it was Byrne. She answered.

'Hey.'

'Where are you?' Byrne asked.

Jessica was so distracted she had to look at the street signs. 'Fifth and Washington,' she said. 'Why?'

'Meet me at Fifth and Christian. I'll pick you up.'

Jessica knew her partner's tone. This was not good. 'Don't tell me there's another body.'

'Times two.'

24

There was little doubt as to which building on this blighted block of the Strawberry Mansion section of North Philadelphia was the crime scene.

Once home to jazz legend John Coltrane, the community was bounded by Fairmount Park to the west, Lehigh Avenue to the north, Sedgley Avenue and the SEPTA rail tracks to the east, and Cecil B. Moore Avenue to the south.

At one time a mixed-income, mostly Jewish enclave, over the past fifty years the neighborhood had gone through a steep decline, although signs of gentrification were occurring on the southern end of the large neighborhood, mostly as it transitioned into Brewerytown.

And while the community got its name from a restaurant that at one time served strawberries and cream, the block on which Jessica and Byrne arrived reflected none of that gentility.

The block – on Monument Street between 32nd and 33rd Streets – had only a handful of dilapidated structures. One row house, the only building that looked occupied, stood bravely between four vacant lots, all of which were dotted with urban detritus – tires, discarded appliances, broken storm windows.

The building on the corner was a two story, dirty brick building with a high gable peak facing 33rd Street. Its Palladian windows were covered in delaminated plywood and spray painted with years of gang lore.

There was a sector car parked at all four corners of the block, lights flashing. Although the day was a brisk forty degrees, there seemed to be a crowd of onlookers surrounding the building. Never an easy task for patrol officers whose job it was to preserve the crime scene for the detectives and crime scene technicians.

Jessica and Byrne parked on Monument Street, about fifty feet from where the other personnel had gathered. Jessica clipped her badge on her jeans belt, then slipped on her leather gloves.

They entered the building by way of a side door, an opening made by a sheet of rotted plywood roughly torn from its nailing. They walked down the narrow hallway that was pocked with what looked to be bullet holes made by many different caliber weapons.

In addition, there was graffiti sprayed and carved into the walls by every known gang in this part of North Philadelphia.

Josh Bontrager stood just outside the doorway. He had his hands on his hips, lost in thought. Jessica knew the look well. With all kinds of people milling around you, sometimes a circus atmosphere, it was possible to be isolated in the middle of the mayhem. Every new job was a puzzle. Some were easier to solve than others. Most, in fact, were. Somewhere around half of the homicides in the city were drug or gang-related, and there was not a lot of loyalty involved. People talked.

Those homicides that were committed in the course of a robbery were rather straightforward. Watch the surveillance tape; follow the tips.

The ability to put the pieces together – be they large or small pieces – in these first crucial minutes and hours, was a talent and ability that, if you were adept at it, you would excel at the job of being a homicide detective. Jessica had met more detectives who were unable to do this than she had met detectives who could.

Josh Bontrager, who had grown up Amish, brought a singularly unique perspective to the job. The younger detectives in the unit – those who got the job since Josh came to Homicide – had no idea that this street-savvy detective had at one time lived on a dairy farm in rural Pennsylvania.

As Jessica and Byrne reached the room where the victims were, they stopped. Jessica saw the shadows spill through the door, and knew what she was going to see. It filled her with rage.

She hoped she was wrong, but the look on Josh Bontrager's face told her she was not.

'Dana says it's a double,' Jessica said.

Bontrager nodded. He gestured to Jessica and Byrne to take a look.

Jessica removed her leather gloves, replaced them with latex gloves. She took a deep, calming breath, peered around the door jamb into the room.

In the center of the room two young teenaged boys were seated on makeshift swings. The swings were attached to the ceiling with loops of nylon rope, threaded through four large steel eyelets. Their victims' heads lolled forward. Around each of their necks was what looked to be tightly knotted silk stockings. Their hands were tied to the ropes with what looked like similar stockings, holding them in place.

The boys were white, dressed in a similar fashion – faded jeans, new-looking running shoes, long-sleeved polo shirts. One boy's shirt was red and blue striped. The other, a solid green. There was an identical crest on the left breast pocket of each shirt.

The seats of the swings were painted in a pale yellow color, a color Jessica had no doubt would be the same color used to paint the bench at the Shawmont station.

Mindful to not fully cross the threshold – the crime scene unit had yet to begin to process the scene – Jessica got down on her knees to get a better look at the boys' faces. When she saw them her heart stammered. She sat back on her heels. Hard.

'*No.*'

'What is it, Jess?' Byrne asked.

Jessica knew what she wanted to say, but for a moment the words would not come. She took a deep breath, her head filled with the chemical scent of the paint.

'I know who they are,' she said.

This, of course, got Josh Bontrager's attention. He walked the few steps down the hall to where Jessica was kneeling.

'You know them?' Bontrager asked.

Jessica nodded, held up a hand, took another moment. Then she shook her head.

'I don't *know* them,' she said. 'But I think I know who they are.'

Bontrager exchanged a glance with Byrne, looked back at Jessica. Jessica reached into her back pocket, pulled out her notebook. She flipped a few pages until she found the entry she wanted.

'The woman I interviewed,' Jessica began. 'The woman whose phone number David Solomon called right before he shot himself.'

'I thought that was a dead-end,' Byrne said. In another circumstance, most notably some gang hit, or drug-related murder, his choice of words would've been taken as gallows humor. Not today.

'I thought so, too,' Jessica said. She found what she was looking for, silently berating herself for not remembering the woman's name. 'Mary Gillen.'

'I don't understand,' Bontrager said. 'Who's Mary Gillen?'

Byrne gave Bontrager a brief rundown on the details of the Nicole Solomon case.

'And you're saying that Nicole's father called this woman? This Mary Gillen?' Bontrager asked.

'He called her number,' Jessica said. 'Her landline. We confirmed with the phone company that the call was made at almost the precise moment Solomon pulled the trigger.'

'And the call came from his phone?' Bontrager asked. 'Solomon's phone?'

'Yeah,' Byrne said. 'I hit the redial on his cordless phone at his house.'

'So, Nicole Solomon's father spoke to Mary Gillen just before he killed himself?'

'No,' Jessica said. 'He got her answering machine. We've got a copy of the recording, but Mateo hasn't been able to clean it up enough for us to get anything out of it.'

Sgt. Mateo Fuentes was the commander of the PPD's A/V Unit.

Bontrager thought for a few moments. 'I'm feeling pretty thick here, guys. I'm not seeing the connection.'

'When I interviewed Mary Gillen, she said she didn't know anybody named David Solomon,' Jessica said. 'I asked her who else lived in the house. She then told me she's divorced, and said the only other people living in her house were her boys. She said her boys are—'

'Twins,' Bontrager said. 'She has twin boys.'

Jessica nodded. 'Twin boys about twelve. She said that they were at soccer practice.'

Bontrager took out his cell phone. He scrolled through some photographs. He studied one of them for a few moments, then tapped it to enlarge it. He turned the phone so that Jessica and Byrne could see it.

Jessica put on her glasses, looked at the picture. She could see it was a photograph of one of the boys in the other room, a somewhat pixelated close-up of the boys shirt, the one wearing green and white.

She recognized the crest. St. Jerome's Academy Soccer Team.

Although it had not been confirmed, Jessica was certain that the two dead boys in the room were Mary Gillen's sons.

Bontrager closed his phone, just as two officers from the crime scene unit arrived. Behind the technicians was an investigator from the Medical Examiner's Office, along with his photographer.

While all of them signed onto the crime scene log, Jessica, Byrne, and Bontrager stepped to the side. They were silent for the moment, processing this new information. There was no question that, if the two boys in the room were Mary Gillen's sons, the investigation into these three homicides had just gotten much wider.

What it did not do, in any recognizable way, at least at the moment, was bring the investigators any closer to the person or persons responsible.

As much as the detectives wanted to enter the room, there was a protocol that had to be rigidly observed. Usually, the first person to make any kind of physical contact with the victim of homicide was the medical examiner. This crime scene, as was the Nicole Solomon crime scene, was a little different.

The evidentiary integrity of the floor had to be preserved. The two CSU officers unrolled a 36-inch wide roll of white paper. They gently placed it onto the floor, a process which would allow the ME and his photographer to enter the scene and begin their investigation. Once the victims were pronounced dead, and the ME's photographer had taken his photographs, the CSU officers could begin to process the scene, and the detectives could start their phase of the investigation.

Jessica stepped outside. Even though the air was clouded with exhaust from the traffic on 33rd Street, it was fresher than the air inside the building. She joined Josh Bontrager, Maria Caruso and Byrne. They stood a few yards from one of the flashing sector cars, parked in one of the vacant lots.

'Who called it in?' Jessica asked.

Bontrager pointed at the police car. 'Mrs Ruta Mae Carver.'

Jessica glanced over to see a heavyset black woman in her late sixties. She sat in the backseat, door open, big legs dangling over the side, eyes closed. She rocked back and forth, perhaps in prayer. She held a white rosary.

'Mrs Carver was walking up 33rd when she looked through the window and saw the victims,' Bontrager said.

Jessica stepped around the side of the building, turned to look. There was indeed a clear view of the two boys through the only open port in the building. The window overlooked 33rd Street, and the park beyond. As with the Nicole Solomon crime scene, the display looked surreal, as if framed by the window opening.

As she was looking, two CSU officers began the process of taping large sheets of paper over the portal. Jessica walked back to Josh Bontrager.

'So she saw them through the window,' Jessica said.

'Yeah,' Bontrager said.

'Did she see anything else?'

Bontrager nodded. 'She saw an old van. She said it had a faded sign on the door, said it looked like, and I quote: "one of them big crawly things, like a cockroach".'

'A cockroach? So maybe it was an exterminator's truck?'

'That's what I'm thinking. She said it was pretty bleached, but the logo looked like it was at one time red and black. I've got someone searching for it online now.'

Bontrager showed Jessica and Byrne a sketch he'd made of the information he'd gotten from Ruta Mae Carver.

'Why was she here?' Byrne asked.

Bontrager pointed to the lone house on the next block. 'She lives there. She was just coming back from church, heard the music and stopped. That's when she saw the victims.'

'The music?' Jessica asked.

Bontrager nodded.

'Coming from in there?'

'That's what she said.'

Jessica glanced back at the woman. She was on her second decade of the rosary, eyes still closed. Jessica lowered her voice. 'So, are we talking *music* music or heavenly voices?'

Bontrager smiled. 'Good question. 'Ruta Mae, it seems, is a rather spiritual person.' He pointed at the woman's house. Even from a half-block away Jessica could see the crosses in every window. She wondered if that was to keep the spirit in or out.

Jessica was just about to ask Josh Bontrager where he wanted her to start her canvass when they all heard the voice coming from inside the house.

'Oh *God*.'

It was a woman's voice. The words were not screamed or shouted, but sounded more like a cry of anguish.

The detectives rushed inside.

A moment later one of the crime scene officers – a young woman in her mid-twenties – came around the corner, into the hallway.

Her skin was pallid, her lips trembling.

Byrne stepped forward. 'What is it?' he asked.

Jessica glanced at the officer's nametag. L Betley. Jessica had seen her around, had worked scenes with her, but it was possible to see members of such a large police force – the sixth largest in the country – on a regular basis, to recognize them by sight, but not know their names.

Officer Betley seemed to swoon. Byrne took hold of her, held her for a few moments. He walked her a few feet down the hallway, away from the room.

'What's your first name, Officer Betley?' Byrne asked softly.

The woman took a second. It appeared she had to think about this. 'Lynn.'

'It's okay, Lynn. You want to take a few moments?'

Jessica saw the young woman relax at Byrne's touch. She had seen it many times before.

Officer Betley nodded.

'Would you like some water?'

'Okay.'

One of the EMTs standing by reached into his pack, took out a fresh bottle. He cracked the seal, handed it to Byrne, who handed it to Officer Betley.

With a trembling hand, she raised it to her lips, took a small sip. She recapped it.

Still holding onto the woman, Byrne asked: 'Can you tell me what's wrong?'

She looked up at Byrne. 'I worked that scene. Last week. I was there.'

'What scene, Lynn? Which one?'

Lynn Betley said nothing. It looked like she might be getting ready to faint.

Byrne squared the young woman in front of him. He looked into her eyes. 'Whatever's in that room, we can handle it,' he said. 'And by *we* I mean you and I, Detectives Balzano and Bontrager here, and every member of the PPD. All of us. We are seven thousand strong. Do you believe that?'

'I do. I guess that it's just, I don't know,' she said. 'I do.'

'Good,' Byrne said. 'Never forget it. For the rest of your time on the job, for the rest of your life, you will never be alone. In this city, any city, if you identify yourself as a law enforcement officer, you will have a brother or sister who will have your back.'

The woman began to sag. Byrne eased her to the floor, caught the attention of one of the nearby EMTs. The firefighter came down the hall, eased Lynn Betley forward. She began to breathe a little more slowly.

Jessica made eye contact with Byrne. He would stay with Officer Betley; she would see what it was that had caused this PPD officer to balk.

Jessica steeled herself, walked back to the doorway. A fresh pair of gloves, another calming breath. She stepped into the room. Everything appeared as it had. As horrifying as the sight of the two dead boys was, Jessica did not imagine this was what set the CSU officer off.

She ran her Maglite around the dimly lit room and saw what had unnerved the crime scene officer so terribly. There, in the left-hand corner of the room – a section that had been shielded from Jessica when she had peered inside earlier – was something so out of place, that Jessica took off her glasses in order to see it better. She had to focus, had to concentrate, to assure herself that it was what it appeared to be.

In the corner of the room, behind the two dead boys, stood a doll. The doll was perhaps twelve inches tall, and appeared to be made of porcelain. It seemed to be looking at the two victims in the center of the room.

But as bizarre as this tableau was, as strange as it was to have a doll deliberately placed in the corner of the room, these things were not what took Jessica's breath away.

She had seen the doll before. She had seen the white blouse, the dark skirt, the dark shoes. She had seen the deep brunette hair, as well as the chocolate brown eyes with irises flecked with gold.

I worked that scene. Last week. I was there.

Now Jessica understood what Officer Lynn Betley meant.

The doll was Nicole Solomon.

25

The four detectives stood at the end of the hallway, staying out
of the way of the now-bustling crime scene.

The command presence was deep. In addition to Sgt. Dana
Westbrook, was their captain and the deputy inspector.

The reasons were obvious.

These victims weren't gangbangers or drug dealers. These
boys weren't part of the game. These were citizens. And while
justice was supposed to be blind, anyone who thought that the
lumbering machinery of crime and punishment moved forward
with the same fervor and purpose for all victims was not being
honest.

Jessica, speaking for herself and just about every other detective in the unit – especially her partner – liked to think that it
didn't matter who the victim was, that she applied herself equally
at all times. This did not always carry over to every other squad
and scientific team.

Two teenage boys – suburban white boys – found dead in a
North Philly building, murdered in such a bizarre and savage

manner, was going to go wide. It was only a matter of minutes before the story went national.

There were no tenants, either residential or commercial in the building or, for that matter, in the next three buildings in either direction. The entire block was blighted.

A section of Fairmount Park was across the street. The likelihood of an eyewitness to the boys being brought to this house was slight.

Again, for the second time in a week, Jessica had to wonder: Why here?

And while the *why* of it all was not yet known, the *when* was pretty clear.

This was the party – the *thé dansant* – to which Nicole Solomon had been invited. Today was November 23. The killers had brought Nicole to the tea dance.

Beneath one of the swings they had found another invitation, nearly identical to the first. Identical in all ways but the date.

You are invited!
November 30
See you at our thé dansant!

It appeared as if they needed one week to crack this case. If not, other children would die.

Jessica and Byrne made notes on getting Josh Bontrager and Maria Caruso everything they had accumulated in the Nicole Solomon investigation, an inquiry that would now be folded into a larger inquiry. Somebody was killing Philadelphia teenagers in grotesque and detailed ways. There would soon be a task force, perhaps even a joint task force with the FBI. There were clearly federal laws being violated here, not the least of which was kidnapping.

Josh Bontrager was about to make a point when Byrne held

up a hand and put a finger to his lips. Everyone stopped talking.

Jessica heard music. She thought she'd heard it before, but figured it was coming from a passing car.

Was this the music Ruta Mae Carver had heard?

Byrne cocked his head to the sound. He looked up, at Jessica, and pointed to the wall that joined the room just north of the crime scene room.

As they walked down the hall the music grew louder. It was piano music, a lively tempo, a standard.

Byrne tried the doorknob. It was unlocked. He pushed open the door.

They rolled into the room, a room cluttered with discarded junk – broken chairs, upended tables, dismantled bookcases.

The music was coming from somewhere in this room. Two things were obvious. There was no piano, and there was no piano player in this space.

Jessica and Byrne holstered their weapons. The sound seemed to be coming from the far side of the room, near the windows that overlooked 33rd Street.

Byrne began to lift the broken furniture from the pile. As he did, the music grew a little in volume. By the time he got to the bottom of the pile he discovered a single drawer, its sides splintered off.

In it was a small tape recorder. The piano tune continued to play. If Ruta Mae Carver had heard this from outside, her hearing had to be exceptional. Perhaps the reason no one on the investigating team had heard it was because they weren't listening for it.

There was no indication that anyone was living in or squatting this space. Anything of value had long ago been taken. There were no switch plates or electrical outlets.

But here, inside a broken dresser drawer, was a tape recorder.

Jessica shone her Maglite on the top of the device. The tape was about to run out.

Jessica turned to the detectives behind her.

'Does anyone recognize this music?'

'It sounds like Scott Joplin,' Byrne said. He pointed at the recorder. 'Mind if we run this?'

'Be my guest,' Bontrager said.

Byrne clicked off the recorder, lifted it carefully, dropped it into a paper evidence bag. 'Let's get this processed then over to Mateo.'

The AV Unit was located in the basement of the Roundhouse. The commander of the unit was Sgt. Mateo Fuentes. In addition to his duties recording and cataloging all city business – the mayor's speeches, press conferences, city council meetings and the like – he had helped to design and establish the ever-growing network of PPD surveillance systems deployed around Philadelphia.

They met in one of the editing bays. They'd given Mateo an hour with the evidence.

Mateo Fuentes was in his forties, a career officer. While much of his job was mundane, there was no one better at divining the clues that resided in the mysterious worlds of audio and video. A denizen of the huge basement, somehow Mateo was never seen anywhere else in the massive building. Byrne once mentioned that no one actually saw Mateo Fuentes come and go. Jessica wondered if the man lived here.

In attendance were Jessica and Byrne, along with Josh Bontrager, Maria Caruso, and Dana Westbrook.

The recorder recovered from the crime scene building sat on Mateo's desk in a clear plastic evidence bag.

Mateo reached into a drawer, pulled out an old catalog, stopped at a page bookmarked with a blue Post-It note. He put the catalog on the desk. The third item from the top of the page was an identical cassette tape player to the one they had found at the Gillen crime scene.

'Not one of the greats, but still working,' Mateo said. 'Obviously.'

'So it's no longer available,' Byrne said.

'No longer for sale in retail outlets, but there are plenty available on eBay and other sites.'

Mateo was ready with this information, too. He maximized a browser window on one of his laptops. It was open to an eBay page where a half-dozen of this model recorder were available to be bid upon. Two had a *Buy It Now* price of $9.99.

Mateo tapped his own cassette player, which was a far pricier Sony. Like all cassette recorders it was vintage, but state of the art for its time. Jessica wasn't even sure if they made new ones anymore.

'This is a 120, right?' Byrne said.

'That's the label,' Mateo said. 'I think it's closer to 125 minutes.'

'I'm lost, guys,' Jessica said.

'Back in the day, audio cassettes were made in specific lengths. Sixty minutes, ninety minutes, one hundred twenty minutes. Hence the designations – C60, C90, C120.'

'So, that's total length?' Jessica asked.

'Yes,' Mateo said. 'One hundred twenty total. Sixty minutes per side.'

'When we found this tape it was right near the end,' Jessica said. 'Are you saying it was started less than sixty minutes earlier?'

'Not necessarily. This model has an auto-reverse feature, which meant the tape would begin to play side B when side A was over. This tape would continue to play on a loop until the batteries wore down.' Mateo tapped the device. 'And to anticipate your next question, the batteries are new.'

'What about the flip side?' Byrne asked. 'Was there anything on it?'

'This *is* the flip side. Same song. I listened from leader to leader.'

'And side A?'

'Halfway through,' Mateo said. 'I made a digital copy of it. I was just listening to it.'

Mateo tapped a few keys. The sound of the piano music came out of the speakers.

'I have to say this is not the best quality recording I've ever heard,' Jessica said.

'Two reasons for that,' Mateo said. 'One is that the tape itself is old. All magnetic tape over ten years old or so is at risk due to the fact that the breakdown of the binder that holds the magnetic particles to the polyester base of tape deteriorates, and the magnetic material literally falls off. Some call this Sticky Shed Syndrome.'

'Okay,' Jessica said, lost again. She thought – and not for the first time – that the only person on the PPD who rivaled Hell Rohmer for Geek Boy Number One status was Mateo Fuentes. 'What's the other reason?'

'The other reason is that this recording is not a direct recording.'

'What do you mean?'

'What I mean is that this is a recording *of* a recording. Or it is a recording of someone playing piano live. Either way, it was probably made with this recorder's built-in microphone. Hence the tinny sound and all the background hiss.'

Mateo turned it up a little. Jessica could now hear what he meant. There was a loud hiss, not to mention an echo.

The group stood in silence, listening to the recording. The longer it played, the more Jessica believed the song itself had significance, not just the placement of the device.

Jessica was just going to ask Mateo about the other recording they had brought to him about this case – the all too brief recording of David Solomon's voicemail message to Mary Gillen, a piece of evidence that became a lot more crucial since the murder of the Gillen boys – when, from the recording, there suddenly came a voice.

A female voice: '*Shut the door.*'

The sound was so unexpected, Jessica nearly jumped.

'Oh *hello*,' Mateo said. He stopped the recording, moved the scrubber bar back. 'You all heard that, right?'

'Yes,' they all said in unison.

'Thank God,' Mateo said. 'You do this stuff long enough, you start to wonder.'

Mateo put on headphones, hit Play. At the same moment in the recording they heard it again.

'*Shut the door.*'

Again Mateo rewound the footage, let it play. This time he let it continue. They listened for a full minute, but there were no other spoken words, nor the sound of a shutting door.

He clicked Stop.

'The voice is definitely female,' Jessica said.

'And young,' Mateo added. 'A teenager.'

'Is there any way of telling when that was recorded?'

'I can tell you that it was probably spoken during the recording of the piano music, so it was recorded at the same time,' he said. 'That was no splice, and I doubt that this was made on a multi-track machine.'

'So whoever made the recording of the music ...'

'Was in the room with the person who said that,' Mateo said. 'Or is one and the same person.'

Jessica thought about this. It would follow. Someone was playing the piano, noticed that someone else was watching them, and told them to shut the door.

'What about the voicemail recording?' Jessica asked.

Mateo tapped a few fingers on his desk. 'There's not too much to work with on that recording. Once again, I'm working with an iPhone app recording of a digital recording from an answering machine.'

Jessica had considered asking Mary Gillen for the answering machine itself, but the sound quality was no better on that device.

'And without a sample of David Solomon's voice, there's nothing to compare it to,' Mateo said.

Jessica made a note to check and see if there were any home movies or videos to be found at the Solomon home, perhaps one from which they could pull an exemplar of David Solomon's voice.

'But I *can* tell you that he's not saying the words "not now",' Mateo added.

'He isn't?'

'No.'

'Any idea what he is saying?'

Mateo just glared.

'I'll take that as a no.'

'If you can find another recording of this subject, one I can use as a control, I might be able to tell you more,' Mateo said. 'But I'll keep at it, though. There are a few things I haven't tried yet.'

As Mateo continued to clean up the recording, moving forward with new purpose now that the element of the human voice on the recording of the piano music had entered his milieu, the four detectives met at the foot of the stairs.

'We made notification before coming here,' Bontrager said. 'Turns out the boys were staying with their father this weekend, a man who is conveniently out of town.'

'He left two boys their age on their own?' Jessica asked.

Bontrager nodded. 'Apparently not up for Dad of the Year.'

'I put in a call to St. Jerome's,' Maria added. 'I'm going to stop there and see what I can find out about the Gillen boys and their routines.'

Bontrager and Maria Caruso took the elevator up. Jessica and Byrne stayed behind.

'The batteries were fresh in that recorder,' Jessica said. 'We were *supposed* to find it.'

'Yes we were.'

26

When Jessica saw her father sitting at the table in Ralph's – the famous Italian eatery on Ninth Street – she almost didn't recognize him. His hair, which had years ago turned a lustrous silver, was a little longer than usual. As an ex-cop – one of the most decorated in PPD history – he had always kept his hair military short. Even in retirement, he visited Dominic Farinacci's barber shop on Eleventh Street every three weeks for a trim.

Now his hair curled over the collar of his white dress shirt. It suited him. He looked five years younger.

In addition, her father was tan and looked to have lost a few pounds. Twice a year Peter Giovanni went to Pompano Beach, Florida to visit family and friends. He always came back with a deep tan, and always seemed to be refreshed and happy. A widower for more than thirty years, Jessica often wondered just what Peter Giovanni was doing down there that cheered him so.

As a good Catholic girl, Jessica never asked.

*

The *giambotte*, as always, was out of this world. After getting the small talk out of the way, while they waited for coffee, they got down to business. Family business.

'What did Vince have to say about it?' Peter asked.

Jessica had debated with herself about how to tell her father that she had decided not to take the bar exam for a while. In the end she just blurted it out.

'You know Vince, Dad. He told me we could make ends meet. Eventually he came around, though. If I stay on the job two more years, we should be in good shape. The DA's office isn't going anywhere.'

Peter thought for a few moments. 'So, how much do you owe? I mean, total?'

'A lot.'

'Okay,' he said. 'Just a round figure, then.'

'A lot *is* a round figure.'

'Jess.'

Reluctantly, Jessica told him. Her father did not react in any way. It was one of the reasons he had been a great detective, and an even better lieutenant. He reached into his coat pocket, took out his checkbook.

'Don't even think about it,' Jessica said.

'Honey, it's not that much.'

'Just put it away, Dad. We'll be fine.'

'Let me give you half, then.'

'Pa, the only Italian I know with a harder head than you is my husband. A real *testa dura*. You *know* Vince. He won't take the money.'

Peter opened the checkbook, took out a pen. 'Tell you what. I'll make out the check, you take it. If you can sweet-talk him into it, you deposit it. If not, tear it up. It's only paper.'

Jessica shook her head. 'We've been married more than ten years. He's impervious to sweet talk.'

'Make him your *sfogliatelle*.'

'Pa.'

'Okay.' Peter held up a hand in defeat, just as the coffee was poured. Still, he didn't put his checkbook away.

They let the matter settle. Jessica told her father about the Nicole Solomon and Gillen homicides. When Peter heard about these cases – murdered children – Jessica could see the anger gather on his face. Once a cop.

'And they left a doll?' he asked.

Jessica nodded, sipped her coffee. 'The doll was made up to look like Nicole. Right down to what she was wearing.'

Despite his Italian heritage, and the fact that he was a cop for nearly three decades, Jessica had heard her father utter the f-word only once in her presence. Had to be some kind of record. She could see that he was mightily resisting saying it now. Instead, Peter Giovanni poured a packet of sugar into his cup, stirred it. And stirred it. Jessica knew that this was one of his affectations, one that meant he was putting something together. She waited him out.

He put down the spoon, asked: 'Have you ever heard of something called the Nutshell Studies?'

'No.'

'Well, they were a little before your time. Actually, they were a bit before my time, too.'

'So, we're talking the mid-1800s here?'

Peter smiled. 'Laugh it up, Jess. You're going to be my age one day.'

'If'n the creek don't rise.'

'Anyway, the studies were created by a woman named Frances Glessner Lee. She founded Harvard's Department of Legal Medicine.'

'As in forensic medicine?'

'Yes. As I understand it, she was born into money, but made it her life's work to create these incredibly detailed representations of crime scenes.'

'Drawings?'

'No,' Peter said. 'She made little dollhouse-sized dioramas that were composites of real court cases. She used miniature dolls to depict the victims.'

Her father now had her undivided attention. 'She used dolls.'

Peter nodded. 'We had someone in Philly who was doing much the same thing. His name was Carl Krause.'

'He was a police officer?'

'No, he worked for the sanitation department, believe it or not. I'm pretty sure he wanted to be a cop at one time, but for some physical limitation couldn't get into the academy. Word is he studied with Mrs Lee, then came back to Philly and began to do the same work she did. I've seen some of them. Amazing stuff.'

'He built these himself?'

'He did. I heard that he got a lot of the material – the wood, the metal, even the fabric he used for the victims' clothing – out of the trash he picked up.'

The waiter poured them more coffee, put the check on the table. Before Jessica could move her father had the check on his lap. He continued.

'So I'm working out of West detectives, a string of burglaries in and around Cobb's Creek. One of them went too far and the owner of this pet store was murdered. Bad scene. They stabbed him in the back. Anyway, we worked the case with the homicide unit. They brought in Krause and he studied the crime scene, snapped dozens of pictures, took a hundred dimensions. Two weeks later he comes back with this one-tenth-scale diorama of the pet store. *Incredible* work. Like nothing you've ever seen.'

'What did you do with it?'

'Well, the guys in homicide studied it, and, I'm not sure what it was, but one of the guys in the squad saw something in the recreation he didn't notice at the scene itself, and it broke the case.'

'They collared the guy.'

'They did,' Peter said. 'Twenty-five to life. The guy is still in Graterford.'

Jessica wondered why she'd never heard of this. It sounded like last-call, cop bar PPD legend.

'Is the guy still around?' Jessica asked. 'This Carl Krause?'

Peter shrugged. 'No idea. I doubt it, though. He was no kid, even back then.'

Before Jessica could ask, Peter read his daughter's face. The look he gave her was one she hadn't seen in a long time.

'Let me make a few calls,' he said.

They walked down the narrow staircase, with Bethany Krause Quinn on point. The cellar was clearly unheated, and Jessica wrapped her scarf a little more tightly around her neck, pulled on her gloves.

After making a few contacts, Peter Giovanni learned that Carl Krause had passed away in 2004. It turned out that Krause had willed a half-dozen of his dioramas to his granddaughter Bethany, who was married to a patrol officer in the Third District.

Calls were made, and Bethany Quinn – a very pregnant Bethany Quinn – talked to her husband, who told her he had no problem with Peter and Jessica stopping by.

'Did you know my grandfather?' Bethany asked Peter as they descended into the cellar. She flipped on the overhead fluorescent lights. Jessica saw that the room was neat and organized, with metal bookshelves on the walls to the left and right, each bearing clearly labeled white boxes.

'I met him on a few occasions,' Peter said. 'He was . . .'

'Really weird?'

Peter Giovanni reddened. 'Not at all,' he said. 'He was an interesting guy.'

Bethany laughed. 'I'm just kidding,' she said. She was about twenty-eight or so, with strawberry blond hair and a light dusting of freckles. 'Not about the weird part. Don't get me wrong, I loved him with all my heart, but when he was down in his basement workshop working, it was like he was in another dimension.'

When Bethany flipped on the track lighting, and the half-dozen dioramas on a table at the far end of the basement room were illuminated, Jessica saw what the young woman meant.

The miniature world of Carl Krause *was* another dimension.

There were seven different dioramas, each a scale replica of a different room. There was a kitchen, a parlor, a garage. There was what looked to be a sewing room, as well as a trio of commercial establishments – a candy store, a pet store, and a tailor shop.

Each diorama was fitted down to the smallest detail. There were tiny light switches, wall sconces, throw rugs, curtains. The sewing room had a miniature ironing board with a small steam iron on it. The candy store had shelves and counter displays with dozens of miniature jars full of brightly colored confections.

The pet store – the crime scene about which her father had told her – had a dozen small cages, each containing a furry, life-like looking animal. There were small plastic water bowls on the floor.

Nothing was left to chance. There were even small-scale blood spatter patterns. The diminutive victim in the pet store – a balding figurine of a man who looked to be in his sixties – had a small knife sticking out of his back. The more Jessica tried to pull herself away from each display, the more she was riveted.

'Do you remember me talking about the Candy Town case?'

Peter asked Jessica, pointing to another display, the one of the candy store.

Jessica did. She was only eight or nine at the time, but because the victims were two young girls, it caught the attention of the news and, subsequently, the kids in her school.

When Jessica looked closely at the display, and saw the two small figures of the girls – both wearing private school uniforms – it brought her mind back to the Nicole Solomon crime scene.

'Do you know where your grandfather got these miniature dolls?' Jessica asked.

Bethany thought for a moment. 'I know he used to make them himself when he was just starting out. After a while, he bought them. I just don't know where.'

'Do you think it was here in Philly?'

'Not sure. I know that he would go to New York a few times a year. He consulted a little with the NYPD. Maybe he got them there.'

Jessica made a note.

'There are a few boxes of his stuff in the attic,' Bethany added. 'If I can get up the ladder, I'll see if there's anything in there.'

Jessica recalled when she was eight months pregnant with Sophie. Climbing a ladder was out of the question. 'We don't want you doing anything like that,' she said. She gave the woman a card. 'If and when you find anything you think might help us, please give me a call.'

The woman took the card. 'Sure thing.'

Jessica took out her iPhone. 'Would it be okay if I took a few photographs?'

'Of course,' Bethany said. 'Just flip off the lights when you're done.'

As Jessica took her pictures, Peter Giovanni offered Bethany an arm, and the two of them made their way slowly up the steps.

27

The basement of Valerie Beckert's house was warren-like, low-ceilinged, with a number of small rooms, all connected by venous passageways.

The electrical wiring was of the old knob and tube variety, single-insulated copper conductors running through the ceiling cavities, passing through the joists via porcelain insulating tubes, supported along their length on nailed-down porcelain knob insulators.

Byrne moved, ghostlike, through the rest of the shadowed house, opening cabinets and doors, running his hands along the wainscoting, tapping the loose windowpanes, wondering what the real reason was that led him here a second time, what dark and unyielding force compelled him.

He stood on the landing on the third floor. Where he thought there might be a small bedroom or sewing room was in fact only a walk-in closet. Inside was more shredded paper, more mouse droppings.

The other end of the hall gave way to an alcove, graced by a bench seat with storage beneath. Just over the stairway landing was an access hole with what Byrne was certain was a pull-down attic ladder.

He had thought that he might brave the attic, but fatigue was getting the best of him. The discovery of the Gillen boys had thrown the Nicole Solomon investigation into chaos, and he knew that he had to be on his game early the next morning.

Besides, whatever feelings and intuitions had drawn him back to Valerie Beckert's house was strongest here, at the third-floor landing, a place where he felt something close in on him, something that seemed to shroud his heart with icy hands.

As a storm lashed rain against the windows, he once more invited the feeling in.

28

On the night Josephine Beckert climbed the staircase for the final time, the storm rattled the windows in the old house.

Valerie spent the early evening deploying a half-dozen pots and pans around the third floor to catch the raindrops that seeped in through the missing shingles.

On nights such as these – indeed, most nights – Josephine would retire to the parlor not long after dinner. Once there she would build a fire, even on nights in June and July, claiming her arthritis needed the heat, despite the ambient summertime temperatures that often rose into the nineties.

Josephine would plop her big body into her favorite chair near the hearth, a soiled, taupe velvet wing back whose springs had begun to show underneath, due to Josephine Beckert's steadily increasing bulk.

Next to the chair would be a table carefully arranged with two boxes of Whitman's Sampler, a pack of cigarettes, a crystal ashtray, and Josephine's ever present bottle of spiced rum, which she would sometimes mix with Diet Rite Cola.

At first, Josephine would struggle from her chair once per hour or so to get ice for her drink. But after a while the effort became too great, and she decided she liked the rum and diet cola warm.

As the evening wore on, and the chocolates and rum were consumed, Josephine would read her romance novels, every so often breaking either into tears or song, mostly songs of the torch variety, perhaps in lament of her lost loves, and rapidly fading beauty. Josephine never saved her romance novels. When finished she would simply toss them on the fire, often accompanied by an epithet.

When the grandfather clock in the foyer chimed eleven, Josephine would push herself from the chair, stoke the remaining embers in the hearth, and tilt the bottle to her lips, drinking any rum she had missed. She would then amble to the stairs, taking them one at a time, slowly, sometime pausing every third or fourth tread.

By the time she reached the final tread, she always had to pause the longest. Valerie knew this as she knew the beating of her own heart. Josephine would steady herself by grabbing the cap on the newel post, then pull herself up onto the landing.

On this rain-swept night, from her sanctuary in the closet, Valerie waited, her eyes closed, counting the seconds.

And then it happened.

First Valerie heard the sound of the loosened newel cap hitting the floor. Then she heard the racket of Josephine Beckert falling down the stairs, the sound of the woman's bones snapping on the oak treads echoing throughout the house.

When the crashing stopped, Valerie closed her eyes, waited for more sounds – the cry of pain, the call for help, the soft wheeze of life leaving Josephine's body.

Valerie did not move for the longest time.

There were no more sounds.

Eventually she opened the closet door, crept down the stairs.

Josephine's body was sprawled on the final four treads, the railing splintered away at the bottom newel post. Her eyes were wide open.

The smell of the sour rum and bile, combined with the stench of *feces – apparently, Josephine's final indignity was soiling herself on her journey to the bottom of the staircase – made Valerie hold her nose.*

In the moments before Valerie called the police, she gathered together her most precious possessions, those being the diary writings and drawings she had made in the basement rooms of her childhood home. She didn't know what, if anything, these writings and drawings would tell the people who came to the house, but she couldn't take the chance.

The authorities mustn't know, of that she was sure.

There were many hiding places in this big house, but none Valerie could yet trust. She sometimes thought of burning her childhood writings in the fireplace, but even then the ashes would scatter and her secrets would be known.

Valerie stole into the sitting room. On one wall was a large dusty painting. She stood on a chair, took the painting down. With a small kitchen knife she began to cut a hole in the plaster. When she felt the hole was large enough, she rolled some of her writings into a tube, and pushed them into the hole, heard them drop. If ever she needed them back, she could cut another hole.

When she felt all was in place, she took a moment to prepare herself.

For a few moments she stopped breathing.

Valerie then picked up the phone. She punched herself in the stomach a half dozen times, taking her wind, surely bringing a frantic quality to her voice.

She dialed the number, out of breath.

'It's my aunt,' she said to the police. 'She's fallen down the stairs. You must hurry!'

Three hours later, after all the tears and the anguish and the forms, after the arrangements were begun, Valerie sat on the top step, looking down the grand staircase.

She liked to sit high up, inaccessible to the dirty little hands of children. From this vantage she had a clear horizon.

Within two weeks, with the help of a man named Albert Hustings – a lawyer who had no problems taking his fees in cash – Valerie became the owner of the Wynnefield house. It had taken a year for her to get her aunt to sign all the necessary papers in her rum-fueled confusion, but Valerie's diligence had paid off.

The next morning Valerie rose early, made herself a modest breakfast. At seven a.m. she parked herself in front of the window in the parlor.

Tomorrow she would follow the girl with the eye patch, a girl named Nancy Brisbane.

She would keep Nancy all to herself, and they would be friends for ever.

29

Byrne stood by the front window in the parlor, his mind returning to the murders of Nicole Solomon, and Robert and Edward
Gillen. He thought of the will it must take to wantonly take
another person's life.

  Byrne had taken more than one life in the course of duty, but
he drew a broad and distinct line between what he did – in the
course of serving justice – and the actions of the person or persons who did what was done to Nicole Solomon and the Gillen
boys. And while he had sympathy for the families of the criminal,
he felt no responsibility toward them.

  He walked across the kitchen, out the back door. The sun was
setting, and the dusk brought with it a deep chill. He looked at
some of the other houses on the street, wondered what dramas
were unfolding in them. Did they contain happy families, families in crisis, families disintegrating under the weight of some
human frailty?

Was there a boy like Thaddeus Woodman inside one of them, frightened and alone?

It was with these dark thoughts in mind that Kevin Byrne descended the back steps, turned the corner, and came face to face with a beautiful woman.

30

Jessica walked across the lobby of the Roundhouse, her thoughts splintered in a dozen different directions. She was still in a state of shock over the discovery of the Gillen boys, and the presence of the doll made in the likeness of Nicole Solomon.

You are invited!

The fact that Nicole Solomon's killer took the time to create a doll in her image, and place it at the scene of a double murder, drew this case to a place of even more profound darkness. Nicole's murder, as well as the murder of Robert and Edward Gillen, were not crimes of passion. These were homicides in aid of a larger, far more evil puzzle.

She thought about the miniature dioramas, the small dolls representing murder victims, and how the diligent work of an unheralded man in a basement workshop had helped bring murderers to justice.

Jessica's phone rang, mercifully breaking her dark trance. It was her husband.

'Hey.'

'I heard about the double. You okay, babe?' Vincent asked.

Jessica didn't want to lie to her husband. He always saw right through most of them anyway. Besides being the love of her life, he was a great cop, and was used to being lied to all day every day. It was the job.

She lied anyway.

'I'm good,' she said. 'I forgot to pick up something for dinner.'

'It's okay,' Vincent replied. 'I'll call Santucci's.'

For the first time in a long time Jessica had no interest in food. She really wasn't hungry. All she wanted was a five-hour bubble bath, and a twelve-hour nap. A *dreamless* twelve-hour nap.

'That sounds good,' she said.

Jessica pushed open the rear door to the Roundhouse, walked down the ramp. She nodded to a pair of young officers, one of whom was cadging a covert cigarette before his tour began. You weren't supposed to smoke within fifty yards of the building, but nobody paid much attention to that.

If you had a problem with it, what were you supposed to do, call a cop?

'I'm leaving now,' Jessica said.

'What do you want on the pizza?' Vincent asked.

Ambien, Jessica thought. 'Anything's good.'

'So, pineapple or agave, right?'

Her husband was trying, bless his heart. He really was trying. 'See you in a bit.'

Jessica ended the call, put her iPhone in her pocket. She closed her eyes for a few moments, letting the chilled night air revive her.

In her mind's eye she saw Nicole Solomon's solitary form on the bench in Shawmont. She tried to imagine the timeline from the moment Nicole was last seen on the street – talking to her friend Naomi Burris – to the moment her killer tightened that stocking around her throat.

What had those moments been like? What had she seen through the kaleidoscope of hallucinations brought on by the magic mushrooms?

What was the connection, the wire that ran from Nicole Solomon to her father to the Gillen boys?

When Jessica opened her eyes she found that she had far more questions than answers. As she retrieved her car keys from her pocket she saw the shadow come up on her right. Fast. It took only a second to approach, but it was a second too long.

Before Jessica could turn around she felt the blow. It connected with a flat thud on the right side of her face.

'... *knew!*' was all she heard.

Jessica saw bolts of lightning behind her eyelids, felt the pain come on in a red roar. Because she had once trained as a boxer – had even fought a handful of professional fights, still worked out at Joe Hand's gym when she could – she anticipated a second blow. It was pure instinct. She didn't know where it would come from, but she got her hands up just in time to block it.

'You fucking *knew!*' her attacker screamed.

The second blow glanced off Jessica's wrists. Jessica pivoted, put her back to her car, just as she heard yelling in the near distance.

'*Whoa!*' someone yelled. 'What the fuck are you doing?' It was a man's voice. Jessica then heard footsteps approaching.

In that next second Jessica was able to focus. She saw her attacker standing in front of her. It was a woman, a few inches shorter than she. The woman tried to launch another punch, but Jessica was able to sidestep it.

A moment later the woman was on the ground.

Jessica looked up to see the two young officers who had been standing at the back of the building. One of them had taken the woman down.

Jessica glanced down at the woman and it all began to make

sense. It was Mary Gillen. The woman tried to scramble to her feet, but one of the officers grabbed her and held her in a bear hug.

'You *knew!*' Mary screamed again. She attempted to kick Jessica but she was too far away. 'You fucking *bitch*! You knew and you didn't say anything.'

The woman tried to spit in Jessica's face, but it went wide.

'You need to calm down, lady,' one of the officers said.

Mary Gillen would not be placated. She was hyperventilating. 'You came to my fucking *house*, I answered your questions, and you knew my boys were in danger. And now they're dead. They're fucking *dead*!'

Jessica held out a hand, palm out. 'It's okay,' she said to the officer holding Mary Gillen.

The officer wasn't so certain. He held onto the woman. 'Are you sure, detective?'

Jessica took a deep breath, tried to clear her head. If she had anticipated the first blow, the way you do in the ring, she might've rolled with it. But this was a sucker punch. And, at this moment, Jessica felt she deserved it. She'd had no idea what fate awaited the two Gillen boys when she visited the Gillen house, but still she felt she deserved it.

'I didn't know,' Jessica said. It sounded weak and incomplete. 'I had no idea that your boys were in danger when I came to your house. I was only there because of that phone call. You've got to believe me.'

The officer still held the woman tightly. The woman kept hyperventilating, but she had stopped struggling for the moment. There was spittle dribbling from her chin. Her eyes were red with rage.

'I *don't* fucking believe you,' she said. 'My boys are *dead*. My life is *over*.'

Jessica made eye contact with the officer. She nodded again.

Reluctantly the officer eased his grip on the woman. Mary Gillen sprang forward and tried to rain blows on Jessica again, but Jessica stepped in close and got hold of the woman, and held her until the woman's volcanic anger began to subside.

'It's okay,' Jessica said. 'It's okay.'

At this moment, standing in the parking lot of the Round-house, holding onto this woman who was as much a victim as the three victims of homicide, Jessica knew two things.

One. It was never going to be okay for Mary Gillen, ever again.

Two. Jessica would do everything and anything she could to catch the person who took this woman's life away.

After icing her face, and calming down her husband – he felt deeply for the woman's terrible loss, but his sense of protection for his wife took over when he saw Jessica's swollen eye – she poked at some food, poured herself a rare double-shot of Jameson, stared past some inane sitcom.

All she could think about was the terrible cocoon of loss and grief in which Mary Gillen must be trapped, and how it would forever be connected to Jessica's life. Every homicide she had ever investigated had, in some way, taken up residence in her heart and mind. She remembered something about each of them.

Four dead.

Nicole Solomon. David Solomon. Robert and Edward Gillen.

There was something that connected all of them to each other, just as they were forever connected to Jessica Balzano.

She would find it.

31

'Sorry,' Donna said.

'It's okay,' Byrne said. 'I was just kind of lost in thought.'

'I remember the look.'

Byrne took a step back, drank in his ex-wife's nearness. He thought he had prepared himself for her proximity. He had not.

'You cut your hair,' was all he could muster.

Donna raised her hand, smoothed the back of her long, elegant neck. 'I did,' she said. 'Do you like it?'

Byrne hesitated for a second. No, it wasn't a second. It wasn't even *close* to a second. It was that nearly infinitesimal length of time measured by people – mostly women – who either are or were in an intimate relationship, the span of time coming right after a loaded question, but before the man could answer.

'I do,' he said. 'I like it a lot.'

'No you don't. You hate it.'

'I don't hate it. It looks good on you.'

'What you really mean to say is, it looks good on a woman my age.'

Since the day the young Kevin Byrne saw the teenaged Donna Sullivan, next to a 7-Eleven in South Philly, he had yet to meet a woman he found more beautiful. She still managed to loose the butterflies in his stomach every time he saw her.

'I'm going to go on the record here,' Byrne said. 'Your new hairstyle is very flattering. It makes you look prettier than ever. Younger.'

Donna smiled. It was the smile he remembered well, the one that all but said she knew that he was slinging the Irish charm, but that, for the moment, she would let him get away with it.

They were now inside the dimly lit parlor of Valerie Beckert's house. 'Well, to put it mildly, and for so many reasons, I was surprised to get your call.'

Since their divorce, Donna had worked as a realtor. Over the years she moved through some of the smaller, mom-and-pop neighborhood agencies, but four years ago landed a job with the largest realtor in the city of Philadelphia, handling mostly Center City properties.

She was also licensed to show any multiple listing. If she made the sale, she would split the commission with the agent of record.

'Well, I haven't made any decisions,' Byrne said. 'I just wanted to get the details on this house.'

Donna looked at him skeptically for a few seconds. She had always been able to read him well, far more accurately than he had been able to read her. Near the end of their marriage it was his job – the long irregular hours, the anger, the way the detectives of the homicide unit bonded even more closely with each other than they did with their families – that brought their relationship to a close. Donna had probably shut off her feelings two years before Byrne noticed the first touch of frost.

Some detective.

Donna walked over to the front window, which was caked with

a decade of soot and grime. She looked for a clean spot to put down her briefcase and, not finding one, held it out to Byrne. Byrne held it aloft while she opened it, took out a folder. She snapped it shut, put the strap over her shoulder.

'Let's see,' she began. She opened the folder, pulled out a thin sheaf of documents. 'The property is four thousand square feet, with six bedrooms, four full plus one half-bath, three-car garage, eat-in kitchen, full basement.' Donna flipped the page, continued. 'The lot size is 8049 square feet, house built in 1928, shows as colonial style but as you probably noticed it is more Tudor. Stucco walls, hardwood floors.'

Byrne looked down. The worn and stained carpeting beneath his feet was probably a deep burgundy at one time. 'There's a floor under here?'

'That's the prevailing theory,' Donna said. She glanced again at the document. 'Public water, public sewer, hot water is natural gas, nice backyard, and the ultimate in luxury, a marble fireplace, which, unfortunately, is bricked in.'

'Who needs heat in Philadelphia?' Byrne asked.

Donna flipped a few more pages, found nothing of interest, put everything back into the folder. 'You probably know this, but I'll say it out loud anyway. There's a rule of thumb in real estate, and that is, if you're moving into a halfway decent neighborhood, and you're looking to rehabilitate a property, you want the worst house on the block.' She handed Byrne the folder. 'Congratulations,' she said. 'You definitely found it.'

Byrne took the folder. 'So, what do you *really* think of the place?'

'I think you should lace up your Nikes and run from this place as fast and as far as you can.'

'Now, see, you're just trying to get me to raise my offer so you can get a bigger commission.'

Donna gave him a sideways glance, and a half smile, the one

that demolished his heart so many years ago. 'You haven't made an offer, detective.'

'What do you think I could get it for?'

'I think you can do a lot better than even the foreclosure price.'

Byrne looked around, as if he might be thinking about it. It was just a stall, and he knew it. He'd made up his mind the minute he walked through the door. There was no choice.

'Let's do it.'

32

Jessica and Byrne spent the morning – wasted the morning was more accurate, if Jessica were asked – by visiting toy stores in an attempt to find a doll similar to the one found at the Gillen crime scene, or someone with some knowledge who might point them in the right direction.

They had done a few Internet searches, found similar dolls and figurines, but that did not give them a direction as to where the doll was purchased. Sometimes shoe-leather police work trumped anything that computers could offer.

As they caught a quick coffee in Center City, Jessica told Byrne about the Nutshell studies. When she showed him the pictures on her iPhone, he was as impressed as she had been when she'd first seen them.

The double homicide of the two Gillen boys was being led by Josh Bontrager and Maria Caruso. While Jessica and Byrne followed up on the doll, the other two detectives interviewed students at the boys' school.

They would meet with command later in the day and compare notes. There was no doubt that the homicides were related.

The fifth store of the morning, a place called The Toy Chest, was located in a converted row house on Germantown Avenue in the Chestnut Hill section of the city. The storefront offered a bright array of the store's wares: games, puzzles, dolls, action figures, models.

Byrne put the car in park, cut the engine. As he walked around the car, and waited for traffic to cross the road, he said:

'Kevin, I'd like you to meet the thousand-pound gorilla in the room. Gorilla, this is Kevin.'

Jessica closed her car door. 'So, what you're saying is, you want to know about the black eye.'

'Not really,' Byrne said. 'My partner shows up looking like she went two rounds in a cage match, and it doesn't really cross my mind.' He glanced at his watch. 'I told myself I'd give it until noon. It's ten after. You should be proud of me.'

'Always,' Jessica said.

'Dish.'

Jessica told him about the encounter with Mary Gillen. Byrne knew her well enough to know that she had not made a decision about what, if anything, she was going to do in response. He didn't press her.

The man stocking the shelves was in his late twenties. He was tall and rail thin, had sandy brown hair pulled back into a ponytail. He wore a red flannel shirt, black Levi's, black Doc Martens.

The man looked up from his task. 'Hi,' he said.

'Hi,' Jessica replied. 'I'm—'

Before she could continue, the young man interrupted her.

'*Wow*. That's one heck of a shiner. I hope the other guy looks worse.'

Byrne suddenly got interested in an item on the shelf, a strange-looking board game called *Oh, Gnome You Don't*. He couldn't look at his partner.

'The other guy is in Laurel Hill,' Jessica said.

Laurel Hill was one of the oldest and largest cemeteries in Philadelphia. Flannel shirt got the message.

'Awesome,' he said.

Jessica noted his nametag. *Florian*.

'What can I show you?' Florian asked.

Jessica produced her ID. 'Is there somewhere we can talk?'

The look on Florian's face said small-time pot bust. The look Jessica returned said not to worry.

Yet.

Florian gestured to the counter at the rear of the store. 'Right this way,' he said.

On the way back, Jessica took note of the inventory on the shelves of The Toy Chest – Winnie-the-Pooh, Raggedy Ann, Curious George and Kewpie dolls, as well as Sesame Street characters, Thomas the Tank Engine, Fancy Nancy. There were also craft kits, costumes, castles, trains, rockets, even old-fashioned paper dolls.

Jessica made a mental note to never bring Sophie here. She had enough money troubles. This place would bankrupt her.

Florian walked around, behind the counter, folded his hands, looked up, clearly not knowing what to expect.

Byrne took out a photograph of the doll found at the Gillen crime scene. 'We're trying to determine where this doll was purchased.'

Florian took the photo, looked closely at it, clearly a concerned citizen. 'This is pricey.'

'You've seen it before?' Byrne asked.

'Not this particular doll, but I go to all the shows.' He gestured to the store. 'Most of my inventory is newer, but I'm always looking. I do a little eBay on the side.'

'Why do you say this is pricey?'

'There's a lot of money in dolls, collectible dolls that is. This is probably an antique. It looks like bisque.'

'Not sure what that is,' Jessica said. 'I know what the soup is, but not the doll.'

'Okay, well, bisque is a type of porcelain. Unglazed, I think. It's what a lot of the older dolls are made of.'

Jessica made the note. 'You mentioned that there is a lot of money in collecting dolls.'

'Oh yeah.'

'How much is a lot?'

'As you can see, we don't specialize, but I get all the trade magazines, too. Barbie is always hot. You'd be amazed how many editions of Barbie are out there. The folks at Mattel are smart.'

'How much would a rare Barbie go for?' Byrne asked.

Florian reached behind the counter, sorted through a stack of magazines. He found what he was looking for, riffled through it, set it on the counter, turned it to face the two detectives. On one page was a picture of a Barbie wearing a little black dress, with a necklace clearly made of precious stones. To the right was an article.

'This is the Canturi Barbie,' Florian said. 'One of a kind.'

Jessica scanned the article, found the price. 'Seriously? Five hundred thousand dollars?'

'And change,' Florian said. 'Now, if you took away the diamonds, of course, she'd be just another Barbie. As far as the doll itself goes, an original, unadorned Barbie – as in Barbie Number One – goes for around eight grand.'

'A bargain,' Byrne said.

'Modern boy dolls go for a lot less. An original G.I. Joe –

sealed in the package – might fetch eight hundred or so. They took it off the market around 1978.'

'Why was that?'

'Not sure,' he said. 'But when they discontinued it the figure measured around eleven inches tall. When they brought it back in 1983 it was around three-and-a-half. I wish I had a box of the originals, I can tell you that much. But those are VHTF.'

Jessica stopped writing. 'I'm sorry?' she asked. 'VHTF?'

'That means—'

'Very Hard To Find,' Byrne said. 'Can you think of a place in Philly that might specialize in this sort of thing?'

Clearly Byrne had had enough of driving around Philly looking for doll data.

Florian once again picked up the photo, scrutinized it, his small pot stash perhaps energizing him to cooperate fully and quickly with police.

Jessica took the opportunity to catch Byrne's eye and mouth the words, *Very Hard To Find?*

Byrne smiled, shrugged.

The man turned back to them. 'I don't know of anywhere in Philly. You might have to go to New York for this.' He handed back the photo. 'There's always the internet. Check eBay.'

As a homicide detective, Jessica had many times tried to track a sale across the World Wide Web. The effort to get the warrants needed to compel an online merchant to turn over records made her feel exhausted just thinking about it.

Before they left the store her phone rang, and Peter Giovanni's daughter Jessica had her belief in shoe-leather police work once again renewed.

Jessica met Bethany Quinn at the door to her house. Somehow, the young woman looked even more pregnant than the last time Jessica had seen her.

'We found this in my grandfather's steamer trunk,' she said.

'In the attic?'

'Yeah.'

'You didn't go up there yourself, did you?'

'No,' she said. 'I made my husband do it.'

'They do come in handy sometimes.'

'He knew about you coming over, of course. When I mentioned your father's name, he was up there in a flash. Your dad's kind of a legend on the force.'

'Please, don't tell him that.'

Bethany smiled, zipped her lips.

Jessica glanced at the card. It was oversized, filigreed, quite fancy as business cards go, definitely from another era.

The address was in West Philly. The name of the shop was The Secret World.

'Do you know if they're still around?' Jessica asked.

'No idea,' Bethany said. 'But my husband saw some old sales receipts from there in the trunk. So, I'm pretty sure my grandfather bought some of his dolls from them.'

Jessica held up the card. 'This was very kind of you.'

'Oh, no problem.'

'Best of luck.'

The woman winced, put a hand on her lower back. 'Thanks,' she said. 'By the way, as you know, my husband is PPD.'

'Yes,' Jessica said. 'Tell him thanks, too.'

'He said to mention that his dream is to one day work in the homicide unit.'

Jessica smiled. In her mind she heard the sound of one hand washing the other. She envied this woman her youth, her faith. 'What's his name?'

'Danny,' she said. 'P/O Daniel Joseph Quinn. He's in the Third District.'

'I'll remember,' Jessica said.

On the way back to the car Jessica called the number on the business card. She got a voicemail greeting that told her that the shop was open Monday, Thursday and Saturday from two p.m. to eight p.m.

She looked at her watch. It was ten to two on a Thursday.

They drove to West Philly.

33

The address on Lancaster Avenue, in the Spruce Hill section of West Philadelphia, was between a number of buildings either in repair, or in dire need. The doll shop was fairly well preserved. It reminded Jessica of stores in her South Philly neighborhood when she was growing up – hobby shops, model shops, variety stores. A few still remained.

As they approached The Secret World Jessica took in the window display. It was like nothing she'd ever seen. There were dolls in chairs, dolls sitting on small dressers, dolls at a table, dolls at a picnic. There was one doll, still in its box, wearing an elaborate satin ball gown.

The entire display window was a cutaway version of a doll house, with pink doors on each side that swung wide.

When they entered, a bell over the door chimed. Jessica noted that the doll house motif continued inside the shop. The space was long and narrow, with a glass counter to the left, shelves floor to ceiling on the right. On them were dolls of every color, every ethnicity. There were baby dolls, child dolls, fashion dolls, boudoir dolls, dolls of every profession – teachers, nurses, ballerinas.

At the back of the shop, over the counter, was an old weathered sign: *E. Rose, Prop.*

Jessica found it a bit disconcerting that she could enter this shop, any shop in her city, be inside for thirty seconds or so, and no one came out of the back room. She wondered if something was wrong.

She decided to give it a little more time. She looked at some of the larger dolls on the rear wall; some were the size of life-size children, some even larger. After a few moments, one of them moved.

Startled, Jessica realized that one of the life-size dolls was really a petite older woman. She had been standing there the whole time, letting Jessica and Byrne browse.

The woman looked to be in her late seventies or early eighties. She had cloud white hair and wore a beautiful lemon yellow cardigan over a white blouse. She wore a sapphire brooch pinned to her collar.

'Are you E. Rose?' Byrne asked the woman.

'I am,' the woman said.

'Would that be *Mrs* or *Ms* Rose?'

The woman took a moment, studying Byrne, considering his question. It appeared as if she might not have heard the query, or felt the answer was beneath her dignity.

'It would be *Mrs* Rose,' she said. She had a slight accent, but Jessica could not immediately place it. It certainly wasn't eastern Pennsylvania, and definitely not West Philly. The woman continued. 'I was married at one time, of course, and for years I took my husband's last name – I keep it still – as was the custom. And, in my opinion, should be now. But with my beloved now these many years in the ground, I haven't seen the need or purpose of calling myself *Mrs* Rose.'

'What shall I call you?' Byrne asked.

'Please call me Miss Emmaline.'

'Miss Emmaline it is,' he said. 'My name is Kevin Byrne, and this is my partner, Jessica Balzano. We're with the Philadelphia Police Department.'

'I am pleased to make your acquaintance,' she said. 'Welcome to The Secret World.'

'Do you own this shop?' Byrne asked.

'Oh, yes. I've been here since 1958.'

Byrne held up the card they had gotten from Bethany Quinn. 'We got this from the granddaughter of a man named Carl Krause.'

'Oh, my,' she said. 'I remember Carl. *Very* intense young man. Liked to work with miniatures. Not much call for them anymore.'

Jessica wanted to interject that the 'young man' had passed away more than a decade earlier, but felt it was not relevant. If the woman asked, she would tell her. Miss Emmaline did not ask.

'May I show you a photograph?' Byrne asked.

'You may.'

Byrne reached into his bag, took out a pair of pictures. One photograph showed the doll they had found at the Gillen crime scene in its entirety, a ruler lying next to it for scale. The other photograph was a close-up of the doll's face. Neither picture provided any context to either the victims or the crime scene itself. Byrne put them on the counter, turned them toward Miss Emmaline.

The woman lifted her glasses – held on a lanyard around her neck – and peered through them. She scanned both photographs carefully.

'What can you tell us, if anything, about this doll?' Byrne asked.

'Perhaps a great deal, young man,' she said. 'But first there is something I'd like you to do for me.'

'Of course,' Byrne said. 'What is it?'

'I need to sit down,' she said. She gestured over her left shoulder to a curtained doorway at the back of the shop. 'My parlor is just through there. Can you help me? I seem to have misplaced my walking stick.'

'It would be an honor.' Byrne walked around the counter, offered his arm. Miss Emmaline took it.

'Would you like me to lock the front door?' Jessica asked.

The woman looked at Jessica. 'Not to worry, my dear. There is a bell overhead, and my hearing is as good as it was when I was a little girl in Metairie, Louisiana, more than eighty years ago.'

A few moments later they stepped through the curtain into the small parlor, into Miss Emmaline's past, into another era. The walls were draped in silk tapestries. The air smelled of lemon oil and mint tea.

And then there were the dolls. Exquisite dolls. All four walls held display cases. If the front window had been like nothing Jessica had ever seen, this was like nothing she could ever imagine.

There were three chairs; two on one side of the room, on either side of a small table; one nearer the curtain. Jessica took the one by the opening, positioned her chair so that she could see through the small gap in the velvet curtains, into the shop. A bell over the door was one thing. A Glock 17 was quite another.

They may have voyaged into the early twentieth century, but this was still West Philadelphia.

'Back when we lived in Plaquemines Parish, my father was a merchant seaman,' Miss Emmaline said. 'He was a big man, you see, well over six feet tall, and he had enormous hands. But still he could thread the finest needle for my mother when she made school outfits for my sisters and me. My mother was a treasured seamstress, known far and wide throughout the parish for her delicate work.'

The woman pointed to a doll sitting in a glass case to her left, a small porcelain figure that looked to be a contemporary of Marie Antoinette. 'Mama sewed this brocade,' she said. 'Isn't it lovely?'

Jessica marveled at the workmanship. 'It's beautiful,' she said.

'Were you always interested in dolls?' Byrne asked.

Miss Emmaline sipped her tea. 'Some, but not more than most girls of an age,' she said. 'My grandfather was a minister, and this was a time when, if you appeared to live above your means, and you were of the cloth, the people of your parish might look upon this as an extravagance, a reason to withhold their coins from the collection basket. Dolls back then were expensive things, long before they were made of plastic. Dolls were a luxury item in my parish, and a little girl with a collection? Well, *chérie*, that would surely have caused a scandal.'

'When did you start collecting?' Byrne asked.

'I think I became interested first in all things old, not just antique dolls,' she said. She stopped, again sipped her tea. 'Now that *I'm* old I find the notion so terribly quaint.'

'Old? Not for *years*,' Byrne said.

Miss Emmaline smiled. 'Heartbreaker.' She glanced at Jessica. 'Is he always this charming?'

'Always,' Jessica said.

Miss Emmaline put down her cup, an elegant china demitasse, continued.

'When my sisters and I were small, my grandmother only took out her doll on special occasions,' she said. 'Mostly on our birthdays, sometimes on holidays.'

'She had just the one doll?' Byrne asked.

'Yes. She was a Bru, very beautiful.'

'What is a Bru?'

'Bru is a line of dolls created in the late 1800s in France. Mostly they were made of porcelain, though some were made of gutta-percha. They are considered by some – myself included – to be the finest dolls ever made.'

'And your grandmother had one of these?'

Miss Emmaline nodded. 'Her name was Sarah Jane. The doll, not my grandmother. We had to be bathed and scrubbed every time we touched Sarah Jane, had to have very clean hands when we held her. When we got older, and took to tomboying, we had to wear our Easter gloves. Imagine.'

While Miss Emmaline talked, Jessica found her attention being drawn to one of the dolls on display. The doll, on top of the dresser to Jessica's left, was big, and its eyes were looking off to the side. They seemed to be looking at Jessica.

'I see you've noticed Carlene,' Miss Emmaline said. 'She's what's known as a Googly doll.'

Miss Emmaline pointed at the doll's face, continued.

'You see how the eyes are somewhat oversized and glancing off to the side? This is a trait of the Googly, although many other dolls and figurines and popular images have this trait.'

'The Campbell kids,' Byrne said.

'Very good, young man,' she said. 'The two children in the Campbell soup advertisements are most certainly in the Googly tradition.'

The headquarters for the Campbell Soup company had for many years been located in Camden, New Jersey, just across the Delaware River from Philadelphia.

Just about anyone in Philadelphia or Camden with the last name of Campbell was nicknamed Soupy.

Jessica thought about the Gillen crime scene, how the doll was in one corner, and the victims directly across.

Was the doll looking at the victims? Was that the invitation?

Byrne held up the photo of the doll found at the crime scene. 'Is this a doll you may have sold in this shop?'

'It is,' she said. 'But I believe I have not seen this *particular* doll before.'

'Is there any way to tell where this doll may have been purchased?' Byrne asked. 'Any markings?'

'Antique dolls can have any number of marks,' Miss Emmaline said. 'The manufacturer's identification mark on an antique doll often appears on the back of the head, which is usually hidden by the wig. But marks can appear on the shoulder plate, on the chest or back, sometimes on the soles of the feet.'

'Are these marks stamped in?'

'Sometimes. It depends on the material. Marks can also be incised into the material, or attached as a label or decal. It depends.'

Jessica felt she knew where her partner was going with this. It made her blood run cold.

Miss Emmaline held up the photograph. 'It's hard to tell much from this photograph. If you could bring the doll here, I might be able to tell you more,' she said. 'If I saw the mark, I could tell you exactly who made this doll, almost to the day when, and perhaps where it might have been purchased.'

'We can do that,' Byrne replied. 'We appreciate the offer.'

'Not at all.'

'May I ask if you run this shop by yourself, Miss Emmaline?'

'Mostly,' she said. 'I live just upstairs, so there is not much of a commute. Then there are a few neighborhood girls who come in and help clean once in a while. It's not too hard to get girls to work in a shop like this. I pay them what I can.'

A few minutes later they stepped back into the shop. Jessica was glad to see the place had not been burgled. She was turning into *such* a cynic in her old age.

Byrne turned to Miss Emmaline. 'I was just wondering. Do all dolls have names?'

Miss Emmaline looked at Byrne as if he had asked her whether or not the sun rose in the east. 'Of course they do, young man,' she said. 'To a lot of people dolls are almost living things. To many, dolls are members of the family.' She gestured to the dolls displayed around the room. 'These are my family now.'

Byrne buttoned his coat. 'Well, again, thanks so much for your time.'

'It has been my pleasure. I have enjoyed this visit immensely, and I hope I have been of some assistance to the Philadelphia Police Department. You have been an assistance to me more times than I care to remember.'

'You've been a great help, Miss Emmaline.'

'Please let me know when you might come by with that doll. I'll try to carve out a moment in my hectic schedule,' she said with a wink.

'May I ask one more question?' Jessica asked.

'You may.'

'What happened to Sarah Jane?'

Miss Emmaline looked out the shop window, perhaps imagining the world as it was when little girls had to wear their Easter gloves to handle their grandmother's prized bisque doll.

'My mother had three sisters, you see. When my grandfather's farm was sold, after his death, the contents were well picked over. My mother was the youngest, so she pretty much got what was left at the bottom. The last time I saw Sarah Jane she was in my cousin Ruthie's hands, looking out the back window of Uncle Frederick's 1937 Ford.'

Jessica wanted to ask if Cousin Ruthie's hands were clean at the time, but the despondent look on Miss Emmaline's face told her they were not.

*

It took a few moments for Jessica to come back to the twenty-first century after walking out of Miss Emmaline's shop. She felt as if she had just time-traveled. She liked whatever place they had gone to, though, she'd liked it a great deal.

They got in the car, buckled up. They sat in silence for almost a full minute.

'You want to know if the killer marked Nicole Solomon and the Gillen boys, don't you?' Jessica asked.

'It crossed my mind.'

'You want to know if there is a mark on the backs of their heads.'

Byrne said nothing. He didn't have to.

'I'll let them know we're coming,' Jessica said.

She took out her phone, and called the ME's office.

Of the eight divisions under the purview of the Philadelphia Medical Examiner's Office, the most active was the forensic investigation unit. In addition to its main charter – that being to determine whether or not a death comes under the jurisdiction of the MEO, and to investigate the circumstances surrounding a death – it sometimes, in conjunction with the city's detective units, aided in notification of next of kin.

Working with the other divisions – pathology, toxicology, histology, as well as forensic odontology and forensic anthropology – the ME's office processed more than six thousand cases of death every year. Add to this the division's bereavement support services, and the recently established Fatality Review program, which strove to find ways to prevent future injuries and fatalities for the citizens of Philadelphia, the office was never silent for long.

All homicide detectives and other police personnel had their ideas about crime prevention, of course, but, for the sake of political expediency, and job longevity, most kept these thoughts to themselves.

When Jessica and Byrne arrived at the huge complex on University Avenue, they pulled around to the rear.

The ME investigator on both the Nicole Solomon and Gillen boys' cases was Steve Fenton.

A fit, athletic family man in his early forties, Fenton took every body he processed seriously. Where there was sometimes a measure of gallows humor within these walls, it never came from Steve Fenton. It was Jessica's understanding that, as a graduate of Westminster Theological Seminary, Fenton had at one time considered the clergy.

They met in the large intake room next to the loading bays. The bodies of Nicole Solomon, Robert Gillen, and Edward Gillen lay on stainless steel tables in the center of the room.

Behind them they heard the sound of insects – mostly blow flies – being zapped by the electronic zapper. If you spent enough time in this room – and mercifully Jessica did not – you almost didn't hear it anymore.

'I missed it on all three of them,' Fenton said.

He brought the lighted magnifying lamp over the back of Nicole Solomon's head. Jessica put on her glasses, leaned in. The mark was small, but unmistakable. Jessica stepped back, allowed Byrne to approach.

'These are really easy to miss, Steve,' Jessica said. 'I can't make out anything. What do they look like to you?'

'They're numbers,' he said. 'The number ten on Nicole Solomon, eleven on Robert Gillen, and twelve on Edward. I had Dr Patel take a look. He concurs.'

Dr Rajiv Patel was the medical examiner for Philadelphia County. If ever there was an overworked, underpaid position, it was his.

'Were these marks done pre- or post-mortem?' Byrne asked.

'Post,' Fenton said. 'No bleeding, no clotting.'

'Do you know what the marks were made with?'

'Not sure, yet,' he said. 'But I'd say presumptively it was some kind of needle.'

'Needle as in knitting needle or hypodermic needle?' Byrne asked.

'Much smaller than a knitting needle. I'd say it was maybe a milliner's or a sharp.'

'A sharp?'

'That's the term for your basic needle used for hand sewing. My mother worked as an in-house seamstress for Wanamaker's, so I grew up around this stuff.'

Fenton methodically, and reverently, pulled the sheets over the bodies, turned back to the detectives. 'I'd say the needles that made these marks are of the kind used for fine tailoring.'

'Did you take any photographs?' Byrne asked.

'I did.' Fenton snapped off his gloves. He walked over to the desk in the corner, retrieved a nine by twelve envelope. He handed it to Byrne.

'Thanks,' Byrne said.

Fenton took a moment, looked at the three small forms beneath the gray sheets in the center of the room, back at the detectives. Whatever he was about to say was not going to come easily. He cleared his throat.

'My daughter Catherine turns thirteen, next week,' he said. 'She goes to the same school Nicole Solomon went to. We have a flyer on our refrigerator door about that movie at the Franklin Institute.' He glanced again at the bodies. The sound of blowflies ceased for a moment. Fenton looked back. 'Cathy had to get her braces tightened that day. If she hadn't, she would have been on that bus.'

For a few moments, no one said anything. The look on Steve Fenton's face said it all.

Let's catch this guy.

*

They rode in silence on the way back to the Roundhouse. Jessica was certain that the images floating through her partner's mind were all but identical to the images in hers.

The killer was marking his victims with a sewing needle, after they had died.

Neither detective said it out loud, but there could be no mistake.

The killer was turning his victims into dolls.

34

The last interior door in Valerie Beckert's house – the final door of twenty-six with a lock that required a skeleton key to open – was to a room off the pantry, perhaps once used as a broom closet. Inside were now the remnants of a corn broom, and a fine layer of dust. An upper shelf was lined with yellowed paper in a gingham pattern.

The skeleton key in Byrne's hand – a tarnished brass key that had been attached to Valerie's key ring, a key that did not work in any other door in the house – locked and unlocked this door. Byrne tried it twice to make sure.

He slipped the key into his pocket, wondering:

Why this door, Valerie?

Why this key?

When the doorbell rang, Byrne's mind was adrift somewhere between the world of antique dolls and the world of antique electrical wiring. At the moment, a few Bushmills into the evening, there was no line of demarcation.

As he crossed the foyer, Byrne found himself relieved that there was a functioning doorbell.

He opened the door.

It was Donna. In her hands was a large brown envelope.

'Kevin Francis Byrne,' she said with finality and a broad grin. 'Homeowner.'

'What's so funny?'

Donna banged him on the chest with the envelope, stepped inside. 'Never thought I'd say those two things in a row.'

'Laugh it up.' Byrne took the papers from her. He hadn't expected Donna. He wished he'd had the chance to clean up a bit. At least a shave.

'What's all this?' he asked.

'My bill.'

Byrne said nothing. He wasn't sure if she was serious or not. She wasn't.

While Byrne closed and locked the door, Donna crossed the front room, slipped the tote bag from her shoulder.

'I love what you've done with the place.'

Donna had brought a full-blown Mexican dinner, as well as two bottles of chardonnay.

They ate on a blanket thrown in the center of the living room. The only light –besides the candles Donna had also brought – was a lamp on the floor in the corner. In anticipation of the deal going through, he'd called in a favor and had the power turned on.

They were halfway through the second bottle of chardonnay.

'I always loved this part,' Byrne said.

'This part?'

Byrne felt he was blowing it. He scrambled.

'This part. When there's no furniture, when there's just a lamp on the floor. Like a picnic.'

'I know what you mean,' she said. 'I sell a lot of properties to young people. I remember.'

Young people, Byrne thought. Before he could say anything, Donna put a finger to his lips.

A few moments later, Donna Sullivan Byrne, the only woman Kevin Byrne had ever really loved, was in his arms.

35

By the last day in April, Nancy Brisbane had lived in the house for two weeks. Thaddeus Woodman had come to live with them just a day earlier.

Nancy was a fussy little girl, never satisfied with anything. No matter what food Valerie prepared for the girl – breakfast, lunch, dinner, or even a sweet evening snack – the girl poked at the food, sometimes throwing it on the floor. Indeed, she had cried for almost the entire fortnight she had been in the house. Even when Valerie put on music for her, Nancy could not find the lilt in the song, nor allow it to lift her spirit.

Thaddeus seemed quite the opposite. He was a quiet boy. He was very polite.

The police had come by just a few hours after the boy went missing – he lived just three streets over – and asked their questions.

The officers were a contrast in age and experience. One young, one older. It was raining that day.

'Can I help you?' Valerie asked.

One of the officers, the younger of the two, touched a finger to the brim of his cap. Valerie appreciated his gallantry. His cap was covered by a clear plastic rain cover. 'Ma'am, we're sorry to bother you. We're looking for a boy.'

'A boy?'

'Yes ma'am. His name is Thaddeus Woodman. He's six years old. Do you know him by any chance?'

Valerie tried to look as if she were thinking about this. She was no actress, and she was certain the police officers would see through her ruse, especially the older of the two, who seemed to be looking at her with some suspicion. Maybe it was her imagination. 'Could you repeat that name for me please?'

'Thaddeus,' the young officer said. 'Thaddeus Woodman.'

'I don't think I know him,' Valerie said. 'Is he a neighborhood child?'

'Yes.'

'Oh, my goodness,' Valerie said. 'Where are my manners? Would you like to come inside, out of the rain?'

In the house, Valerie heard a banging noise. It was coming from a locked room on the second floor, and was surely that Nancy Brisbane. Whenever Nancy felt neglected – which was almost constantly – she would take to stamping her feet on the floor. Valerie looked closely at the officers. They didn't seem to hear it. Maybe the sound was masked by the passing traffic.

'No, ma'am,' the young officer said. 'But thank you.' Held up a photograph. It, too, was wrapped in clear plastic.

'May I?' she asked.

'Please.'

Valerie took the photo, looked carefully at it. It was a school picture of Thaddeus. In it he wore a white shirt and a thin black neck tie. Somehow, his mother had managed to tame that cowlick. 'This is the missing boy?'

'Yes, ma'am.'

Valerie pored over the photograph a few more seconds, handed it back. 'I'm sorry,' she said. 'I haven't seen him.'

The younger officer pocketed the photo. He took out a small notepad.

'May I have your name, ma'am?'

'My name is Valerie,' she said. 'Valerie Beckert.'

He wrote this down. 'Didn't someone else live here recently?'

The banging grew louder. Valerie was certain the older officer reacted to it. He glanced over her shoulder, into the darkness of the foyer.

'That was my aunt Josephine,' Valerie said. 'She passed away recently.'

'I'm sorry to hear it,' the officer said. He handed her a card. 'My name is Officer Cooper. My number is on that card. If you see Thaddeus, I'd appreciate it if you give me a call.'

Valerie took the card. 'Do you think he's all right?'

'I'm sure he's just fine,' the officer said. 'He's probably playing with friends and just lost track of the time. You know how kids can be.'

Oh, I do, Valerie thought.

'I'll keep a watchful eye out the window,' she said. 'If I see anything, I'll be sure to give you a call.'

A few moments later, as Valerie watched the two policeman walk down to the sidewalk, she heard Nancy Brisbane begin to bang on the floor again. Valerie wanted to be cross with her, but she just couldn't.

Instead, even though it was before supper, and would surely spoil their appetites, she went into the kitchen and made a batch of oatmeal raisin cookies.

36

Byrne stood on the porch for a long time after his ex-wife drove away. He tried to remember the last time they had made love.

He could not. He certainly recalled the first time, but he could not remembered the last.

As they'd drifted away from each other in the last months and weeks of their marriage they had stopped sleeping in the same bed, had all but ceased even the most casual of human contact.

Byrne could smell her perfume on the collar of his shirt.

What did this mean? He had no idea.

But whatever the house he'd just bought originally meant to him, it had just come to mean something else. He firmly believed that a space was the sum total of the events and energies that had been spent between its walls – days, weeks, years, centuries – and these energies remained.

There were now new echoes.

37

I tried to imagine a metaphor so great it could explain the way I felt.

I am no poet, no great wit – just ask Mr Marseille, he'll tell you – and thus felt ill-equipped to describe the breathtaking vista before me.

I have many times stood on the western bank of the Delaware River (less frequently on the eastern bank, during my two trips to Camden, New Jersey), and have, more than once, had my breath stolen by the majesty of it all.

But to stand in front of the Atlantic Ocean – something about which I have dreamed my entire life – brought tears to my eyes. Mr Marseille anticipated this, as he has most of my moods for as long as I can remember, was at the ready with one of his soft white handkerchiefs.

I smiled through my tears of joy, dabbed at my eyes.

'Where is it?' I asked.

Mr Marseille knew what I was asking. He always did. Sometimes he surprised me with this ability, although this time I fear I was obvious. He pointed somewhat to his right.

'Right there, I believe.'

I looked out over the water, squinted, as if this would help me see it.

'How far away is it?' I asked.

'Three thousand six hundred fifty-two miles.'

This made me smile. 'That sounds precise,' I said.

'There is no reason to be anything else.'

I looked at the ocean again, wondering if there was a boy and girl, at that very moment, standing on the sand in France, wondering the same things about America, having the same conversation.

I liked to think there was. I made a game of wondering what their names might be.

We drove back from Atlantic City. This time we were in our own car, a much older model that, according to Mr Marseille, had quite a robust and powerful engine. I loved to hear him talk of such things. Inside it was very quiet. We recited poetry to each other.

We stopped for our evening meal at a restaurant called Friendly's, but neither Mr Marseille nor I found that the place lived up to its name.

When we arrived home, Mr Marseille pulled the big car into the garage we had long ago hired just a few blocks away from where we lived.

When he opened the trunk I heard the birds complain in their caw-caw manner, the sound climbing into the pitch black sky.

Were there seagulls in Philadelphia? Of course there were. But being so far inland, they did not fill the need.

That night, when I closed my eyes, I could still taste the salt on my tongue, and wondered about the French boy and girl.

38

The Home Depot on West Cheltenham Avenue was the closest location, geographically, to the Shawmont crime scene. There was no reason to think that the person responsible for the deaths of Robert and Edward Gillen, of Nicole Solomon, had purchased the rope, paint, and/or the section of two-by-eight common board pine at this store, but there was no reason not to.

If there was any facet common to the profile of a murderer it was that they tended to do things near their nest: shop, work, hunt.

Of the four items entered into evidence from that scene – the paint, the lumber, the hardware, and the rope – the one likely to yield a direction was the paint.

When Jessica and Byrne arrived, about ten a.m., the store was relatively empty. Home Depot opened at six a.m. on weekdays, and the contractors were in and out by seven-thirty or so.

When Jessica and Byrne approached the long stainless countertop there were two patrons ahead of them.

The paint sample they had gathered at the Nicole Solomon

crime scene was a small piece cut from the seat of the bench. According to CSU, and their presumptive tests, the paint – an exterior flat latex – had been applied less than three hours before Nicole Solomon's body had been found.

While they waited Jessica and Byrne looked at some of the folders located on the racks to the right of the counter. The number of colors available was staggering. There looked to be thousands.

They found a large brochure for Behr latex. Inside the color samples ranged from ultra pure white to something called Rosemary, which was a deep green. In between were colors such as Lemon Wedge, Pewter Gray, Crisp Celery, and Spicy Cayenne.

Byrne pointed to one of the paint samples on the third row of the large foldout brochure, something called Tranquil Retreat.

'This looks pretty close,' he said.

'I think our sample is a little lighter,' Jessica said. She pointed to a sample called Soft Feather. 'Maybe this one.'

'Welcome to Home Depot.'

Jessica and Byrne turned around. Before them stood a petite black woman, perhaps in her early forties. She wore a spotless Home Depot smock in the company's favorite color, orange. Her name tag read *Tonya T*.

'How may I help you today?' she asked.

'We just have a few questions about paint,' Byrne said.

'Then Tonya T is your girl,' the woman said. 'If it's about paint, and I don't know it, then it ain't about paint.'

Byrne gestured to the long rack of sample cards. 'Are all these colors really available?'

Tonya T nodded. 'And then some.'

'And you mix them all here in the store?'

'We mix them all back *here*,' she said, pointing to a computer mixing machine behind the stainless steel counter.

'I imagine getting the shade exactly right is a challenge,' Byrne said.

'Well, the computer does most of that. What the computer cannot do is tell you what color you're going to like in a few years.'

'I understand.'

Tonya T took a half-step back, looked Jessica and Byrne up and down. 'Now, see, I deal with a lot of couples such as yourself,' she said. 'Most of the time Tonya T maintains harmony. But once in a while the devil rears his ugly head in the Paint Pit.'

'Bad?' Byrne asked.

'Oh *laws*, yes,' she said. 'The discussions are usually over color selection or techniques of application, but I once saw a woman throw a can of Satin Espresso Rustoleum 2X at her man over nothing more than the quality of a drop cloth. Can you imagine?'

'I can see it happening,' Byrne said. 'Drop cloth choice is a personal thing.'

Tonya T just nodded. Apparently, Byrne was right. 'Caught him right in the kisser, too. I hope he has dental.'

'So, if we wanted to get some paint and have it match a paint sample *exactly*, how would we go about that?' Byrne asked.

'Well, if you still have the can, and the lid, you just bring it to Tonya T, and I can scan the code on the lid. If you don't have the lid, I can match from whatever paint is left in the can.'

'And it's fairly accurate?'

Tonya T took a step backward. Apparently, this was a personal affront. 'It's *always* accurate.'

Byrne held up a hand in surrender. He reached into his shoulder bag, retrieved the piece of wood, a four-by-four-inch section cut from the material on which Nicole Solomon had been seated. It had been processed, so there was no reason to handle it with care.

'We're looking to match this,' Byrne said.

Tonya T put on her glasses, took the material from Byrne. She took a few long moments to scrutinize it.

'Yeah. All right,' she said. 'I know this color. It's called Candle-light.'

'You could tell just by looking at it?'

Tonya T took off her glasses, if for no other reason than to glare at Kevin Byrne.

'Okay,' Byrne said. 'Fair enough.'

Tonya T smiled. 'Where are you thinking about using this?'

'We're not sure yet.'

Tonya T took a full step back. 'You two ain't married, are you?'

'No, ma'am,' Byrne said. He next took out his shield wallet.

Tonya T shook her head. 'I *thought* you had the look about you.'

'The look?'

'My daddy was a *police*. Big strong man like yourself. Thirty-six years.'

'Here in Philly?' Byrne asked.

'No, in South Carolina. He was a statie. He passed in '02.'

'Sorry.'

'Thank you.'

'The reason we're here is that the sample you have there turned up in a current investigation,' Byrne said. 'We'd like to know if someone has had it mixed recently.'

'And you want to find that person.'

'Very much so.'

'I can certainly tell you whether or not we recently mixed this color. But it will only be in this store, and only in the last ten days,' she said. 'We only keep the records for ten days.'

'All good,' Byrne said.

Another smile. 'This ain't *Undercover Boss*, is it?'

'Ma'am?'

Tonya T winked at Jessica. 'Come on over to the Paint Pit.'

Before she could take a step Byrne asked: 'Do you need to run this by your manager on duty?'

Eyebrows up, along with hackles. 'Tonya T *runs* this here department. I don't need to ask no damn MOD for permission to do nothin.' Especially for the PPD.'

While Tonya T searched through the records, looking for a recent order of Candlelight, Jessica and Byrne stood near one of the self-service checkout lanes.

Even with the store mostly empty there were a lot of people. Jessica began to feel that this line of inquiry was an even longer shot than she had thought on the way in.

'Wow,' Byrne said.

'What's wrong?'

Byrne pointed to the small LCD monitor over the register. 'That's me, isn't it?'

Jessica looked at the five-inch screen. 'Yeah,' she said. 'That's you.'

'Am I that fat?'

'You're not fat.'

Byrne turned to the side, sucked it in. 'So, what you're saying is, if you were watching this on TV, and this guy walked across the screen, you wouldn't think he was fat?'

Byrne had a point. He did look a little heavy on the monitor. But Jessica knew him well enough not to help him make that point.

'Television always adds ten pounds,' she said.

'Yeah, well, this isn't television. This is a security camera at Home Depot.'

'Same thing. And they don't really light a Home Depot all that well, unlike the *Real Housewives of Wherever*.'

Byrne seemed transfixed by the image. 'I can't believe I'm that big.'

Jessica was just about to continue with her intervention when she was saved by Tonya T approaching.

'I found it,' she said.

'Someone had Candlelight mixed?' Jessica asked.

'They did indeed,' she said. 'I wasn't here that day, but my associate Donte mixed a gallon of Candlelight a week ago Saturday at 10:06 a.m.'

'Do you know who it was mixed for?' she asked.

'That I don't know.'

'What about your surveillance cameras? Might there be a recording of people checking out around that time?'

'Now that's something you *will* have to talk to the MOD about. His name is Rufus and he is most irascible. I recommend having your handcuffs at the ready.'

On the way back to the car, they took a moment to absorb what they'd learned. It was not a break, but if they could put their hands on surveillance video that showed whoever bought the Candlelight paint, they would have a direction. They'd put in a request to have the surveillance video from that morning retrieved and put on a disk.

'Oh, I forgot to mention,' Byrne said, as he was unlocking the driver's side door.

'What?'

'I bought a house, and I might be getting back together with Donna.'

'Are you out of your fucking *mind*?'

Byrne just stared for a moment. They were standing in the middle of the Home Depot parking lot. If Byrne had expected to calmly discuss this on the way to the Roundhouse, he was clearly mistaken.

'Is that a trick question?' Byrne asked.

What Byrne had told Jessica – that he had bought a house once occupied by a murderer scheduled to be given a lethal injection in just a few weeks, no less – did not immediately compute.

'Jesus *Christ*. I mean, there's not enough real estate available in Philly?' Jessica asked. 'You have to buy a haunted house?'

'I'm sure there is other real estate, Jess. It's just that—'

'I can't *imagine* trying to sleep in a place like that. I'd levitate every time a branch hit a friggin' window.'

Jessica wasn't particularly superstitious, but that didn't mean there *wasn't* such things as ghosts. She'd always felt that there was plenty of trouble around without asking for it.

'I don't sleep anyway,' Byrne said. 'It will probably be a good fit.'

Byrne went on to tell her about his suspicions that Valerie Beckert had been responsible for the murders of other children. When he framed his decision in this way, it began to make *some* sense. Not a lot, but some. Jessica still wouldn't do it, but she was beginning to understand why *he* was doing it.

Byrne also told her about meeting with Theresa Woodman, about driving all the way out to Muncy, about talking to Father Tom Corey, about his brief but exasperating call to Brandon Altschuld, Esq.

'Why do you like her for the others?' she asked. 'Is there any evidence?'

Byrne looked out the window. 'I don't have anything except a feeling, Jess. Six kids are still out there. This house was ground zero.'

Jessica considered this. She knew how cases got under your skin. She had a few of her own. 'I guess I understand the why *you* part,' she said. 'But why *now*? Because of her status?'

'Partly,' Byrne said. 'Plus, If I didn't buy it, it was going to be demolished.'

'What do you expect to find there?'

Byrne took a few seconds. 'I really don't know. I just figure if

I can walk the same hallways she did, maybe something will come to me. It's worth a shot. I tried everything else I could think of.'

If it were anyone other than Kevin Byrne telling her this, she would take him to the nearest mental health facility and walk him through intake.

But her partner for these many years had never once been wrong about these intuitions – feelings he had never really discussed with her, and that was okay – so she did all she could do in a situation like this. She put a reassuring hand on his shoulder, and said:

'If something *does* come to you, or you need a sounding board, even in the middle of the night, you call me. You don't even look at the clock.'

Byrne said nothing.

'Kevin Francis?'

He turned to her and smiled. He knew that she only used both names when she was serious, just as his mother had.

'I will, partner,' he said. 'And thanks.'

Back at the Roundhouse the task force met. In addition to Jessica and Byrne were Dana Westbrook, Josh Bontrager, Maria Caruso, and John Shepherd. Shepherd was a veteran detective who had retired a few years earlier, gone into hotel security, then came back. An extreme rarity for the homicide unit, but they were extremely fortunate to have him back.

Byrne began with their findings at the ME's office.

'Do we have any idea what that number mark means?' Westbrook asked. 'By that I mean the context.'

'Not yet,' Byrne said. 'Jess is going to revisit the doll shop, and see if the owner there can shed some light on it.'

Westbrook nodded at Bontrager.

'Josh?'

'I tracked down the father,' Bontrager said.

'The boys' father?' Westbrook asked.

Bontrager nodded. 'His name is Michael John Gillen, forty-eight, late of Torresdale and Miquon. He used to be—'

'A judge,' Byrne said. 'Judge Gillen.'

'Right,' Bontrager said. 'You know him?'

'Not exactly, but I testified in his courtroom a few times,' Byrne said. 'They used to call him Killin' Gillen.' Byrne turned to Shepherd. 'You remember him, don't you, John?'

'Oh yeah,' Shepherd said.

'Where is he, Josh?'

'Well, he was in Germany at a conference,' Bontrager said. 'They've had some serious weather there in the past few days, apparently. He's been trying to get back to Philly. He should be here tomorrow.'

'So he knows about his boys,' Westbrook said.

Bontrager nodded. 'I talked to him early this morning.'

'How did he react?'

Bontrager shrugged. 'Dead silence for a long time. For a while there I thought the call was dropped. I tried to ask a few questions, but I didn't get far. I asked if he had any ideas about who might have done this.'

'What did he say?'

'He said he was on the bench for thirteen years. He said there were probably a thousand people who wanted to.'

It was true. A day didn't go by when members of the law enforcement community, as well as the judiciary, weren't threatened in some manner. But a cop's or a judge's family? There were stone-cold gangsters who would find this off limits.

'He was a municipal court judge?' Westbrook asked.

Byrne nodded. 'Yeah. Common pleas too, I think.'

Bontrager looked at his notes. 'He was both. About three years ago he ran for the Superior Court and lost. He went into private practice after that.'

'Criminal defense?' Westbrook asked.

'No,' Bontrager said. 'Real estate law. Some copyright stuff. No violence.'

They all knew that what was done to the Gillen boys, and Nicole Solomon, transcended street violence.

'Let's take a look at his cases for the last few years he was on the bench,' Westbrook said. 'Let's isolate the worst of the worst offenders he ruled on, and cross-reference them with what we have so far.'

Jessica thought this was a reasonable avenue of investigation, but she wasn't sure how this was going to connect with Nicole Solomon's murder.

Westbrook nodded at Jessica.

Jessica looked at her notes. 'We've tracked down the color and brand of the paint that was used at both the Solomon and Gillen murder scenes. It's called Candlelight and the Home Depot on Cheltenham Avenue mixed a gallon of it the day Nicole Solomon was killed.'

'They only mixed that color once?' Westbrook asked.

Jessica nodded. 'The records in the paint department only go back ten days, and only the records for that store are logged on the computer there. But, yes. Only one customer had that color mixed in the previous ten days.'

The detectives took this in.

'We've got a request of surveillance footage for the hour or so after the paint was mixed.'

'Of the checkout lanes.'

'Yes,' Jessica said. 'We should have it today.'

Westbrook nodded at Maria Caruso. She went through her notes. 'We've got preliminary results back on the cigarette Nicole was holding. It's a specialty brand called Gitanes Brunes. French manufacture, not available anymore in the US.'

'Why not?' Westbrook asked.

'Not sure,' Maria said. 'I talked to the owner of a specialty shop on Sansom called Avril 50, and he told me that both Gitanes and Gauloises are not allowed to be imported anymore. They might be available at duty-free shops, or through the mail. I'm looking into it.'

'Nicole was a smoker?' Westbrook asked.

'No,' Jessica said. 'Autopsy showed no signs of it. But what is strange is that there is lipstick on the filter, and it doesn't match the lipstick Nicole was wearing. CSU collected everything in the drawers in Nicole's bathroom – makeup, perfumes, cosmetics – and none of it matched.'

Westbrook looked to John Shepherd. He stepped forward.

'The stockings that were used to strangle Nicole Solomon – and it looks like the Gillen boys, too – are vintage, as well,' he said.

Shepherd put six photographs on the whiteboard. Three of them showed the heels of the stockings in close up. The others showed the tops.

He pointed to the close-up of the heel.

'The stockings are all the same manufacture, in two different shades. The material is a pure silk chiffonette,' Shepherd said. 'Reinforced Lisle tops with what's known as a French heel.'

Jessica took this in. The stockings were more than seventy years old.

'There are stains on all three that do not match the DNA profile of the victims. Two of the three have been mended with a contrasting silk thread. By that I mean mended *recently*.'

He pointed to the top of the stocking used in the Solomon murder. 'All three of the stockings have identical initials embroidered at the top. They all have *FdP*.'

'Do those initials show up anywhere else in the investigation?' Westbrook asked.

'Not yet.'

'Are silk stockings like these available anywhere? Maybe eBay or vintage clothes stores?'

'Both,' Shepherd said. 'I'm checking eBay now to see if transactions for any stockings with these initials were recently closed. Nothing so far.'

Jessica made a column in her notepad, drawing the common elements in the murders.

All the victims were sitting on a recently painted seat. Nicole Solomon on a train depot bench; the Gillen boys on swings, crudely made of a pine two-by-eight.

All the victims had a mark drawn into their scalps – the numbers 10, 11, and 12 – all made with a sharp needle, all made post-mortem.

At both crime scenes were found handwritten invitations, apparently inviting one victim to the next tea dance, the next murder scene.

At the Gillen crime scene was found a porcelain doll, an almost perfect replica of the first victim, Nicole Solomon.

Before meeting with the task force, Jessica had received a fax from Hell Rohmer. In it he said there was no doubt that the author of the second invitation was the same person who wrote the first.

After the meeting ended, Jessica and Byrne caught up to Josh Bontrager near the elevators.

'Hang on, Josh,' Byrne said.

'What's up?'

'How long ago were Gillen and his wife divorced?' Byrne asked.

Bontrager flipped through his notes. 'Around ten years ago.'

'And he moved out then?'

'I can't say for sure, but that would be my guess.'

Byrne thought for a few moments. 'Maybe David Solomon wasn't calling Mary Gillen,' Byrne said. 'Maybe he was calling Judge Gillen, and it was the last phone number he had for him.'

'David Solomon had no criminal record,' Jessica said. 'Neither did Nicole.'

'It had to be something else. Do we know how long David Solomon had been a social worker?'

'I don't know about that, but I know he worked at AdvantAge for nine years,' Bontrager said.

'What about before then?'

'No idea,' Bontrager said. 'I'll find out.'

'Let's see if he ever did any work for the city or the county.'

Before leaving for the day, Jessica revisited the ViCAP database, inputting the new data – the presence of a doll, victims posed on swings, victims given magic mushrooms. She found no signature that even came close to the combination of these elements.

She also did a general keyword search with some of the data. The results seemed to be even more scattershot. She got hits for songs by Ella Fitzgerald and Big Joe Turner, videos on how to paint a swing set, as well as a link to the 1957 film *Silk Stockings* with Fred Astaire and Cyd Charisse.

The one hit that seemed to have an outside chance of relevance – as in way outside – was a painting called *The Swing* by a man named Jean-Honoré Fragonard. In it, a young man hides in the bushes, watching a young woman being pushed on a swing by an elderly man.

Jessica put her notes on all this into an email to Byrne, shut down the terminal.

She looked at her watch. Late already. She had ten minutes to get halfway across town.

39

The bar was about half full. A standalone low brick building, The Ark was located at 52nd and Chestnut, near the heart of University City in West Philadelphia, an unincorporated neighborhood that was home to both the University of Pennsylvania and Drexel University.

There were enough people in their late twenties and thirties in the bar that Vincent and Jessica did not attract much attention. It was one of those West Philly taverns that brought in people from the universities, including faculty and grad students, as well as locals.

One of Vincent Balzano's great attributes – one that made him a great undercover detective – was his ability to look like anyone he wanted to be. Tonight he wore a Flyers jersey and jeans, a three-day beard. He looked like the guy who delivered the beer. Jessica wore a short leather jacket and her favorite black Levi's. No one gave them a second look.

They made their way to the middle of the bar, sat on stools. The bartender was a man in his mid-twenties, probably a grad student. He gave Jessica his best younger guy smile, Vincent a nod. He put a pair of napkins on the bar. 'Welcome,' he said. 'What can I get you?'

'I'll have a diet Coke,' Jessica said. 'And a Miller Lite.'

'You got it.'

He took a few steps away, put some ice in a glass with a scoop, put the glass beneath the Diet Coke tap. While it was filling he grabbed a Miller Lite from the cooler, twisted off the cap. From order to serve was no more than thirty seconds. This was not his first bartending job.

'My name's Kurt,' he said. 'If you need anything else, just holler.'

Jessica leaned in. 'We're supposed to meet Denny Wargo,' she said. 'Have you seen him?'

Kurt held Jessica's gaze a few seconds, as if summing her up. Jessica knew she could be mistaken for a lot of things, but trouble was not among them. Besides, she'd done things like this a hundred times. She could stare down just about anyone. A few seconds later the bartender looked around the bar. Left, right, back to the left.

'I don't see him,' Kurt said.

Jessica pushed a five across the bar. 'Let me know if he comes in.'

The five was off the bar in a flash. 'Will do.'

Jessica turned, leaned against the bar, sipped her Coke. Suddenly the crowd looked a lot younger to her. When she had gone to Temple – the first time, when she got her undergraduate degree in Criminal Justice – the people in this bar would have skewed older. On the rare instance when she'd gone out with some of her classmates in law school – her second time at Temple – she felt like somebody's mom. Now she felt like a fossil.

At the jukebox, someone put on House of Pain's 'Jump Around,' and the place went nuts. The song was a little too raucous for someone of Jessica's refined sensibilities, but at least it was her era.

A few songs later Jessica found Kurt at the end of the bar. She saw that he was looking at the door. Jessica couldn't see what he was looking at, but when he turned to look at Jessica, and nodded, she knew that the man they had come to see, Denny Wargo, had arrived.

'We're on,' Jessica said to Vincent.

A few moments later Jessica saw a man in his late twenties making his way over to them. He wore a black down vest and a blue flannel shirt, beige chinos, expensive watch. He had about him the look of the over-privileged and under-employed.

'Hey,' he said to Vincent. 'You Hector?'

'Yeah,' Vincent said. 'Denny?'

'Yeah.'

The two men shook hands. Vincent gestured at Jessica. 'This is Marta.'

The man looked Jessica up and down, nodded. 'How ya doin.'' He looked back at Vincent. 'You a cop?'

'Yep.'

The man just stared. Vincent smiled.

Wargo returned a nervous smile of his own. Vincent clapped the man on the shoulder, said: 'Don't say I didn't warn you.'

Wargo clearly didn't know what to do. He decided to believe Vincent was bullshitting. Vincent Balzano was very good at this. He started laughing and Wargo laughed with him.

'What are you drinking?' Vincent asked.

'Johnny Black double, neat.'

'Dream on, sport.'

Vincent ordered the man a Miller Lite.

Kurt pulled the bottle, uncapped it, slid it over. He made himself busy at the other end of the bar. It was clear he had a pretty good idea what Denny Wargo did for a living, and he wanted some real estate between himself and the transaction.

Wargo sipped his beer. After what he considered the right amount of foreplay, he said: 'Luis said you guys want some 'shrooms.'

Luis Rodriguez was a confidential informant that sometimes worked with the Narcotics Unit. If Vincent had thought there was a possibility that this night might end badly, he would not have used Luis for the meet. Once you burn a CI, that CI stayed burned.

'You double parked?' Vincent asked.

'What?'

'You in a hurry?'

'No, I was just—'

'Relax, Denny,' Vincent said. 'Enjoy your beer.'

Wargo looked to Jessica. Another nervous smile. Jessica began to wonder if Denny Wargo was cut out for this business. On the other hand, he wasn't selling heroin or crack. The worlds of hallucinogens and hard-core street drugs were night and day.

Thirty minutes later they stood at the back of the small parking lot next to The Ark. The temperature had dropped. Jessica wished she had worn something other than her leather jacket.

'So,' Wargo said. 'You're looking for 'shrooms.'

Vincent nodded. 'Luis said you've got some satori.'

'The best there is.' Wargo looked up the street, back. 'But they're expensive.'

Vincent held the man's stare for an uncomfortable amount of time. He then reached into the front pocket of his jeans, pulled a roll that could choke a Clydesdale.

Wargo's eyes widened. He reached into his pocket, took out a twist of baggie, handed it to Vincent. When Vincent didn't hand him any money, he knew.

'You're not Hector and Marta, are you?'

Vincent smiled. 'Man, haven't you ever seen *Scarface*?'

Wargo shook his head. 'Damn, man. I *knew* I'd heard those names together somewhere.'

They were talking about the scene when Al Pacino, as Tony Montana, goes up to the motel room to meet with the Colombians. The woman on the bed – the hard-looking woman with the machine gun – was called Marta. Jessica wasn't thrilled with the casting decision, but she'd done enough undercover work to know you take the role given, and do your best.

Jessica loved Al Pacino, but she'd never understood the appeal of that movie.

'Man, I *asked* if you were cops.'

'And I told you the truth.'

'Am I busted?' Wargo asked.

Vincent gave the question the appropriate weight. 'That depends.'

A look of relief came across Wargo's face. It turned quickly into one of concern. 'On what?' he asked.

'The answer to my next question.'

'Okay.'

'I need to know who has bought this recently.'

'The satori?'

'Yes, Denny. The Schedule One, illegal narcotic I have in my hand at this moment.'

'Nobody.'

'And why is that?'

'It's a little bit beyond the college crowd, price-wise. And Pink Floyd isn't touring.'

The joke, if that's what it was, fell flat.

'How did my guy get this drug, Denny? We're not going to part company until this question is answered to my complete satisfaction.'

Wargo took a few seconds. 'The only way to get this cheaper is to grow it yourself, but growing mushrooms is not that easy, okay? It's really easy to catch a mold, then the whole batch goes south.'

'I'm listening.'

'There are a few things that people need to start a grow. Syringes and substrates. I sell those, too.'

Vincent said nothing. Wargo kept talking.

'There is this one guy I've sold syringes and some satori substrates, too.'

'More than once?'

Wargo nodded. 'More than once.'

'What does this tell you?'

'It tells me he's no chemist.'

'Who is this guy?'

'Just a guy,' Wargo said. 'Young fella. Name is Mercy or something.'

'Mercy?'

Wargo shrugged. 'What do *I* know? You told me your name was Hector.'

Vincent let the attitude slide for the moment. 'How young?'

'A freshman, maybe. Maybe a sophomore.'

'He goes to Penn or Drexel?'

'I don't know.'

'How did he find you?'

'How does anyone find me? How did *you* guys find me? A guy who knows a guy who knows a guy.'

'How does he get hold of you?'

Wargo held up his phone. 'He has my cell number.'

'When was the last time he called?'

'Maybe a month ago,' Wargo said.

Vincent held out his hand. Wargo started to roll his eyes, thought better of it. He handed over his cell phone.

Vincent began to scroll through recent calls. 'About when was this?'

Wargo thought for a few seconds. 'Late October.'

'Remember the day of the week?'

Wargo snapped his fingers. 'I do. Funny the way you remember things.'

Vincent looked up, waited. 'It's much funnier when you answer the question, Denny.'

'It was a Saturday.'

'And you remember this how?'

'I get my daughter on weekends.'

Jessica could see that her husband wanted to mention that this guy was doing drug deals on the phone while he had custody of his daughter, but he'd save that for later.

'When did you get the call?' Vincent asked.

'Afternoon,' Wargo said. 'Late. Three or four.'

Vincent went to the second last Saturday in October. He showed Wargo the screen, scrolled slowly down. There were a dozen incoming calls between three and five p.m.

'That's it,' he said, pointing to one of the numbers, a 215 area code, meaning it was Philadelphia metropolitan.

'You're sure.'

'Yeah,' Wargo said. 'I know all the others.'

Vincent wrote down the number. If Jessica knew her husband – one of the most feared narcotics detectives in the city – she knew that he memorized another half-dozen numbers from Wargo's phone. It was an uncanny ability he had.

Rule one for drug dealers, Jessica thought: Never hand your phone to a narco unless you have to.

Vincent handed the phone back, let Wargo twist for a few seconds.

'Can you describe this guy to a sketch artist?' Vincent finally asked.

For Wargo, the night just got worse. He looked across the parking lot for a second or two. Vincent Balzano, at his most patient, was like a Rottweiler looking at a brisket. That is, not so much.

He grabbed Wargo by the wrist. 'All right. Let's go.'

'Wait!' Wargo said. 'Yeah, okay. I can describe him.'

Vincent pulled the man close. 'Fuck with me one more second, Denny. One second.'

'I'm sorry.'

After the right amount of time, Vincent let go. He then reached into his pocket, handed Wargo one of his blue cards. Blue cards, while not technically a get-out-of-jail card, when presented meant that Vincent would get a call the next time Wargo ran afoul of the law, and was caught at it. Might never happen. Probably would.

'This is a one-time only call,' Vincent said. 'If you fuck up too badly, or you sell to kids, I will personally supervise your trip to hell.'

Wargo just stared at the ground.

Vincent continued. 'You are now going to drive to the Roundhouse. We will follow you, and walk you in. When you're there, you will give a highly detailed description to our sketch artist.'

Wargo listened.

'Run one stop sign, or make one funky turn, and the next year of your life will look like *Scared Straight*. Feel me?'

Wargo nodded.

'Say it out loud.'

'I feel you.'

'That's the Denny Wargo we have all come to know and love,' Vincent said. 'Which one is your car?'

Wargo pointed to a ten-year-old Taurus. Jessica had spent half her time in the department in one just like it. Truly glamorous. Maybe the 'shroom business wasn't so good.

Vincent nodded to the driveway leading to 52nd Street. 'We'll be right there.'

Wargo turned to leave. Vincent put a hand on his arm.

'By the way,' Vincent said. 'They *are* touring.'

'Who?'

'Pink Floyd. Next summer. Let me know if you need tickets. I know a guy who knows a guy who knows a guy.'

40

At ten o'clock the next morning Byrne received a call from the Loss Prevention manager of the Cheltenham Avenue Home Depot. While Jessica followed up on the doll they had found at the Gillen crime scene, Byrne took a ride back to the big box store.

The morning's status report included the information that Jessica and Vincent had gotten the night before, that being the name 'Mercy,' a suspect sketch, and a phone number, which turned out to be a pay phone at a gas station near the West Ridge Pike exit on the Blue Route.

These were all long shots – the possibility that the man who purchased the mushroom-growing accessories from the dealer was not the man they sought, or was simply someone who grew the mushrooms, and sold them to someone else, was likely – but every lead needed to be followed. There was, at that moment, a detective from West Division sitting on the pay phone, and the homicide unit was running the name 'Mercy' through NCIC.

While at the Home Depot, in addition to watching the surveillance footage, Byrne decided to pick up twenty-five gallons of exterior paint for his new house, an order Josh Bontrager promised to pick up later in the day. Josh drove a Subaru Forrester.

While Byrne was there he had a brief conversation with one Donte Williams, the young man who had mixed the gallon of Candlelight. Donte said he recalled mixing the paint, but couldn't remember the customer. He said the reason for this was that the customer probably knew exactly what he wanted. If he'd had to do some selling, it would be more likely that he'd remember.

If it had been a woman – any woman – Donte said he'd remember. He was asked to sit in when Byrne watched the surveillance video.

The manager of the Loss Prevention office at Home Depot was Tony Walton. African American, in his mid-fifties, Walton was a gregarious man in a job that would surely chew up and spit out anyone who thought they would eliminate the petty theft at a store with over ten thousand items on its shelves, a lot of it able to fit in a pocket.

Gregarious, however, did not mean he was an easy mark. Even in the short time they spoke, Byrne could see that nothing slipped by Tony Walton.

They met in the cluttered security room, where there were a half-dozen monitors, showing two dozen vantage points in and around the busy store.

Walton offered coffee; Byrne accepted. It was surprisingly good for hardware store java. They sat in front of one of the monitors. Walton took out a book of discs, pulled one that had the date in question written on it in black felt tip pen.

As he slipped it into the optical drive of the desktop computer under the table, Byrne asked, 'Were you ever on the job?'

Walton nodded. 'I was,' he said.

'Here in Philly?'

'No,' he said. 'I was in Pittsburgh.'

'What squads did you work?'

'I was a detective in Zone Three.'

'Do you miss it?' Byrne asked.

'Only every day.'

The two men kicked around the vagaries of the job, the life. Then it was time for business.

'I pulled this from the time frame that the paint you were asking about was mixed,' Walton said. 'The time stamp on this video is for three minutes after the paint was mixed.'

'Are we sure that this subject is buying the Candlelight paint?'

'We are not,' Walton said. 'But I ran the register receipts starting at the same moment the paint was mixed, and moving forward for the next thirty minutes. There were only eight cans of paint purchased in that time, only four of them were gallons. Two of those customers bought a number of other things – plywood, drywall, one bought a space heater. Of the remaining two, only one bought only the paint.'

Byrne took this all in. He was grateful for the work Walton had done, the thought he'd put into this. Once a cop, right?

'Now this might lead to nothing, but if this is your guy, this will be your guy.'

'Okay,' Byrne said.

Donte Williams sauntered into the room.

'Thanks for finding the time,' Walton said.

'Huh?'

Walton turned to Byrne. 'Ready?'

'I am.'

'Here we go.'

Walton hit a key on the computer keyboard, and an image came onto the monitor. The angle was from above and to the left of the checkout line, the one closest to the north exit doors. This was one of the two open lines.

The first man in line had what appeared to be a half-dozen lengths of PVC electrical conduit, along with a Home Depot plastic bucket. Byrne knew that, for some odd reason, Home Depot did not offer its customers handheld shopping baskets. Either they thought baskets were a little too fey for their testosterone-heavy clientele, or they wanted their clientele to accidentally buy an orange bucket on every visit.

The guy with the conduit wasn't fooled. He looked like a tradesman. He dumped the contents of the bucket on the counter, and put the bucket underneath.

Byrne watched this with casual interest. His focus was on the next man in line. He felt that familiar feeling, that low level electrical current begin to pass through him, that feeling that he might be laying eyes on a suspect for a very first time.

Byrne tapped the monitor. 'That's him?'

'That's him,' Walton said.

Byrne turned to Donte. 'Do you think this might be the guy you mixed the gallon of Candlelight for?'

Donte leaned in, squinted at the monitor. 'Could be,' he said. 'I don't know. I mix a lot of paint, yo.'

On screen, from above and behind, the man with the paint appeared to be young – early twenties perhaps. He had dark hair, swept back from his forehead. He wore a well-tailored dark overcoat.

When the man with the conduit was finished, the man behind him stepped forward. He put the gallon can of paint on the counter. The young lady behind the counter took it, and swiped her handheld scanner across the bar code on the can's lid. She didn't put it in a bag, but instead put on a PAID sticker.

As the man reached into his coat pocket – Byrne noted immediately he did not retrieve his wallet from his pants pocket, but rather from an inside pocket of his coat or suit – he said some-thing to the checkout girl, something that made her smile. Byrne noted that the girl curled one foot behind the other leg, a rather obvious sign that she was being flirted with, or charmed at the very least.

This was the first moment where there might have been a breakthrough. If the man paid for the purchase by credit card, they would have a substantial lead. But there was no such luck.

The man handed her cash, then returned his billfold to his inner coat pocket.

As he walked out of the top of the frame, heading for the exit, he paused for a moment. He set down the can of paint, buttoned his coat, reached into a side pocket and retrieved a pair of gloves. He slipped them on, then once more picked up the can.

At the top of the frame, at the upper left-hand corner, a woman approached him. Byrne could barely see anything, other than she wore a knee-length overcoat, and wore low heels.

The two hesitated a moment, then they were gone.

Walton stopped the recording.

'Do we have video of them leaving the store?' Byrne asked.

Walton shook his head. 'No,' he said. 'We have cameras on the parking lot, but they only fire when we need them. Keeping video of the lot 24/7 is expensive. This is all we have, I'm afraid.'

He rewound the recording, let it play again. There was no mistake. The man waited for a moment until he was joined by a woman.

Byrne wondered: *Wife? Girlfriend? Sister?*

The two did not appear to join hands, so it really could be any of the above.

Walton ran the recording one more time, stopped it just as the man crossed the end of the checkout lane. For an instant the man turned to his left, and they saw a very fuzzy profile. The subject was white, no older than twenty-five, well dressed. Although they couldn't be certain, he appeared to be wearing a white shirt and dark tie.

'What do you think, Donte?' Walton asked.

Byrne turned to look at Donte. The kid was checking his Twitter feed on his phone. Byrne wanted to give Donte a few hours in the basement of the Roundhouse, just to give him an idea of the importance of this. He decided to let it go for now.

'Go mix some paint,' Walton said.

'Now?'

'Now.'

Donte sniffed, slow-rolled out of the office.

When he was gone Byrne asked: 'Can I get a printout of that frame?'

'You got it.' Walton hit a few keys. Seconds later the laser printer on the floor beneath the desk came to life. Walton grabbed the printout and handed it to Byrne.

Byrne thanked the man. They made their parting remarks.

At the door Byrne asked: 'Can I ask a personal question?'

'Are you really a cop?'

'I am.'

Walton smiled. 'Then there's no such thing as personal.'

'May I ask how old you are?'

Walton told him. He was younger than Byrne had originally thought. Just a few years older than Byrne, actually.

'How do you like this job?' Byrne asked.

Walton shrugged. 'I'd rather be chasing brown women around Bimini, but it pays the bills. Some of them anyway.' He fixed Byrne in a knowing look. 'You want to know what you're going to do when you take your twenty.'

'Thirty, actually.'

Walton looked impressed. 'To tell the truth, I never thought I'd be doing this. What I mean is, you have no idea the volume of theft from a store like this. You learn really quickly what matters here and what doesn't. I didn't like being a housecat at first, but the job grows on you.'

On the way out of the store, as Byrne stood at the Pro Desk, paying for his own paint purchase, he glanced up, at the smoked glass dome cameras hanging from the ceiling, wondering if Tony Walton was watching. He also observed the checkout lane where his subject had paid for the Candlelight paint, as well as the door the young man had exited, but not before meeting up with his companion.

Shut the door, the woman said on the piano recording.

Were they looking for a man *and* a woman?

Byrne had the afternoon off, but his mind would not leave the image of the man and woman on the surveillance tape.

It was with that mental image that he stood in his driveway, measured the small flower beds. He hadn't even considered the landscaping costs.

Before he could write down the dimension he heard a soft thump. Then a second thump, which was a bit louder than the first.

Then he heard a baby cry. Or was it?

He stepped into the driveway, trying to determine where the cry came from when heard another thump – this time quite loud. And it was accompanied by a louder cry.

He stepped into the flower bed next to the house.

There, in the bushes, just a few feet away, was a cat. Or, more accurately – at least from his perspective – a former cat. The cat was stretched out on the mulch below the spirea, a pair of fallen bricks on its head.

Bricks that would almost certainly be on top of Byrne's head if he had not stepped into the driveway. He stepped back just as another few bricks tumbled off the roof, a safe distance away.

The chimney was crumbling.

He stepped back to the cat, gently removed the bricks. The cat was dead.

'Ah, shit.'

Byrne looked around for something with which to cover the animal. He retrieved a small tarp he kept in the trunk of his car. When he tried to put it over the cat, the cat opened its eyes, and extended all four paws, claws out, ready to rumble.

'How is it?'

Byrne had made a call to a friend in the Animal Protective Services, and found the nearest vet.

The vet gave him a sideways glance. 'It?'

'Well, yeah,' Byrne said. 'The cat. How is it?'

'Not your cat then, I take it?'

'No.' Byrne decided against telling the doctor how he and the cat met.

'Well, the cat – it's a he, by the way – is just fine. Just a concussion.'

Byrne had not had a pet of any kind in a long time. Although it made perfect sense, he had not considered that cats could suffer a concussion. Of course they could. Cats and dogs had brains. Where there are brains, there are concussions.

'Great,' Byrne said. 'So he's going to be okay?'

'He is.'

Byrne pulled into the driveway, looked over at the cat. He still appeared to be a little groggy, perhaps wondering who threw the bricks at him.

'It wasn't me, buddy.'

Byrne opened the car door, the cat leapt out, followed him. He went in the house, grabbed a couple of small Dixie Cups and a bottle of Jameson. He stepped back onto the porch, tore off the top of one of the cups, poured a half-inch of whiskey into it. The cat, who had been lying on the porch, perked. He struggled to his feet, sniffing the air. Byrne pushed the cup closer.

'This is probably wrong on so many levels, but if anybody has earned a thimbleful of Irish today, it's you.'

Byrne poured himself a shot, tapped his cup against the cat's cup. They both took a sip. The cat looked at him. No reaction at all. No cat-grimace. Byrne wondered if he'd done this before.

A few minutes later Byrne stepped back into the driveway, looked at the chimney. The mortar that had at one time been tuck-pointed between the courses of bricks – the tuck pointing that had disintegrated to the point where the bricks came loose – was scattered along the shingles. He picked up the cat, pointed to the chimney, by way of explanation. The cat wasn't interested.

'On the outside chance that you and I meet up again, I'm going to call you Tuck.' He put Tuck down in pretty much the same place he had found him. The cat struggled to maintain his legs, but soon found them. He glanced up at Byrne and then, with a speed and strength Byrne would not have thought possible – considering the brick concussion and the shot of Irish – took off like a rocket.

'Tuck,' Byrne said. 'Nice to have met you. Next round is on you.'

41

When Jessica and Sophie entered the shop, Jessica immediately smelled the scent of lavender.

She scanned the room, did not immediately see Miss Emmaline. Instead she saw that there were two teenaged girls dusting the shelves.

'Hi, ladies,' one of them said. She had short blond hair, and wore a U Penn sweatshirt. 'Welcome to The Secret World!'

'Hi,' Sophie said.

'Is Miss Emmaline around?' Jessica asked.

'Sure,' the girl said. 'She's in the back. Do you want me to get her?'

'Maybe you could just tell her I'm here, and ask if it's okay if I come back to her sitting room. My name is Jessica. She's expecting me.'

'Sure thing.'

The other girl – taller, with deep auburn hair – slipped on her coat and gloves. 'Got to catch my bus,' she said. 'See you next week.' A few moments later she left the shop.

The blond girl got down from her step stool, crossed the shop.

'I'll tell Miss Emmaline you're here.' She parted the curtains that led to Miss Emmaline's parlor.

Before Jessica stepped through she looked at her daughter.

Sophie was starstruck. She'd had a few dolls when she was younger, but it was never anything like an obsession. As far as Jessica knew, none of her dolls had been off the shelves in her bedroom for a few years.

When Jessica turned in the doorway, and saw the expression on Sophie's face as she scanned the shelves, it looked like all of that was about to change.

Jessica hoped not. Swimming was a lot less expensive than collecting antique dolls.

The blond girl stepped back into the shop.

'Miss Emmaline said to just come on back.'

'Thanks,' Jessica said. 'Is it okay if my daughter looks around? She won't be a bother.'

'Of course!' she said. 'She'll be fine.'

'I won't be long, sweetie,' Jessica said to Sophie.

No answer. Sophie's mouth was open, but she didn't make a sound.

Today Miss Emmaline wore a teal dress and a single strand of pearls. Her brilliant white hair was pulled back into a single braid.

Jessica hoped she'd be able to pull off such elegance and grace at Miss Emmaline's age. Actually, she hoped to be able to pull it off next week.

'Thanks for seeing me,' Jessica said.

'Not at all, my dear. You are always welcome here.'

Jessica put down her shoulder bag. 'I've brought the doll with me.'

Miss Emmaline said nothing.

'Do you have a few moments to take a look at it?'

'Of course,' she said. 'Shall I put on gloves?'

'Only if you want to. The doll has been processed.'

Miss Emmaline raised an eyebrow. 'Processed?'

'What I mean is, we've processed the doll for fingerprints. It's okay if you touch it.'

Miss Emmaline looked at Jessica's bag for a moment, back at Jessica. 'So, what you are saying is that this doll is somehow relevant to a crime?'

Jessica had thought this might have been obvious, but she could see how it might not.

'It was found at a crime scene, yes, ma'am.'

Miss Emmaline nodded. The moment had taken on gravitas, but perhaps not more than Miss Emmaline had experienced in her eighty-plus years.

'May I?' Jessica asked.

'Please.'

Jessica unzipped the bag, took the doll out, set it on the table. Miss Emmaline put on her glasses.

The woman nodded.

'I thought as much, but there is no substitute for having an item right in front of you.'

'Ma'am?'

'This is a bisque doll, made in the style of the French.' She ran a finger gently over the doll's face. 'In the early twentieth century the French and the Germans were the undisputed masters of the craft, you see. For more than eighty years, no one could touch them in terms of quality and design and craftsmanship.'

'So you're saying this doll is an antique?'

'No,' she said. 'It's a Sauveterre.'

'Could you spell that for me?'

Miss Emmaline did. Jessica wrote it down. As she did this, the blond girl from the front brought a pot of tea, set it down on the corner table next to Miss Emmaline's chair.

'Would you like a cup, my dear?' Miss Emmaline asked.

'No, thanks,' Jessica said. 'I'm fine.'

The girl walked back into the shop as Miss Emmaline poured herself a cup, and then turned her attention back to the doll.

'The face has been painted over, of course. These are not the original eyes.'

The lab had confirmed as much, but Jessica wanted an expert's opinion. The eyes were a dead-on match to Nicole Solomon's eyes.

'I would say the hair is different as well.'

'The hair is newer?'

'No, but I believe it has been dyed,' she said. 'And then there's the clothing.'

'What do you mean?'

'The clothing is modern. Even in terms of comparison to a Sauveterre. Whoever dressed this doll sewed the clothing herself.'

'*Her*self?'

Miss Emmaline looked up.

'Funny how we believe ourselves to be tolerant and open-minded,' she said. 'But when presented with something that dovetails with our preconceptions, we just presume. I just assumed that the person who sewed this clothing was a female.'

'Don't worry about it.'

'Still, I am probably correct in this. The stitching is a hand-kerchief stitch. Very fine work.'

'What can you tell me about Sauveterre?'

'Not much, I'm afraid. He was French, but not in the league of the major doll makers. Those would be Bru and Jumeau, of course. Jean Marie Sauveterre, in essence, made replicas of their works. Rather hastily made and obvious copies.'

'He was from France?'

'Originally. The rumor was that he went a bit mad, then moved here to the States.'

'Do you have any of his dolls here?'

'I did have a few, but I believe they were sold.'

Jessica consulted her notes. 'The last time I was here you mentioned that doll makers sometimes mark their dolls on the back of the head.'

The crime lab had examined the Nicole Solomon doll's head, and found the number 10, which matched the killer's mark on Nicole's scalp.

'That's correct.'

'Would you happen to know how many dolls Jean Marie Sauveterre made?'

'I don't know.' She gestured to the bookshelf against the far wall. There, on the top shelf, were a dozen bound reference books. 'I'd have to do a little research on that. But if an answer to your query is to be found, it will be found here.'

Jessica took a moment, prepared her thoughts. 'I think I know the answer to this, but I'll ask it anyway ... '

Miss Emmaline smiled. 'I've always found this to be the best way to find out what you need to know.'

'Who collects dolls?'

Miss Emmaline gave her answer some time. 'Dolls are ancient, as is the practice of collecting them. Doll collecting is similar to the collecting of anything, as you might imagine. Some, as with those who collect stamps, or paintings, or even classic cars, do so for the beauty of the object. Others care only about the acquisition, and many more care only about the value, treating an object – even a rare and exquisite object – like a commodity.'

'So there is no one type of person who collects dolls.'

'Collecting dolls can be a wonderful way to be part of a community, a worldwide community,' she said. 'On the other hand, some of the most antisocial people I've ever met have been doll collectors. To them, it is akin to hoarding.'

There was something here. Jessica just couldn't see it yet. She was just about to ask another question when the blond girl poked her head through the curtains.

'I'm going to leave for the day, Miss Emmaline.'

'Okay. Thank you, *chérie*.'

'*Je t'adore*.'

It was only a few seconds later that Jessica realized that she was holding her breath. She heard the bell over the front door of the shop tinkle, then the door close.

Seconds later she found herself on her feet.

'The girl, the one who was just here,' Jessica said.

'What about her?'

'When she left, what did she say?'

Miss Emmaline thought for a few agonizingly long moments. 'She said "*je t'adore*". Why?'

'What does that mean?'

'It is French. It is a term of endearment. It means "I adore you".'

In an instant Jessica was out of the back room. She found Sophie sitting alone in the shop, leafing through a doll catalog.

'That girl,' Jessica said. 'The one who just left. Which way did she go?'

Sophie pointed north. 'That way.'

Jessica ran out of the shop and onto the street. There were a number of people passing by, perhaps thirty or forty people on the block, on both sides of the street. Young men on cell phones, women with young children, older people walking slowly to and from the corner store.

There was no blond girl.

Jessica reentered the store.

'What's wrong, Mom?' Sophie asked.

Jessica locked the front door to the shop. 'Everything's fine, sweetie.'

Sophie looked worried. 'I don't think so.'

'Come stand back here,' Jessica said, indicating a spot behind the counter, near the doorway into the back.

Sophie didn't ask any more questions. Being the daughter of two police officers, she knew there were different states of alert. Yellow for thunderstorms. Red for the boogeyman. She knew instinctively that this was one of the latter.

As Jessica stepped around the counter, there were two certainties in her mind. One: There was no doubt that, on the recording, the tape they'd found at the Gillen crime scene – the recording of the piano music – the girl on the tape did not say 'shut the door.'

She said '*je t'adore*.' 'I adore you.'

The other thing about which Jessica was certain was that the girl who spoke the words on that tape had just left the shop.

When Jessica walked into the back room Miss Emmaline was in her chair, her eyes wide open, her hands folded in her lap. She looked to be in a trance. Or worse. Jessica vaulted across the room.

'Miss Emmaline,' she said. 'Are you okay?'

For a long moment, the woman said nothing. Jessica reached down, felt for a pulse. She found one.

'Miss Emmaline.'

No response.

Standing this close to the woman, Jessica noticed that the scent of lavender perfume had an undernote, something she had not noticed before. She glanced at the teacup on the table. She picked it up, sniffed it. There, beneath the aroma of tea leaves, was something else, something earthen and organic, something that smelled like . . .

Mushrooms.

The blond girl had brought her the tea.

42

As much as I liked working in the shop, I disliked wearing the blond wig. It was quite itchy, and I don't think it was all that flattering. I wore it at Mr Marseille's insistence. A compromise, if you will.

I had always fancied being a shop girl, and when we visited Miss Emmaline's store for the first time – in search of a pair of crystal eyes – I saw the *Help Wanted* sign in the window, and knew that I wanted to work there. I felt it was meant to be.

But now that the police had found The Secret World, I knew I couldn't go back there.

I placed the wig in a trashcan.

As I boarded the bus I thought of how I would miss the shop, and all the beautiful dolls. I thought of Miss Emmaline and her many kindnesses. I felt terrible about making her our special tea – due to her advanced age I feared the consequences to her well-being might be dire – but I made it in the hope that the woman from the police might have some, therefore buying me and Mr Marseille some time to complete our preparations.

I thought of the many people I had met at The Secret World, how each and every one of them had a place on my shelf.

As the bus passed the shop, I looked through the front window, perhaps for the final time. I thought of my new friend, Sophie.

I began thinking about how I might paint her beautiful brown eyes on a Sauveterre.

BOOK TWO

Mr Marseille

43

They met in the emergency room intake of Penn Presbyterian Hospital.

When Byrne arrived Jessica was on the phone with Dana Westbrook, giving her a status report. Westbrook told Jessica that detectives from the homicide unit were currently searching the doll shop for any leads on the shop girl, and that neighborhood interviews were underway.

When Jessica saw Byrne crossing the ER waiting room, she signed off. She took a few minutes to fill Byrne in on the meeting with the dealer, Denny Wargo. She showed Byrne the sketch, which turned out to be none too detailed. All three times Wargo had met with the young man – the man he called Mercy – had been in the parking lot of The Ark. According to Wargo, they did their deals car window to car window, so at best, he got a three-quarter profile at night.

The sketch was a white male, dark hair, no facial hair. Not much to go on.

The good news was that, if this particular strain of mushroom –

a chemical found in the bloodstreams of Nicole Solomon, as well as Robert and Edward Gillen – was purchased or grown in Philadelphia, it came through Denny Wargo.

Both Jessica and Byrne were all but certain that this sketch was of the man they sought.

'How is Miss Emmaline?' Byrne asked.

'She's sedated. They're calling her condition stable.'

'Has she said anything else?'

Jessica shook her head. 'No. I only had a few minutes with her in the ambulance and in the ER before they kicked me out. She wasn't making sense.'

'And you're sure?' Byrne asked. 'You're sure about the girl who was in the shop?'

'I've never been more positive about anything in my life,' Jessica said. 'The girl who was working in that shop is the girl on that tape. I've listened to it ten more times in the past hour. It's her.'

'And you say there was another girl working there with her?'

Jessica nodded. 'CSU is processing the shop now. Dana told me that they haven't found any pay stubs for either girl yet, but that's probably because Miss Emmaline paid the girls in cash, under the table. West Division detectives are fanning out in the neighborhood, seeing if anybody knows them.'

Byrne considered this for a few moments.

'Everything in there is a non-porous surface,' Jessica added. 'The dolls are all plastic and porcelain, the counters and break-front windows are all glass. If this girl's fingerprints are anywhere in the system, we'll find her.'

'About how old was she?' Byrne asked.

'She looked seventeen. Maybe a little older,' she said.

They both knew that there was not a great likelihood that the girl was in the system. Add to that the chance that a girl her age would be involved in such horrendously evil acts, and there was not much about which to be hopeful. Still, it was a direction.

'Josh told me that he did a quick search on Facebook and Twitter for both Nicole Solomon and the Gillen boys.'

'Anything turn up?' Byrne asked.

'They all had Facebook pages, of course, but only Nicole had a Twitter feed. Josh said that there was no cross-posting that he could locate yet.'

'What about Mary Gillen?'

Jessica understood what her partner was asking. He wanted to know what, if anything, would be the fallout from the attack in the parking lot at the Roundhouse.

'She's in hell, Kevin. She doesn't need any more heat.'

An ambulance pulled into the intake bay outside the sliding glass doors. Jessica and Byrne stepped back. An EMT wheeled in an older man holding an ice pack to the man's forehead. The ER team geared up for another patient.

'I'm going to stick around for a while,' Jessica said. 'Then I'm going to head over to Woodside.'

The Woodside Health Group was a consortium of healthcare providers that offered outpatient services ranging from home care to outpatient group wellness and psychotherapy. David Solomon had worked for Woodside in the six years previous to his coming to AdvantAge.

'Do you want me to go with you?' Byrne asked.

'I've got it,' Jessica said. 'Can you take Sophie home?'

'No problem,' Byrne said. 'I have to make a stop at my house. I'll get her there in an hour or so.'

When Jessica arrived at Woodside – a standalone building in a commercial complex near Pennsport – she met with the managing director, a woman named Jane Grasson. Grasson was in her late fifties.

Jessica gave the woman a brief rundown of what had happened, and what brought her to Woodside, that being the suicide of David Solomon.

'What a terrible thing,' Grasson said. 'I just can't believe it.'

'Yes,' Jessica replied, echoing the sentiment. She gave it a moment. 'How long did you know Mr Solomon?'

'Not very long. Just a few years.'

'You met him when he came to be associated with Woodside?'

'Yes.'

'Would you say you knew him well?'

She thought about this. 'As well as you might know anyone in a workplace setting. Other than the occasional birthday or holiday party, I never socialized with him.'

'Did you ever visit him at his home, or did he ever come to yours?'

'No.'

'Did you ever meet his wife?' Jessica asked.

'No, but he talked about her a lot.'

'How so?'

'Not anything specific, but I could tell he was deeply in love with her. You know how some people sound so cruel when they talk about their spouses? Like they can't say anything nice about them?'

'I do.'

'David Solomon was just the opposite. He always talked about his wife and baby daughter in the most loving way.'

'You're referring to Nicole?'

'Yes,' Grasson said. 'She was born when David worked here.'

Jessica made a note. 'What about his work here? What can you tell me about it?'

'As you might expect, when you work in the mental health

field, you come in contact with all kinds of people. More than once David spoke of one particularly difficult patient or another – never in detail, of course – and the possibility that he might not be giving that person the proper treatment or advice.'

'In what way?'

Jane Grasson appeared to be looking for the proper way to put what she had to say next. 'As you know, Woodside does some work for the city and the county, as well as the department of corrections. And while this is not *pro bono* work, it *is* offered for what amounts to little more than expenses – travel costs, meals, et cetera.

'In doing this work, especially for a licensed clinical social worker, the patients present with a wide spectrum of conditions. Everything from mild depression to bipolar disorders. By law, and by training, there is only so much an LCSW can do.'

'And Mr Solomon had concerns about his safety?'

'I would have to say he did. More than once I heard him wonder whether or not one of his patients, upon their release from custody or rehab facility, might come looking for him. There are all kinds of transference.'

While far from having a deep understanding of the phenomenon, Jessica knew that, in a therapy context, *transference* referred to the rerouting of a patient's feelings for a significant person in that person's life to the therapist.

'Do you recall if Mr Solomon ever referred to a specific patient with whom he was having doubts or fears?'

'No,' she said.

'But you believe he feared for the safety of his family.'

'Yes,' Jane Grasson said. 'I believe he did.'

44

When Byrne turned the corner onto his street his mind was a deadfall of questions.

First and foremost was the elusive connection that tied Nicole Solomon directly to the Gillen boys. They did not yet have a link between them. The victims did not attend the same schools or churches or social clubs and, as far as they knew, the families did not know each other. The relationship between Judge Gillen and David Solomon had not been established, if indeed it was Michael Gillen who Solomon meant to reach.

Before leaving the hospital Byrne learned that, at the request of the homicide unit, the ER doctor had taken a blood sample from Miss Emmaline, and by the end of the day they would know if the psilocin in Miss Emmaline's bloodstream – if indeed it was used in the tea – matched the substance found in Nicole Solomon's bloodstream.

As he neared his address Byrne saw a pair of pickup trucks parked at the curb a half block south. One Ford F150; one

Dodge 1500. One of the trucks had folded scaffolding in the back, the other had a plastic bed liner with a bay in which to lock your tools.

Seeing these trucks was a positive thing. If other people on the street were keeping up with their repairs, and doing basic remodeling and rehabilitation work, it was good for the block.

Byrne pulled into his drive, parked the car.

'Oh, my gosh!' Sophie said. 'Your house is so cool!'

'Thanks.'

As Byrne exited the car, and turned to head down the driveway, his heart plummeted.

There was a cloud of smoke rising into the sky, coming from behind his house.

'Stay here,' he said to Sophie.

She got back in the car.

In his time on the police force, especially as a rookie patrol officer in a sector car, he had run into countless buildings, not having any idea the depth of the danger to be found within. Part of the job was not thinking about it.

As he sprinted down the driveway towards the garage, he fully expected to see the back porch, maybe even the rear of his house – a more than ninety-year-old, dry-as-kindling house – fully engulfed in flames.

By the time he rounded the corner he had the *nine* and the *one* punched in to the touchpad of his iPhone. He stopped at the end of the driveway.

His house was not on fire.

Instead, in his backyard, were fifteen or so men. Men who, for some bizarre reason, all seemed to be dressed identically – straw hats, overalls, and work boots. They all had beards, except for one. They were sitting on the ground in a loose semicircle, and they were all smoking pipes.

Corncob pipes.

Byrne was just about to say something – all the while pledging to hop on the wagon, now and forever – when one of the men stood up. He was the only one without a beard.

'Kevin!' the man said.

Somehow the man's voice was familiar, but his face was not. Then the man took off his straw hat.

It was Josh Bontrager.

'Josh,' Byrne said. 'What's . . . what's going on?'

Bontrager gestured to the group of men. 'I'd like you to meet the guys.'

He started at one end of the semicircle. 'This is Caleb, Abram, Isaac.' As he counted them off, each man removed the pipe from his mouth and nodded a greeting at Byrne, only to replace the pipe between his lips and continue to silently puff. 'Over here we have another Caleb – we call him Eli's Caleb – and next to him is Mark, Lemuel, and John.'

When he got to the last man – who looked to be about 350 pounds, at least one third of that beard – he stopped, and said: 'And, saving the best for last, this is Silo Mervin.'

'Gentlemen, I'm pleased to meet you all,' Byrne said. 'Welcome to my home.'

Bontrager crossed the yard, stood next to Byrne. He put the straw hat back on his head, shoved his hands into the pockets of his overalls, and rocked back on the heels of his work boots. Byrne imagined he looked every bit the country boy he had been growing up in Berks County. It was now clear that these men were family, or friends of the family.

'So,' Bontrager said. 'What do you think?'

Byrne was just about to ask what he was talking about when it hit him. The trucks out front, the scaffolding in the bed of the F150, the flecks of white paint on the men sitting in his backyard. He took a step back and looked at his house, the first time since arriving home.

His house was completely and expertly painted. All of it. Every square inch, from the finial on the gable end, to the soffits, from the back porch all the way around to the side door, it was a bright and gleaming white.

'Josh,' Byrne said. 'I don't—'

Bontrager held up a hand, stopping him. 'I know, I know,' he said. 'It's amazing, isn't it?'

'I was only gone a couple of hours,' Byrne said.

Bontrager looked at his watch. 'Four hours and forty minutes to be exact.'

'How did you guys manage to do this so quickly?'

Byrne heard one of the men chuckle. It might've been Caleb. Or Eli's Caleb.

'This is a spectacular crew, even by Amish standards,' Bontrager said. He glanced at one of the men, the one called Abram. 'Tell him the record, Abram.'

Abram took the pipe from his lips. 'Seven barns in six days.'

Byrne was almost speechless. 'Wait. You're saying you painted seven barns in six *days*?'

'We *built* seven barns in six days,' Abram said. 'Plus a silo.'

'We had to do a little patching around the upstairs windows,' Bontrager said. 'Luckily the boys had some caulk with them. She should be airtight and draft free for a while. But you're going to want new windows in those rooms over the garage.'

Byrne hadn't even concerned himself with whatever was over the garage. It was way down the list. 'Can I talk to you for a second, Josh?'

'Sure.'

The two men stepped over to the garage.

'Whatever these guys charge is not going to be enough,' Byrne said. 'This job is as professional a job as I've ever seen. They should get paid what a union crew gets. More. You tell me, and I'll write the check.'

Bontrager looked toward the rear of the property, rocked back on his heels again. Byrne wondered if that was an affectation struck by all men who wore straw hats, overalls, and work boots. He looked back at Byrne. 'I just have one question for you regarding this matter.'

'Okay,' Byrne said. 'What is it?'

'Do you have any beer?'

When Byrne realized he'd almost forgotten about Sophie, he went out to his car. She was calmly sitting in the front seat, reading a book. He brought her inside, took a soda out of the fridge, put it on the counter. Sophie sat down at one of the two stools in the kitchen, opened her book.

'Will you be okay for a few more minutes?' Byrne asked.

'I'll be fine,' she said. 'This house is *great*.'

Byrne opened his refrigerator door and was instantly reminded that he had not yet begun to think of this place as a residence. There was mustard, ketchup, and mayonnaise, one half loaf of Italian bread – surely gone stale – and a sixpack of Coors. He picked up the sixpack, walked onto the back porch, looked at the congregation in his yard. He held up the beer.

'This isn't going to be enough, is it?' he asked.

All the men, including Josh Bontrager, looked at Silo Mervin.

Silo Mervin shook his head.

'So are all these guys Bontragers?' Byrne asked as the two trucks pulled away. He'd made a quick beer run, and sent them off with three cases of Yuengling. There were smiles all around.

'Oh my, no,' Bontrager said. 'There's some Ringenbergs, Beachys, Albrechts, Troyers, a Schrock or two.'

'To be honest, I wasn't even sure if the Amish drank beer.'

Bontrager laughed. 'Man. You've got to get out of the city a little more, detective.'

'Hey, I saw *Witness*,' Byrne said. 'I think it's safer in Phila-delphia.'

When they walked in the kitchen Sophie was still reading her book, the untouched soda on the counter next to her.

'Hey, little darlin',' Bontrager said.

'Hi, Josh.'

Byrne sat down next to Sophie. He noticed she was on the same page she was on a half-hour earlier. Something was wrong. 'You okay?'

Sophie just nodded. Byrne knew better. He read the concern on her face.

'Don't worry about your mom,' Byrne said. 'She's all right.'

'Somebody punched her in the face the other day.'

'I know,' Byrne said. 'That woman was just upset. It happens sometimes. I've been punched a lot.'

Sophie almost smiled, but decided against it. She said nothing.

'Your mom is the toughest person I know,' Bontrager said.

Byrne often thought about Sophie, about her unique situation, about what it might be like to have two detectives as parents. It couldn't be easy.

'I hear you're a really good swimmer,' Bontrager added.

Sophie shrugged, picked at an imaginary piece of lint on her sweater. 'I came in second.'

'Correct me if I'm wrong about this, but that's a silver medal, isn't it? Most people never get anywhere near a silver medal. And you're just getting started.'

Another shrug. 'I guess.'

Byrne reached over, opened the can of soda, slipped a straw into it. Sophie took a small sip.

'You have to have a party,' Bontrager said to Byrne.

'A party?' Byrne asked.

'Yeah. Some kind of housewarming get-together.'

'Yeah!' Sophie said. 'You could have a *huge* party here.'

'I don't know . . .'

'All houses have to be blessed,' Bontrager added. 'Maybe Donna will come.'

Byrne felt himself redden. 'How do you know about *that*?'

Bontrager gave him the look that reminded him that police departments were as bad as junior high schools when it came to gossip. Maybe worse.

Byrne looked at Sophie. 'If I have a party, will you come?' he asked.

'Am I invited?'

'Of *course* you're invited,' Byrne said. 'What kind of party would it be without you?'

Sophie beamed. She was looking more and more like Jessica every day. 'Not a very good one.'

They did a quick fist bump.

'Will Colleen be here?' Sophie asked.

It seemed the decision to have a party was made. 'Sure,' he said. 'Colleen will be here.'

'I'll spread the word,' Bontrager said. 'Big board or small board?'

What Bontrager meant was, should he put a notice about the party up at the Roundhouse only, or on bulletin boards at all the district headquarters, as well.

'Let's keep it small board,' Byrne said.

'You got it.'

As Byrne watched Josh Bontrager walk out to his car, he began to warm to the idea of a party. Maybe it was just what this house needed. Maybe it would establish that he was, at long last, a real homeowner.

45

While Jessica was heading back to the Roundhouse to write up her notes from her visit to Woodside, it came to her.

It had begun to come into focus when Byrne had walked across the ER lobby at Penn Presbyterian. Byrne had kissed Sophie on the top of her head, then took her hand and the two of them walked out.

Earlier in the day, before Jessica and Sophie left for the doll shop, Sophie had wanted to change from her school clothes. Jessica had mentioned that the store was a quaint and elegant place, and Sophie had wanted to dress appropriately.

They spent the most time on Sophie's hair, about which her daughter was most fussy. Jessica had never seen a kid spend more time in the shampoo aisle at Rite Aid than Sophie Balzano.

The only thing Sophie was fussier about were her hair ornaments and accessories – bows, bands, clips, combs, and barrettes.

Today, to visit the doll shop, Sophie chose a pretty black acrylic clip with a French closure. The design was dancing flowers.

At the ER, when Byrne stood up, and the light caught Sophie's barrette, it dawned on her.

She made the first call, then called Byrne.

'What's up?' Byrne asked.

'Are you still with Sophie?'

'Yeah,' Byrne said. 'I was just about to drop her off. Vince is home.'

'Look at her hair.'

'What about it?'

'Humor me,' Jessica said. 'What do you see in her hair?'

'She has a hair clip or something. You know, a . . .'

'Barrette,' Sophie said in the background.

'Right,' Byrne said. 'A barrette.'

'Remember the Nicole Solomon crime scene? Remember what she was wearing?'

'I do. Black sweater, black skirt, white blouse, black loafers.'

'She was also wearing a barrette,' Jessica said.

'Yes, she was. It was in the shape of a swan.'

'Exactly. So why would the killer, who went through all that trouble to dress the Nicole doll, right down to the last button, zipper, and stitch—'

'Leave out the barrette.'

'Right again.'

'Maybe it wasn't Nicole's,' Byrne said. 'Maybe it belonged to someone else.'

'My thoughts. I just called the ID Unit. Guess what one thing from that scene wasn't processed?'

'I'm going to go out on a limb and say the barrette for a thousand, Alex.'

'Have you ever put a barrette on a kid?' Jessica asked.

'It's on my bucket list.'

Jessica subconsciously wiggled the fingers on her right hand. 'I've done it a million times, partner. More. Absolutely *impossible* to keep your fingers off the barrette.'

46

When Anabelle told me the news, I was initially distressed. It was no secret that I didn't approve of her working in that shop at first, but I could see what it has meant to her over these few years.

We strolled through the park, arm in arm.

'Please don't be sad,' I said.

'I can't help it,' Anabelle replied through her tears.

As we headed to our car, I saw that we had drawn the attention of a pair of boys, perhaps sixteen. From their outward appearance they appeared to represent everything I disdain – slovenly appearance, poor hygiene, vulgar manners.

I took Anabelle's hand. We began to walk further into the park. The sun was setting and it became chilly. I took off my coat and draped it over Anabelle's shoulders.

'*Merci*,' she said. Her voice sounded so small, like a child's. It broke my heart.

I glanced behind us. As I suspected, the two boys were following.

'We are being followed,' I said to Anabelle. I felt her tense.

One thing that might be known about me is that I've never been one to raise my voice. I've always believed that volume is a poor substitute for substance. If you do not have a valid point to make, you shout, hoping to bully your point home.

I detest bullies.

For as long as I have been shaving, I have used a straight razor. I have tried many, but my favorite is a Thiers-Issard Eagle with a 5/8 inch blade and tortoise handle. It is very light and agile, and extremely sharp.

As I turned on my heel I slipped the razor from my pocket, and under the cover provided by the gathering darkness, opened the blade.

The two boys continued toward us. I brushed the leaves from a bench for Anabelle. She sat down. I walked up the path and chose a spot under a copse of shedding maples. I greeted the boys.

They were no more than ten feet away.

'Gentlemen,' I said. 'Is there something I can help you with?'

The boys looked at each other, as if they had never been referred to as gentlemen before. This was entirely understandable.

'Gimme your cell phone, motherfucker,' one of them said. '*That's* what you can help me with.' He wore a brown, hooded sweatshirt. There was some sort of sports team logo on the left front breast.

'I'm afraid I don't own a cell phone,' I said. It was true. I can't imagine a life so rubbled with useless information that one would be compelled to share it every second of every day.

'I think you do,' said the other boy. This one wore a black hooded sweatshirt with something that looked like FUBU written on it. 'You look rich. Rich people got cell phones.' As he said this he took a knife from his waistband. It was a fixed blade dagger with what looked to be a five inch blade.

I have had a keen interest – if you'll allow the *bon mot* – in steel weaponry my whole life. The handle of my razor, which was open, rested against the backs of my curled fingertips, its length shielded by my right wrist.

'Sorry to disappoint you,' I said. 'And now, if we have no further business with which to attend . . . '

'Fuck you, asshole.'

The boy with the knife closed the distance to where I stood in two quick strides. Leading with the knife in a forward grip – what is known as a modified saber grip, with one thumb on the side of the blade – he was ill-prepared for anything that might result from a failure to plunge the knife into my chest.

He, being large and oafish, and more than a few pounds overweight, stumbled past me. I managed to dodge the assault with ease. As he passed by I raised my right foot and brought it forcefully down to the back of the boy's left knee.

He fell to the earth, face first, the wind momentarily stolen from his lungs.

I dropped a knee to the center of his back, pulled down his hood, and placed the blade of the straight razor against the center of his neck. Just this slight touch drew blood. I felt his body jitter.

'Do not move,' I whispered.

He did not.

I looked at the other boy, who had been about to join the fray. He was now frozen in place.

'This is a Thiers-Issard,' I said. 'It is French steel, inarguably one of the finest shaving instruments made. Aside from a DOVO, you cannot buy a better blade.'

I had taken the chance that the other boy was not equipped with a firearm. It was a calculated risk. I was right. He certainly would have produced it by now.

'What will happen now is that I will count to three.' I pointed to a light pole, perhaps forty yards away, down the path. 'If you do not reach that pole by the time I count three, I will sever your colleague's spinal cord. He will live, but not well. If you turn around, even once, I will cut his throat.'

The boy vibrated with fear.

'I need to know that you understand. Say "I understand".'

The boy said nothing. Instead, he just nodded. It was enough.

'One.'

I did not need to count to three.

I eased the blade from my attacker's neck, and smelled the unmistakable odor of urine. Before I let him up I picked up his knife. I threw the offensive weapon into the wooded area that bordered Kelly Drive. It was a thug's pride, useful for nothing more than whittling.

'Stand,' I said.

The boy didn't move.

'I never say things twice.'

The boy slowly got up, but did not turn around.

'If this were all about me, this moment would be where you and I part ways. But you have upset the person most important to me in the world.'

I pointed to where Anabelle sat.

'We will now walk over there, and you will apologize to her.'

The boy didn't know what to do.

'You *do* know what an apology is, do you not?'

He nodded slowly, turned, glanced at my right hand, which still held the Thiers-Issard.

'Let's go,' I said.

The boy ambled over the bench. When he was ten feet or so from Anabelle, I touched his shoulder. He stopped.

'I'm ... I'm sorry,' he said.

My heart bled with pathos. 'When you called me that crass and vulgar name you were much louder than this.'

'I'm sorry,' he repeated, this time a little louder.

'To whom are you speaking?' I asked.

The boy again tensed, not having any idea what was coming next.

'You are speaking to a lady,' I said. 'You address her as "miss".'

'I'm sorry, *miss*,' he said.

'Very well,' I said. I looked at Anabelle. 'Dear heart?'

Anabelle looked up. 'I accept.'

I turned the boy around. 'And so,' I said. '*D'accord.*'

With the boy facing me, the smell of urine was overbearing. I wanted nothing more than to conclude our business. I brought the razor up and across, the blade coming to rest a mere inch from the boy's face.

'Run.'

A few minutes later Anabelle and I sat in our car. We were silent for the longest time.

'I lost my temper,' I finally said. 'I feel quite the ruffian.'

'It's okay,' Anabelle replied. She patted my hand.

'You're not angry with me?'

'Never.'

I started the car, turned the heat on low. Anabelle was always cold at this time of the year. I tapped my vest pocket.

'It seems I dropped my pocket watch during the encounter.'

'Oh *no*,' Anabelle said. 'The Verge Fusee?'

'Yes.'

'But you love it so.'

I looked out the driver's side window, toward the park, back. 'I think I know where it is,' I said. 'I'll just run back there for it. You'll be fine for just a minute?'

'Yes. I'll be fine.'

I opened the door, stepped out. 'Lock the doors. I won't be long.'

*

I found the boy sitting on a bench near the river. He smoked a cigarette with one trembling hand, held a cell phone in the other. Apparently he already *had* a cell phone, just as I had never dropped my watch.

We are defined by the breadth of our lies, *n'est-ce pas?*'

I was upon him before he could make a sound.

He had frightened Anabelle, and for that there was no clemency.

Twenty minutes later Anabelle and I pulled into the garage. I cut the engine. For a few moments the only sound was the click and clack of the cooling engine.

'There are four dolls left to mend, then we'll be done,' I said.

Anabelle looked into the gloom of the dark garage, the weight of our small and cosseted world on her slight shoulders. 'Then what will become of us?' she asked. 'Where will we go?'

'We will go to Paris, and there live out our days.'

'Really?'

'Yes,' I said. 'We'll live in a warm little *chaumière* and we will have many friends.'

Anabelle sat up straighter. I could see the visions of my plan capering in her eyes. I hadn't the heart to tell her the truth.

'We have *so* many preparations to make,' she said.

'Yes, we do.'

'Our final tea will be our grandest ever!'

'Yes,' I said. 'A *grande fête.*'

We exited the car, and walked the few blocks to our home.

I was pleased to see that we were not followed.

Safely home, I washed the last of the blood from my hands.

When I stepped from the bathroom, Anabelle was curled on the divan, reading a book on French country living. She looked up at me and smiled.

I loved to make my Anabelle smile.

47

In homicide investigations, a break in a case can come from any quarter. Sometimes, although rarely, a confession is gleaned. Sometimes a witness suddenly recalls a key detail omitted from an initial interview, or a previously unknown surveillance video surfaces. Most of the time, it comes from the science.

This time, it came from the ID Unit, the section that collects and compares fingerprints, and from IAFIS – the Integrated Automated Fingerprint Identification System – maintained by the FBI.

One of the best officers in the ID Unit was Eddie Dunbar. He met with Jessica and Byrne by the first-floor elevators.

'I've got some interesting news and some strange news,' Eddie said.

Jessica looked at Byrne, back at Eddie. 'In my experience those are often the same thing,' she said.

'Not this time.'

'Okay,' Jessica said. 'You pick.'

'We've got a hit on your print.'

'Wait,' Jessica said. 'You mean *the* print?'

'I'm pretty sure I do.'

'The one we lifted from Nicole Solomon's barrette?'

'The very one.'

'And, of course, we compared it to Nicole's prints and her father's prints,' Jessica said. 'We ruled them out.'

In police work, when you were stating the obvious, you often used *we*. That way, the other cop knew that *you* knew you were stating the obvious, but still giving them an out in case it slipped by them. If they screwed up, the blame would be spread around.

'Yes, we did.'

Eddie was a lifer. He understood.

Jessica felt her pulse begin to race. It was the break they were waiting for. 'Dish, big man.'

Eddie looked at the fax in his hand. 'The print – a beautiful eight-pointer, by the way, the kind I love to testify about – belongs to a woman name Crystal Anders. Thirty-two, Caucasian, pretty lengthy record. Mostly drugs and prostitution.' He tapped the fax. 'She was probably kind of hot before she got hit by the Meth Express. Maybe she still is. But, then again, I'm not that picky.'

'Please tell me we have a current address,' Jessica said.

'The most current there is.'

'What do you mean?'

'She's in custody.'

The best news just got better. '*Whoa*.' They high-fived. 'Dinner at *home*.'

'I haven't gotten to the strange part.'

Nothing could dampen Jessica's spirit. 'I don't care how strange it is, this is good news,' she said. 'Hit me with your best shot.'

'She's in custody in Cleveland.'

48

The Cleveland Police Department operated out of the Justice Center, a 26-story monolithic building located on Superior Avenue, near the heart of the city. Covering five districts, the 1500-member force was only slightly younger than the Philadelphia PD. It was established in 1890.

The flight from Philadelphia lasted just under an hour and, as the plane banked over the city, Jessica was amazed at the size of the lake. She'd been to the ocean many times, had experienced the Delaware at its widest, but this was her first Great Lake. She'd never seen anything like it from the air.

Byrne slept through the whole thing.

The special operations division of the CPD was similar to that of the Philadelphia Police Department. The units – arson, fraud, theft, narcotics, and special victims/sex crimes – were the same. The major difference was that the homicide unit of the CPD was folded into a robbery/homicide division.

In a city of roughly 500,000, the per capita ration of citizen to officer was about the same, but the land mass covered by patrol was much larger in Philly. The PPD had jurisdiction over all of Philadelphia County. The CPD worked only a small portion of Cuyahoga County.

After signing in in the lobby of the Justice Center Jessica and Byrne took the elevator up to the fifth floor.

No matter how many times Jessica visited other big city police departments, she was always amazed by the similarities. The same dismal walls, the same crappy elevators, the same smells – a prying blend of sweat, disinfectant, and cherry air freshener.

The man who came around the corner looked to be in his late forties or early fifties, good-looking in a beat-up city cop way. He wore a blue dress shirt, sleeves rolled up, a navy blue striped tie, good watch.

The man saw Byrne first. At six-three, it happened to Byrne all the time.

'Are you Detective Byrne?' the man asked.

'I am,' Byrne said. 'And it's Kevin.'

'Kevin it is,' the man said. 'Jack Paris. Welcome to Cleveland.'

'Thanks.'

The two men shook hands. Byrne stepped to the side.

'This is my partner,' Byrne said. 'Jessica Balzano.'

'It's a real pleasure,' Paris said. 'Welcome.'

Jessica shook hands with Detective Paris.

Paris gestured to the room around them. 'As glamorous as the stories, right?'

Byrne mugged. 'The cabbie gave us a mini-tour on the way in,' he said. 'I like your town.'

'Never been?'

'Never had the pleasure.'

'I hope he didn't take you to Lake County.'

'No,' Byrne said. 'I asked him to give us the nickel tour. I always like to get a feel.'

'I'm the same way,' Paris said. 'I haven't been to Philly in years. We used to go to Wildwood every summer when I was a kid. We'd always stop for cannoli at this place in South Philly.'

'Termini's,' Jessica said.

'Man,' Paris said. 'Corbo's on the Hill here is good, but I might have to return to your fair city.'

'You are welcome any time.'

'Are you staying over?' Paris asked.

'No,' Byrne said. He glanced at his watch. 'We've got a flight back in five hours or so.'

'Then let's get to it.'

The documents sat on a holy mess of a desk, as did a framed photograph of a pretty young woman.

'My daughter, Melissa,' Paris said.

'She's beautiful,' Jessica said.

'She is my light.'

'Grandkids?' Byrne asked.

Paris smiled. 'Bite your tongue, brother,' he said. 'I mean, I want them, but just not tomorrow.'

Byrne held up both hands in surrender. 'Couldn't agree more.'

They took a few moments, discussing their children. Then it was time to get to the reason for the visit.

Paris tapped the documents on his desk. 'I don't know about the PPD, but we don't get a lot of requests like this.'

'Same here,' Jessica said. 'We saddle up with the county and the Feds now and then, but most of the bad guys who aren't homegrown get to meet our Fugitive Squad.'

Paris read over the document in front of him.

'Crystal Anders was picked up last Saturday on a drug charge. And by drug charge I mean trafficking. Bail was set at 100K. Judges here are feeling the heat, passing it down.'

'I read her sheet on the way in,' Jessica said. 'I didn't see any violence.'

Paris nodded.

'So she was here last Saturday?' Byrne asked.

'Yes.'

'What time was she arrested?'

'She was picked up at 30th and Chester at 11:45 p.m. Part of a long – and I mean long – sting operation. We pulled in sixteen people that night, all of some weight.'

The time frame didn't rule Crystal Anders out of anything. Jessica now knew that Cleveland was just under an hour from Philly. Crystal Anders didn't look like a frequent flier, but stranger things have happened.

'Did she cop to the drugs?' Byrne asked.

Paris shook his head. 'It wasn't my interview, but I read the notes.'

'Let me guess,' Byrne said. 'She was just getting a ride.'

Paris laughed. 'Something like that.'

'Think she may have been muling the weight from Philly?'

'It's possible.'

'We checked her for a sheet on NCIC,' Byrne said. The National Crime Information Center was a national database of criminal justice information. It offered a wide array of data helping police apprehend suspects, locate missing persons, and recover stolen property. 'We didn't find any Philly connection.'

'Neither did we,' Paris said. 'She was born in Weirton, West Virginia.'

'But she lives here now?'

'Crystal is kind of hard to pin down in that regard. She certainly doesn't own a home. She hasn't had a driver's license in almost ten years.'

'Did you check with TSA?'

Paris nodded. 'We did. If she flew, she did it with a false ID.'

They agreed that Detective Paris would handle the beginning part of the interview.

Crystal Anders was a woman who had surely at one time been considered pretty. The scourge that was methamphetamine had slowly eroded her face, her teeth, her body, her life. Jessica was a little surprised at how small she was. Maybe it was all the meth. She couldn't have weighed more than ninety pounds, even though her sheet said 5'3'/120.

There was a thick keloid scar on the right side of her neck, a deep crimson in color, that stood out in stark relief to her ashen skin.

They met in a small interview room on the fifth floor. By comparison to the equivalent in Philadelphia, the room was downright spacious – perhaps one hundred square feet – and had somehow managed to camouflage that monkey house smell.

Crystal Anders wore a bright orange jumpsuit. And despite her emaciated appearance, she was shackled to the table. Jessica understood the play. More than one cop had backed off on this, only to sorely underestimate the speed and strength of a seemingly harmless or defeated suspect.

'Crystal, my name is Detective Paris,' he said. 'This is Detective Byrne and Detective Balzano.'

Paris sat at the table, across from Crystal. Jessica and Byrne sat slightly behind him. The door was closed.

The woman looked up for a split second, divided her attention between the three of them, then looked down again. Jessica could see that she'd been in a very similar situation to this many times. She could also see that the woman was in withdrawal.

'What we'd like to talk about is—'

'Y'all need to talk to D'Shawn,' Crystal said. 'I told t'others. Talk to D'Shawn. Not me.'

Paris sat back in his chair, steepled his fingers. He gave the moment some heft. 'D'Shawn?'

The woman nodded, chewed on one of her dirty nails. She remained silent.

'You mean D'Shawn Thomas?'

'Yeah,' she said. 'I didn't do nothin.' Talk to D'Shawn. All that was his. I told t'others. I was just getting a ride.'

'All *what* was his?'

'Them drugs. I don't mess with all that.'

Paris opened the folder in front of him, slid out a rap sheet, slid it to his right so Jessica and Byrne could see it.

Jessica saw that D'Shawn Dixon Thomas was a piece of work. Thirty-nine years old, incarcerated about thirty percent of that – gun charges, ag assaults, forgery, extortion. Suspect in a cop killing. Real citizen.

'Now, see, Crystal, I would *love* to talk to D'Shawn,' Paris said. 'He killed a police officer a few years back so, trust me on this, everybody in this *building* would love to talk to him. We just don't know where he is. Can you help us with that?'

'He never kilt nobody.'

'Where is D'Shawn right now, Crystal?'

'I don't know.'

'Then I can't talk to him, can I?'

No response.

'We'll come back to D'Shawn,' Paris said. 'Right now he's only one of your problems.'

She looked up again, this time chancing a slightly longer glance at Paris. She didn't seem to know what he was talking about.

'I'd like to go back to last weekend,' Paris said. 'Let's start with last Friday night.'

'What about it?'

'Where were you that night?'

The woman shrugged, said nothing.

'Did you stay home? Did you go out?'

'I was home.'

'All night?'

'Purt near.'

'Not sure what that means,' Paris said.

'I was home purt near all night.'

'So that means that you went out.'

Another shrug.

'What time did you leave the house, Crystal?'

The woman looked at her now bloodied, raw fingernails, as if the timeline might be located there. 'I don't know,' she said. 'Maybe eleven, some.'

'Was there anyone else at your house with you at that time?'

'Gingerbelle was there.'

'Who is Gingerbelle?'

Another shrug.

'You don't know who that is? Is that a person, a dog?'

'My friend.'

'Gingerbelle is a woman?'

Crystal looked up at Paris as if he were crazy, as if a man would be called Gingerbelle. Jessica could think of a hundred scenarios where a wisecrack would be called for. This wasn't one of them. The woman just nodded.

'What is Gingerbelle's last name?'

'Wallace or Watkins,' she said. 'Like that.'

Jessica thought: How many Gingerbelles could there be? She made the note.

'Was there anyone else there Friday night?'

'No.'

'Okay,' Paris continued. 'When you left the house, did Gingerbelle go out with you?'

'Yeah,' she said. 'She had to get some formula for her baby, so we went to the Food Mart.'

'Which one?'

'The one up to 71st Street.'

'Where did you go after that?'

More squirrelly moves. 'We went to Billy's for a spell.'

'That's the biker bar? The one on Payne?'

Crystal obviously knew that *he* knew that it was. She just nodded.

'Did you score while you were there?'

'Score?'

Paris moved on. 'Tell me about Saturday.'

A one-shoulder shrug this time. 'I slept late.'

'Until what time?'

'Noon, some.'

'What time did you leave town?'

Because Jessica knew this question was coming, she watched the woman closely. Crystal Anders was hard to read.

'Leave *town*?'

'Yeah,' Paris said. 'What time did you go to the airport?'

The woman took a moment to glance at Jessica and Byrne, as if maybe this was a joke. Neither Jessica nor Byrne were smiling. Crystal didn't either.

'Airport? I didn't go to no airport.'

Paris shuffled a few papers, leaned back, crossed his legs. 'You know that there are records of all this now. If you took a flight to anywhere on last Saturday – or any day, for that matter – I can get that information in about thirty seconds,' Paris said. 'If you tell the truth about anything here today, Crystal, this would be the time.'

'I ain't lying.'

Paris took another moment. 'I may not have mentioned this, but detectives Byrne and Balzano are from Philadelphia.'

Another quick glance up, then back to chewing her nails.

'They would like to talk to you about some things that have been happening in their city.'

Byrne pulled his chair forward. 'Crystal, once again, my name is Detective Byrne. I think you know you're already in a lot of trouble. I'm not going to insult you by trying to sugarcoat it for you.'

After a long uncomfortable minute, when Byrne didn't continue, Crystal was forced to look up.

'As Detective Paris said, there have been some events in Philadelphia recently. In the course of our investigation, we've discovered an item that brought us here, to Cleveland.'

'I don't know nothin' about it,' she said. 'I ain't never been.'

'Not only did this evidence bring us to Cleveland, Crystal, it brought us to you.'

This got her full attention.

'To *me*?'

Byrne reached into his bag, removed a folder. From within he produced a glossy color photograph of the swan barrette found at the Nicole Solomon crime scene, the barrette bearing Crystal Anders's fingerprint.

When he set it on the table, and pushed it toward Crystal, all three investigators watched her reaction.

When Crystal looked at the picture of the barrette, something happened to her, something Jessica had seen before, but not for a long time. It wasn't something that was a behavior characteristic common to drug addicts, or meth addicts in particular. It was something that happened to mothers, especially those who have dark and troubled histories with their children.

When Crystal saw the barrette she imploded.

The untrained eye might not have seen it, but Jessica did, and she was certain both Kevin Byrne and Jack Paris saw it as well. It seemed to be the final step in the dismantling of a human being. There was no doubt that Crystal recognized the barrette, and her reaction told Jessica it could only have one connection, one visceral link to her life, and that link was a child.

She was finally able to choke out the words. 'Where . . . where did y'all *find* this?'

'We'll get to that in a while,' Byrne said. 'For the moment, tell us what you know about it.'

Crystal shook her head. 'I can't.'

'I'm sorry,' Byrne said. 'Are you saying you can't remember, or you can't tell us what you know about it?'

'I-I can't,' she repeated.

'Were you in Philadelphia last Saturday, Crystal?'

She again shook her head, then dabbed at her eyes with the back of her right hand.

'I need you to help me understand, then,' Byrne said.

'Understand *what?*'

'I need to understand how this item, with your fingerprint on it, ended up at a crime scene in Philadelphia last Saturday.'

Seeing the barrette, and being hit with the questions, might have been too much. The color was rapidly draining from the woman's face. It appeared as if she might be getting ready to faint.

Byrne pressed on. 'Tell us about the barrette.'

'I . . . I ain't seen that in years.'

'So you do recognize it?'

She rocked back and forth, nodded slowly.

'Okay,' Byrne said. 'Tell me about it. How did you come across this before?'

'I . . . I stoled it.'

'You stole it?'

She nodded.

'From where, Crystal?'

She pointed at one of the walls. 'It was one of them places with all the sunglasses and things at the mall.'

'You mean a kiosk? A vendor that sets up in the middle?'

'Yeah.'

'What mall?'

Another point. 'The Richmond one.'

'Okay, then,' Byrne said. 'What did you do with it afterward?'

Now came the real tears. Jessica had no idea what complicity, if any, this woman had in murder. She still couldn't just sit there. She reached into her bag, pulled out some Kleenex, reached across the table and handed them to Crystal. The woman nodded a thank you.

'Crystal,' Byrne said. He had softened his tone. 'Tell me what you did with that barrette.'

'I gave it to my baby girl.'

'Your daughter?'

Crystal nodded.

'When was this?'

She shrugged. 'I was eighteen, some.'

'How old was your daughter then?'

'She was three. It was her birthday.'

Jessica looked at the sheet. Crystal was now thirty-two. This was fifteen years ago.

'Where is your daughter now, Crystal?'

More tears. This time the woman leaned forward, placing her face almost on the battered metal table. For a long time no sound emitted, then:

'*I . . . don't . . . know.*'

Byrne looked at Paris. Paris nodded.

'Crystal, we're going to take a little break,' Paris said. 'Can I get you a water or something?'

The woman didn't look up.

They stood outside the interview room. Paris had gotten them both a cup of coffee. It was truly awful.

'I've had this coffee before,' Byrne said. 'I thought it was a Philly blend.'

'I think it's universal,' Paris said.

The door to the interview room was closed. Still, they spoke in hushed tones.

Jessica had read the rest of the notes on Crystal Anders. According to the report, Crystal was found to have left two children at Richmond Mall, a mall on the city's east side. The children were put into emergency foster care. When Crystal was picked up, she spent three days in county jail. When she was bailed out, she skipped town.

'The report says two kids,' Jessica said.

'It's my understanding that she had two, a boy and a girl.'

'Do we know where they went?' Jessica asked.

'As you know, this is ancient history,' Paris said. 'But I can make a few calls. Chances are they went into the county system, and they tend to keep better records than the city.'

'What do we know about the father?'

'Not a clue,' Paris said. 'I haven't really dug into this yet. The only reason she's on my radar is because of your department's request. I ran across her three years ago when D'Shawn Thomas killed one of our own, but she wasn't directly involved. She was just a KA.'

Jessica knew what he meant. Crystal Anders was a known associate.

'I've got a younger detective pulling everything we can find together for you,' Paris added.

'Much appreciated,' Byrne said.

Paris looked at the monitor on the nearby table. It showed a high angle shot of the interview room and its occupant.

'It looks like she's calmed down a bit,' Paris said. 'Ready for round two?'

Byrne just nodded.

'Crystal, it's important that we trace the history of this barrette, from the time you gave it to your daughter, right up until last

Saturday,' Byrne said. 'I can't promise you anything on your other charges, but everything you do – good or bad – goes into the file.'

No response.

'Are you with me, Crystal?'

She nodded. At Byrne's request, they had taken off the shackles. She dabbed at her eyes and nose with a big wad of tissue.

'The report says there were two children at Richmond Mall that day,' Byrne said. 'Is that accurate?'

She nodded.

'Was the boy your son?'

A few more tears, but not like earlier. Crystal Anders was understandably cried out. 'My baby boy.'

'How old was he?'

'He was three.'

'So the boy and girl are fraternal twins?'

She did not respond. It was possible that she was unfamiliar with the term.

'Where was the father in all this?'

This time there was not a shrug or a tear. This time Jessica saw the woman stiffen, and shift her eyes side to side. She raised her right hand to touch the scar on her neck.

'Crystal?'

'We was never together like that,' she said. 'We was never a couple or nothin'.'

'Do you know where he is now?'

'I ain't seen him or heard from him in years. No mind to.'

Byrne made the note. 'Did he give you that scar?'

She shook her head, but she wouldn't look up. She was lying.

'What's his name?' Byrne asked.

Another shrug, but Crystal knew immediately this wouldn't fly. 'Crystal?'

'His name is Ezekiel,' she said. 'They call him Zeke.'

'Ezekiel what?'

Crystal mumbled something unintelligible.

'I'm sorry?'

'Moss.'

Jessica had been looking in Paris's direction when Crystal said the name. As soon as Paris heard it Jessica saw the color rise in his face. He uncrossed his legs, sat a little straighter. It looked like he wanted to jump into the interview, but he said nothing.

This name had meaning for him.

'So a man named Ezekiel Moss is the children's father,' Byrne said. 'Do you think the children may be with him now?'

She shook her head.

'And why is that?'

'He was a trucker. He didn't call no place home. Not mine, sure.'

'Okay,' Byrne said. 'Where and when did you meet him?'

She pointed at the wall again. 'Down to Weirton.'

'And when was this?'

'I was fifteen, some.'

'Is that where the children were born?'

She nodded.

'We'll need to know the name of the hospital.'

Crystal looked up. She almost smiled, as if this were the dumbest question imaginable. 'Weren't no *hos*pital.'

Byrne stared at her for a moment. 'So you're saying there are no birth certificates for the children?'

She shook her head. 'No.'

'When was the last time you saw your children?'

At this Crystal looked at her hands. She began to shake. Jessica figured that this was as much from this interview as it was from her paroxysms of withdrawal.

The interview was over.

*

The detective that Paris had put on background had made a few hits. When the two children were put into emergency foster care it was at the county level. The group home was located on the city's near east side.

When the children went through intake, the case worker did not have an ID on them, so they entered as a John and Jane Doe.

Jessica knew this often happened, especially if the father was unknown. The children were not given the last name Anders because there was no birth certificate for them, no birth records of any kind.

The detective learned that, at this group home, there were eight children that were unidentified at the time – four boys and four girls –ranging in age from three to seven. They were all Jane and John Does, so the trail on Crystal Anders' children grew a little fuzzy at that time.

When the home was closed due to cutbacks, the forty-one children were sent to different homes. Where the two children in question went was still unknown.

The CPD detective was working the phone and fax machines at that moment.

He did provide a lead that might have been useful. Crystal Anders's probation officer still worked for Cuyahoga County. His name was Marc Santos, and he had first met Crystal about a year after she had abandoned her children.

Marc Santos was in his mid-forties, rotund and easy going. Jessica could see how that affability could turn to discipline in short order. If there was a profession that heard more lies on a daily basis than a police officer, it was a probation officer.

What the two jobs had in common was that each of them had the legal right to take away a person's liberty.

They met in the lobby of the Justice Center. Santos had brought with him some documents.

'I remember her well,' he said. 'She was one of my cases at two different times. Once when she was nineteen, and once when she was twenty-six.'

Santos put two photographs down on the bench. They were not police mug shots, but rather Polaroids taken at the probation officer's office. Both had a painted white concrete wall as a background.

But that's where the similarities ended.

At nineteen, Crystal Anders had been a pretty young woman. Her blue eyes were clear, her skin was smooth. The photograph, and its lighting, was not particularly flattering, but despite this she was quite attractive.

The photograph of her at twenty-six was a shock, especially in contrast, side by side, to her younger self. In the second photograph she had open sores on her forehead and chin. She had cut off the left side of her hair – or had it roughly done for her. As bad as the woman looked today, at thirty-two, she did not look quite as bad as she had six years earlier.

'I'd like to tell you that her appearance in these two photos is a rarity, but I see it every day,' Santos said.

'These were both for drug offenses?'

Santos nodded. 'She did a year and change on the first one, about ten months on the second.'

'And she never violated her probation?'

'Hard to say. Random drug testing back then was expensive and infrequent. But I can say she kept her appointments with me.'

'Did she ever mention her children?'

'Just once, that I can recall.'

'How so?'

'She knew they were in foster care, and she wanted to see them. I told her that it wasn't going to happen.'

'This was during her first probation?'

'Yeah.'

'How did she react?'

'Not well,' Santos said. 'I see it all the time. At first, when I started – I'd been a PO about a year when I got Crystal's first case – I was a lot more sympathetic to it all. Now, I'm sorry to say, I'm unmoved. I've seen women who have sold their new-borns for a five dollar rock, then come crying about how they love their baby. Once you cave, you crumble.'

'What was the upshot?'

Santos looked out at the huge lobby, back. 'I probably shouldn't have done this – and it's something I've only done a few times since, and not for a long time, now – but I told her that seeing the kids was not a possibility, not until she cleaned up her act, and went through court-appointed rehab. But I told her that, if she wanted to write a note, without using her name, I would get it to the director of the foster home.'

'Did she write one?'

'She did.'

'Did you pass it along?'

Santos took a few moments. He nodded to a pair of officers passing by. He seemed to be organizing his thoughts.

'There's this little piece of the world you get, you know?' he said. 'Some eight by ten room, some mansion, some cave, some utility room off a basement in Detroit or Baltimore or Mexico City. Maybe the room smells like mildew and mice, maybe you only get a moldy sandwich to eat, maybe not even that, but it's some place where four walls meet, some place where you can be safe from all the knives this life throws at you, even if it's just for a little while.'

Jessica and Byrne just listened.

'These two kids got dealt a shit hand, and their mother probably did, too. I knew that someone else was going to make the decision on whether or not to give those kids Crystal's note, if and when they were ready to read it. At the moment she handed it to me, I couldn't think of a single reason not to pass it along. I've thought of a hundred since. But then? I just did it.'

Jessica didn't want to ask if he'd read the note, but she had to. Marc Santos said he did not.

'When you got Crystal's case the second time, did she ask about the note?' Byrne asked.

Santos shook his head. 'No,' he said. 'She didn't ask about the children, either.'

'Any idea where the kids are?'

The man shrugged. 'That's above my pay grade, I'm afraid.'

As Santos walked out onto Superior Avenue, Paris got off the main elevator. He found Jessica and Byrne, walked across the lobby. He'd put his suit coat on, and had a smile on his face.

'You know how a day starts off being about one thing, then it turns into something totally different?'

'I do,' Byrne said.

'Well, I've got one for you and one for me.'

'We could use one,' Byrne said.

'I found out about Crystal's kids, and where they might have gone when the group home here was closed.'

He opened the envelope, took out a document, continued.

'The forty-one children were sent to five different facilities.' Paris read from the list. 'Six went to Columbus, eight went to Indianapolis, ten went to Youngstown, eleven went to Toledo, and six went to Erie.'

None of this was good news to Jessica and Byrne.

'Do we know where Crystal's children went?' Jessica asked.

'One of two places. The John and Jane Does went to Toledo and Youngstown. Four each.' Paris held up a document, but did not show it to either Jessica or Byrne. 'I called the Youngstown facility, and was told that the home closed a year after the children got there. From there they went to a home outside

Pittsburgh. I called *that* home, and found out they closed eleven months later. All twenty-one kids living there at the time went to one facility.'

Paris handed Jessica the document. It was a fax from the Commonwealth of Pennsylvania Department of Welfare.

When Jessica saw the address of the group home, she felt her pulse spike.

The foster home was in North Philadelphia.

Jessica wanted to hug detective Jack Paris, but it would have been inappropriate. Instead she smiled, wagged a finger. 'You could have just told us this.'

'Now what would be the fun in that?'

'I'm never playing poker with you,' Jessica said. 'Mind if I ask a question?'

'Not at all.'

'When Crystal mentioned the father's name, I saw you react.'

Paris raised an eyebrow. 'You should be a detective.' He gestured to a corner of the lobby, overlooking Superior Avenue. They walked over.

Paris lowered his voice. Most of the people passing by were cops, but there were a number of civilians, as well.

'She said the children's father was a man named Ezekiel Moss.'

'What about him?' Byrne asked.

'About twenty years ago we had an Ezekiel Moss on radar. Very bad actor. Allegedly killed eight prostitutes, that we know of, over the course of thirty-six months. Long-haul trucker used to make a Georgia to Detroit run.'

'And you're thinking he may have passed through Weirton, West Virginia.'

'If it's the same Ezekiel Moss.'

'It's certainly on the route,' Byrne said. 'What happened to him?'

Paris shrugged, ran a hand over his chin. 'In the wind. I walk by that wanted poster every day. I still think he's going to pop up one day, but he's probably gone underground or dead. Either way, he's stopped hunting.'

'You think he's the father of her kids?'

Paris held up his iPhone. On it was a mug shot of a wiry, hard-looking man in his thirties. 'Let's find out.'

They passed through a series of locked doors, went down in an elevator to the basement. There Jessica saw a pair of holding cells, one of which held Crystal Anders.

Paris excused himself, walked past a security station, and into her cell. When Crystal saw him, she stood up.

Jessica and Byrne watched as Paris showed her the picture on his phone, the mug shot of Ezekiel Moss.

Crystal Anders fell to her knees.

They had their answer.

Paris dropped them at the USAir gate at Hopkins International airport.

He got out, flashed a badge at one of the TSA agents. The man nodded.

Paris shook hands with both detectives.

'I can't thank you enough for this, detective,' Byrne said.

'Any time. If we hadn't put Crystal in the box, I wouldn't have this fresh page on Ezekiel Moss. Strange how things work in this business.'

'If you ever think about moving, the PPD would be lucky to have you.'

'Thanks, but I'm happy here. After all, we did get the Rock and Roll Hall of Fame. Sorry about that.'

'You did, indeed,' Byrne said. 'But we have the Mario Lanza museum.'

Paris smiled. 'Sounds like a draw.'

The two men shook hands. 'Be safe.'

This time Jessica did hug Paris.

After checking in, Jessica turned to see Paris standing on the sidewalk, hands on hips, looking toward his city. She had the feeling that they would one day again cross paths, and that whatever route Detective Jack Paris had pointed them down, they had helped do the same for him.

Paris's case began when a man named Ezekiel Moss first lifted his hand in madness to another human being.

Their case might just turn on the same legacy of evil.

49

Byrne was fatigued – travel always exhausted him – but found some energy around eight p.m.

Tonight's project was the room off the parlor, the one with the smallest of the three fireplaces in it.

When he had knocked out the brick in the fireplace, he found a number of old issues of *Life Magazine* lying across the andirons, all but intact. He glanced briefly at the covers, all from within a six-month period in the early 1960s. The faces staring out at him brought him back.

Marilyn Monroe, Rock Hudson, an impossibly youthful, incredibly blue-eyed Paul Newman.

They were all so very young in the pictures. They were all gone now.

As were a young girl named Nicole Solomon, and boys named Robert and Edward Gillen.

Against his better judgment Byrne stacked the magazines on the mantel. There was a pretty good chance that after he died, someone would be going through the house and find them again.

He had never been much of a pack rat, but now that he was living – although he was far from taking occupancy – in the largest place of his entire life, he had no intention of starting.

Byrne's first order of business was to remove the old plaster from the walls. He had priced out restoring the plaster and had almost laughed into the phone when he heard the estimate. For a fleeting moment he thought the man had given him a price on the entire *job*, that being six rooms. Even *that* seemed high.

The truth was, he was being quoted a price on just the parlor.

Hearing that, making the decision to use drywall instead was a no-brainer.

By ten, Byrne had three of the four walls done. The hard part was knocking off the dried plaster that was keyed between the horizontal slats of wood lath.

There was one wall left.

He brought the lamp with the 200 watt bulb in it across the room, plugged it in. On this, the wall opposite the fireplace, he saw that there was a large rectangle, a shape that was lighter in color than the rest of the room. It appeared that there had, at one time, been a rather large painting in that space. The number of nail holes supported this theory. Unfortunately there was a fist-sized hole in the wood lath. Not a big deal, if the studs on either side were in good shape. They would still be able hang drywall.

He got a keyhole saw out of his toolbox, returned to the room, proceeded to cut out the splintered sections of wood lath.

When he got down to about waist level, he looked into the opening. There was something at the bottom. It looked like a wad of paper, folded into quarters. He walked to the kitchen, poked around his makeshift toolbox. None of the tools looked like they could do the job.

Byrne found a piece of door trim, drove a nail through it, bent

317

it forward. He went back into the room in which he had been working, shone a flashlight down between the studs with one hand, and attempted to spear the paper with the other.

After a few attempts he got it.

He carefully brought the sheaf of papers up and out from behind the wall.

In the kitchen he unfolded the pages, and carefully smoothed them out on the table. They were large, perhaps ten inches by fourteen, and yellowed by time. On the front of the first page were a pair of drawings, clearly made by a child. The top drawing was of a rectangle, hastily – perhaps angrily – drawn in blue crayon. In the lower left-hand of the rectangle was a black mark, a vertical slash no more than a half-inch high.

Below this drawing was a large stick figure. It was drawn in brown crayon and appeared to be a man with big white gloves and a top hat.

A man with no face.

At the bottom were six words, all written in a child's careful hand.

Room is blue. Room is dark.

Byrne looked at the drawing at the top of the first page. There was no question that the rectangle, furiously colored, was indeed blue. But what was the mark in the lower left-hand corner of the rectangle?

He went to the kitchen, opened up the box he had brought containing some basic office supplies – envelopes, rubber bands, his one and only stapler, a rubber-banded group of pencils. At the bottom was an old magnifying glass. He fished it out, gave it a shot of Windex, cleaned it off. He positioned himself under the overhead light and looked at the blue rectangle again.

What he had thought was merely a vertical black mark in the lower left-hand corner, was a drawing of a little girl. The stick figure drawing beneath the rectangle, the man wearing a top hat and big white gloves, was extremely crude.

The drawing of the little girl, even though no more than one inch high, was far more detailed. It looked to have been drawn with a fine-tipped pen, perhaps a fountain pen.

Byrne put the paper down on the table. He looked at all the other pages – six in all. On them were drawings of children; some were carefully rendered, some were primitive. One was a full page drawing of a girl. It was highly detailed – mouth, hair, dress, legs, feet, fingers – but the whole drawing was scribbled over, as if the child wanted to obliterate it.

All the drawings of adults, always a man, had some part missing.

There were no drawings of women.

At midnight he sat at the small card table in the kitchen, three fingers of Black Bush in a glass. The Thomas Rule binder was open in front of him.

On the night he had come to this house for the first time – the night Valerie Beckert had been arrested – he had signed into the crime scene log. It took nearly four hours for him and a pair of West Division detectives to search the premises, all to no avail.

The crime scene log in front of him showed him signing in, then out four hours and six minutes later.

But there was something in the log that he was not able to explain, something that had haunted him for ten years. Now, sitting in the very house, it hit home.

The crime scene log showed him signing back in at midnight that same night, then signing out forty-four minutes later.

Forty-four minutes. Not unusual, but he had no memory of doing so.

It was at a time in his life when he suffered from migraines with aura, but even then he had never lost track of time.

Why had he come back to the house that night? What had he done while he was here? What, if anything, had he discovered? And, most importantly, if he had found something, where was it now?

He did not have an explanation for any of this.

He thought of these things as he pulled up a chair, placed it before the front window. He shut off the kitchen light, poured himself another drink, brought the drawings with him, sat in the chair.

As fatigue overtook him, he lost all sense of time and place.

When he was startled awake, two hours later, he was still in the chair. His dreams had been violent. The house had been filled with cries of anguish and pain.

Forty-four minutes. Six children missing.

Byrne looked out the window, his heart pounding. The street was silent and still, the shadow of the house a long di Chirico painting on the pavement.

What was happening to him?

Room is blue.

Room is dark.

50

Jessica was so preoccupied walking across the parking lot at the Roundhouse that she almost walked right into the man.

She had gotten up early, got the kids ready, made breakfast for herself and Vincent, and managed to get in a three mile run all before seven a.m. She was still in her running clothes when she drove in to work.

'Oh, I'm *sorry*,' she said. She stepped back, looked at the man, and had that strange feeling of *déjà vu* – not based on having done this precise thing before, but rather the feeling of having met this man in a different situation, a different life.

'Hello, detective,' he said.

When he smiled, she placed him. The man was FBI Special Agent Terry Cahill.

'*Terry*,' she said. 'My God, how long has it been?'

He smiled, thought for a moment. 'A long time.'

She gave him a hug. Not professional, but she liked Terry, and they were far from being deployed in the same squad.

Agent Terry Cahill worked out of the Philadelphia field office of the FBI. His office had worked with the PPD on many notable joint task forces over the years, quite often with the Narcotics and Auto Units, and just as often with Homicide. If a body crossed state lines, or a victim was kidnapped, the FBI offered assistance. Many times it wasn't an offer, but rather a request from PPD brass.

Jessica and Byrne, as well as the entire PPD, had once worked with Terry Cahill and his team to hunt down a very bad man nicknamed The Actor a few years earlier, a case during which Cahill had been injured.

You would never know that now. Terry Cahill looked great.

'You're so tan,' Jessica said.

'It's a full time job,' he said.

'So, have you been assigned to the Miami office or something?'

'Actually, I've been liaison with the consulate in Mexico City for the past year or so. The cartels keep us pretty busy. Back in Philly to stay.'

'Well, *hola* and *bienvenido.*'

'*Gracias.*'

'What brings you to our humble *casa*?'

'Got something I think you should see.'

Jessica waited for more. More was not forthcoming. '*Me* or *us* or the whole of PPD?'

'Are you still partnered with Kevin?'

'For life,' she said. 'We're like pigeons and Catholics.'

'I think you should call him.'

The ride to the rest area off I-476, just south of the Borough of Emmaus, in Lehigh County, took a little over an hour. On the way, Jessica and Byrne rode in virtual silence. The fact that they had discovered – more accurately, the FBI had discovered – additional evidence concerning this series of murders, broadened the investigation even further.

They followed Cahill's departmental sedan, which rode at a respectful and legal sixty miles per hour the entire way.

Cahill left the turnpike, took the spur to the other side – the southbound side – and pulled into the rest area. The stop had a huge parking lot, in which a half-dozen or so eighteen-wheel rigs were parked.

There was also a fueling station, an RV dump, and a small diner called Dot's.

They all exited their cars, slipped on their winter gloves. Cahill put on a knit watch cap. The temperature had dropped fifteen or so degrees in the past hour.

Cahill led them to a far end of the lot where a worn-out big rig sat. It was the kind of semi with a studio sleeper behind the driver compartment.

A pair of Pennsylvania state troopers sat in their car next to the truck, engine running for heat.

'The rig has been here about three weeks,' Cahill said. 'The owner of the diner – who leases the lot from the Commonwealth – was going to call in the plates to see if he could contact the owner and get it off the lot, but there are no plates.'

'Has this happened to him before?'

Cahill shook his head. 'People don't abandon eighteen-wheelers. Not like some rusted out old Toyota. Even one in this shape could fetch eighty grand.'

'When did he suspect something was wrong?' Byrne asked.

'He said he came out to look in the truck last night, opened the driver's door, and freaked out.'

Cahill opened the driver's door.

'There was blood all over the wheel, the door handle. Forensics say there were trace amounts leading toward that path, but not enough to make a match.'

Cahill walked over to his car, reached inside, took out a large envelope. He opened it, handed Byrne a document.

When Jessica looked at the photocopy, a shiver went up her spine. She thought about how it had surfaced more than forty miles away from any of the other crime scenes.

The date coincided with the Nicole Solomon murder.

You are invited!
November 16
See you at our thé dansant!

'Your open investigation was posted on our secure site, so when the state police logged on and put in the information, it flagged,' Cahill said. 'State called us, we called you.'

'Much appreciated,' Byrne said.

'It looks like the same handwriting,' Cahill said.

Cahill went on to tell Jessica and Byrne that he'd sent exemplars to the FBI document section at Quantico. Their databases and resources were vastly superior to any municipal police department's.

'We'll run it by our documents examiner, but it looks identical,' Byrne said. He held it up. 'Where was this found?'

'It was in the visor on the driver's side.' Cahill reached into the truck's cab, flipped down the visor. Clipped there was a smudged, half-silvered mirror, as well as an index card of a logo, a tongue coming out of the back of an eighteen-wheeler. Beneath the logo it said *Rolling Stoned, LLC.*

'Rolling Stoned,' Byrne asked.

'We're looking into it,' Cahill said.

'And the truck was unlocked?' Byrne asked.

Cahill nodded.

Jessica could see the black powder on the visor. The truck had been processed for prints.

'After the diner owner – his name is Richard Kendall – saw the blood on the door and the seat, he called the state troopers. When they didn't show within ten minutes or so, he admits that his morbid curiosity got the better of him. He walked the path over there. The snow had melted a bit, and that's when he found the bodies.'

'How long do you think they've been out there?' Byrne asked.

'Our anthropology team says three weeks, give or take.'

'Can you show us where they were?'

They walked across the parking lot, into the forest. The path was about three feet wide, but not paved. It was a hardpan clay, well traveled.

'Is there something back here?' Jessica asked, pointing to the other end of the path.

'There's a tavern, not part of the township,' Cahill said. 'You can't sell liquor within a mile of these rest stops, but that only counts for establishments in the same township.'

The yellow tape ringed an area about fifty by fifty feet where the bodies were found.

Cahill took out the crime scene photos. They were grotesque.

The dead woman looked to be in her forties. She wore a short denim shirt and jacket, no blouse. Her face looked to have been severely burned. She had no eyes.

'Any ID on her?' Byrne asked.

Cahill consulted his notes. 'The victim is Deirdre Emily Reese, forty-six, late of Richlandtown. We talked to the manager of the tavern, and learned that Ms Reese was last seen there on the night of November nine or so in the company of the other victim.'

'Hate to be indelicate, but was she a working girl?' Byrne asked.

'The bartender says yes, but added he hadn't seen her in maybe a year until that night. I ran a check and found out she had done nine months for soliciting and possession, getting out of county just this past October.'

'What about the other victim?'

'No ID, and nothing in the truck. Running the VIN.'

'Where are the bodies now?'

'They're at the county coroner's office. We have a team and equipment on the way from Quantico. The county's not really equipped to perform an autopsy on victims that are this compromised.'

Jessica glanced again at the photographs. The dead man's face was all but obliterated. It was clear that any number of animals had been at him. But that wasn't the worst part. The worst part was that his arms and legs had been severed from the trunk of his body, and were stacked in a neat pile next to him.

Jessica pointed at the photo. 'Any idea on a weapon?'

'Team says an ax, perhaps a machete,' Cahill said.

'Nice,' Jessica said. She held up the photos. 'Can we get copies of these?'

'You're holding them.'

'Call us if and when you make an ID,' Byrne said. 'We'll be working on that on our end, too.'

'Sure thing,' Cahill said.

'Thanks, Terry,' Jessica added. 'Don't be a stranger at the Roundhouse.'

'I won't,' he said. 'Be safe.'

They sat in silence for a few minutes while the car warmed up.

'Rolling Stoned, LLC,' Jessica said.

Byrne didn't bother stating the obvious. 'Do you want to make the call first or go to Shawmont?'

'Let's call,' Jessica said. 'He's earned it.'

'I'll tell Terry.'

While Byrne got out of the car and walked across the lot, Jessica searched her bag for the business card, found it. She took out her phone and called Detective Jack Paris, Homicide Division, Cleveland Police Department.

They had found Ezekiel Moss.

*

Jessica and Maria Caruso stood on the platform, looking at the dark woods around them. Because Byrne was expecting his family for dinner, Maria had agreed to drive to the Shawmont station to help Jessica conduct the search.

Jessica had thought about asking other detectives to join them, but decided against it. There was no threat in this place. Not any longer.

As they stepped from the platform, fanning out into the darkness, Jessica tried to find the path easiest to travel. As she moved through the low scrub she heard things scurry in the darkness. Squirrels, perhaps rabbits. Every so often she would turn, look back at the train platform.

Twenty minutes later, as she was just about to give it up for the night, opting to come back in daylight, her boot tapped up against something solid.

She crouched down, moved some of the ground cover to the side, and found it.

There, on the ground, was a doll that looked like Ezekiel Moss.

Next to it was a stack of doll arms and legs.

51

Of all the people whom Byrne was nervous about seeing his new house – and they really weren't that many – his daughter Colleen, by far, made him the most anxious.

When she pulled in the driveway, in her Kia Rio 5 – which she purchased on her own, even though Byrne had offered to pay for it – he stepped out onto the porch.

All of his worry was for naught. He could see through the windshield the look on his daughter's face. Although she had been deaf since birth, like many in the deaf community she relied quite a bit on facial expressions to communicate.

'Oh my God, dad, I love it,' Colleen signed.

Byrne felt a huge weight lifted from his shoulders. 'Thanks, honey,' he signed. 'It's coming along.'

If Byrne had learned anything since buying the house it was that the standard response to people saying nice things about the project was 'it's coming along.' If he owned the house another twenty years, and replaced every floorboard, door, fixture, cabinet, and appliance, he was probably going to say the same thing.

Colleen opened the hatch at the back of her car, reached in, and extracted a large healthy houseplant with a bright red ribbon and bow wrapped around the ceramic pot. She closed and locked the hatch and walked up the walk.

Byrne smiled. 'You know you've just signed a death warrant on that plant, don't you?'

Colleen smiled back. 'I predict many years in the appellate process.'

Although his daughter was majoring in business administration at Gallaudet University, the first and preeminent higher learning institution in the country for deaf and hard of hearing students, she had been around the cop life most of her life, and knew the vagaries, terms, and jokes.

Byrne took the plant from his daughter, placed it on the porch. They hugged. Byrne felt his heart soar. He had not seen his daughter in a few months and he felt his emotions running away. It seemed to be happening increasingly of late.

He leaned back, looked at his daughter's face, her beautiful aquamarine eyes.

'I've missed you,' he said aloud. There was no need to sign such a thing.

His daughter smiled, and Byrne saw her eyes began to mist.

'What's wrong?' he signed.

Colleen shook her head, hugged him again. When she pulled away, their attention was drawn by something at the far side of the porch. They both turned to look.

It was Tuck. The cat was just sitting there, as if he owned the place. Maybe he did.

Colleen beamed. 'Is he yours?'

'I don't know yet,' Byrne signed. He went on to tell Colleen how he'd met the cat.

'And he still likes you after you brained him with the brick?'

'Jury is out on that one. On the other hand, if he knew I spent two hundred sixty dollars with the vet, he might be a little more appreciative.'

When Tuck jumped on the railing, and began to preen, they saw what he had been hiding. There were two dead mice, set like a gift beneath the window sill.

Having been dropped off by one of his old dockworker buddies, Paddy Byrne arrived, a six-pack of Harp lager in hand.

The entire, immediate Byrne clan sat around a card table in the eat-in kitchen. The food was from an Indian takeout. Byrne had never had Chicken Tikka Masala before, but Colleen admitted to a twelve-step-sized addiction to it. Byrne could see why. It was delicious.

Halfway through the meal, well in his cups, Paddy Byrne raised his bottle of Harp. 'To being around a table like this for many years to come,' he said. *'Sláinte chuig na fir, agus go mairfidh na mná go deo.'*

The three of them touched bottles.

There was no need to translate the toast into sign language – a toast that meant health to the men, and may the women live forever – for Colleen. It was her grandfather's one and only tribute.

While Colleen did the dishes, Byrne fetched a fresh six pack for himself and his father. Byrne sat on the floor, his back to the wall. Paddy took the easy chair, the only stick of furniture in the living room.

After a few minutes of silence, Paddy said: 'Your mother always wanted a house like this.'

They had lived in a few different small apartments in and around Pennsport when Byrne was growing up, mostly because of Paddy Byrne's job as a dockworker. Byrne never recalled a time when there wasn't enough room.

'You know, I've never asked you . . . ' Byrne said.

'Asked me what?'

'How you met.'

'Me and your mom?'

Byrne nodded. 'Yeah. I can't believe I don't know this. Do you remember the first time you set eyes on her?'

'Do I ever.'

Byrne cracked open another beer, handed it to his father. Paddy took it. It gave the old guy a few seconds to gather the tale. Byrne had been thirty-eight when he'd lost his mother to cancer. He and his father had never really discussed it. He imagined they never would. The Irish, for all their passion, for all the raucous energy of their wakes, did their real grieving alone.

'I was twenty years old,' Paddy said. 'I was working Pier Eighty-Two with your Uncle Michael in those days. Davy's dad.'

Byrne smiled. 'I know who Uncle Mike is.'

Paddy glared. 'Do you want to hear this or not?'

Byrne tipped the neck of his beer, meaning: *Sorry. Go on.*

'Anyway, we were working Eighty-Two – this was before they built the Packer Avenue Terminal – and we would hit this little place called Katie's over on West Oregon. The food was crap, but the beer was always cold.' He sipped his lager. 'So anyway, there was this little dress shop across the street, and every day, when we were getting to Katie's – maybe around five-thirty – the ladies at the dress shop were getting ready to close at six. Three years we went to Katie's and I never paid that dress shop any mind.'

Byrne just listened.

'So, one day I'm sitting there, maybe checking the *Daily News*, and I look across the street, and I see this woman locking up. I only see her from behind, right? Beautiful strawberry blond hair. And she had on this fine red coat.'

'I remember that coat,' Byrne said.

'I couldn't get her out of my mind. A few days later I'm sitting in a booth by the front window, and I see a shadow to my right. I look up, and there she is. Never a more beautiful woman born. She was standing on the sidewalk, wearing that red coat, putting on her lipstick, using the front window at Katie's for her mirror.'

'Did you go out and talk to her?'

Paddy shook his head. 'I was wordstruck. She was way out of my league, boyo – as you probably know –and, believe it or not, I didn't have the gift then.'

'Hard to believe.'

'For the next three months I wore out the sidewalk in front of that dress shop, trying to work up the nerve to talk to her. Finally, I did.'

'Did she say yes the first time you asked her out?'

Paddy smiled. 'She did. She said she'd wondered when the crazy man walking up and down the block was going to walk in and get it over with. She also told me she was beginning to wonder whether putting on her lipstick right in front of me that first time had been a bad idea.'

Byrne smiled, glanced out his front window.

There were two times a year, somewhere in spring and some-where in late fall, when the gloaming light in Philadelphia was perfect. This was one of those times. Or maybe it was the lager, and this moment with his father.

'I see her face sometimes,' Paddy said.

Byrne expected his father to continue. He did not. 'What do you mean?'

'When I look at you. I see your mother's face. Not always, but sometimes.'

Byrne said nothing.

'You have this look, when something isn't quite the way you thought it was going to be,' Paddy said. 'Your ma used to do that. Every time I saw that look I knew I was in trouble.'

'As I recall, you were in trouble a lot.'

'I was,' Paddy said. He sipped his beer. 'Do you see Donna's face when you look at Colleen?'

All the time, Byrne thought. 'Yeah,' he said. 'I do.'

'Funny, that, isn't it?'

It occurred to Byrne, and not for the first time, that he and his father had to be the only two Irish Catholic men in Philly – maybe the world, for that matter – with one child each. Paddy Byrne still harbored the notion that his son would one day meet a woman, get married, and have a few more children. Paddy Byrne still thought of him as if he were twenty-five years old.

Byrne stood up. 'Go for a wee dram, Da?'

'Okay,' Paddy said. 'Maybe a short one.'

Byrne went for the bottle of Black Bush he kept in the small broom closet off the pantry. When he opened the door he

didn't mean to break the vase with the yellow flowers in it

knew that this small space was once a place of confinement.

He touched the brass key in his pocket.

It felt like an amulet.

52

Valerie sat at the kitchen table, a cup of chamomile tea in front of her. She'd made a tray of brownies for the next day's dessert, but her mind had been elsewhere, and she'd left out the sugar. The kitchen still smelled of chocolate.

At just after midnight she stepped into the pantry, took out the brass key, and opened the broom closet.

'You can come out now,' she said.

A full minute later Thaddeus emerged from the darkness. Valerie helped him onto a chair in the kitchen, sat across from him.

'Do you have anything to say?' she asked.

The boy looked at his hands.

'I'm sorry,' he said softly. 'I didn't mean to spill the water on the floor.'

'And what about the vase?'

Thaddeus glanced at the sideboard, where the crystal flower vase had once stood, filled with daffodils. Now the flowers were in an old ceramic water pitcher, a chipped jug with a missing handle.

The boy looked back at Valerie, his eyes red from crying. She had locked him in the small closet off the pantry before supper. None of the other children had asked where he was.

'I'm sorry,' he repeated.

Valerie gave the apology the proper amount of time to settle. 'Okay,' she said. 'You are forgiven.'

The boy didn't move.

'You didn't have any supper,' Valerie said. 'I kept a plate warm for you. Are you hungry?'

Thaddeus shook his head.

'Are you sure? It's fried chicken. Your favorite.'

'No thank you.'

Valerie waited a few moments. Children were always changing their minds. Thaddeus did not.

'I have something for you,' Valerie said. 'A present. Do you want to see?'

He brightened a little. 'Yes.'

Valerie walked across the kitchen, into the dining room. When she returned she had in her hands a Macy's bag. From it she pulled out a pair of new pajamas, handed them to the boy.

'Do you like them?' she asked.

'Very much.'

'They are dark blue. Just like your eyes.'

Thaddeus held the package tightly to his chest, but didn't open it.

'Okay,' she said. 'Off to bed with you, young man.'

Thaddeus slipped off the chair, and all but ran to the steps. Seconds later, Valerie heard him reach the top.

She turned off the oven, took out the boy's plate, wrapped it in foil. Before heading off to bed herself, she crossed the pantry, opened the door to the broom closet. The ceiling light in the pantry shone inside.

The mop and duster were hanging from eightpenny nails, as always, but the broom was leaning against the wall. Next to it, in the corner, was a small pile of dust.

While he was locked in the closet, Thaddeus Woodman had swept up.

53

Andi looked at her watch for what had to be the twentieth time in the last hour.

How long could one friggin' day last?

When she'd gotten the job at American Apparel at King of Prussia Mall – the massive shopping center in Upper Merion Township, anchored by Lord & Taylor, Neiman Marcus, Bloomingdale's and Nordstrom – she'd taken on a thirty-hour week because she thought she could pull it, along with school-work, and save up some money for a trip to New York next summer.

Saturday was her only full day, and she had figured that hanging around a mall all day – something she'd done anyway since she was about thirteen – would be kind of cool. Fun, even.

As it turned out, not so much.

She'd applied at a number of places in the mall, places she'd really *wanted* to work: Armani Exchange, Diesel, J. Crew, Lacoste, even Gucci, Hermès, and Burberry. No dice at any of them. Either they weren't hiring, or thought Andi didn't have 'the look,' whatever the hell that was. She'd browsed at all those stores many times and, yes, everyone who worked there was well dressed, everyone there was well groomed, but none of them were all that. Not a Jennifer Lawrence or Selena Gomez among them.

In the end, American Apparel was an okay fit.

Except today. Today it was a graveyard.

Andi stepped out from behind the counter, trying to look busy. She folded and refolded some crewneck sweaters at the front table, straightened some purses on the two end caps, straightened sleeves on the rack of skater dresses which, Andi had to admit, were pretty cool. She got a pretty good employee discount. Maybe she'd get one.

Of course, she'd probably have to lose five pounds first.

She was just about to head to the back of the store to unbox some new stretch denim pencil pants – also cool, a seven-pound loss required – when she heard the soft tone that sounded when someone entered the store.

She turned to greet the customer, but the words froze on her lips.

He was that good-looking.

'Hi,' Andi finally managed. 'Welcome to American Apparel.'

He smiled. Andi's knees went a little watery.

'Thank you,' he said.

He wore a navy blue suit, white spread collar shirt, and a deep burgundy tie. The shirt was a French cuff. He wore tasteful sterling silver cufflinks in the shape of the letter M. Or maybe it was a W.

Andi was pretty good at spotting designers, but his suit looked to be a bespoke.

'I hope you don't mind, but I've been watching you,' he said. He pointed to the benches by the fountain, just outside the entrance. 'I've been sitting just there most of the morning.'

Try as she did to stop herself, Andi blushed. 'I don't mind.'

'I'm wondering if you'd like to sit and chat with me,' he said. 'Perhaps after work, or whenever you get a break.'

Andi glanced at her watch. 'I get a break around two.'

'Wonderful. I noticed that there is a small court near the entrance to Nordstrom. Will you meet me there?'

'Uh, sure,' Andi said. 'Okay.'

He once again smiled. 'Two o'clock it is.'

Andi turned and almost walked into the front table.

When Andi entered the Café Court, she saw him sitting at a table. He wasn't reading a magazine, he wasn't looking at a cell phone, he wasn't drinking coffee or eating some crap food available at the food court. He was just sitting there, legs crossed, hands folded on the table, his bright white cuffs pulled a perfect inch from the cuff of his dark suit.

Just sitting there.

When he saw her approach he stood, held a chair for her.

'I'm so pleased you came.'

Andi sat. Since he came into the store she had been rehearsing things she might say. Being this close to him, however, it all left her head, as if someone opened one side of her brain, and walked across it with a Swiffer.

'Tell me about you,' he said. 'I want to know everything.'

Andi tried to think of something clever to say. Instead she said: 'There's really not much to tell.'

'I'm sure there is.'

Andi took the next few minutes to give her brief life story: mom and dad, school, work, her favorite music, her favorite movies, her favorite foods. It all sounded so boring, like some suburban nightmare compared to whatever and whoever this boy was.

'By the way, I really like your suit,' she added.

'Thank you,' he said. 'I think it is important to always look your best.'

'Most of the boys I know dress like slobs. I hate all that saggy-pants crap.'

'As do I.'

'They come in the store and they never buy anything. Half the time my manager just kicks them out. I can't tell you how many times she's had to call mall security.'

He touched the lapel of his suit, flicking away a spot of lint. 'The boys are probably just trying to impress you.'

'Why would they want to do that?'

'Because you are beautiful.'

Andi almost choked. 'You think I'm *beautiful*?'

He reached out a well-manicured finger, gently moved a strand of hair from her face. 'You are the smile of Garbo and the scent of roses.'

'Wow,' she said. 'What's that from?'

'Just an old song.'

None of this seemed real. But Andi decided to just go with it. 'I don't even know your name.'

'I am Marseille.'

So the cufflinks were an M, not a W, she thought. 'That's a *very* cool name.'

Andi wanted to ask him if that was his first name or his last name, but she didn't want to pry. She didn't want to give this guy any reason to end this conversation, either. Even though she had to get back to the store. Amazing how a day that was dragging could speed up and fly by.

'And you are Andrea,' he added.

Andi was surprised. 'How do you know my name?'

He smiled, held her gaze. A few seconds later it hit her.

Andi closed her eyes, realizing she'd just said the dumbest thing she'd ever said. Seventeen years – seventeen and two months, thank you – and she'd chosen this moment to utter the dumbest words of all time.

Great, Andi.

She lifted up her nametag. 'I'm so stupid.'

'Not at all,' he said. He leaned forward. 'When are you through for the day?'

Andi looked at her watch. She knew she was off at four o'clock, so whatever time it was now didn't matter. She just needed something to look at. She glanced back up.

'I'm off at four.'

'Do you have plans for after work?'

She didn't. She never did. 'No.'

'I'd like to invite you to tea.'

Of all the things she expected him to say, an invitation to tea was probably last. 'Tea?'

'Yes,' he said. 'Every Saturday we have a tea dance – a *dansant*, if you'll allow. It is quite the formal affair. You'll love my friends. They are quite a lively and eccentric lot.'

'It's a dance?'

'Yes.'

This was a first, Andi thought. But why not?

'Sure,' she said. 'It sounds like fun.'

'Wonderful,' he said. 'Where shall we meet?'

Andi was going to get a ride from her friend Tacy, who worked at the men's fragrance counter at Nordstrom. This was way better.

'I'll meet you by the south entrance to Saks,' she said.

He looked deeply into her eyes for a few moments, then said: 'I shall count the moments.'

54

It was Saturday. The Homicide Unit was on tenterhooks.

Every time the phone rang, the six detectives working the task force expected it to be news of another body, another invitation to die.

Byrne had worked the phones all morning and early afternoon, trying to track the history of the two children who went into the Philadelphia County welfare system – specifically into a long-shuttered foster care home in the Nicetown section of Philadelphia, a group home called Vista House.

At two he found a direction. He spoke to a woman, Dr Meredith Allen, who had done some work with Vista House when the eight children were transferred from Pittsburgh more than twelve years ago. She agreed to meet him.

Meredith Allen was an attractive, dark-haired woman in her late thirties. Her office was on Tenth and Spruce, a converted double row home on a fully restored block.

Twelve years earlier Dr Allen had been a psychology fellow,

and told Byrne that there had been a program in place at that time, one that served to document the psychological status of children who became residents of Vista House, as well as a number of other foster care homes in the tri-county area.

They met in her office.

'So you evaluated all the children who came into intake for Vista House?' Byrne asked.

'Myself and another fellow, yes. It was all supervised by a psychiatrist who was on the board.'

'As I said on the phone, we're trying to locate a boy and a girl who came to Vista at that time. They would have been about six years old.'

'What are their names?'

'That I don't know. They entered and left the Mahoning and Allegheny County welfare systems as a John and Jane Doe.'

Dr Allen nodded. 'There were a few at Vista House at the time.' She stood, crossed the office, opened a file drawer. After a few minutes she returned. She had eight photographs in hand. She arrayed them on the desk. Four boys, four girls.

She pointed at two of the pictures. 'These children were older. They were closer to eight.'

Byrne looked at the other six children. Two were biracial. Two looked similar enough to be brother and sister, though not enough alike to be twins. He pointed at those photographs.

'I think these might be the children.'

Dr Allen looked at the pictures. 'Yes, okay,' she said. 'I remember them.'

'There are no names on the photographs.'

'No,' she said. 'We only knew them by their case numbers.'

'Do you remember anything about their session?'

'I can do better.'

'What do you mean?'

'For three years every child's intake, county wide, was videotaped. I made copies of all the sessions in which I was involved for a documentary I considered producing at the time, a film about the long-term effects of foster care. Something akin to the *Seven Up!* series.'

'What happened to your film?'

'Life, work, my own children, but mostly funding.'

'And you're saying you still have some of the taped interviews?'

'I have them all.'

Byrne tapped the two photographs on the table. 'Do you know where these children went when Vista House closed?'

'No idea,' she said. 'Could have been anywhere. There may be records buried somewhere in the county system. I can try to find someone who might know where to begin looking.'

Byrne made the note. 'Before we get started, do you mind if I ask your opinion on something?'

'Not at all.'

Byrne reached for his bag, took out the drawings he'd found buried in the walls of his house. He smoothed them out on the desk.

Dr Allen put on her glasses, looked at the drawings.

'Can you tell me anything about them?' Byrne asked.

Dr Allen pointed to one drawing, one that depicted a boy with a large head and arms. 'This might display a central language disorder in the child. You see how there was poor planning? No room for legs.'

She picked up a second picture. This one was of a tree. 'This shows an unhappy child, but one of higher intelligence.'

'Unhappy how?'

'The leaves are falling off the tree, and there are dark clouds overhead. Plus, the drawing of the tree's roots continue underground. This is a smart child, but quite a sad one. Unless the scene is in bright colors, and there's a sun shining, falling leaves is never a good thing.'

'So dark colors are a warning sign?'

'As a rule of thumb. Children generally have the full palette from which to choose. If they pick dark colors exclusively, it's for a reason.'

Room is blue, Byrne thought. *Room is dark.*

He picked up a drawing. 'What can you tell me about this one?'

'This is quite compelling. You see how all the elements of the figure are present – head, eyes, ears, nose, mouth, arms, and legs?'

'Yes.'

'But notice also how the figure is disjointed. Nothing is attached.'

Byrne just nodded.

'This means that the child was from a dysfunctional, broken home. Very insecure. And probably excessively fearful of the unfamiliar.'

Byrne took a moment to absorb the information. He gathered the pictures together.

'I can't tell you how grateful I am for all of this.'

'Happy to help,' Dr Allen said. She stood up. 'Shall we begin?'

The play therapy room was small, windowless, the walls painted a cheerful primrose yellow. Along one wall was a series of two-way mirrors. At the far end was a 24 × 36 inch box filled with white sand, standing about 24 inches from the floor.

The other side of the room, floor to ceiling, were shelves.

'And this room is essentially the same as it was twelve years ago?' Byrne asked.

'It is,' Dr Allen said. 'The carpeting has changed. Twice, I think. It's certainly been painted. When you have children passing through all day every day things can get messy.'

Byrne pointed at the bookshelves. 'What about these objects?'

'We've added some things, got rid of some. Many have been broken, of course, and had to be replaced.'

Byrne walked over to the built-in shelving, looked a little more closely at the objects. Because everything in the room was scaled for children, he felt like Gulliver among the Lilliputians.

On the two top shelves on the right were buildings – houses, school, stores, castles, churches, a gas station. Two of the larger structures on the shelf looked to have doors that opened and closed. Beneath those objects were two shelves of vehicles. There were a number of cars and trucks, bicycles, airplanes, a pair of steam shovels. The lower shelf was devoted solely to prams and baby carriages, bassinets and high chairs.

The shelves on the left, floor to ceiling, were people – babies, children, teenagers, adults. The adults appeared to represent every imaginable profession, plus, as expected, kings, queens, princesses, and superheroes.

'I'm not sure I know what play therapy is,' Byrne said.

'Play therapy is a way for a child to convey thoughts and feel-ings – what's happening inside of them – without using words,' Dr Allen said. 'We ask them to create a world in the sand tray using figurines and other toys. There they can address their problems in a non-threatening environment.'

'Is it easy to spot aberrant behaviors?'

'Not easy,' she said. 'But young children aren't yet practiced in hiding or masking their feelings. What we do is really equal parts art and science.'

'How so?'

'It is an art because a good deal of the therapy is based on the therapist's ingenuity, sensitivity, and impulsiveness.'

'And the science?'

'This is where the research and clinical studies come in.'

Byrne looked back at the shelves. He thought about his own childhood, one about which he held no bad memories. He wondered what world he, as a six-year-old, would have created in a sand tray.

'Are you ready to watch the video?' Dr Allen asked.

'I am.'

The adjoining room was long and narrow, and ran the length of the mirrored wall in the play therapy room. Along one wall was a built-in desk with four computer monitors.

Dr Allen sat down at one of the monitors. She motioned for Byrne to do the same at another. At the moment the screensaver on all four terminals was Winnie the Pooh and Tigger.

'What you are going to watch is a play therapy session which I had with the two children. It's about ten minutes long.'

'Did you have contact with them before or since?'

Dr Allen shook her head. 'What you're about to see is my first contact with the children. And my last.'

She tapped a key. The same image appeared on both monitors. The first shot was a title and time code. The image then cut to the room next door.

It was an eye-level shot about three feet from the floor, perhaps slightly higher. It allowed a clear view of the sand tray.

When the boy and girl walked into the frame, Byrne felt a prickling sensation at the back of his neck.

Was he really looking at a pair of cold-blooded killers at six years old?

The girl was pretty and prim. She wore a white cardigan sweater and dark skirt, along with a white hat. The boy's hair was neatly combed. He wore a white shirt, buttoned to the top, and dark trousers.

For ten minutes or so Byrne watched the girl and the boy create scenarios in the sand tray. The girl went to the shelves first. She seemed to hesitate before taking any of the dolls from the shelf.

'When you present a grouping of dolls like this, what choices do they generally make?' Byrne asked. 'Do they pick a mom and dad and kids? Do they pick just themselves and one parent?'

'It depends. Their choices often reflect their home environment.'

'And if they were abandoned?'

'Then they might not choose any of the adult dolls.'

As if on cue, the little girl brought a handful of dolls to the sand tray. None were adults. Only one was a boy. She put them in a circle, facing in. She put the boy behind one of the girls.

A few moments later the boy brought over an adult doll, a woman. He placed the doll outside the circle, behind the boy doll, facing the other way.

After a few moments, he began to dig a shallow hole, a hole into which he placed the woman doll, burying her up to her neck.

Was this his mother? Had the boy gotten the note from Crystal Anders, and now she was all but dead to him?

Byrne watched the little boy and girl carefully. They were never more than a few feet from each other. Every so often, when the girl dropped something, or got sand on her skirt, the boy would pick up the object, or brush her off.

He was very protective.

Every so often, the girl would turn two of the dolls to face each other, pairing them off, two by two.

'Why is she doing that?' Byrne asked.

'The dolls become the child's family. They will act out, with the dolls, often what happens at home. So, if they are experiencing violence, they may bang the doll's head, or hit another doll. They can act out not only what they see, but what they wish would happen.'

'Is this typical of play therapy?'

'I expected to see them again, so I treated this as a first session. I allowed them to see a spectrum of things, and do whatever they wanted,' she said. 'You don't allow a child to hurt themselves, of course, but you want them to tell their story and feel comfortable doing it.'

The boy and girl stood next to the sand tray. The girl held a doll that could have been herself. The boy held the adult woman doll. He held it upside down.

'Whenever you approach the child, you allow them to displace what is going on in the home with these creatures,' she said.

Onscreen, the little girl took out the tea set, and placed a small cup in front of each one of the dolls. As she lifted each cup to the doll's lips, the boy followed her. When the girl moved on – after every doll had a sip of tea – the boy took each doll, and placed it face down in the sand.

When they were done, the little girl sat on a chair, facing the camera. She took off her hat, and placed it on her lap.

There, on the left side of her head, was a barrette. A barrette in the shape of a swan.

The same barrette they'd found on Nicole Solomon.

A few minutes earlier Byrne had wondered if he was looking at a pair of cold-blooded killers at the age of six.

Now he was certain.

Byrne stood on the bank of the Schuylkill River, near the East Falls Bridge. He often came to the rivers to think.

Dr Allen had graciously allowed him to take the videotape with him, and promised to make the calls necessary to try and track the path of the boy and girl after Vista House closed.

They now had a direct line from that moment, eighteen years ago, when a teenaged girl in Weirton, West Virginia met a long-haul trucker, a malevolent spirit that haunted the corridor from Atlanta to Detroit.

When Byrne got back in the car he looked at the drawings on the seat next to him. The picture on top was the one with the obliterated little girl.

Room is blue. Room is dark.

By the time he reached the expressway he understood.

55

When Jessica entered the Video Monitoring Unit, located on the first floor of the Roundhouse, Maria Caruso was chatting with one of the officers assigned there.

The large room was arrayed with three tiers of long tables, each with a handful of wired terminals where a technician could jack in a laptop, or an all-in-one desktop, and from there monitor any of the city's hundreds of pole cameras.

At the front of the room was a huge, ten-foot diameter screen, a display available to mirror any of the terminals. Right now, on the screen, was a frozen, high-angle daytime shot of a Philadelphia street corner.

'What do we have?' Jessica asked.

'This is surveillance video of the street corner where Nicole Solomon was last seen with her friend, Naomi Burris.'

'We have a pole cam there?'

'No,' Maria said. 'This is a SafeCam video.'

SafeCam was a fairly new citizen outreach program whereby the location of private surveillance cameras – those owned by homeowners and business owners – were mapped by the PPD and Homeland Security.

If and when a crime occurred near the location of a particular SafeCam camera, the department would contact the homeowner or business owner to see if there was any footage. Not all SafeCam participants had systems that recorded audio and video to a hard drive, or Secure Digital card, and they were in no way legally bound by law to share the footage, if it existed.

The program had, to date, been a resounding success, at least as far as the department was concerned. With more than 2400 SafeCams in the program, in a little over a year there had been nearly two hundred cases solved.

On the screen, the angle showed Nicole Solomon, with her back to the camera, waiting at the light to cross the street.

Jessica found that she was holding her breath. It wasn't often – in fact, she could only remember a handful of times, via videotape or surveillance footage – that she got to see a victim of homicide alive in the minutes or hours before they were killed. She couldn't help but think that Sophie was just a few years younger than Nicole Solomon.

Soon a group of four people approached Nicole from behind. One was an older woman, with a cane in one hand, and a shopping bag in the other. The other was a tall man, African-American, talking on a cell phone. The other two – a young woman and young man – stepped up to the curb on Nicole's left.

Was this the girl from Miss Emmaline's shop? Was this the young man in the sketch they had gotten from Denny Wargo? It was impossible to tell.

After a few moments, the young man on Nicole's left turned to her. Nicole looked at him. They spoke for a short while. Other people gathered behind them and to Nicole's right, further obscuring the view. It was maddening.

When the light changed, the group proceeded across the street, then disappeared from the frame.

'Do we pick them up on another cam? One of ours?'

'No,' she said. 'I checked all our pole cams for three blocks.'

'What about private security?'

'Nothing yet,' Maria said.

Jessica was just about to pick up the phone and call the Comm Unit when she heard hard-soled shoes coming down the hallway. Fast. Both she and Maria looked at the doorway, and saw Josh Bontrager nearly run by the entrance to the Video Monitoring Unit.

Josh Bontrager had a tendency to run whenever he had important news.

'I followed up on your visit to Woodside,' Bontrager said to Jessica. 'And also on the lead that David Solomon – along with other personnel from Woodside – did some consulting work with Philadelphia County, as well as the Pennsylvania Department of Corrections.'

'What kind of work?' Maria asked.

'Well, they had two psychiatrists and four social workers on staff then. If the sheriff's office or the courts were backlogged with the therapists they usually contracted with, and they needed help with an evaluation, they called Woodside, or some other mental health provider, and they sent someone over.'

'And you're saying Solomon did some of this work for the courts?'

'Yes,' Bontrager said. 'But only six times. I cross-referenced his name on the log-in sheets with every name associated with these cases. I found one instance that jumped off the page. I think you'll see why.'

Bontrager put the printout on the table. It was an intake log of people signing into one of the hearing rooms at the Criminal

Justice Center. The readout listed names, room number, as well as the date and times signed in and out.

The date was ten years ago.

Jessica scanned the names. When she saw them her blood ran cold. Those in attendance were:

The Honorable Michael J. Gillen
David Solomon LCSW
Marvin Skolnik, Esq.

'Why were they there that day?' Maria asked.

'It was a competency hearing,' Bontrager said.

'Whose hearing?' Jessica asked.

The voice came from behind them.

'It was Valerie Beckert's.'

They all turned to see Byrne standing in the doorway.

'How do you know?' Jessica asked.

'I was supposed to be there.'

Byrne explained to the task force the details of Valerie Beckert's arrest, and that he had been scheduled to testify at her competency hearing, but was never called. He never entered the hearing room, and did not know who else was present.

'So, David Solomon knew,' Jessica said. 'When Nicole was killed, her father saw that invitation, and *knew*. Someone was getting back at him for helping to put Beckert on Death Row.'

'You were right,' Bontrager said to Byrne. 'Solomon probably believed Judge Gillen still lived in that house. That's why he called.'

Byrne held up a fax. 'Just got this from Mateo. He sent the voicemail recording of David Solomon to the Philly field office of the FBI, who sent it off to Quantico. They cleaned it up enough to hear what Solomon said. He did not say "not now" on that recording.'

'What did he say?' Jessica asked.

Byrne put the fax down on the table. The other detectives looked at it. It read:

Sha'aray dimah lo ninalu.

'It's Hebrew,' Byrne said. 'From The Talmud.'

'Do we have a translation?' Bontrager asked.

'We do,' Byrne said. He read from a second fax. 'It means "the gates of weeping are not closed".'

'He thought he was warning Judge Gillen,' Jessica said.

'Probably so,' Byrne said. 'Obviously he was pretty unstable at that point.'

Byrne handed the videotape he had gotten from Dr Allen to Bontrager, who cued it on a VCR. For the next ten minutes everyone watched the recording of the boy and girl. At the moment the camera showed the little girl wearing the barrette, Byrne hit Pause.

'Does that look like the girl who was working in Miss Emmaline's shop?' Byrne asked.

Jessica had no doubt. 'It's her,' she said.

The next two videos to be played were the security video from Home Depot – in which the male subject who purchased the paint met up with a woman by the door – and the SafeCam video of the young man and woman meeting up with Nicole Solomon on the street.

They were the same people.

They were hunting a man and a woman.

'I'll get hard copies of these still frames out to the districts,' Maria said. She sat down at a laptop and began the process.

'Does this attorney, Marvin Skolnik, still practice in Philadelphia?' Dana Westbrook asked.

Bontrager sat down at a computer terminal. 'Hang on.'

He did a search, and soon came up with a website. *Skolnik Powell Reedman*. He clicked on a tab labeled *The Partners*. A fresh page loaded with three photographs. The top photograph and bio was for a Marvin Skolnik.

'It has to be him,' Westbrook said.

Jessica picked up a phone, put it on speaker, called the office number.

'Good afternoon, Skolnik Powell Reedman. How may I direct your call?'

'My name is Jessica Balzano. I'm a detective with the Philadelphia Police Department. May I speak with Mr Skolnik, please?'

'I'm afraid Mr Skolnik is gone for the day. Would you like to—'

'Who am I speaking to?' Jessica asked.

'This is Julie.'

'Julie, it's important that I speak with Mr Skolnik. Do you have a number where I could reach him?'

As Jessica said this she looked at Josh Bontrager. He shook his head. He had done a search for Marvin Skolnik's home address. It wasn't listed. This was not surprising.

'I'm afraid I can't give that information out.'

Jessica had, of course, hit this wall many times before. It didn't make it any less frustrating.

'I'm going to trust you here, Julie. By that I mean I'm going to tell you something, and I need it to stay between you and me.'

Pause. 'Okay.'

'Do I have your assurance on this?'

Another pause. 'Yes.'

'It's possible that Mr Skolnik might be in danger. So, here's what I want you to do. I'm sure part of your reluctance to give me this information is based on you not knowing that I am who I say I am. Yes?'

'Yes.'

'I understand. I want you to take two phone numbers down. Are you ready?'

'Yes.'

Jessica gave Julie the non-emergency number for the PPD, followed by her cell number.

'I want you to call Mr Skolnik,' Jessica said. 'If you reach him, have him call the second number I gave you. Tell him it's extremely important that he calls me immediately. If you don't reach him, I want you to call the first number I gave you – that's the main number for the police – and ask for me. They will patch the call through to me. Again, my name is Detective Jessica Balzano.'

Jessica spelled her last name.

'Will you do this?' Jessica asked.

'Yes.'

'Good. If you don't get hold of Mr Skolnik, I want you to be prepared, when you call me, to give me all of Mr Skolnik's phone numbers, as well as his home address. Are you okay with this, Julie?'

A long pause. Too long.

'Julie?'

'Okay,' she said. 'I just ... okay.'

'What time do you have?' Jessica asked.

'It's four-fifty.'

Jessica started the timer app on her iPhone. 'Okay. I expect you or Mr Skolnik to call me within three minutes. Have you got that?'

'I do.'

Two minutes later the desk phone rang. Jessica picked up the receiver, punched the blinking red button. 'Homicide, Balzano.'

'This is Julie Glassman over at Skolnik Powell Reedman.'

'Yes, Julie.'

'I got Mr Skolnik's voicemail, on both his home phone and his cell.'

'Did you leave the message we discussed?'

'I did,' she said. 'I left your cell number, and told him to call you immediately.'

'Fine,' Jessica said. 'I'll need both his numbers, as well as his home address.'

This time the young woman hesitated again, but not nearly as long as the first time. She gave Jessica two phone numbers, as well as an address in Mt. Airy. Jessica wrote it all down.

'You did the right thing here, Julie,' Jessica said. 'I appreciate it.'

'Is Mr Skolnik going to be okay?'

'I'm sure he's just fine. Most of my job is just about taking precautions. You've been a big help.'

'Okay.'

'And if for some reason you talk to Mr Skolnik, and he didn't get your voicemail, the message still stands. Have him call me immediately.'

'I will.'

Jessica clicked off, punched the button for another line. She called dispatch.

Within seconds, four PPD sector cars would be heading to the Skolnik home.

56

When Andi opened the door, she was glad to see that the cleaning service had come to the house. It wasn't as if they were slobs or anything – far from it. But things did tend to get untidy from time to time. Friday night was usually movie night in front of the sixty-inch plasma in the living room, and the popcorn bowls and soft drink cans and potato chip bags had a way of lingering on the end tables until Saturday night, or even Sunday morning, all depending on how much her stepmother had to drink.

Now the place looked pristine and *Architectural Digest* pretty: pillows fluffed, carpet vacuumed, glass sparkling, magazines cascaded.

'What a lovely home,' Mr Marseille said.

'Thanks,' Andi said. 'I'll just be a minute.'

She flew up the stairs.

*

I could not seem to stop glancing at my pocket watch.

I looked out the front window. The street was calm and still. I expected that it would not remain so for long.

The home of Marvin Skolnik, Esquire was indeed lovely. A little too modern for my taste, but clearly well-appointed, with quality furnishings. In a small den off the large living room I noticed a beautiful mahogany desk. On it was an answering machine, red light blinking.

I glanced at the door at the top of the stairs, then stepped into the office, slipped on a single leather glove. I tapped the answering machine's volume to low, then pressed the button to play the single unheard message.

From the machine, softly:

'Andi, it's Dad. I tried you on your cell phone, but got your voicemail. I'm terribly concerned about a call I received from the police. Please call me the moment you get this.'

I once more looked at my watch. We did not have much time.

I deleted the message, and walked to the foot of the stairs.

As Andi clanged through her closet, she suddenly wished she'd bought that skater dress.

Hanger after hanger: *No, no no, no no.*

In the end she selected a burgundy Lola dress, ran a brush through her hair, spritzed herself with two blasts of Houbigant *Quelques Fleurs* from an atomizer, slipped on her best heels.

Record time.

She was out of breath.

Before she could leave her room her cell phone beeped in her purse. She'd either gotten a text or a voice message. Whoever it was, they would have to wait.

Calm, Andi. She tried to remember her yoga practices, her Andrew Weill meditation courses. Zip. Her pulse was probably 120 and her blood pressure 200 over 190.

A few seconds later, when she walked down the steps, the young man who called himself Marseille was glancing through an issue of *Travel & Leisure*.

He looked up and smiled, put down the magazine, held out a hand.

'Miss Andrea Skolnik,' he said. 'You are a living doll.'

57

The Skolnik home – a large, well landscaped stone colonial in West Mt. Airy – was lit by the flashing bar lights from a pair of sector cars deployed at the curb.

When Jessica and Byrne pulled up, Jessica saw Dana Westbrook standing on the sidewalk in front of the entry door. Next to her was a tall, tanned, well-dressed man of about fifty.

Jessica and Byrne clipped their badges to their coats.

'Mr Skolnik, this is Detective Byrne and Detective Balzano,' Westbrook said. They all shook hands. The fact that the first PPD personnel on scene – besides the patrol officers – was a supervisor, spoke not only of the seriousness of the possible crime, but also the community and political standing of Marvin Skolnik, Esq.

'I was in meetings all afternoon,' Skolnik said. 'I had my phone off. I just got Julie's message about five minutes ago. On the way I called Andi's cell and the landline here. Nothing.'

'Is there anyone else home now?' Byrne asked.

Skolnik shook his head. 'My wife and son are at our house in Key West.'

'Where does your daughter work?'

'At King of Prussia Mall.'

'Which store?'

The man looked gutted. He didn't know. He said so.

'Are you certain she's not here?' Byrne asked.

'I looked,' Skolnik said. 'She's not home. But she was just here, I know that.'

'How do you know?'

'I checked her room. She's usually pretty neat and tidy. Plus, I can smell her favorite perfume. She only wears it for special occasions. It's expensive.'

'Do you know if she had a party, or maybe a wedding to attend?' Byrne asked.

'No. We have a big calendar in the mud room. One of those dry erase white boards. We all put down things we have planned on there. We have a different color for each of us. Andi uses red. There's nothing on the calendar for today.'

'Can you call your wife and ask her about this?'

'I just did,' Skolnik said. 'I got voicemail. I tried my son, too. Same result. They're probably at a show.'

'Would it be all right if we gave a quick look around the house, inside and out?' Byrne asked.

'Of course.'

Jessica, Byrne, Bontrager and Maria Caruso entered the home. Jessica and Maria went upstairs, Byrne and Josh took the first floor.

Upstairs were four bedrooms and two full baths. Everything seemed to be in place. Jessica saw what Marvin Skolnik meant about Andi's room. There were a few items of clothing on the floor. Jessica picked up a dark, long-sleeved crewneck sweater. On it was attached a nametag from American Apparel.

Jessica took out her iPhone. She quickly got the number for American Apparel at King of Prussia Mall. She dialed, heard:

'Thank you for calling American Apparel. This is Martina. How can I help you?'

'Martina, my name is Jessica Balzano, I'm with the Philadelphia Police Department. No cause for alarm, but I have a couple of quick questions for you.'

'Um, *okay*.'

'I'm trying to reach Andrea Skolnik,' Jessica said. 'Is she there, by any chance?'

'Andi? No, she got off at, I think, four. Let me check.'

Jessica heard the tapping of keyboard keys.

'Yeah. She got off at four. She'll be here tomorrow at noon. Can I give her a message?'

'Did you see her at all today?'

'I did, actually. I got to the mall around two. I had some shopping to do.'

'And you saw Andrea?'

'I did. She was sitting in the food court.'

'Was she by herself?'

'No,' Martina said. 'She was with this cute guy.'

'Can you describe him for me?'

'Dark hair, good-looking. And he was wearing a suit. Real dreamboat.'

'Have you ever seen him before?'

'The guy? No way. I'd remember.'

'Did you see them leave together?'

'No. When I came into the store at around quarter to four Andi was in the back. When she came out I was with a customer. We just waved. I was going to ask her about Mr Movie Star, but she was gone.'

'I'm going to give you my number,' Jessica said. 'If you hear from Andrea, please ask her to give me a call.'

'Sure.'

Jessica gave the girl her cell number, clicked off. She looked around the girl's room. A feeling of dread began to creep slowly up her spine.

She was with this cute guy.

Where are you, Andrea Skolnik? What's happening to you? What are you doing at this very second?

When Jessica looked up, and saw Byrne standing in the door-way, she knew.

58

There was a section of Center City, Philadelphia – from approximately Seventeenth to Eighteenth Streets, from Walnut to Sansom – that was known as the French Quarter. Although not an officially designated neighborhood, around 1999 the area was recognized by the city with orange signs bearing its name.

Contained within the area were French restaurants, French cultural societies, as well as Sofitel, one of the French upscale chain hotels.

Jessica and Byrne parked at Eighteenth and Moravian Streets, about a half-block from where the sector car was deployed. A group of PPD personnel were gathered at the mouth of an alley. They had learned on the way that John Shepherd had been assigned the case.

Shepherd was partnered with a young detective named Bình Ngô. Bình was second generation Vietnamese American. Different homicide detectives bring different skills and assets to the job. Among other skills – including obvious language assets – Bình was one of the best at defusing tense situations when two warring parties were about to escalate their disagreement. Quiet and observant, Bình was proving himself a more than capable investigator.

When Jessica ducked under the yellow tape at the mouth of the alley, she was once more struck by how dreamlike the setting was.

At the end of the alley, just beneath a security light in a mesh cage, was a bench. Even from twenty feet away Jessica could see that it was painted a pale yellow.

The girl lay across the bench, her hands folded across her chest. Beneath her head was a pillow. It smelled of gardenia perfume.

Between her hands was a small container of what looked like strawberries.

While Byrne was briefed by John Shepherd, Jessica approached, hugging the wall. When she got to about ten feet from the bench she stopped. The victim was pretty, had light blond hair, nails painted a pastel pink. Jessica took out the picture they had been given by Marvin Skolnik. There was no doubt.

Beneath the bench were four objects, each with a yellow crime scene marker next to it, each tented by a piece of white paper, paper put there by CSU officers to preserve the integrity of the evidence, and to shield it from the elements.

Jessica heard someone approaching from behind her. It was Bình.

'What do we have there?' Jessica asked, pointing to the objects.

'You're not going to believe this,' Bình said. He crouched down, lifted the small paper tent. Underneath was a bird.

'It's a seagull?'

Bình nodded. 'Yeah,' he said. 'There are four of them.'

'All dead?'

'All dead.'

Jessica pointed at the victim, at the container in her hands.

'Are those strawberries?'

'Believe it or not.'

Jessica was having a hard time believing any of it. It was clear that they had missed Andrea Skolnik's killer by hours, if not minutes. What they had in their favor was that, in this part of Center City – an area that contained hotels, upscale restaurants, just a block or so from the city's toniest addresses at Rittenhouse Square – there were the highest concentration of police and private surveillance cameras.

When Jessica returned to the street, John Shepherd was talking to a man in his thirties. The man wore a dark blazer, white shirt, patterned plum tie. There was a nametag on his vest, *Yves*, and the logo for Sofitel.

He appeared to be badly shaken.

'I'm here almost every night,' Yves said. 'I've never seen anything like this.'

'Why do you come down here?' Shepherd asked.

'I step out for a smoke when I'm on break,' he said. 'You're not allowed to smoke within a hundred feet of the hotel. They're really strict about it.'

'You tend bar?'

The man nodded. 'I work the lobby bar at Sofitel Liberté.'

'Did you see anyone when you came down the alley?'

Yves shook his head. 'No,' he said. 'Except for Jazzie.'

'Jazzie?'

Yves pointed to a man – late fifties, clearly homeless – who was leaning against a sector car, talking to one of the patrolmen.

'Where was Jazzie when you saw him?' Shepherd asked.

'Right about where he's standing now. By the mouth of the alley.'

'Was he walking in or out of the alley?'

'Neither. He just kind of hangs out there. Sometimes he panhandles from the people coming in and out of the hotel. Management doesn't really like it, but he's not on hotel property. Besides, he's harmless.'

'Do you recognize the victim?'

'No,' Yves said. 'I've never seen her before.'

'What time did you take your break today?'

'Right at six o'clock. I only get fifteen minutes, so I was probably here at around 6:02.'

Shepherd made the note. 'We might need to talk again tonight. What time do you get off?'

Jessica saw some color drain from the man's face. Perhaps it hadn't occurred to him that he had to go back to work after all this.

'Eleven,' he said. 'I get off at eleven.'

Shepherd handed him a card. 'Sorry you had to see this. If you think of anything else, call me immediately. My cell is on the back.'

The man put the card in his pocket, then pulled out a cigarette with a shaking hand.

Shepherd and Bình stood at the mouth of the alley, interviewing Jazzie. Jessica and Byrne observed.

Norman 'Jazzie' Garrett wore three or four sweaters, a pair of patched workpants, fingerless gloves.

'Why do they call you Jazzie?' Shepherd asked.

'I used to play a little piano back in the day. Brubeck, Bill Evans, O.P. Mind you, this was back when Philly was a jazz town – not like now – back when a white boy with fat fingers could make a living.'

Shepherd nodded. 'What, if anything, did you see tonight?'

'Nothing, really. Same tune, different arrangement. I hang around here because sometimes he brings out food.'

'Yves?'

'Yeah. He's a good guy.'

'Did you see anyone come in or out of this alley?' Shepherd asked.

'No, sir,' Jazzie said. 'But my eyes ain't what they used to be.'

Shepherd produced the subject sketch. 'Did you see this man anywhere around here tonight?'

Jazzie squinted at the drawing they had obtained as a result of interviewing Denny Wargo. The man called Mercy.

'Yeah, yeah. I seen him. But only 'cause he walked right by me.'

'Where?'

Jazzie pointed down Sansom Street.

'Show me exactly where,' Shepherd said.

Jazzie and the four detectives walked a half block down the street.

'Right here?' Shepherd asked.

Jazzie nodded.

'What was he doing?'

'Nothing,' Jazzie said. 'But he had one of those things with him.'

Shepherd stared at the man, as did the other detectives. When the man didn't continue, Shepherd prodded. 'He had *what* with him?'

'One of those ladder things,' he said. 'But smaller.'

'Like a stepstool?'

'Yeah, but taller. When he came back he got into this red van.'

'Where was the van?'

Jazzie pointed across the street.

'Can you recall anything about the van?'

Jazzie shrugged. 'It was rusty. No rims. Rims don't last too long around here these days.'

'Anything else?'

'License plate said "Moochie".'

'Can you spell that for me?' Shepherd asked.

Jazzie did. Bình Ngô opened his phone, stepped down the sidewalk a few paces, called it in.

'And you say he came out of this other alley?' Shepherd asked.

'Yeah.'

Jessica and Byrne took out their Maglites, walked down the short passageway, a narrow corridor that met the end of the alley where Andrea Skolnik's body was found. They ran the beam of their flashlights above eye level, along the brick window sills.

Halfway to the end, they saw them.

There, on the window ledge across the alley, looking down at the dark and grotesque display that was Andrea Skolnik's body, were two porcelain dolls.

Boy dolls.

One wore a blue and red striped polo shirt. The other wore an identical shirt in solid green.

The dolls were Robert and Edward Gillen.

As they waited for the ME's investigator to release the scene, Bình Ngô returned.

'We have a hit on the red van with the Moochie vanity plate,' he said. He checked his notepad. 'It's registered to a man named Anthony Mucinelli.'

'Let me guess,' Byrne said. 'He's either in jail, on parole, or out on bail.'

'Door number three,' Bình said. 'Charged with assault. I cross-referenced him with Jeffrey Malcolm, and it turns out they both used the same bail bondsman.'

'And that bondsman is Liberty 24 Bonds,' Byrne said.

'Right again,' Bình said. 'They're located on—'

'Lancaster Avenue,' Jessica said. It all started to click. Liberty 24 Bonds was two doors down from Miss Emmaline's shop, The Secret World.

'Okay,' Bình said. 'You guys are spooky. I heard about this.'

'And I'll bet you called Liberty 24,' Byrne said.

'I did,' Bình replied. 'The guy told me they were broken into about three months ago. He said they had some files stolen.'

'That's how they're targeting the vehicles they're using,' Jessica said. 'They're stealing cars from people who would never call the police.'

'I asked the guy at Liberty 24 to compile a list of the other files that were missing,' Bình said. 'He jacked me around for a few seconds, but I let him know that these files are related to homicides, and that I was going to make his life quite difficult. He came around. I asked him if he had any clients who worked for an exterminating company. He said yes.'

'The van that was spotted near the Gillen crime scene in Strawberry Mansion,' Jessica said. 'The one with the faded cockroach logo on the door.'

'The same. It turns out the man in question *used* to own his own bug service, but that was before he turned to a life of crime, and before his current stint in Curran-Fromhold, where he's been for the past three months.'

'What about the other files?' Westbrook asked.

Bình held up his cell. 'Waiting for that call now.'

At this, the ME's investigator emerged from the alley, having pronounced Andrea Skolnik dead. The detectives were now free to begin to process the scene.

Jessica snapped on a latex glove, stepped forward. She looked beneath the bench on which the victim was in repose. As expected, there was an envelope.

Knowing that CSU had photographs of the envelope *in situ*, Jessica reached under, carefully peeled off the tape, removed the envelope. She handed it to Bình, who was on the lead team with John Shepherd.

It was another invitation.

371

You are invited!
December 2 at Midnight
See you at our thé dansant!

Jessica glanced at the card. Unlike the first two invitations, it was not a week away. The killers were stepping up the game. It was two *days* away.

And, for the first time, there was a time of day listed.

'There's something else in the envelope,' Bình said.

He held it up to the light.

'Two invitations?' Shepherd asked.

'I don't think so.'

Bình reached inside, pulled out the card by its corner. It was a rectangular document, light blue in color. It looked to be old, corners bent, colors faded. He handed it to Jessica. It read:

Pan American World Airways System
Passenger Contract Ticket
Baggage Check

It was an old airline ticket from the now defunct carrier, Pan Am.

Byrne took out his phone. 'You remember that email you sent me? The email about the search you did after the Gillen boys were found?'

'What about it?' Jessica asked.

Byrne found what he was looking for. 'Some of the hits were about how to paint a swing set, one was about the oil painting of the girl on a swing, another one was about the Fred Astaire movie.'

'I remember.'

'And one of the hits was about an—'

'Ella Fitzgerald song,' Jessica said.

Byrne showed her the screen on his phone.

These Foolish Things.

The song lyrics were the templates for the killings.

THE DOLL MAKER

The sigh of midnight trains in empty stations.
Silk stockings thrown aside, dance invitations.

All the references were there. The allusions to painted swings, to the tinkling piano in the next apartment, to the cigarette with lipstick traces, and now, at the Andrea Skolnik crime scene, the Île de France with gulls around it.

And an airline ticket to romantic places.

Jessica scanned the ticket.

It was issued to Jean Marie Sauveterre.

When Jessica and Byrne arrived at The Secret World there was only a solitary spotlight on in the display window.

Although they were not exactly following procedure, they decided not to take the chance of upsetting Emmaline Rose with the request. She was still in Penn Presbyterian, still sedated.

Byrne called in a favor from a friend who worked as a locksmith. He had them inside in seconds.

They entered the shop, deciding, for the moment, to keep the lights off in the main area. As they made their way to the back parlor, Jessica noticed the glow from the front window display washing over the dolls on the shelves. It was eerie. It seemed as if they were watched by a thousand crystal eyes.

The back room was much as Jessica remembered it. Nothing seemed out of place. Because there was no overhead light, they switched on the three table lamps. It helped chase the gloom.

They walked to the bookshelves. Five of the large volumes dealt with the history of doll making. One dealt with French doll-making from 1530 to 2000. The other dealt with doll making in the US during the twentieth century.

Jessica scanned the book on France, found only a single mention of Jean Marie Sauveterre. While Byrne paged through the book on US doll makers, Jessica pulled some of the other volumes from the shelf. Most were catalogs. Out of four books, she found only one other mention of Jean Marie Sauveterre, a listing that mentioned him having been a member of a doll-maker society.

When she slipped the books back onto the shelf, she glanced over at Byrne. He had put his book down, opened to a page near the back. He was staring out through the opening that gave way to the shop, his phone in hand.

'What is it?' Jessica asked.

He pointed to the book.

Jessica picked it up, read the short bio. From it she learned that Jean Marie Sauveterre was born in Colmar, France, the son of a cobbler and a homemaker. He was educated at the Sorbonne, dropping out after only one year to pursue the craft of doll making. He moved to Paris and apprenticed with a man who had, in his youth, apprenticed himself with Emile Louis Jumeau, the son of Pierre-François Jumeau, considered one of the premiere doll makers of the nineteenth century.

At the age of thirty-two, Sauveterre moved to New Orleans, where he opened a shop in the French Quarter. At thirty-six he married, only to lose his wife a year later as she gave birth to their only child.

Beneath the article was a picture of the doll maker and his child.

'Oh, my God,' Jessica said.

59

On the night Paulette Sauveterre gave birth to her only child, a girl born two weeks early – a girl Paulette would name Valérie after her late grandmother – a series of powerful storms lashed the Delta. The former Paulette Giroux, once a celebrated actress on the stages of Paris and Avignon, died from complications from the birth two days later.

She had been just twenty-four.

It would be a week before Valérie's father, Jean Marie Sauveterre, learned of either event. On those seven days he had been lost to his absinthe fever dreams, consorting, as he would for the rest of his life, with la fée verte.

Jean Marie Sauveterre, newly widowed at the age of thirty-seven, and ill-prepared for fatherhood, had his workshop on Royal Street in New Orleans. The small shop was tucked between a cozy brasserie and a cobbler shop, both popular with the local merchants and residents.

Sauveterre was a doll maker, a craftsman and artist in the tradition of Bru and Jumeau. Unlike his predecessors in the world of bisque porcelain, he never became famous, nor did his work become lauded and collected by the wealthy.

When he saw his daughter for the first time – a full two weeks after her birth, swaddled in blankets at the newborn ward at the hospital – he knew what he must do. Fueled by the hellish delusions, he decided he would keep his daughter a child for her entire life, crafting each of his creations in her image.

This line, which he called Bébé V, *produced hundreds of molds, but only a handful of finished dolls.*

Over the next years Valérie was allowed out of her basement room for school, for church, but nothing else. She took her meals from a tray left at her door, and each night, at precisely eight o'clock, her door was locked and bolted from the outside.

In this place that sunlight never graced, a place of small shadows, Valérie's world was lighted by candles. Her only friends and playmates were the dolls her father could not sell, each one imperfect in their own way, each one a miscreation. Like Valérie herself, each a slightly distorted mien of a girl.

By day Valérie Sauveterre lived in fear and isolation.

It was at night that her broken dolls gathered to play.

As a young teenager, Valérie would awaken before dawn each morning and, via the ducts and stone plenum space beneath the old shop, begin to explore the house and the surrounding buildings. It was then that she discovered the room next to her father's workshop, the makeshift kitchen where he prepared his absinthe and other homemade potions, keeping company night after night with la fée verte.

At around seven, each morning, she would watch the children pass by her basement window, each of them growing in health and stature.

None of her playmates grew. Each doll was to be a child forever.

One night, when she was thirteen, her father left her door unlocked. Valérie braved the corridor, and snuck into his workshop, a place she had never been. There she saw the doll parts – bisque heads, leather bodies, mohair lashes, crystal cut Bluette eyes – all displayed on racks and shelves. She touched them all, wondering which of them were her eyes, her lashes, which of the long tresses were her own.

She went through the drawers, being careful to not disturb any of the contents. She found letters from a woman named Josephine Giroux Beckert, a relative of Valerie's deceased mother, a woman of means who lived in a place called Philadelphia.

Two years later, as another storm ravaged the Delta, Valérie heard shouting, tortured cries of pain and anguish. It was her father's voice, her father's torment.

She awoke to a steaming dawn, the mist coming off the blistered cobblestones outside her basement window.

Her door was wide open.

With great apprehension, Valérie stepped out of her room. As she passed her father's workshop she chanced a glance through the open doorway. Every doll in the shop – hundreds of figurines in various stages of creation – had been smashed to bits. The fireplace in the corner was piled high with charred arms and legs and torsos. The floor glistened with shattered crystal eyes.

Valérie crept up the stairs.

There was a man in the kitchen, a heavyset policeman with skin the color of boiled shrimp. The policeman nodded a greeting, averted his eyes. Valérie wondered why. She glanced out the kitchen window, to the courtyard behind the shop. There Valérie saw her father on an ambulance gurney, his face and neck covered in dried blood.

He did not move.

Two weeks later, another stranger entered her home. This one was old and bent, and wore a shiny black suit that draped off his skeletal shoulders.

Without saying a word, the man handed Valérie a train ticket, along with a small, battered valise.

Jean Marie Sauveterre was dead, and his daughter, his imperfect doll, was free.

Two days later, Valérie stepped into her new home in Philadelphia.

60

'Valerie Beckert is the doll maker's daughter.'

'Yes,' Byrne said. 'Did you read the last paragraph?'

Jessica had not. She turned back to the book.

The final entry in the brief article was about Sauveterre's body of work. It stated that Sauveterre had crafted hundreds of dolls in his career, but a total of only sixteen dolls in his time in New Orleans. It said that, right up until his death, he seemed to be obsessed with making the perfect doll, a small bisque figurine in the visage of his *poupée parfaite*.

Sixteen dolls, Jessica thought.

CSU found the number 9 on the Ezekiel Moss doll. The number on Nicole Solomon's head was 10. The Gillen boys were 11 and 12. The ME's investigator confirmed that there was a number carved into Andrea Skolnik's scalp, the number 13.

If the killer's plan was to take a life for each of these dolls, it meant that there were three more dolls to go.

'Do we know if John and Bình have made the official notification to Marvin Skolnik yet?' Byrne asked.

Jessica took out her phone, called John Shepherd. He answered on the first ring.

'John, it's Jessica.'

'What's up?' Shepherd asked.

'Have you made notification yet?'

'We're at the Skolnik house now.'

Jessica looked at Byrne. 'John's there now.'

Byrne held out his hand. 'Let me talk to him.'

61

That summer in the house, all her friends were there – Thaddeus Woodman, Nancy Brisbane, Aaron Petroff, and Jason Telich.

It was a glorious time.

Though she could not bring the children to the park, Valerie made the house come alive with daffodils and roses. Each night they played music and games.

Valerie had never been happier.

A few weeks after meeting her newest friend, Aaron Petroff, Valerie visited the Philadelphia Zoo. She loved to come to the zoo in the off-peak season. It was far less crowded, and she had ample opportunity to watch the children.

Lost in thought about how to best handle her growing coterie of friends, Valerie turned the corner near Solitude House – the elegant manor house built by William Penn's grandson John Penn, near the zoo's Peacock Pavilion.

She almost didn't notice the boy and girl at first. They seemed so small, dwarfed by the white stone manor. When she approached them the boy looked up. He had dark hair, fair skin, and deep green eyes. The girl had lighter hair than the boy – a chestnut shade – and blue eyes. They may have been brother and sister, though the resemblance was not that strong. They were, perhaps, seven or eight years old.

They were just sitting on a bench near the house, holding hands, not speaking to each other. There was no adult anywhere to be seen. Valerie wondered if they were being punished, or were told to sit on the bench while their caregiver went for some food or something to drink.

Somehow Valerie knew they were different. They were broken, yes, but not in a way that Valerie was.

Above all, what drew Valerie up the path to Solitude House – and into their world for the first time – was that the boy and girl were beautiful.

As beautiful as a bisque Sauveterre.

When they entered the house for the first time the boy and girl hesitated before stepping across the threshold.

'It's okay, mes chatons,*' Valerie said. 'You are safe here.'*

After a brief tour of the first and second floors, she introduced them to the other children. She then led them to her secret rooms, a place to which Valerie had never brought the others.

All the time they held each other's hand.

When Valerie opened the door, and flipped on the light, she watched their faces. The girl was all but overwhelmed. The boy was as well, but he tried to mask it. It was clear to Valerie that the boy was very protective of the girl.

Over the next days and weeks Valerie watched the newspapers, waited for a knock on her door.

If the children were missed, it could not be proven by the media.

She taught them the basics of doll mending.

They watched her with fascination as she made her special tea, watched as she crushed the mushrooms, poured the hot water over it, then strained the liquid. Sometimes she would use licorice tea, sweetening it with stevia from her window box herb garden.

They seemed to understand the need to fix that which is broken.

'All dolls are mended here,' Valerie told them. 'This is our workshop.'

There were shelves of doll parts: heads, bodies, eyes, lashes. There was row after row of clothing. A dozen shelves held the wigs.

When Valerie felt they were ready, she put on the old record. The children just sat on the sofa, listening intently. It was a recording of her aunt Josephine, a collection of standards from the 1950s.

'My aunt Josephine was a great singer,' Valerie told them one day in July, slipping onto the turntable an old 45 rpm single record. 'This was her favorite song. It will be yours, too. It is called "These Foolish Things".'

Over the next few months Valerie played the song every evening, played it so often that the children had begun to sing along with the old recording. Sometimes, Valerie heard them humming the tune while they did their chores.

A few weeks after the boy and girl arrived she began to teach the boy to play the piano. He took to it very quickly, and with great enthusiasm. While the other children watched and listened, he often accompanied the record. After a while, Valerie, while listening from another room, could not tell which was the boy, and which was the recording.

It was during that summer that Valerie began to make her trips to Fairmount Park, stealing through the shadows of the night, her cargo as heavy as the growing burdens of her heart.

Sometimes, she thought, even with the help and company of her friends, it seemed that no amount of care could make the dolls whole again.

62

While Byrne waited for the video feed to be set up, he paced the small room next to the Video Monitoring Unit, attempting to calm himself. He tried to recall a time, any time, when he had been faced with what he was about to do. He could not think of a single instance.

Jessica, along with the other detectives, and the brass, were giving him space, perhaps grateful that the weight of this was not on their shoulders.

Byrne glanced at his watch. He had less than ten minutes.

He was just about to walk into the main room when his phone buzzed. He looked at the screen. It was Dr Meredith Allen. He thought about letting it go to voicemail, but considered that, if ever he could use some advice from a therapist, it was now.

He answered.

'Dr Allen,' he said.

'Hello, detective. Am I catching you at a bad time?'

Byrne had no answer to this. There had never been a time like this. 'Not at all.'

'Well, I made a few calls, and was able to persuade an old colleague to visit the archives at what was once Vista House.'

Byrne just listened. She continued.

'None of these files were digitized, of course, so it took a bit of digging through paper records,' she said. 'He did find some information on the two children you saw on the videotape. The boy and the girl.'

Byrne felt his pulse quicken. 'What do we have?'

'It's not the best news. They were at Vista House for twenty-two months, then they were transferred to a group home called New Outlook.'

Byrne remembered the name. 'That was in West Philly?'

'Yes,' she said. 'But it looks like they were only there for a few weeks.'

'Why?'

Byrne heard Meredith Allen take a deep breath, exhale. 'They disappeared.'

'What do you mean they *disappeared*?'

Byrne instantly realized that he was sounding accusatory, as if Dr Allen's profession was more culpable for what happened to these children than his own. He didn't mean it that way.

'There wasn't a lot in the file,' she said. 'It appears that they went on a group outing at the zoo, and never rejoined the group.'

Byrne knew that this happened far too often. Caseworkers didn't always file reports when foster children went missing or ran away. The courts and the justice system were overburdened and underfunded. Add to this a lack of communication between law enforcement and coroner's office – yielding a disconnect between unidentified dead children and those who have slipped through the cracks of the child welfare system – and it was easy to see how there would be a long list of children who are either missing or dead.

'So they were reported missing as a John and Jane Doe?' Byrne asked.

'No, I have their names right here,' she said. 'Their names were Martin and Cassandra White.'

Byrne felt the floor drop away.

Martin and Cassandra White were two of the children on the list of twelve missing children that Byrne had, at that moment, in his wallet. Two of the children who disappeared when Valerie Beckert had been hunting. He had not had their DNA tests done because they had lived in foster care.

'Who gave them these names?' Byrne asked.

'It sometimes happens with John and Jane Does, if they are young enough. When they come into the system, and become legal wards of the county, they are sometimes given names. As simplistic as it sounds – and I'm not sure what to think about it, even now – some white children are given the name White, black children Black. The sensitivity of it all is questionable, in my opinion, but it happens.'

'And there's no record of what happened to them?' Byrne asked.

'That's more in line with your office than mine, detective. I'm afraid that's all I have.'

Byrne was just going to ask Dr Allen about how to approach what he was about to do, but Jessica poked her head into the room, and said:

'It's time, partner.'

63

It was just after putting away the groceries in the pantry that late August day that Valerie heard the boy's voice for the first time.

A month earlier she had watched Thomas Rule walk up her street, hand in hand with his mother, a woman so distracted and consumed by her cell phone that it amazed Valerie that she didn't just leave the boy standing on a street corner.

One day Valerie had followed them to the small park on Woodbine Avenue. While there, she observed the boy walking with his slight limp, gamely trying to keep up with the other children. Around and around the edge of the small park the children ran, trying desperately to get a large blue kite airborne. After a few revolutions, the children came up behind little Thomas, already having lapped him once. The boy did not give up.

Valerie knew that if ever there was a doll that needed mending, it was Thomas Rule.

Then, one day – through no effort of her own – the boy was in her house.

*

Thomas Rule sat in the kitchen, right next to the pantry door.

Valerie had gone to the market early that morning, and when she returned home she found the boy and the girl seated around the table with Thomas.

'Who is this?' Valerie asked. She knew who the boy was, but she'd had the question she'd wanted to ask – what is he doing here? – momentarily stunned out of her.

'This is Thomas,' the girl said. 'Thomas Rule. We invited him to tea.'

'Where did you meet him?'

The girl looked at the boy, back. 'We met him at the park. I hope it's okay that we invited him into our home.'

It was unlike the boy and girl to venture out on their own. She had taken them out through the stairwell that was concealed in the garage a number of times. She knew that door was always locked.

Had they found her extra keys? Had they learned how to push the buttons on the door to keep it from latching?

They must have.

When Valerie put down her handbag, she noticed that on the table was a pot of tea. Valerie did not recall making the special tea before leaving, but it appeared that the boy and the girl, from many hours of observation, had learned the recipe, just as Valerie had from secretly observing her father. The thought made her a bit cross at first, but she had by this time found herself reluctant to scold the boy and girl.

Strangest of all was that when Valerie had entered the room, Thomas did not look up from his drawing. Instead, he had a fistful of crayons in each hand, trying frantically to get all the colors in the rainbow down onto the paper as fast as he could. One by one he would finish a page and cast it to the floor, colors bleeding into one another, shapes morphing from trees, to horses, to people. Drawing after drawing, each one slashed with orange and red and yellow.

After a while he slowed down, and his palette began to run to more somber colors – roan, crimson, deep blue.

Eventually, exhausted, he slipped from the table, crossed the room, crawled onto the divan, and closed his eyes. Soon he was fast asleep.

The boy and girl followed Thomas across the room, and there stood over him, watching in something close to fascination, as if the boy were a specimen in a jar.

That evening, when Valerie had finished with the supper dishes, she returned to the parlor. She thought about taking Thomas back over to the park. She had not been prepared to make another friend so soon, but now Thomas Rule was in her house.

When Valerie went into the basement, on that final day, she knew what had happened.

The boy and girl were reading, as usual. They seemed to have grown so much in the past year. The boy especially.

She had shopped for them at all the vintage stores, and the boy had taken quite a fancy to fashion. The girl had begun to become proficient with a needle and thread. Each day the boy would put on a fresh white dress shirt and tie. Even though they each had a few pairs of jeans and slacks, the girl always chose to wear a dress, or a smart blouse and skirt set.

They had grown so steadily that it was hard to keep up.

When darkness fell that night Valerie eased the car from the garage, keeping the lights off until she had reached the corner.

Before leaving for Fairmount Park she had taken everything that belonged to the boy – all but a single drawing, a drawing of cows in a field of bright sunshine – and burned it in the fireplace.

64

The State Correctional Institution at Rockview is a medium-security facility located near State College, Pennsylvania, about two hundred miles northeast of Philadelphia.

Opened in 1915, Rockview became the only facility in the Commonwealth at which the death penalty was carried out. While the prison itself is a medium-security facility for men, the death chamber – in the former prison field hospital just outside the main perimeter – was renovated in 1997 to became a maximum-security building.

Between 1915 and 1962, three hundred forty-eight men and two women received the death penalty at Rockview. And while there was no death row at Rockview, prisoners were transferred there just days before the ultimate sentence was to be carried out.

When told of the potential information that could be gleaned from an interview with Valerie Beckert, Marvin Skolnik, her former attorney, made a call to both the district attorney of Philadelphia, and the United States Attorney's Office for the Eastern District of Pennsylvania.

As a result, the PPD was granted a five-minute interview with the condemned.

Because Rockview was two hundred miles from Philadelphia, the interview would be conducted by video conference.

At the time the video link was established, Valerie Beckert was scheduled to be executed in less than twenty-eight hours.

Byrne sat at the long table in the Video Monitoring Unit, a camera on a tripod in front the of the table.

The image at the far side of the huge room – projected onto the massive monitor – showed a date and time code on a black screen, as well as SCI Rockview in the upper right-hand corner.

To Byrne's right was a digital timer set at 5:00.

In the room, out of range of the camera, were more than thirty police officers, including Jessica, Josh Bontrager, Maria Caruso, Dana Westbrook, Captain John Ross, as well as lawyers from the District Attorney's office.

At exactly eight p.m. the onscreen image flickered, then went to color bars.

Another flicker.

Then, they saw her.

Byrne had not set eyes on the woman in ten years. At that time she was a slight, pale young woman of nineteen. When he had interviewed her in the box she had been less than cooperative, never offering more than one- or two-word answers to his questions. Still, she had been polite and respectful, something different from the demeanor most people would ascribe to a person who would strangle a four-year-old boy to death.

Sitting in front of him now was a mature woman of twenty-nine. She had put on a few pounds, but not to excess, which is easy to do with institutional, carb-heavy food. Her hair was much shorter, and the pallor that had at one time made her look sickly was gone. She did not look robust, but she looked healthy.

It was Valerie Beckert's eyes that struck Byrne. Her eyes all but said she had resigned herself to her fate.

They were the eyes of the condemned.

'Hello, detective,' she said.

It suddenly struck Byrne that she could see him, too. He knew this, but was still caught off guard. He wondered how he looked to her.

'Hello, Valerie.'

'It's been ten years,' she said.

'Yes, it has.'

Byrne found himself scrambling to find a way to begin a conversation such as this. He'd never *had* a conversation such as this. Normally, you say how good someone looks, ask after their family and job and, when signing off, say something like 'see you soon,' or 'talk to you later.'

Byrne had none of these things available to him. The woman sitting before him would be put to death in less than twenty-eight hours. There *was* no later.

In addition, he had no idea what, if anything, Valerie knew about the murders that had been occurring in Philadelphia over the past few weeks.

Unless, of course, she was behind them.

'Whenever Papa fired a new doll, I could hear it, of course,' she said. 'I could hear it being born.'

Byrne just listened. He wanted to grill her, but she was talking and he didn't want her to stop. He glanced at the clock. Somehow, almost ninety seconds had passed.

'Whenever he failed, whenever he made an imperfect Sauveterre, I could hear that, too,' she added. 'There was always a red rain when that happened. Oh my, yes there was. There was hell on account.'

'Valerie, I need to—'

'But it always meant that I was getting a new friend. All my friends were broken dolls. As was I.' She looked away for a second, then directly back at Byrne. 'You are broken too, are you not, detective? I knew it the moment we met in Fairmount Park that day.'

Byrne had no answer for this. Nor the time to create one. He looked at the clock. Two and a half minutes to go. He pushed forward.

'Tell me about Martin and Cassandra White, Valerie.'

She just stared, remained silent.

'Martin and Cassandra. Where are they, Valerie? I need to know.'

'They are on the shelf now. Or soon will be. There's nothing you can do.'

'Okay,' Byrne said. He felt the anger build. He tried to contain it. 'This *shelf*. Where would I find this *shelf*?'

'I wanted so much more for them, but I think they are beyond mending. The others? Nancy and Aaron and Thaddeus and Jason? I'd speak to Mr Lundby.'

'Who is Mr Lundby?' Byrne asked. Out of the corner of his eye, Byrne saw Josh Bontrager sit down at a laptop, and begin a search for the name.

Valerie Beckert said nothing.

Before he could stop himself, Byrne shot to his feet.

'Martin and Cassandra White, Valerie! Where the fuck *are* they?'

'Language.'

'You kidnapped them, brought them into your sick fucking world, and now they are murderers, Valerie. Just like you.'

Byrne knew he was blowing it. She had baited him, he'd taken the bait, and now he was blowing it. He took a deep breath, exhaled slowly, and said:

'Valerie, please listen to me. In these last few moments, you can do the right thing. Help me stop them.'

Precious seconds ticked by.

'I've dreamt about you, Kevin.'

'*Valerie!*'

'Tell them I love them.'

'I will, Valerie. I promise. Just tell me where they are, and I will tell them anything you want me to. You have my word.'

'They are the last Sauveterres. They are the most beautiful of all.'

Byrne glanced at the clock. He had thirty seconds left. He didn't know what to say. He knew he would never again have the opportunity to speak to Valerie Beckert. He sat back down.

'Valerie, I need your help. There isn't much time. Maybe I can do something for you.'

It was a lie, and Byrne knew that *she* knew it was a lie. He saw a shadow on the wall next to where Valerie sat. It was the corrections officer coming to get her.

With five seconds left, Valerie raised her eyes, looked directly into the lens, directly at Kevin Byrne, and said:

'Enjoy your new home, detective.'

65

The six detectives gathered outside the room. For a few long moments, no one said a word.

'They're doing it for her,' Byrne said. 'She took them in, and they're punishing the people who put her on death row by taking something most dear to them.'

'Their children,' Shepherd said. 'Christ.'

'So she's directing all this from her death row cell?' Bình asked.

No one had an answer to this. The crimes were so well choreographed, so well timed, it was hard to believe it had been planned in advance. Too many variables, not the least of which was weather, which was starting to turn nasty. The forecast was for rain turning to snow.

'It's not like she has a phone,' Shepherd said. 'And only family, clergy and counsel can visit.'

'What about a log of phone calls coming in to her?' Bình asked.

'I've got a request in on that,' Byrne said.

He took out his phone, called Barbara Wagner's cell. She answered after two rings.

'Kevin,' she said. 'I was going to call you tonight.'

He put the call on speaker.

'Barb, you're on speaker,' Byrne said. 'I'm here with the task force.'

'It took a little doing, but we've got a log of recent calls to Valerie Beckert,' she said.

'Since she got to Rockview?'

'Yeah. She's only gotten two calls.'

'Counsel or clergy?' Byrne asked.

'Neither. According to the log, it was her children.'

Byrne looked at Jessica.

'I didn't know she had children,' Byrne said.

'Neither did we,' Barbara said. 'But at this late date, the rules can get a little bent. Not broken, but bent.'

'What can you tell me about the calls?'

'Not much. One came in at 3:36 p.m. six days ago. And one came in four days ago at 10:22 a.m.'

'How long did they last?'

'First one lasted six minutes. Second one lasted five.'

'Do we have the number from which the calls were placed?'

'We do.'

Barbara gave him the number. 'Thanks, Barb,' Byrne said.

'You got it.'

Byrne hung up, took out his notebook. Jessica had her notebook out as well. They both found it at the same time.

The number they had gotten from Barbara Wagner, the number from which two phone calls were made to Valerie Beckert, was the same number they had gotten from Denny Wargo.

The man who purchased the accessories to grow magic mushrooms, the man Wargo called *Mercy*, was Martin White.

Jessica was just about to contact West Detectives to see what was happening with the surveillance on that pay phone when Byrne's phone rang again.

He answered, listened for a few seconds, then hung up. He grabbed his coat.

'What's up?' Jessica asked.

'We found the other girl who worked at Miss Emmaline's shop.'

66

The Kilroy home was a white brick row house on Sixth Street near Washington.

Bridget Kilroy was a tall, skittish girl of about seventeen. She wore an oversized Swarthmore College sweatshirt and plaid flannel pajama bottoms. Jessica recognized her immediately as the other girl who had been in The Secret World that day.

With Bridget's mother sitting in, they met in the cramped eating area of the kitchen. Placed between them, untouched, sat a plate of Pepperidge Farm Milano cookies.

'What can you tell us about Cassandra?' Jessica asked.

The girl looked confused. 'Who's Cassandra?'

'The girl you worked with at The Secret World,' Jessica said. 'Her real name is Cassandra White.'

'I only knew her as Anabelle,' Bridget replied.

Jessica held up the photograph of Miss Emmaline and the two girls, the picture taken in the parlor at the rear of the shop. The girl to Miss Emmaline's right was Bridget Kilroy.

'Is this other girl the one you're calling Anabelle?'

The girl just nodded.

'Okay,' Jessica said. 'What can you tell us about her?'

Bridget coiled a strand of hair behind her left ear. 'I don't really know her that well.'

'Let's start with how you two met,' Jessica said.

'Okay,' she began. 'I think it was in June or July.'

'Of this year?'

Bridget nodded. 'Yeah. I needed to find a job, and I was walking down Lancaster and I saw the sign in the window.'

'At Miss Emmaline's shop?'

'Yeah. I'd never been in there, but I always thought it was really cool.'

'Are you a doll collector?'

'Not really,' Bridget said. 'I mean, I have *some* dolls, but I was never a real fan girl or anything. Not like some of the people who come in the shop.'

'What do you mean?'

'Well, some of the people seem a little ... '

'Obsessed?' Jessica asked.

'*Oh* yeah. Like *really* obsessed.'

'Would you put Anabelle in that category?'

She thought for a few moments. 'I guess so. She seemed to know a lot about them. But maybe that's because she worked there, and hung around Miss Emmaline.'

'So you met Anabelle that day?'

'Yeah. She was working behind the counter when I went in.'

'Did you two ever socialize?'

'Not sure what you mean by that.'

'Did you ever go to the movies together, go to the mall, hang out?' Jessica asked.

'No.'

'So, you've never been to her house?'

The girl shook her head. 'No. We were never really friends like that.'

'Did she ever tell you where she lives?'

'No, but I always thought it was nearby.'

'Why is that?'

'I mean, I never saw her drive up in a car or anything. I just assumed she walked to the shop.'

'What about other things? Did she ever talk about her friends or family? Where she liked to eat?'

Bridget chewed on a nail for a few moments, considered all this. 'She never mentioned any family. I think I asked her once and she changed the subject. She was kind of a secretive person.'

'So, no one ever stopped by the store that she knew? No one ever showed up to give her a ride home?'

'No.'

'Did she ever mention someone named Mercy, or someone named Valerie Beckert?'

'Sorry. I don't know those people.'

'That's okay.'

'Wait. I do remember something. I know that she likes to sew,' Bridget said. 'She would really perk up when she talked about sewing.'

Jessica thought about what Miss Emmaline had said about the stitching on the doll dressed as Nicole Solomon.

'What kind of sewing?' Jessica asked.

'Well, sometimes she would come in to work with a new dress or a skirt or something, and I would ask her where she bought it. Most of the time she said she made it herself. She's really good.'

'Why do you think that this is important?'

'Well, she once told me that she bought all her fabric and stuff at this store on East Fourth.'

'Do you remember the name of the store?'

'It has a funny name. Something with "Johnny" in it.'

Jessica took out her iPhone, tapped her browser icon. She put in a search string for Philadelphia fabric stores plus the name Johnny. In short order she had a hit.

'There's a fabric shop on Fourth called Johnny B. Dry Goods,' Jessica said. 'Does that sound right?'

'Yeah,' Bridget said. 'That's the one.'

67

I have always been happy to indulge Anabelle her interests and passions.

I don't know much about the art and craft of sewing, but I have a keen interest in fashion. Whenever I see older films, I feel a sense of nostalgia – if indeed that is possible to feel for a time and place that predates, by many decades, the time of your birth – for stories that depict life in the 1940s and 1950s.

In these stories people dressed for an occasion in their finest. Attending a church service, enjoying a meal, even shopping. Indeed, in many of these stories, the father in a family would wear a suit and tie at the dinner table with his family.

Now, sadly, those practices are all but unheard of. Whenever I see a teenager walking down the street, wearing flannel pajama bottoms, I fear for the world.

It is for this reason and others that I have never minded at all coming to this shop with its bolts of fine gabardines, its rainbow of bright silk threads, its reams of fine lace.

While I find it enjoyable, Anabelle is in heaven here, and that is enough for me.

On the day of our final tea, I found myself at the back of the shop, daydreaming about the things to come, when I heard it. The two words made the blood freeze in my veins.

'Miss White?'

It was spoken by the woman behind the counter. I had not been paying her any mind because my attention was on other things, that being the preparations for our tea later today. The woman had dark eyes, long dark hair managed into a ponytail. She was very pretty, and had about her an air of competence.

If I'm not mistaken, when we entered the shop, this woman had been sorting through a pile of old buttons on the countertop, separating them as to material and style. Old buttons and lace were one of the reasons Anabelle had chosen this shop.

'Anabelle?' the woman said.

I quickly stepped through the curtains into the back of shop. Once there, hidden from sight, I peered through the opening. Anabelle did not look my way, nor did the man and woman now standing on either side of her.

A few moments later they all left the shop together. I did not move for the longest time, the dark reality of what had just happened descending upon me.

It had been many years since Anabelle and I had spent more than just a few hours apart, and the thought of it made me feel sick inside.

They had my Anabelle.

They had my life.

68

The girl sat quietly in Interview A, her feet crossed beneath the table, her hands clasped above, fingers interlaced. The door was propped open.

She wore a navy blue skirt, a navy pullover in an argyle pattern, a white blouse.

In her time in the homicide unit Jessica had probably seen every criminal type sitting in that chair. She had seen dead-eyed gangbangers; men who had come home to find their wives in flagrante, and picked up the nearest blunt object; drunk drivers who had no idea that they had taken someone's life.

This girl, if she was culpable in the deaths of Nicole Solomon, Robert and Edward Gillen, and Andrea Skolnik, was a cipher.

She just sat there, her expression blank.

The old police adage of knowing whether or not someone was guilty of a crime by how relaxed they were in the box was true.

If you did the crime, and you knew you were caught, you got some rest. The next day or so were going to be taxing to say the least.

The girl in the room now – a girl whose true identity and connection to a series of homicides, if she was connected at all, was
still a mystery – was as calm as Jessica had ever seen anyone in
that claustrophobic, windowless, six by eight foot room. A space
that was, not by accident, the same size as a prison cell.

Jessica had never seen anything like it.

Jessica and Byrne reentered the room. Jessica sat to the girl's left;
Byrne sat across the small table from her.

'Are you comfortable?' Byrne asked.

'Quite comfortable,' she said. 'Thank you.'

'As I said earlier, we just need to ask you a few questions.'

'We have to wait for Mr Marseille, of course.'

Mr Marseille, Jessica thought. This is the man named 'Mercy'
that the drug dealer, Denny Wargo, had mentioned.

'I'm sorry?' Byrne asked.

'We must wait for Mr Marseille.'

'Mr Marseille?'

'Yes.'

'I don't know who that is.'

The girl looked up at Byrne. She smiled. When she did this
her eyes brightened and her face seemed to light up. Jessica had
initially thought the girl was very pretty. But when she smiled she
was beautiful. She had delicate features, flawless skin. Her eyes
were a midnight blue. She looked like—

Don't think it, Jessica.

She did anyway.

She looked like a doll.

'Don't be silly,' the girl said. 'Of *course* you know who Mr
Marseille is.'

Byrne took a moment. 'What I meant to say, of course, is that
I know a few *different* men named Mr Marseille. I'm just not sure
which one you mean.'

The girl wagged a finger. 'There is only one.'

'Is Mr Marseille on his way here now?' Byrne asked.

The girl shrugged. 'I don't know for certain, but he has never been late for tea, and we are never apart for very long.'

'May I ask your relationship to Mr Marseille?'

'My relationship?'

'Yes,' Byrne said. 'Is Mr Marseille your boyfriend, your husband, your brother?'

Another smile. 'A gentleman would not ask such a question.'

Byrne nodded. 'Fair enough,' he said. 'You mentioned tea. Can we get you a cup?'

The girl looked up. 'Oh I don't think you have our favorite kind. It is *very* special. We brew it ourselves. Thanks for the offer, though.'

Jessica thought: *She's talking about the magic mushrooms.*

Byrne clicked his pen, leaned forward, and asked: 'You haven't yet told us your name.'

'How could you *not* know my name?'

Byrne returned the smile. 'Well, when you get to be my age, you forget things all the time,' he said.

'My name is Anabelle.'

Byrne wrinkled his brow. 'That's odd, because I have here that your name is Cassandra.'

Jessica watched the girl closely. No reaction.

'Cassandra? That is a perfectly lovely name, but it is not mine.'

'Your name isn't Cassandra White?'

'No,' she said. 'You see?'

'See what?'

'You have the wrong girl. This is a big misunderstanding. It's Cassandra White you want!'

'You might be right about that. But we'll go with Anabelle for the time being.' Byrne made a note. 'It's nice to meet you, Anabelle.'

Another sly smile. 'We haven't quite met yet, sir. All I know is that you call yourself Detective Byrne. I don't know your first name.'

'How rude of me,' Byrne said. 'My name is Kevin.'

'Another perfectly lovely name.' She extended one small, delicate hand. 'Pleased to make your acquaintance.'

Byrne offered a hand. 'Charmed, I'm sure.'

They shook hands.

'May I know your last name?' Byrne asked, his pen poised over his notebook.

The girl looked quizzically at him. 'I don't have a last name, of course.'

'My boss is rather picky about such things. She always wants to know the full names of our visitors here. Is there some kind of last name I can just put in the blank here?'

The girl perked. 'Your boss is a woman?'

'Yes.'

'Oh my,' she said. 'How very modern.'

Byrne waited a few seconds. He asked again. 'Anabelle? Is there a last name I can put down here?'

She thought for a few moments. 'There simply is not. I am, and always have been, simply Anabelle.'

Jessica saw Byrne write N/A in the box for last name. He clicked his pen again, put it down on the notepad. He then reached into his folder, took out a form they used in circumstances similar to this, rare as they may be.

'If I don't do this, I'll be in a world of trouble,' he said.

'We don't want *that*.'

'I just need you to write your first name, and today's date on here. Then we'll be done with this portion of the interview, and we can move on. Can you do that for me?'

'Of course.'

Byrne turned the document to face the girl. On it were two lines of text. My name is _____. Today's date is _____.

Before the girl could ask for Byrne's ballpoint pen, he reached into his suit coat pocket, took out a different pen. A Staedtler Calligraph Duo. Black ink.

Anabelle took the Staedtler, uncapped it, wrote her first name on the appropriate line. She did the same for the date. She then capped the pen, and handed it back to Byrne.

'I can't thank you enough for this,' he said, returning the pen to his pocket. 'You've saved me a lot of grief.'

'We couldn't have your boss be angry with you, could we?'

Byrne smiled. On cue there was a knock at the door. The door opened; Josh Bontrager popped his head in.

'Sorry to bother you,' Bontrager said. 'Jess, you've got a call.'

Jessica stood, gathered a few documents, including the form Anabelle had just filled out.

'Excuse me,' she said. 'I'll be right back.'

She stepped out of the interview room, closed the door behind her. Sitting at a nearby desk, just a few feet away, was Hell Rohmer. In front of him were photocopies of the invitations they had found beneath the bench at the Shawmont train station, on Sansom Street, beneath one of the swings at the Gillen crime scenes, as well as Ezekiel Moss's truck.

Jessica put the exemplar that Anabelle had just made down on the desk.

Hell Rohmer put on his glasses, studied the documents side by side. He took out a lighted magnifying glass, pored over the documents one by one. He took off his glasses, sat back.

'No,' he said. He picked up a photocopy of one of the invitations, as well as the newly created form. 'These two documents were not written by the same person.'

Shit, Jessica thought. It was the kind of evidence they would need to hold this girl.

They would have to find something else.

*

407

Jessica reentered the interview room, sat down. She studied the girl for a few moments. The girl did not look away, did not break eye contact with Byrne.

Who is this girl? Jessica wondered.

'While we're waiting for Mr Marseille, are you sure I can't get you something to eat or drink?' Byrne asked. 'Maybe a water?'

'A water would be lovely.'

At this, Jessica again walked out of the interview room, turned the corner into the small coffee room next door, the room with the two-way mirror. Sgt. Dana Westbrook and Josh Bontrager were watching.

Jessica took a bottled water from the small refrigerator, as well as a fresh clear plastic cup from the stack. She walked back into the room, put the cup on the table, opened the bottle and poured half a cup of water. She put the cap back on the bottle, set it down.

'Thank you very much,' the girl said. She picked up the cup, sipped daintily from it.

Byrne made a dramatic gesture of looking at his watch. 'You know, I'm not sure that Mr Marseille knows you're here,' he said. 'I'd be happy to call him if you like.'

The girl put down her cup of water. 'I'm afraid he does not have a telephone.'

'Was he nearby when we met at the fabric shop?'

'Of course.'

'How could he know where we've gone?'

'He just knows,' the girl said. 'He has always known.'

'Now, Anabelle, I'd like to mention a few names to you, and see if you know these people. Would that be okay?'

'Like a game?'

'Something like that,' Byrne said.

'Okay.'

'I'll mention a name, and you just tell me – yes or no – if you know the person.'

'I will.'

'Nicole Solomon.'

'No.'

'David Solomon.'

'No.'

'Robert Gillen.'

'No.'

'Edward Gillen.'

'No.'

'Andrea Skolnik.'

'No.'

'Ezekiel Moss.'

Jessica had been watching the girl carefully. At the mention of this name – the name of a man they were all but certain was this girl's biological father – there was the slightest hesitation. Then:

'No.'

'What about Valerie Beckert?'

This time, it seemed, the girl was ready. She didn't even flinch.

For the past few questions Byrne had been nudging his note-book ever nearer the girl, toward the plastic cup in front of her. On top of Byrne's notepad sat his iPhone. Right on cue, the iPhone rang. Byrne reached for it. In doing this, he knocked over the plastic cup, spilling the inch or so of water onto the table.

'Oh my God,' Byrne said. 'I'm so *sorry*.'

Byrne reached for the box of Kleenex on the other side of the table. He handed a few of them to the girl.

'No bother,' the girl said. 'I've been known to be somewhat clumsy in my time, too.'

As the girl blotted the water, Byrne picked up the plastic cup by its rim, excused himself, left the room, where he found Josh Bontrager just outside the door with a paper evidence bag.

Bontrager would now run the bag to the ID unit, just down-stairs. They needed to confirm that the young woman in the room was the same person as the young woman who worked in the store. They had collected a number of prints from the porcelain dolls, the figurines that were on the shelves at The Secret World, where Jessica had seen the girl in the blond wig – the girl in Interview A – dusting and cleaning.

They had visual evidence, but they needed the science.

Byrne reentered the room, sat down. He put a fresh cup on the table, poured water into it.

'Sorry about that,' he said.

The girl said nothing.

Byrne settled into his chair. 'I'd like to show you something, if I may.'

'Of course!'

Byrne took his laptop out of its case, opened it. He pulled his chair to the other side of the table, positioned the laptop so that all three of them could see it.

'This is a short video I'd like you to watch.'

The girl sat up straighter in anticipation. Jessica noticed that so much of her body language, so many of her gestures, were in many ways childlike.

Byrne tapped the space bar on the laptop. The video began.

It was the recording Byrne had gotten from Dr Allen.

Jessica watched the young woman as the tape began to play. There could be no mistake. The little girl on the tape, and the young woman in the room, were one and the same.

Byrne said nothing at first. He let the recording play.

'What a delightful room,' Anabelle said. 'So cheerful.'

'What do you think the dolls are doing?' Dr Allen asks.

Byrne hit PAUSE. 'Do you recognize this little girl?'

Anabelle pointed at the screen. 'This little girl in the movie?'

'Yes.'

'No,' she said. 'I don't know her.'

'Look again.'

Anabelle glanced at the screen. After a few seconds, she turned back to Byrne. 'Once again, I'm so sorry. I don't know her. I hope nothing bad has happened to her.'

'What about the boy?' Byrne asked. 'Do you recognize him?'

Another glance. 'I feel I am being no help to you and Detective Balzano whatsoever. I'm afraid I don't recognize him either.'

'Isn't that little girl you?' Byrne asked. 'And isn't that little boy Mr Marseille?'

At this the young woman burst out laughing, then quickly covered her mouth. After a few moments she said: 'I am *so* sorry. I don't mean to make light of all this. I mean, the fact that I am here, in a police station, means that something bad has happened. It's just that the notion of this little girl being me is quite amusing.'

'This recording was made about twelve years ago, in the office of Dr Meredith Allen. You do remember Dr Allen, don't you?'

The young woman gave Byrne a look that Jessica could only describe as one of maternal concern, as if she were trying to figure out how to tell a child the truth about Santa or the Easter Bunny.

'You have a wonderful imagination, Kevin. I'm wondering if you may have missed your calling.'

Byrne held the look for a few seconds. 'There is one more thing I'd like you to look at,' he said. 'May I?'

'Of course,' she said. 'But don't be cross with me if I cannot be of any help to you.'

'I won't.'

Byrne tapped a few keys, then the spacebar. This time the video was from the SafeCam. On the screen, Nicole Solomon is standing alone at the intersection. A few seconds later, the young man and young woman approach. Unlike the video shot at Dr Allen's office – an image made almost at eye level to the children – this was a high-angle shot, and from behind.

The young woman watched intently. There was no audio.

'This looks *terribly* covert,' she said.

'Do you recognize anyone in this video?'

For a long time, Anabelle said nothing.

Byrne stopped the recording, took out his phone, opened the photo folder to a still photograph of the video transmission from SCI Rockview.

It was a picture of Valerie Beckert.

'Do you recognize her?' Byrne asked.

The girl sat back in her chair, smoothed her skirt. 'I'm afraid all of this has been quite exhausting for me. I still have a great deal of work to do today.' She looked up at Jessica. 'I'm sorry I couldn't be of any help to you, but I must be going. Unless I am compelled to stay. Am I?'

They were being played. The young woman was trying to see what they had. She was going to ask for a lawyer.

'Could you excuse us for a second?' Jessica asked.

'Of course.'

Jessica and Byrne stepped out, closed the door. They were joined by Josh Bontrager, Dana Westbrook, and ADA Paul DiCarlo.

What did they have? They had a high-angle pole cam shot of two people talking to Nicole Solomon on the day she was murdered, one of who might have been the young woman in the other room. The person on the recording could have been any one of fifty thousand other young women in the city. Add to that the fact that, even if it was 'Anabelle,' there was no crime committed on the tape.

They had a twelve-year-old recording of a six-year-old girl that Jessica would swear under oath was their suspect. Again, no crime.

They had no prints, no DNA, no hair or fiber, no eyewitness to put the young woman at the Solomon or Gillen or Skolnik crime scenes.

What connected the young woman, however tenuously, was the fact that she worked at the doll shop, a place where the dolls found at a crime scene may or may not have been purchased.

If they could put the young woman's fingerprints on the teapot from which Emmaline Rose drank her tainted tea, they might be able to work with it. However, the fact that they could not prove that Anabelle had made the tea, or, even if she had, Miss Emmaline might have known what she was drinking, meant that it would take a first-year public defender about ten minutes to get the girl released.

'Has she asked for a lawyer?' Dana Westbrook asked.

Byrne shook his head. 'Not yet.'

DiCarlo considered their options. 'Has the older woman regained consciousness? This Miss Emmaline?'

'Yes,' Jessica said.

Byrne stepped away, took out his phone, called the hospital. Within a minute he returned. 'She's still sedated. Still listed as stable.'

'Well, if we can get her on the record saying it *wasn't* her magic mushroom, we have a shot at holding this girl on a misdemeanor assault charge.'

'As soon as we charge her, she's going to ask for a lawyer,' Westbrook said.

'And then I'm going to have to cut her loose,' DiCarlo said.

Jessica glanced back through the mirror. The girl had not moved an inch. She just sat there, expressionless, her hands folded on the table, as enigmatic and impenetrable as the moment she walked in.

'Let's see if we can get her to sit tight,' Westbrook said.

DiCarlo looked at the three detectives, said: 'Give me something to work with.'

69

How does one dress to be put on a shelf?

It surely is a question pondered by all of my kind for ages.

I layered the clothing on the bed. I had selected a classic notch lapel, three button. The material was a fine wool and silk, a glen plaid and blue windowpane design.

Anabelle's clothing, unbeknownst to her, had been packed for weeks. I do so hate to deceive her, but protecting her heart is far more important.

I knew what she would want to wear.

If all went as planned – as had been written in our story since that dark moment when an eighteen-wheel truck pulled to the side of the road so many years ago, the moment a slender young backwoods girl was observed practicing her cartwheels in the yard, the Blue Mountains rising from the mist in the distance, the moment the past and the present met and linked forever – I intended to return to this room but one more time.

I looked at my watch, my heart falling.

In just a short time our *maîtresse des marionnettes* would be dead.

414

70

Byrne wanted to be alone, to decelerate, to clear his mind, but decided to go ahead with the get-together.

He had given serious thought to cancelling, based on the recent events – he certainly wasn't in a festive mood – but too many people were invited, people who had nothing to do with the department or the justice system as a whole.

He was on call, and could be back at the Roundhouse within fifteen minutes. Paddy Byrne was on the way, and there was no one better at hosting a party if need be.

So far their suspect, Cassandra White, had not asked for a lawyer. Her fingerprints were not in the system.

Byrne stood in the center of the front room. There were a half-dozen candles on the mantel, a dozen or so folding chairs scattered about the room, chairs he had managed to borrow from a friend of his who ran a funeral parlor in South Philly. The good news was, the Grace Brothers funeral home was not stenciled on the back of the chairs.

He'd borrowed Colleen's iPad for the evening, and had it plugged into a stereo system, also borrowed. On it he had programmed three or four hours of music. Old blues, mainstream jazz, some modern stuff for the under eighteens.

Byrne again looked at his watch, far more nervous about this than he thought he would be. It was only a get-together for a small group of family and friends, after all, every one of whom had his back.

He was so nervous that he'd even set the timer on the oven, just to remind himself to take a shower and clean up.

At five-fifteen – two hours before the first guests were expected – there was a knock at the door. It would be the delivery from Finnigan's Wake. He flipped on the light in the dining room wincing at how his makeshift buffet table – in reality, a four by eight sheet of plywood, on a quartet of sawhorses, draped with a plastic picnic tablecloth in the red and white checkerboard style – looked under the callous glare of the old chandelier. As soon as the food was set up, he would turn the light off.

He opened the door, saw the van in the driveway, idling, the Finnigan's Wake logo on the door.

'How are you doing?' he heard from behind the van.

The delivery man, wearing the distinctive Finnigan's Wake green shirt and ball cap, came around the side of the van with three big trays of food.

'Are you Mr Byrne?' he asked.

'I am,' Byrne said. 'Call me Kevin. Do you need a hand with that?'

'No thanks,' he said. 'I got it.'

The man walked in the foyer, wiped his feet, then crossed the living room to the dining room. He set the trays down on the makeshift table, looked around.

'Great house,' he said.

'Thanks. It's coming along,' Byrne said. 'Are you sure I can't give you a hand with any of this?'

'There are two more trays,' he said. 'It would be great if you could grab them. I can set up the steam trays.'

'No problem.'

Byrne walked out to the van, noticing that the sky was crystal clear, the temperature unseasonably warm. He walked back inside, put the trays on the table, the aroma of fish and chips reminding him that he hadn't eaten.

'Well, that's everything.'

Byrne took out a twenty, tried to hand it over.

'No need,' the man said. 'But I will have a beer. As long as you don't tell my boss.'

'You got it.'

Byrne grabbed a beer from the cooler, twisted off the cap. He retrieved his tumbler of Kessler's from the table.

'To your new house,' the delivery man said.

'Thanks.'

Byrne raised his glass, downed it. The whiskey was serviceable, but it wasn't Black Bush or Tullamore Dew. He reminded himself to never go on the cheap again.

Glass drained, Byrne once again held up the twenty. 'Sure you won't take this?'

'I'm fine.'

Byrne pocketed the bill, turned back to check on the steam trays, trying to calculate whether or not there was going to be enough food.

'Actually, there *is* one thing you can do for me.'

'Sure,' Byrne replied.

'You can let Anabelle go.'

At first, Byrne thought he had misunderstood the young man.

In an instant, though, he understood. Everything came rushing toward him. Why the young man looked familiar, was the first thing. When he saw him walking up the dark drive, he chalked it up to having seen the young man at Finnigan's Wake.

He now knew where he recognized the young man from. He'd seen him on surveillance tape. He saw him as a six-year-old boy. He was the boy known as Martin White, a name Byrne now knew was given to him by the foster care home.

He was Mr Marseille.

The other thing that came quickening toward Byrne was the fact that his service weapon, and his secondary weapon, were upstairs, in a box on a nightstand table.

'Anabelle?' Byrne asked, slowly turning around.

As expected, the young man had a handgun pointed at him. The front door was closed.

'I think you know who I mean.'

'You mean Cassandra White,' Byrne said.

'I know of no one by that name.'

'And you are Martin White.'

The young man remained silent.

Byrne pointed at the logo on the green Polo shirt. 'Is he dead?'

Again, silence. Then the young man said: 'I'd like you to sit down. '

'If I refuse?'

'You are just another doll,' the young man said. 'You mean nothing to me. Broken or whole. If you refuse I will pull the trigger.'

Byrne knew he would have to find another way out of this, if there was one to be found. He looked over the young man's shoulder, waiting for headlights to wash the front of the house, hoping that the first guests to arrive would be cops. No headlights shone.

Byrne reached back, pulled a chair, sat down.

'So you are Mr Marseille,' Byrne said.

'I am.'

'I knew I would one day meet you.'

'And here we are.'

'Maybe you could tell me exactly what you want,' he said. 'I'll see if I can make it happen.'

'I want you to make a call, tell your superiors that you made a mistake detaining Anabelle, and that they are to let her go immediately.'

'It's not that easy,' Byrne said.

'It's not my problem.'

'You have to know that you are just prolonging the inevitable. Even if they do let her go, and you two do get together, it will only be a matter of time until you're caught.'

'Like you caught me tonight?'

'Fair enough,' Byrne said. 'But there are now at least four bodies on your sheet. It's not going to go well.'

'Let me worry about Mr Marseille and Anabelle.'

Third person, Byrne thought. Never a good sign. 'So, this is all about Valerie Beckert, yes?'

'Yes,' he said. 'When she took us in we were merely a boy and a girl. Now we are Sauveterre.'

'She is Jean Marie Sauveterre's daughter.'

'She is every Sauveterre ever *made*,' he said. 'She is perfect. And soon you will take her life.'

'I don't think my bosses are going to do this.'

'Then it will be up to you to convince them.'

Byrne considered his options. There were few. 'If there is more bloodshed there will be nowhere on the planet for you to hide.'

'We have been hiding in plain sight for years,' he said. 'No one looks at dolls on a shelf.'

'Why tonight?' Byrne asked. 'Because she is scheduled to die at midnight?'

Mr Marseille pulled up a folding chair, positioned it by the front window, peered through the curtains. He turned back, sat down.

'There is one more tea,' he said. 'When that is over we will both turn our lashes to the light, and you can put us on a shelf forever.'

'They were all there at the competency hearing,' Byrne said. 'You blame them for Valerie getting the death penalty.'

The young man said nothing for a few seconds. Then:

'Have you ever lost a doll, Mr Byrne?'

He was talking about loss. Real loss. Byrne thought about losing his mother to cancer, how thin she grew in her final weeks, how much he missed her, and always would. He battled back the sorrow.

'Yes,' he said.

'Then you know the pain of grief.'

'I do.'

Mr Marseille looked at the stairs leading to the second floor. 'I remember the first time I climbed these stairs. I thought they might reach to heaven.'

Byrne needed to bring him back to the moment.

'What if I can't do what you're asking? What if I call my bosses and they say no?'

'Then I will greet your guests at the door, and one by one I will send them to their rooms.'

Send them to their rooms, Byrne thought. This is how this man thought of cold-blooded murder.

'In the meantime, I cannot have you down here,' he said. 'Please stand up.'

Reluctantly, Byrne stood up.

He started up the stairs with Mr Marseille behind him. When they reached the third floor, Mr Marseille opened the closet door. He reached beneath the bottom shelf. Byrne heard a latch triggered. The young man then gripped the bottom shelf and pulled.

The entire shelf unit opened as one, hinged on the left. In front of Byrne was a long hallway.

'What is this?' Byrne asked.

'Welcome to my home,' Mr Marseille said.

He flipped a wall switch. Ahead Byrne saw a half-dozen iron wall sconces come to life, bathing the corridor in an amber glow.

On either side was a wall of dolls, nailed to the plaster, at some places three deep. There had to be hundreds.

When they reached the end of the hall, Marseille unlocked a steel door, pulling two large barrel bolts to the side. Ahead was a windowless double bedroom. And still more dolls. But here the walls were lined with posters and photographs, as well.

Pictures of Nicole Solomon, of Robert and Edward Gillen, of Andrea Skolnik, scores of others, many of them black and white pictures turned sepia by time.

'Please have a seat,' Marseille said, gesturing to a chair near a small rolltop desk.

Before he could move Byrne heard a buzzer go off. It was the kitchen timer he'd set, but it sounded far too close. He suddenly understood. He looked down, at the heating vent at his feet.

'That's how you knew,' Byrne said. 'You heard everything that was said in the kitchen. All my conversations.'

The young man didn't respond to this. Instead, he repeated: 'Please have a seat.'

In his mind, Byrne knew what he meant. But the sound was strange, full of reverberations and echoes. For a moment, he thought it was the music, which was coming from just below them.

But he knew it wasn't.

It was why the bottom shelf whiskey had tasted so bad. Marseille had done it while Byrne was at the van. It was why Marseille wanted a beer, to make a toast.

He had laced Byrne's drink with magic mushroom.

A few moments later, as Marseille closed and bolted the steel door from the other side, the world began to change.

Byrne looked around. Every corner of the room watched him with dead eyes, eyes that, two by two, began to open, to come to life.

The forty-four minutes he had lost that night.

He'd been here before.

71

I left the policeman to his thoughts. He seemed a bright and reasonable man, but that in no way meant that he would not put me on a shelf at the first opportunity or sign of weakness.

I gave him time to think about his guests, and what he could do to save them.

I pulled a chair to the front window, looked out at the street, my heart brimming with sadness. The idea of hosting a tea without Anabelle filled me with a deep longing for the time when we first came to this house, when Valerie took us in and made us Sauveterre. It was a splendid summer, the house filled with all our little friends. Aaron, Nancy, Thaddeus, Jason. And Thomas. Little Thomas Rule with his slow gait and fierce determination.

There had been other friends over the years, but it had not been the same without Valerie. When we read in the paper that the Commonwealth of Pennsylvania was going to take her life at the stroke of midnight – in just a few hours' time – I knew what we had to do.

Lost in my reverie of things past, I almost did not see the headlights wash the front of the house.

A guest had arrived early.

I surveyed the parlor and dining room. All appeared as it should. I put the Finnigan's Wake cap back on my head, a smile on my face.

The doorbell rang.

I made sure my handgun could not be seen.

I crossed the foyer, and reached for the door.

72

Jessica waited at the door, impatient for any number of reasons. She knew it was a big night for her partner. He deserved every happiness.

She also knew that the weight of the cases was heavy on his shoulders, on all their shoulders. They were both on call this night, in case there was a significant break. Or, God forbid, another killing.

Jessica's cousin Angela was watching Carlos. Vincent promised to stop by later, provided the drug dealers of North Philadelphia could behave themselves for a few hours. Jessica was not going to hold her breath on that one.

She thought about what her life might be like – indeed, the life of her family, as well – if and when she ever joined the district attorney's office. For at least the first few years there would be irregular and uncertain hours. In Philadelphia, there had to be a handful of ADAs on call twenty-four hours a day for arraignments.

Still, even if she was on call for the DA's office on a night like this, the disposition of the justice would not involve weapons and arrest procedures, and all the danger that lies within.

She put her hand on the doorknob, called out.

'Ready?'

Jessica glanced up to see Sophie come down the stairs, looking adorable in a blue velvet, empire waist dress, even though there was nothing much yet to *empire*, thank God. No heels yet either, also thank God. Strappy shoes.

'How do I look?' Sophie asked.

Jessica had to bite her lip. Like a grown-up, she thought.

'You look beautiful, honey.'

Two minutes later Jessica started the car, pulled away from the curb, and headed to Kevin Byrne's house in Wynnefield.

73

Byrne listened to the sounds, his head swimming in the colors and textures around him. The room was lit by candles, and as the flames danced, the wall of dolls around him seemed to move.

No, he thought, they *were* moving.

The dolls on the shelf to his left glared at him, each with Valerie Beckert's eyes.

All about him he heard the rustling of crinoline and satin, the tick of plastic and bisque arms and legs moving, saw tiny hands and feet try to grasp the air.

'Whenever Papa fired a new doll, I could hear it. I could hear it being born,' said the small doll just to his left. Byrne glanced over. The doll wore a paisley shawl, had feathered eyebrows, painted upper and lower lashes.

Byrne closed his eyes to the hallucination, tried to will it away. How much of the mushroom had he taken? There had only been a few inches of whiskey in his glass. It couldn't have been much.

When he opened his eyes the doll who had spoken to him was replaced by Nicole Solomon. In his mind's eye Byrne saw the silk stocking around the doll's neck growing ever tighter, heard the hyoid bone begin to crush, saw her eyes fill with blood.

'Why couldn't you save my father?' the doll asked. The voice was young, trusting. A tear shone on her porcelain cheek.

'I didn't know,' Byrne replied. 'I tried.'

When he looked back the Nicole doll's eyes were closed. On either side were Robert and Edward Gillen.

'We were only twelve,' they said in unison.

'I know,' Byrne said. 'I'm sorry.'

Time passed.

Byrne heard the wind in the eaves. It was as mournful and terrible a sound as he could ever remember hearing.

Around him, the broken dolls began to sing.

Byrne knew the song.

It was 'These Foolish Things.'

His cousin Paul, dead these many years, sat on the floor in front of him, cross-legged, his back to the door. Long before anyone in the neighborhood ever heard the word 'yoga' Paulie sat like this. It wasn't a mannerism, it was how Paulie sat on the floor. He was always taller, always skinnier, always more limber than any of them. He couldn't play touch football for shit, but he was fast.

'Never got laid, Kev,' he said. 'Only got drunk that one time with you.'

'Wild Irish Rose,' Byrne said. He could still taste it.

Paulie smiled. He had no teeth. He'd lost them in the accident, along with the rest of his face. Not to mention that steering column through his chest. 'King of the bum wines.'

Paulie got clipped at 26th and Lombard. He was only sixteen. They say the guy in the Camaro was doing sixty or seventy per, blasted through the red. They also said that Paulie died instantly.

For those who loved Paulie, that was the good news. The bad news was that Byrne was supposed to be driving Paulie to work that night.

Everyone in the Pocket said they heard the impact. Maybe it was legend.

'You got close that one time with ... what was her name?' Byrne asked.

'Linda,' Paulie said. 'Linda Vecchio.'

Linda Vecchio still wore that glittery nylon sleeveless shell, and a denim skirt. She had a tattoo on her right calf, an eighteen-wheeler with a big red tongue coming out. Rolling Stoned, LLC. She sat on the floor where Paulie had been sitting.

'Fucking liar.'

Linda was now Deirdre Emily Reese, the prostitute found in the woods off I-476, her body next to Ezekiel Moss's, the one with no eyes. She had eyes now, though. They were painted on.

'That trucker said he had a bottle,' Deirdre said. 'All he had was a razor blade.'

Some time later, Byrne heard the door open and close. He looked up.

It was Marseille. For some reason, Byrne saw him as he had looked on the videotape, as a six-year-old boy, the tape he had seen at ... what was the doctor's name?

He couldn't recall.

'Do you like our tea?'

He was once again a young man. Byrne said nothing.

'What did you see?' Marseille asked.

Byrne opened his mouth, but no sound came out. He knew what he wanted to say, but he couldn't seem to speak.

'This is the view from the shelf, detective.'

The young man was right. *Partially* right. For a moment Byrne saw the room from above.

Marseille stood behind him. Byrne tried to rise to his feet, but his legs were unsteady.

'Are you familiar with Xanax?' Marseille asked.

The young man was now in front of him again. Byrne opened his mouth. This time a word emerged. 'Yes.'

Marseille unfurled his hand. In it were two oval blue pills.

'Do you trust me that this will help?'

Byrne did not. But he had no choice. 'I do.'

'Take them, please.'

Byrne took the pills, put them in his mouth, dry swallowed them.

'Your guests have begun to arrive,' Marseille said.

'What are you telling them?'

'I'm telling them the truth. That you have been detained.'

'That's not the truth.'

Marseille smiled. 'They are helping themselves to your bounty. The one young lady – the pretty one with the dark eyes – said she will play hostess until I return.'

Maria Caruso, Byrne thought.

'I will be back in one half-hour,' Marseille said. 'Then we will make that call.'

74

Byrne opened his eyes, fearful of what he might see.

He was alone. The room was mercifully silent. He looked at the candles, and noted that they had begun to burn down.

How much time had passed? He had no idea.

The dolls were no longer moving.

Somehow the man was sitting next to him.

'How do you feel?'

Exhausted, Byrne thought. Sluggish from the Xanax. But better.

'Fine.'

'Did you go to a place of happiness or one of fear and regret?'

Byrne said nothing. The mushroom had opened a portal within him, a corridor through which he did not have the courage to pass.

Marseille stood up. 'I think we should begin the process now,' he said. 'Unless you have decided you will not do so.'

Byrne knew there was no choice. If he said no, or in any way tipped off the cavalry in the process, there could be a bloodbath downstairs. He had to concentrate.

'Okay,' Byrne said.

'How do we begin?'

'My first call will be to Paul DiCarlo.'

'Who is he?'

'He is an assistant district attorney. He will have to sign off on Anabelle's release.'

Marseille nodded. 'What would be the step after that?'

'Paul would then call the county sheriff's office.'

'Why them?'

'The holding cells in the Roundhouse are their jurisdiction. As soon as Mr DiCarlo talks to a deputy sheriff, Anabelle will be released.'

Marseille thought for a few moments. 'When you say released, what do you mean? Released where?'

'What I mean is she would be free to go. She would walk out of the Roundhouse, and be free to go wherever she wants.'

'That is across town from here.'

Byrne nodded. 'Yes, it is.'

'I'm afraid Anabelle is not very worldly. She has always depended on me for such things.'

Not my problem, Byrne wanted to say. Instead, he said nothing.

'In addition, I am certain she has very little money for things like cab fare,' he said. 'None, in fact.'

'I can have her driven to anywhere you say.'

Marseille nodded. 'That is most kind.'

The man pulled up a chair, sat across from Byrne. Outside, just under the eaves, the wind whipped around, rattled the dormer windows, loose in their mullions.

'This Mr DiCarlo. Does he know your voice?'

The answer to this question, of course, was yes. Byrne had spoken to ADA DiCarlo hundreds of times, had been questioned on direct examination in a courtroom by him dozens of times. Byrne had to consider the play. If he said no, and Marseille placed the call, pretending to be Detective Kevin Byrne, DiCarlo would surely know something was wrong.

But DiCarlo, as streetwise an ADA as there was, would not know the play. Byrne couldn't take the chance. There was only one option.

'Yes,' Byrne said. 'He knows my voice.'

'Will he be at the office at this hour?'

'I don't know,' Byrne said. 'But I have his cell number.'

'Would he think it odd that you would be calling him at this hour, or that you would call him on his cell phone?'

'No on both counts,' Byrne said. 'I've called him at all hours. I've also called him on his cell. We work well together. Providing we follow procedure, he will do what I ask.'

'Are you ready to place the call?'

'I am.'

The phone rang once, twice, three times. Byrne had not even considered the possibility that it would roll over to voicemail.

On the fourth ring Paul answered.

'This is Paul.'

'Paul, Kevin Byrne.'

'Hey, detective. How's the party?'

Byrne had forgotten that an invite went out to the ADAs, and that Paul had left a message, respectfully taking a rain check. 'Two hours in and they're already swinging from the chandeliers.'

DiCarlo laughed. 'Sorry I can't make it. I'm up to my ass in RICO alligators. And, needless to say, there's a pall over the office about Marvin Skolnik's daughter.'

'I won't keep you. The reason I'm calling is Cassandra White.'

As soon as Byrne said this, he considered that it might have been a mistake to call her Cassandra White and not Anabelle.

433

He'd had no choice. Cassandra White was the name on the paperwork. Paul DiCarlo would have no idea who Anabelle was.

'What about her?' DiCarlo asked.

'I want to cut her loose.'

Silence. Expected, but still a little unnerving. 'What do you mean? Why?'

'I don't think we have anything that we can make stick. We're already past six hours.'

According to the law, a person had to be charged or released within six hours.

DiCarlo hesitated a few moments. Then:

'I'll make the call.'

'Thanks, Paul,' Byrne said. 'I owe you one.'

'You want that on the big tab or the little tab?'

'Be well,' Byrne said.

'You too.'

Marseille hit the button, ending the call. 'Thank you, detective.'

Byrne said nothing.

'What is the next step?'

'In a few minutes I'll call the desk sergeant. When Anabelle walks into the lobby she'll be expecting her. I'll tell her to have one of the patrol officers take Anabelle anywhere you'd like.'

Before Marseille could respond, Byrne's cell phone rang.

Both Byrne and Marseille looked at the caller ID at the same moment.

It was Jessica.

'If I don't answer she'll know something is wrong,' Byrne said.

'Perhaps she'll think you're busy and couldn't get to the phone.'

'You don't know my partner. She won't give up.'

Marseille considered this. 'I needn't tell you what's at stake.'

'No,' Byrne said. 'I know what's at stake.'

Marseille pressed the button, answering the call. He then tapped the icon, putting the phone on speaker.

'Hey, partner,' Byrne said.

'Hey yourself,' Jessica said. 'Where are you?'

'Don't ask.'

'Too late.'

'Are you ... at my house?' Byrne asked. He winced. He'd almost asked if she was downstairs.

'I'm about two blocks away. I'm with Sophie. Vince is going to try and stop by. Where are you?'

Byrne knew he couldn't continue to avoid answering that question. 'I'm on my way home in a bit. I'm at SVU.'

'SVU? What's going on?'

This was getting deeper. He should have said something else, something other than the Special Victims Unit. Jessica could check on this if she suspected something was wrong.

Byrne could sense the man with the gun getting agitated.

'I'll explain later,' he said. 'I think we have a break.'

'I'll be right there,' Jessica said. 'I'll drop Sophie at the party and head over.'

'No,' Byrne said, a little more forcefully than he wanted to. 'I'm walking out the door now. This can wait. I'll explain.'

Jessica was silent for a few moments.

'Can you help Maria play hostess until I get there?' Byrne asked.

'I guess so,' she said. 'I just think—'

'Thanks,' Byrne said. 'I'll be there as soon as I can.'

'When do you think that will be?'

'After midnight,' he said.

'*Midnight?* I'll probably be—'

'I'm getting behind the wheel now.'

'Okay,' Jessica said. 'If you need me to—'

Marseille pressed the button, ending the call.

'I want you to call this desk sergeant. Tell her that when Ana-belle comes to the lobby to call you at this number.'

Byrne gave Marseille the number for the desk at the Round-house. Marseille dialed, put the phone on speaker. When the call was answered, Byrne gave the desk sergeant at the Roundhouse – a veteran named Tina Willis – the information.

They waited.

Byrne knew how agonizingly slow the wheels could turn at times. He couldn't tell Paul DiCarlo to hurry this up. It would certainly have raised suspicions in a man suspicious by nature. Byrne was certain that Jessica had only bought half the loaf he was selling.

A full five minutes later, the phone rang. Byrne nearly jumped from his chair. They both looked at the readout. It said: NO CALLER ID.

Marseille tapped the icon to answer. He put the phone on speaker.

'This is Kevin,' Byrne said.

'Detective Byrne, this is Sergeant Willis.'

'Hey, Tina. Thanks for calling back.'

'No problem,' she said. 'I've got Cassandra White right here.'

Byrne knew how this was going to sound, but he had to ask it anyway. 'Are we on speaker there, Tina?'

As expected, a pause. 'No, detective.'

'Okay, thanks. Put her on please?'

A few seconds later, from the phone: 'Mr Marseille?'

Byrne could hear the anticipation in her voice. She sounded like a child.

'Yes.'

It was clear that the young woman had begun to cry.

'Please don't cry, *mon cœur*,' Marseille said.

'Okay. It's just that . . . '

'It's just that what?'

'We've never been apart this long. Ever.'

'I'm going to give you an address to which I want the police to take you. They'll know where it is.'

Byrne heard the address. It was one block south of his house.

What is this man preparing to do? Byrne wondered.

'*Au revoir,*' the girl on the phone said.

'*A bientôt.*'

Marseille ended the call, took out his weapon. 'It is not always easy to do the right thing.'

'You think this – all of this – is the right thing?' Byrne asked.

'It will all be over soon, detective.'

75

Jessica decided to drink only mixers, for any number of reasons. Not the least of which was that she didn't know where this night was going to take her.

She didn't buy for a second Byrne's story. Something was wrong. He wanted her to *know* something was wrong, but she felt he was hamstrung from telling her so.

She'd put in a call to Paul DiCarlo and had gotten his voicemail.

The next call was to the Special Victims Unit. As she suspected, Byrne had not stopped there this evening.

The next went to the Roundhouse. What she learned was disturbing, but not surprising. They had released Cassandra White.

Dana did not know the details, but the lead investigator, Kevin Byrne, and an attorney from the DA's office, Paul DiCarlo, had signed off on it and that, as they say, was that.

For almost any detective, that would be enough.

Unless you were Lt. Peter Giovanni's daughter.

Jessica Giovanni Balzano knew something was wrong.

Even though Byrne said he would not be home until after midnight, every few minutes Jessica stepped onto the porch, watching for his car.

By eleven o'clock the party was in full raucous swing. There had to be forty people milling around the house. Sophie had found a new best friend in Maria Caruso's niece, Jennifer. They were stuck in a corner, gossiping like loopy fishwives, talking about God only knows what.

Both Paddy Byrne and Colleen were there. Paddy, being the default elder statesman – not to mention the ranking clan Byrne family member – was the *de facto* party chief and bartender in lieu of his son. He was in his glory.

Jessica looked at her watch for the hundredth time, found a space along the wall next to the fireplace in the front room. She stood next to a young man in his late twenties, a civilian who worked at the forensic lab. She could not recall his name or his discipline.

Like most people who worked in the science divisions, he strode to his own rhythms. He was a sheet or two to starboard, leaning against the wall for balance, but still rocking steady to the music.

'You're Detective Baldacci, right?' he asked.

'Balzano.'

The young man went cherry red. For a moment it looked as if he thought this might be a firing offense. 'Sorry,' he said.

'Not a problem.'

He stuck out a hand. 'Ronnie Meldrum. I work in the drug lab.'

Jessica shook hands. They'd met before, but there was no reason to get into that now.

Meldrum held up his beer, tipped the neck toward the stereo. 'Clapton,' he said.

'What about him?' Jessica asked.

'I didn't know there was a live version of this. This is *awesome*. I'm going to have to get this.'

Jessica listened closely. She knew the song, but just couldn't place it. 'What song is this again?'

'*After Midnight*,' Meldrum said. 'It was originally on Clapton's first solo album, I think, but he didn't write it. I think it's a JJ Cale tune.'

'Ah, okay,' Jessica said.

After Midnight. Odd coincidence that Byrne would say that he would be there *after midnight*, and it would be one of the songs on his playlist. Then it hit her.

When she'd spoken to Byrne, she'd been a full two blocks from the house. Yet she'd heard the Clapton song. She'd heard music through the *phone*.

It was faint, but it was there.

Now she was certain.

Byrne was in the house.

76

With the party raging below, Jessica reached the top step. It creaked under her weight. She walked the length of the hall, edging open each of the doors. Most of the rooms were empty; two of the rooms had some boxes stacked in the corners.

None of the other partygoers had ventured up.

After checking all the rooms, Jessica got to the end of the hall. She opened the door, expecting to find a bathroom, or maybe yet another bedroom, but instead found a linen closet.

She looked up, saw the attic door. Would he really be in the attic?

Anything was possible.

She was just about to go downstairs and try to covertly sneak a chair on which to stand out of the dining room, when she sensed movement to her right. She spun around, the image of any number of bogeymen in her mind – this house did give her the creeps – only to find that it was the cat, precariously perched on the railing.

'You scared the *shit* out of me.'

The cat looked at her, nonplussed. It soon jumped off the rail, and paced around her legs, nuzzling. A few seconds later Tuck jumped onto the bottom shelf of the closet. He turned twice, sat down, glanced up at Jessica.

'Come on,' Jessica said. 'Get out of there. I'm sure Kevin doesn't need you on his face towels. Let's go.'

No dice. The cat dug in.

'What is it?' she asked. 'Do you have a toy in here?'

Jessica poked through the towels and washcloths on the top shelf. Nothing.

The middle shelf held a six-pack of bath soap, shampoos, a Water-Pik in a box.

The cat spun again. This time he pawed the back of the closet.

Jessica got down on her hands and knees. Something didn't look right, but she wasn't sure what it was. Then she saw it. A pair of large hinges, painted white to match the inside of the closet.

Jessica pulled on the left side of the shelf unit. Nothing. She planted her feet and pulled again. The shelving began to move. Seconds later it swung open.

It was a door.

Ahead was a long hallway.

Jessica thought for a moment of going downstairs and getting Maria to come with her, but she didn't want to alarm anyone at the party.

She wasn't certain there was anything to be alarmed *about* yet.

Jessica stepped into the hallway, felt for a light switch. A few steps in she found one. She flipped it on.

'You have *got* to be kidding me,' she said under her breath. Ahead, lighted by a half-dozen sconces, was a corridor of dolls, floor to ceiling. They were bolted and screwed to the walls – baby dolls, adult dolls, dolls of every race, size, material. Hundreds and hundreds.

When she got to the end there was a door. At the top and

bottom were two barrel bolts, thick steel slide bolts. From behind the door Jessica heard pounding. *Loud* pounding. When she slid the upper bolt to the left the noise stopped.

She put her ear to the door, heard nothing, then gently pushed back the bottom bolt.

A few seconds later she stood to the side, nudged open the door with her foot. She could see that this room was lit with candles. She took one cautious step in, and heard the sound of broken glass under foot. She looked down. It wasn't glass, but broken porcelain. She saw that this room, too, was lined with dolls, but many of them were broken – half-faced dolls, dolls with smashed limbs and skulls.

There was a large shadow to her left.

She drew weapon more out of instinct than a sense of danger.

It was Byrne. He had dug halfway through the wood lath and plaster with the body of a broken doll. He was covered in plaster dust.

As Byrne brushed himself off, Jessica noticed a large poster on the back of the door. It was for a nightclub in New Orleans, and featured a singer named Josie Giroux, the *Fleur de Paris*, who had made a recording of the standard, 'These Foolish Things.'

'Valerie's aunt Josephine,' Byrne said. 'That was her maiden name.'

'The embroidery on the murder weapons,' she said. 'The FdP.'

'Yeah,' Byrne said. 'It was all hers – the stockings, the old cigarettes.'

Jessica took out her phone. She called Maria Caruso.

'This is Maria.'

'Maria, it's Jess. I need you to not react in any way to what I'm going to tell you.'

'Sure.'

'Our subject is in the house. Martin White. He's wearing a Finnigan's Wake polo shirt and cap.'

'Okay,' she said, sounding upbeat. 'Sounds great.'

Jessica could hear that Maria was moving from the living room, away from the music.

'Do you see him?' Jessica asked.

The music grew fainter and fainter.

'He left,' Maria said.

'You're sure?'

'Yes. I saw him leave.'

'Do you know how long ago?'

'Maybe ten minutes?'

'Watch the front of the house. Ask John Shepherd to watch the back. Our suspect does not come inside.'

'We need the rest of those lyrics,' Byrne said.

'Hang on, Maria.'

Jessica made a search on her iPhone for the lyrics of 'These Foolish Things.' She found them. It seemed the killers had made some sort of reference to every verse in the song.

Except two.

'I need you to call in the entire department,' Jessica said to Maria, filling her in. She gave her an address on Delancey. 'Send half to Delancey Place, we'll take the other.'

As Byrne walked to one of the bedrooms on the second floor, retrieving his weapon and shield, Jessica looked around the room. On one crowded corkboard were what looked like hundreds of photographs, large and small, new and older.

There were many of the front of this house. Some had older cars, circa 1985 parked out front. Some were of people standing on the porch. As Jessica reached the last photo in the stack, she sensed Byrne standing behind her.

He saw the photo at the same moment she did.

77

We stood across the street from the house, the home that had been ours for more than ten years. Anabelle held my hand, but I could feel her trembling. She knew we would never be coming back.

I had changed back into my best suit. I wore a navy blue cashmere coat.

We observed the people at the party, the young and the old, watched the children play their games of tag, weaving through the adults as if they were trees in a forest. We watched the handful of teenagers, adrift on their sea of angst. We watched the young woman speaking in sign language.

We saw them all.

'She seems so sad,' Anabelle finally said.

'Yes.'

Anabelle put her head on my shoulder. 'She is beautiful.'

'"The beauty that is Spring's",' I said.

I could not see my Anabelle's face, but I knew this made her smile. Our song, 'These Foolish Things,' always did.

I looked at my pocket watch. 'It is time to go.'

I saw the single tear glisten on Anabelle's cheek. She pointed at the form walking down the front steps, heading toward one of the cars parked on the street. 'Shall we bring her with us?'

'Yes,' I said. 'She is *numéro seize*. The last Sauveterre.'

78

The photograph was of Colleen Byrne standing on the porch of the house. She was talking to Byrne. The picture was no more than a few days old.

Before Jessica could say a word, Byrne was out of the room, and down the hall. She heard him on the stairs before she made it out of the doorway.

By the time Jessica reached the bottom of the stairs Byrne had woven his way through the crowd, into the kitchen. Jessica moved through the partygoers, trying her best not to alarm them. When she reached the kitchen, she saw Colleen Byrne in her father's arms.

Colleen was safe.

A few seconds later John Shepherd, perhaps sensing that something was wrong, opened the back door.

'Our subject?' Byrne asked.

'Haven't seen him,' Shepherd said.

'I need you to shut this down.'

'The party?'

Byrne nodded. 'Quietly as possible. Our killers are on the move.'

'You got it.'

As Shepherd relayed the message to the people in the living room, Jessica found Paddy Byrne. 'Paddy, I need you to take Sophie home with you. I'll pick her up at your house later.'

'Sure,' Paddy said. He knew enough not to ask why. 'I'll get the car.'

Jessica threaded her way back through the crowded living room. She found Maria's niece Jennifer sitting on a folding chair in the dining room.

'Where's Sophie?' Jessica asked.

Jennifer stood, looked around the room. 'I think she went outside.'

Jessica felt her fear begin to rise. 'Outside? Why?'

'She said she wanted to get something from your car.'

Jessica's heart fell. She made her way frantically around the room, looked on the porch, up and down the dark street, at her empty car parked at the curb.

Sophie was gone.

79

The Delaware River Port Authority of Pennsylvania and New Jersey was a regional transportation agency that served the people of Southeastern Pennsylvania and Southern New Jersey.

The agency owned and operated the Benjamin Franklin, Walt Whitman, Commodore Barry, and Betsy Ross bridges.

At Pier 82 was the SS *Clermont-Ferrand*. At one time a French luxury passenger liner, the steamship – launched in 1952 to set an Atlantic crossing speed record – was decommissioned in the 1990s, and has since been permanently docked in Philadelphia.

By the time Jessica and Byrne arrived at the pier there were a half-dozen sector cars on scene, lights flashing, blocking off the streets.

As they made the turn onto the pier, they could see an EMT van near the end of the gangway. A paramedic was tending to someone on a gurney. Byrne took it in, and knew what had happened. Their suspects had attacked a night security guard or one of the cleaning crew to gain access to the ship.

When Byrne looked up at the bow, his heart sank. There,

silhouetted against the bright moon, were Martin and Cassandra White.

It looked like Sophie Balzano stood between them.

Jessica saw it too.

Before Byrne could bring the vehicle to a halt, Jessica was out of the car and heading for the ship. Byrne was out like a shot after her. He barely caught up with her before she could head down the pier and onto the vessel.

He wrapped his arms around her and held her tight.

'Let me go!' she screamed.

'Jess.'

She began to struggle, to kick her legs. Byrne knew his partner was very fit, that from time to time she still trained as a boxer, that she ran a couple of miles every day. She was one of the most physically able people, man or woman, in the entire department. Add to that the fact that she was a mother whose daughter was in danger, and it took Byrne every bit of his strength to try to contain her.

'Let me fucking *go*, Kevin. I swear to *Christ*.'

Byrne felt that he was about to lose his grip on her. She was that strong at this moment. He locked his hands together and held on as tightly as he could. All around them police personnel were arriving on scene. Byrne could hear the outboard motors of the boats from the Marine Unit coming up on either side of the SS *Clermont-Ferrand*.

'Jess, you have to listen to me.'

'*I don't want to hear it,*' she said. 'Let me. Fucking. *Go!*'

'I can't. I can't let you go. You *know* why.'

Byrne felt Jessica relax just the slightest bit. But he knew her well enough to know that it might be a con. He still held on.

He looked over Jessica's shoulder and saw the command presence arrive. Dana Westbrook and John Ross. He also saw a four-member SWAT team arrayed in full tactical gear.

'Jess. Listen to me. *Listen*. If I let you go, you've got to promise me something.'

Jessica said nothing.

'The longer we do this, the worse it gets up there.'

Byrne stole a glance at the bow of the great ship. The three figures there had not moved.

'I'm going to let you go, but I need you to promise me that you'll listen to me for ten seconds. Just ten seconds. After that, I'm not going to stop you from doing what you need to do. I just need you to listen, and to promise me.'

Jessica remained silent.

'Promise me.'

Jessica took a few deep breaths. She nodded her head. Still, it took Byrne a number of seconds before letting her go.

When he eased his grip Jessica sprang out of his grasp, but she did not run down the pier. She took a few steps in the other direction, then spun on her heels, all but hyperventilating. She glanced at the bow of the ship, and for a moment Byrne thought she would bowl him over and run toward the entrance. She did not.

She looked him in the eye.

'I'm going up there, Kevin.' She took out her weapon, checked the action. This put everyone nearby on alert. This was a very fluid scene, and no one really knew what was going to happen next.

As a pair of SWAT officers ran past them, and deployed on either side of the entryway, Byrne put one hand on each of his partner's shoulders.

'You can't go up there, Jess. You know you can't.'

'They've got Sophie, Kevin.'

'I know,' he said. 'And that's exactly why it has to be me. If one thing goes wrong up there, any little thing, this whole thing could go wrong.'

'I don't give a fucking *shit*, Kevin. That's my little girl.'

'I know,' Byrne said. 'But you could end up in prison, Jess. Then where would you be for your daughter? There isn't a lawyer, on either side of the aisle, anywhere in Philadelphia County, that wouldn't ask the question of why you didn't stand down. We need you down here. Please. Let me do this.'

Jessica took a few steps away, made another glance at the bow of the ship. She holstered her weapon. She walked right up to Byrne's face.

'Kill them,' she said.

'Jessica, I can't—'

'If you don't, I swear to Christ I will.'

Byrne looked over his partner's shoulder, saw Josh Bontrager, John Shepherd, and Maria Caruso arrive. He made eye contact with Maria. She understood. She would take care of Jessica as long as she had to.

Byrne then glanced at Dana Westbrook, who nodded. She was letting him know that he would be on point.

He left Jessica with Maria, took off his suit coat. Josh Bontrager reached into the open trunk of the department sedan, took out a Kevlar vest. He fitted Byrne with it. While they were doing this an officer from the communications unit slipped a two-way radio onto Byrne's belt, and ran the earpiece up to Byrne's ear. In his hand they put a printout of the blueprint of the front of the massive steamship.

As Byrne reached the entrance, he turned and found Jessica at the end of the pier. No matter how long he lived – and there was a possibility that it was all ending right here and right now – he would never forget the look on his partner's face.

Kill them.

80

The wind was fierce. The air was cold, but the moon was full and bright. I wished that I had been more dutiful in preparing our outfits. I had not planned on the elements. It was unlike me.

Below us the lights of the city, the lights of all the police cars, made a festive gouache of the view, but there was no joy in my heart.

We stood on either side of the little girl, the daughter of the policewoman. I knew that, if it were not for her, then the men with guns would certainly have taken a shot at us by now.

When I listened to their conversation in the kitchen that day, the day the men with beards painted the house, I knew it would be the sad little girl. She was the last Sauveterre.

I turned, looked into Anabelle's beautiful eyes. She was softly crying. In her eyes I saw the abandoned little girl sitting in front of the toy store in Richmond Mall. I saw the girl who, for nearly a year, would not speak to anyone but me, the first of nearly three years we spent in that terrible foster home.

In her eyes I saw the girl sitting next to Solitude House.

Anabelle, who has no memory of a time before the wall of dolls, before we met Valerie, and came to live in her doll house.

For my dearest heart, there was no past.

When she saw the huge ship, perhaps she thought it would be the vessel that would take us to France. I did not have the heart to tell her otherwise.

I took out the small silver flask, one that belonged to Valerie's father, Jean Marie Sauveterre. I uncapped it, handed it to Anabelle.

'Here,' I said.

'What is it?'

'Tea,' I said. It was the strongest I had ever made. 'It will warm you.'

Anabelle looked confused for a moment, then she understood. We were to be our own guests. This was our *thé dansant*. We were as much responsible for Valerie's fate as anyone.

Indeed, more responsible.

We belonged on the shelf for eternity.

81

Byrne made his way slowly up the ladder, his weapon in hand. As he neared the access hole to the deck he heard the sound of the wind growing ever louder.

He keyed the microphone button on his two-way. He got a response from John Shepherd.

'Everyone in place?' Byrne whispered.

'Affirmative,' Shepherd whispered. 'SWAT's deployed to the east and south of the subjects. If you can get Jessica's daughter to the deck they will engage.'

'Copy,' Byrne said.

He took a deep breath, holstered his weapon behind his back, turned the volume in his earpiece even lower, and stepped onto the deck of the *Clermont-Ferrand*.

The two groups stood on the bow, thirty feet apart. Sophie looked so small between the two of them. The gusts whipped the flags overhead.

'Detective,' Marseille said.

Byrne just nodded. He made eye contact with Sophie. She was shivering, but she nodded back.

'How did you find us?' Marseille asked.

Byrne tried to consider his answer, but there was not time. 'It came down to two possibilities. There's the line about Garbo, and we considered the collection of letters from Greta Garbo at the Rosenbach Museum on Delancey Place.'

'But you came here,' Marseille said, 'Why?'

'*The scent of smould'ring leaves, the wail of steamers,*' Byrne said, quoting the song.

Marseille smiled. He took Anabelle's hand. '*Two lovers on the street who walk like dreamers.*' He looked at Sophie, back at Byrne.

'I expected you, detective, just not quite this soon.'

Byrne heard soft footsteps behind and below him. It would be the two other SWAT officers. Out of the corner of his eye he saw them on the iron ladder, just below deck.

Byrne looked back toward the bow, took a few tentative steps. Marseille had his free hand in his pocket. Byrne had no idea if he was armed. He took one more step. The man did not tell him to stop.

'This can end here and now,' Byrne said. 'There's no need to harm the girl.'

Marseille took Sophie's hand.

'If it weren't for her we would not even be having this conversation, *n'est-ce pas?*'

Marseille had, of course, seen the SWAT officers deployed on the pier.

'Tell me what you want and I'll get it for you,' Byrne said.

'Can you rewind the world?'

'What do you mean?'

'Can you take us back ten years, to the day when Anabelle and I visited Solitude House at the Philadelphia Zoo?'

'Believe me, if I—'

'Because that is where our lives began. Before then, there was no Anabelle, no Mr Marseille.'

Byrne waited for the man to continue. He did not. 'I wish I could do that. I wish it for everybody involved. I wish it for Thomas Rule, too.'

Marseille looked out at the city for a moment, back. 'Thomas,' he said.

Byrne took a few more steps. 'You don't have to hurt this girl. I was there the night Valerie was arrested. I arrested her.'

'I know.'

'So take me instead. If you blamed David Solomon and Judge Gillen and Marvin Skolnik for what happened to Valerie, fine. But I'm more responsible than any of them.'

'You don't understand.'

'You're right,' Byrne said. 'I *don't* understand. *Help* me to understand. Take me instead.'

Byrne slowly reached behind, slipped his service weapon out of its holster, put it on the deck of the ship. He then turned slowly, 360 degrees, showing the man he was unarmed.

'If I wanted to mend you I could have done so at the house,' Marseille said. 'You are broken. We watched you many a night.'

Byrne did not want to think about what they might've seen and heard from their secret room.

'Yes, you could have. But you didn't. That means something.'

Byrne glanced at the girl, at Anabelle. There was little doubt in his mind that she had taken the mushroom. Her eyes were glassy and distant.

Before Byrne could say another word he saw all three of them take a step backward. They were right up against the rail now.

He was losing them.

82

For Detective Jessica Balzano, the concept of time no longer existed. When she saw her daughter on the bow of the ship, time stopped.

As she paced on the pier, as the machinery of a hostage situation deployment unfolded around her, as the flashing of lights and the crackle of two-way radios and the sound of an ambulance siren approaching assaulted her senses, time had no meaning.

She had never felt more helpless in her life. No woman ever had. Her daughter was just a few hundred feet away, and she couldn't reach her, couldn't protect her. The sacred oath she had taken the day Sophie Balzano was born was now broken.

Right now her daughter was a tiny silhouette on the bow of a massive steamship, flanked by a pair of monstrous people, and there was nothing she could do.

She wanted to be able to pray, but right now she didn't believe. Where was God at this moment? Where was St Michael?

She put her hand on the grip of her weapon. Right now, this was her God, her saint, her archangel.

Jessica looked at the SWAT officer on top of the shuttered ticket kiosk, in full tactical gear, his high-powered rifle on a tripod, his cap backwards, his eye to the scope.

She had seen this tableau a hundred times before, but it never had any meaning for her. She thought it had, but it hadn't. Not really. She knew that now.

As time stood still, she had but one thought.

Take the shot.

The more she willed it, the more time refused to budge. Still, the mantra screamed in a never ending loop in her mind.

Taketheshottaketheshottaketheshot . . .

83

Byrne was now fifteen feet away.

He still had a second weapon in an ankle holster. He had no way of knowing if it was visible. To look at it might mean giving it away.

Martin and Cassandra White, still holding hands with Sophie, were backed up all the way to the railing.

Sophie looked so small.

'You okay, kiddo?' Byrne asked.

Sophie nodded.

'It's not too late to stop this,' Byrne said. He gestured to all the lights and people surrounding the ship. 'We can end this with no one else getting hurt.' He tore the earpiece from his ear, the two-way from his belt. He threw them both overboard. A strong gust of wind hurtled them into the blackness.

'It's just us now,' Byrne added. 'No one else is listening.'

'Did you know her?' Marseille asked.

'Who?'

'Our *maîtresse des marionnettes.*'

'You mean Valerie? No. I did not.'

'And yet you judged her.'

'I never judged her,' Byrne said, realizing, as he said the words, how inadequate they were. 'I just did my job. She had a fair trial.'

'She was our kind.'

'What do you mean?'

Before Martin White could say another word, Byrne heard the footsteps behind him. Someone had given the order.

The SWAT officers had breached the ship's deck.

Byrne looked into Sophie's eyes.

Jessica's eyes.

No.

84

At the moment the world began to end, I looked at Anabelle. I know it is not possible for a doll to feel love, but at that moment I loved her.

I always have.

'Is it beautiful?' I asked her.

She nodded. 'It is the most beautiful thing ever.'

'Do you trust me?'

'Of course,' she said. 'Always.'

She looked down. In my free hand was the cameo brooch we had been given by our *maîtresse des marionnettes* so many years ago. I handed it to her.

'These foolish things,' I said.

A tear rolled down Anabelle's cheek. 'Never foolish, Mr Marseille.'

She saw the gun in my hand just as the men came up through the floor. She looked into my eyes. She brought the girl closer to her.

*

'No, Mr Marseille.'

Anabelle and the girl took a step away from me.

'It has to be this way,' I said.

'No.'

To my left I saw the shadows moving quickly toward us. I looked into Anabelle's eyes.

'My dearest heart.'

I wrapped my arms around Anabelle and the little girl. We all fell backward, over the railing, into life, into the eternal fire that is the moment of creation for all our kind.

85

When the three figures fell from the bow of the ship, Jessica was standing at the end of the pier. For an agonizing moment it didn't seem real.

She heard a bloodcurdling cry, a heart-rending scream of pain and anguish. It seemed to come down a long, echoing tunnel.

The screams were her own.

She found herself running down the pier. When she reached the end she tore off her coat and her shoes. The water beneath her was black and roiling. Before she could dive into the water, strong arms grabbed her from behind and pulled her back.

'*Let me go!*'

There were now four arms around her. From somewhere she found the strength to fight them off. She heard the siren *whoop* on the marine unit boats. Lights flashed. More hands grabbed for her. She pivoted, lashed out with her fist, connected. The pain burned up her arm.

Jessica was free for one moment, no hands on her. It was long enough. She vaulted the few steps, jumping for the back of the marine unit boat as it left the pier. She barely landed on the rear deck. In the process she slipped, hitting her head. Hands pulled her on board. For a few seconds her face was near the outboard, the smell of fuel and heat from the engine clogging her senses.

The sound of the sirens became louder. More shouting. Jessica tried to stand, but the blow to her head was dizzying. She lost her balance, struggled to her feet.

'*Sophie!*' she screamed.

On unsteady legs she made her way to the front of the craft. The water was lighted by a pair of halogen spotlights as it neared the bow of the SS *Clermont-Ferrand*. Jessica saw a figure in the water, no more than thirty yards away. Again she tried to dive into the water, but was held back.

'You can't go in, detective!'

'*Get your fucking hands off me!*'

As the officer held her, Jessica saw her daughter. Sophie was trying to swim against the tide. Every stroke brought her head under the frigid water. Stroke after stroke she tried, but the tide was too strong. She was pulled under.

Two divers went in. More shouts.

The longest moments of Jessica's life passed. She tried to battle the arms holding her back, but she had no strength.

Moments later the divers pulled Sophie on board. Her skin looked blue. She wasn't moving.

She wasn't breathing.

Jessica did not remember anything after that. All she could see was her dark-haired toddler, struggling to her feet next to the coffee table at her father's house on Catharine Street.

Then, amid the sound of the rescue team shouting, amid the smoke and noise and chaos, there was only darkness.

86

Hour dissolved into hour. Night into day into night.

The sound of sirens and screaming had become the sound of a blood pressure monitor, the whoosh of the oxygenator, the soft murmur of doctors, nurses, aides, orderlies.

Jessica opened her eyes to a gray light filtering in a window. She felt her head. It was bandaged. As was her right hand.

She fought the pain, tried to sit up. She looked around the room. She was in a hospital bed. Someone was sleeping in the chair next to her.

It was Vincent. Somehow he sensed she was awake. He stood up, rubbed the sleep from his eyes. She had never seen him look so pained. He took her hand.

'No,' she said. 'Jesus Christ, *no.*'

'Jess.'

'*Sophie*,' Jessica said.

'Mom?'

Jessica turned. Sophie was sitting up in the bed next to hers.

Jessica tore the nasal cannula from her nose, the IV from her arm. She rolled out of bed, knelt next to her daughter.

'My baby girl,' she said. 'My baby girl.'

Sophie stroked her hair. 'Did I beat Angie Alberico?'

For Jessica, the tears came, and would not stop.

Nor did her prayers.

87

The marine unit of the Philadelphia Police Department was one of the elite divisions in the country. With hundreds of square miles to patrol, as well as the not infrequent performance of rescue and recovery operations – on both the Delaware and Schuylkill rivers – their equipment and their training of officers and divers was world class.

In the weeks that followed the events on the SS *Clermont-Ferrand*, the unit found no trace of Cassandra and Martin White. Police departments in Camden, New Jersey, and other departments from New York to Maryland were also alerted.

The two had vanished.

This was not unusual for the Delaware River. The current was so strong, and the river – in some places three miles wide and more than fifty feet deep – had concealed and consumed shipping vessels, fishing boats, human beings, and myriad secrets for centuries. Investigators conceded that they might never know the fate of the young man and woman who called themselves Anabelle and Mr Marseille.

On December 12 the District Attorney of Philadelphia announced that the execution of Valerie Beckert was halted indefinitely, while the case for which she had been tried and convicted – the murder of Thomas Rule – was reopened.

Each day Jessica read the overnight reports, as well as the *Inquirer* and *Daily News*, hoping and expecting to read of the recovery of the bodies, but it never came.

Far more troubling was that Kevin Byrne had taken a leave of absence, and Jessica had not been able to reach him.

She stood in front of the Wynnefield house. Although it had been less than two weeks since the party, it seemed much longer.

Jessica had to admit that, although she still thought the place haunted, it looked far less threatening in daylight.

She stepped onto the porch, knocked on the door, waited. She knocked again, put her ear to the door, listened for footsteps. Nothing.

She made her way to the rear of the house, looking at the windows for signs of damage or foul play. She found none.

Once on the back porch she knocked again. Again there was no answer. She tried the door, and was surprised to find it unlocked.

Byrne would never leave his door open. He was the type of man who would lock his car if he was going to take eight steps into a dry cleaners. Not paranoid, just practical.

Something was wrong.

Jessica pushed open the door. 'Kevin?'

No answer.

Jessica drew her weapon, kept her finger on the trigger guard. She held the Glock at her side.

'Kevin?'

Silence. She listened for sounds. All she heard was the wind rattling the old window panes.

Jessica turned the corner into the front room, and there found a disaster.

She took the room in all at once. There was destruction everywhere – plaster, wood lath, drywall, light fixtures, heating vents, wall switches, glass – all in piles scattered about. It looked like the aftermath of a tornado.

In the middle of it all sat Kevin Byrne. He looked worse than Jessica had ever seen him.

'You okay?' she asked. He was clearly *not* okay.

Byrne looked up, his face a coil of anguish. For a horrifying moment Jessica thought he might have his service weapon in his hand.

He did not.

'What's up?' she asked.

Byrne said nothing.

Jessica took a moment to once again assess the room. The walls were completely torn apart. What had been fresh drywall and paint just a few weeks ago was on the floor in piles. She glanced into the dining room. It was the same. Ditto the kitchen. She had a feeling the whole house was going to look like this.

'What happened?' she asked.

Byrne remained silent, reached for the bottle of Tullamore Dew. Jessica noticed an empty nearby. Byrne took a sip.

'He liked squirrels,' he said.

It took her a moment to realize what Byrne had said. 'Squirrels?' she asked. '*Who* liked squirrels?'

Jessica stepped closer. She now saw that, scattered around Byrne, were dozens of drawings and notes, all sketched and written in a child's hand. Four of them had names.

Byrne held up the half-full bottle of Dew.

'Buy you a drink?' he asked.

Jessica smiled. 'Sure, sailor.'

'I'd offer you a glass, but I think there's a pretty good chance I broke them all.'

'Bottle's fine,' she said. 'South Philly girls don't need a glass.'

Jessica cleared a spot on the floor, sat down, glanced at the ceiling. It was intact. At least that was something.

'How's Sophie?' Byrne asked.

'She's good. Day at a time. But the days are getting better. She's sleeping through the night.'

'Tough kid,' Byrne said. 'Wonder where she gets it.'

'Her father,' Jessica said. 'Trust me on that one.'

There were so many things Jessica wanted to say, so many thoughts and feelings that had come together over the past two weeks. Thoughts about her job, thoughts about what happened on that pier, thoughts about putting her daughter in harm's way. She had no idea where to begin. She decided to just start talking, and hope it all came out right.

'Kevin,' she said. 'That night on the pier. I didn't mean to—'

Byrne held up a hand, stopping her. He passed her the bottle. She'd said all she needed to say, and for that, and so many other reasons, she loved him.

They sat in silence for a while. Byrne picked up one of the pieces of construction paper on the floor next to him. He handed it to Jessica. At first she didn't know what it was, but soon it made sense, and she then understood why the house looked the way it did.

In her hand was a crude map of Fairmount Park. On it were five stars, drawn in red crayon. Byrne had torn apart his house looking for it.

'It's them,' she said.

Byrne didn't answer. He didn't have to.

The paper was a map of where the other children were buried – Jason Telich, Nancy Brisbane, Aaron Petroff, and Thaddeus

Woodman – as well as a star where Valerie intended to bury Thomas Rule.

'I found it in the kitchen,' Byrne said. 'Behind the stove. Remember how Valerie said "speak to Mr Lundby"?'

'Yeah.'

'Turns out there was once a company called Lundby that made tiny stoves for dollhouses.'

'Did you call it in?'

'I did,' Byrne said. 'Dana said she put a call into the FBI. They're going to go to these locations with their equipment. But I know. They're there.'

Jessica thought about the case, the madness that was Valerie Beckert, the obsessions of Martin and Cassandra White, the anguish of David Solomon.

'One thing I don't get,' Jessica said. 'What spooked Solomon? What was it about the invitation we showed him that clued him in as to why Nicole had been killed, and that they might be coming after the Gillen boys?'

Byrne reached to his side, sifted through a short stack of what looked like a court reporter's transcripts. He handed one of the documents to Jessica. It was a partial transcript of a therapy session between David Solomon and Valerie Beckert. Jessica scanned it. She saw it at the bottom of the second page.

'It was *thé dansant*,' she said. 'Valerie told him she'd see him at the *thé dansant*.'

Byrne said nothing.

Before leaving the Roundhouse, Jessica learned that the straight razor they had recovered in the secret rooms upstairs was matched to a wound inflicted on a homicide victim found in the Lemon Hill section of Fairmount Park, a teenager named Latrelle Hopwood. One of Hopwood's wounds – a cut to the back of the neck – was consistent with a wound found on the body of Ezekiel Moss.

When brought in for questioning on an unrelated matter, Hopwood's cousin George identified Martin White as someone he and Latrelle tried to rob in the park.

Jessica looked at the other papers scattered around the room. She noticed a stack of drawings near the hearth. On top was a drawing of a black sky and a tiny crescent moon. She pointed at it.

'I take it those aren't your memoirs.'

Byrne offered a sad smile.

'May I?'

'Sure.'

Byrne handed her the drawings.

Valerie Sauveterre's drawings.

88

They sat in the parlor.

'We've done terrible things,' Valerie said. 'I'm going to leave now. I should be back soon, but if I am not, you know what to do. You will be all right. You know where everything is. I've signed all the necessary papers.'

'What terrible things have we done?' the girl asked.

Valerie just looked at the girl, her beautiful face, her flawless skin, a priceless Bru.

Valerie closed her eyes for a moment, hoping the image would last. It would not, of course. They were children, not dolls.

Only dolls remained children forever.

Valerie stood, paused in the doorway, considered the question. She wondered what they would understand, then remembered that they were far more worldly than she in many ways. In other ways, they lived in a world of counterweighted eyes, bright colors, and pretty bows.

'You are our maîtresse des marionnettes,' the boy said. 'We can't lose you.'

'The big people will try to hurt you, but first they must find you. You know where to hide.'

Valerie knew that the children knew what could be seen, and what *must remain unseen. The groceries would come every two weeks, delivered to the back door. Aunt Josephine had arranged for the real estate taxes, as well as the utilities, to be paid monthly, for many years.*

By the time this was all discovered the children would be old enough to strike out on their own.

Valerie just hoped that the authorities would blame her for what went on here, not the children.

She touched the girl's cheek. 'You will be Anabelle.' She touched the boy's cheek with her other hand. 'You will be Mr Marseille. I want you to be strong, little man.'

'I will,' the boy said.

'You must always look after Anabelle.'

The boy took the girl's hand in his. 'I promise.'

'The big people will not understand what went on here. They will put you on the shelf.'

'Just like Vista House,' the boy said.

'Just like that.'

Valerie opened her bag. From it she retrieved a pair of photographs. One of the boy, one of the girl.

She held up their pictures.

'Ces petites choses,' she added, 'me parlent de vous.'

She reached into her pocket, took out the cameo brooch.

'This belonged to my mother,' she said. 'Keep it always as a remembrance of me.'

She handed it to the boy.

'We will,' he said.

Valerie glanced at the door, at the small form of Thomas Rule, wrapped in the shower curtain liner, then back at Anabelle and Mr Marseille.

They really didn't know it was wrong.

She kissed them each on the forehead, turned, and walked out the door, closing it behind her.

She never came back.

89

One by one Byrne explained what he had learned from Dr Allen about Valerie Sauveterre's childhood drawings.

'She didn't do it, did she?' Jessica said. 'She didn't kill the children.'

'No,' Byrne replied. 'It was the boy and girl. Martin and Cassandra White. Valerie may have brought the children here, but she only wanted friends. All she had growing up were the imperfect dolls. That's why she went after the kids she saw as damaged. She wanted to fix them.'

Jessica shuddered at the thought of young children, no more than eight years old at the time, causing the death of other children. She wondered what, if anything, they would find in and around the grounds of this house.

Byrne went on to explain the secret rooms. When the house was built for one of Philadelphia's railroad barons, the man had included in the design three small rooms in which he kept and consumed his liquor during Prohibition. The deliveries were through a trapdoor in the garage ceiling, the same door by which Martin and Cassandra White made their entrances and exits.

'I didn't like the color in here anyway,' Byrne said.

Jessica laughed. She wanted to cry, but she laughed.

'I'll make some coffee,' she said.

Byrne held up the bottle. There were a few inches left.

'Not just yet,' he said.

As Jessica took the bottle, the cat came around the corner, considered them.

'Who is this guy, anyway?' Jessica asked.

Byrne looked over. 'His name is Tuck.'

Byrne told her about how he and Tuck met, about the bricks tumbling from the roof that had almost killed the cat.

Jessica then told Byrne how it was the cat who had alerted her to the hidden door in the closet, maybe saving his life.

'He did that?' Byrne asked.

'Yeah.'

Byrne thought for a moment. 'I guess we really are even, then.'

Tuck, perhaps sensing the balancing of the books, jumped onto Jessica's lap, curled around once, and lay down.

Within moments, he was fast asleep.

90

Byrne stood on the porch, rang the doorbell. He smoothed his tie, ran a quick hand through his hair, Father Tom Corey's words caroming in his mind:

Faith is the substance of things hoped for, the evidence of things not seen.

It had been a month since the disappearance of Martin and Cassandra White. In the weeks that followed, the remains of four small bodies had been found buried within a few hundred yards of each other in Fairmount Park.

Somehow it had taken this long to complete the paperwork, clearing a path for Byrne to do what he was about to do. It took only a second to end someone's life, but it took a month to complete the paperwork.

Over the past two days he had met with the other families. Aaron Petroff's, Jason Telich's, Thomas Rule's, and Nancy Brisbane's.

Thaddeus Woodman had been the first of the victims.

*

Theresa Woodman had poured coffee. It sat cooling between them.

'Do you have children?' she asked.

'Yes.'

'Boys?'

'No,' Byrne said. 'One daughter.'

'I always wanted one of each. God said no.'

Byrne wanted to say that she was young enough to try again, but it was not his place. 'I always thought I would have more,' he said. 'We're blessed to have them in our lives, even if it's not for very long.'

Byrne reached into his bag, handed Theresa the drawing he'd found in his house. The big green yard with the skinny squirrels in the trees. The drawing was signed *Thad W*.

Theresa Woodman touched a hand to her heart.

'His grandfather's house in Bucks County,' she said. 'He loved to go to the farm. He loved to watch the squirrels.'

She began to softly cry. Byrne reached over, pulled a few tissues from the box on the counter, handed them to her.

'He would be sixteen now,' she said.

Byrne just listened.

'I'm not even sure I would know what to do as the mother of a sixteen-year-old boy.'

'You would have figured it out,' Byrne said.

He thought about all the drawings he'd found in the house, and how he had, for a moment, contemplated keeping them, perhaps one day taking them out as a talisman against some as yet unimagined evil, the innocence of each scribbled line an armor around him.

In the end he burned them all, except for five, sending the ashes aloft over the city he loved.

Theresa held up the drawing. 'Thank you.'

From the moment he'd found the map, he knew he would do

479

this. The Woodman home was the fifth out of five. This was a good thing because Byrne did not have one more ounce of energy – neither physical nor spiritual – left to spend.

As Byrne stood in the driveway he considered the wire, the malleable but unbreakable filament that began with a monster named Ezekiel Moss, and ended with a boy and girl who inherited his legacy of evil and committed these terrible crimes. He wanted to lash out, to assign blame, but he had no idea where to begin.

He looked through the kitchen window, at Theresa Woodman putting the drawing he'd given her on the refrigerator.

It fit perfectly in the space that had only moments ago held the calendar, the calendar Theresa Woodman would no longer have to tend, crossing off the days and weeks and months until either her son returned, or his remains were found.

Byrne got into the car. He felt as if a veil had been lifted from his heart.

'You okay?'

Byrne turned to look at her. He didn't know what the future would hold for them – or what their past together had wrought – but, at this moment, he knew he didn't want to be anywhere else in the world than sitting next to her.

'I'm good,' he said.

Donna Sullivan Byrne leaned over, kissed him on the cheek, then thumbed off her lipstick. It had always been her way.

She started the car, buckled her seatbelt.

'Where to?' she asked.

Byrne said: 'I need to stop somewhere.'

The crime scene unit had found the doll that was made to look like Andrea Skolnik at the base of the ladder leading to the deck of the SS *Clermont-Ferrand*. On its head was scratched the number 13, matching the number etched into the scalp of the victim.

On either side were two other dolls, faithful replicas of Martin and Cassandra White, who called themselves Anabelle and Mr Marseille. These dolls were numbered 14 and 15.

It wasn't until a week later, while Byrne considered the presence and placement of these dolls, that he began to further tear out the interior walls of the secret rooms.

He knew the other doll had to be there.

He was right.

Standing in a grove of trees, in Fairmount Park, just a few feet from where Thaddeus Woodman's body had been found, Byrne took out the small garden trowel, made a hole deep enough for what he had to bury.

He had lost two nights' sleep wrestling with what he should do with the doll, and everything he'd come up with did not seem right. Everything seemed to have the potential to backfire, to one day be discovered or, worst of all, hurt someone he loved.

When he looked down, at the just-turned earth, he realized that this, too, was wrong. He firmly believed that, in this life, energy echoed across time, and that the spirit of Thaddeus Woodman – a boy who loved the outdoors, a boy who loved to laugh – would watch over this small figurine for all eternity, keeping it safe.

Still, he could not do it.

He knelt, smoothed the dirt, put the small garden trowel back into his bag, along with the doll marked 16, the last doll ever made by Jean Marie Sauveterre.

The doll that looked like Sophie Balzano.

Epilogue

It seemed like just a few days since she had stood in front of the Roundhouse that morning in November, her future uncertain. Somehow, five months had passed.

She thought about that horrible night on Pier 82.

In the days that followed, Sophie had not slept. For two nights Jessica sat up with her daughter, holding her close. On the third day, exhausted, Sophie had slept for a few hours. Each successive night it got a little easier. At least on the outside.

Jessica recalled looking at little Miranda Stovicek, the two-year-old daughter of the woman who had found Nicole Solomon's body at the Shawmont train station. She recalled wondering whether children had these terrible things imprinted in their memory. Jessica was all but certain the memory of falling from the bow of the SS *Clermont-Ferrand* would live in Sophie's mind for the rest of her life.

Because Sophie was a far more forgiving person than Jessica could ever hope to be – and the fact that the man and woman who called themselves Anabelle and Mr Marseille had not yet been found – Sophie one day told Jessica that she forgave them, and wished them well.

And, because she was a Balzano, Sophie added that she wished them well, as long as they spent the rest of their lives in a penitentiary.

Jessica glanced up, at the tall building at Three South Penn Square, then at the plaque over the entrance.

Office of the District Attorney.

Come Monday morning she would walk into this building, and begin a whole new set of challenges. Because of her experience on the street, and her time working homicides, she knew she would be fast-tracked to one of the elite divisions. She wasn't supposed to know this, but she did. She just hoped she wouldn't step on too many toes in the process.

Had they paid off her loans? Not even close. But they would. They would find a way. Based on his stellar work holding the car-wash sponge for his father, Carlos Balzano had his stash up into the low two-figures. It was only a matter of time until they were flush.

As she stood in the shadow of this massive structure she thought about her late brother Michael, and how he was always walking next to her. She thought about her late mother, about how she would always sing when she made dinner, how those songs would always live in her heart. She thought about her father, his legacy, his reputation in the department and the city.

Mostly she thought of Kevin Byrne, and how they would forever be partners.

If all went as planned, she and Byrne would be working together again soon – same row, different aisles – and God help the criminal element in the City of Brotherly Love.

Acknowledgements

With deepest thanks to:

Jane Berkey, Meg Ruley, Peggy Boulos Smith, Rebecca Scherer, and everyone at the Jane Rotrosen Agency;

Josh Kendall, Garrett McGrath, Pamela Brown, and the great team at Little, Brown / Mulholland Books;

Dominic Montanari, Kathleen Franco MD, Gaille Ruhl, Theresa and Leah Najfach, Jimmy Williams;

The men and women of the Philadelphia Police Department;

Barry Hay, George Kooymans, Rinus Gerritsen, and Cesar Zuiderwijk – the incomparable Golden Earring – for the music, and the kind consideration.

Strange wings, indeed.

About the Author

Richard Montanari was born in Cleveland, Ohio, to a traditional Italian-American family. After university, he travelled Europe extensively and lived in London, selling clothing in Chelsea and foreign-language encyclopedias door-to-door in Hampstead. Returning to the United States, he started working as a free-lance writer for the *Chicago Tribune*, the *Detroit Free Press*, the *Seattle Times*, and many others. His novels have now been published in more than twenty-five languages.